White Light

WILLIAM BARTON and MICHAEL CAPOBIANCO

AVON • EOS

This is a work of fiction. Names, characters, places, and incidents either are the product of the author's imagination or are used fictitiously. Any resemblance to actual events, locales, organizations, or persons, living or dead, is entirely coincidental and beyond the intent of either the author or the publisher.

AVON BOOKS, INC.
1350 Avenue of the Americas
New York, New York 10019

Library of Congress Catalog Card Number: 98-17586
ISBN: 0-380-79516-7
www.avonbooks.com/eos

First Avon Eos Mass Market Printing: August 1999
First Avon Eos Trade Printing: October 1998

AVON EOS TRADEMARK REG. U.S. PAT. OFF. AND IN OTHER COUNTRIES, MARCA REGISTRADA, HECHO EN U.S.A.

Printed in the U.S.A.

WCD 10 9 8 7 6 5 4 3 2 1

Crystalline spheres filling up the sky. Choirs of bright angels orbiting round and round and round, spiraling inward toward a center of unseeable, unknowable light.

Listen. *Listen to them* sing.

"THIS IS THE BIG ONE: A JOURNEY TO THE END OF THE UNIVERSE AND THE END OF TIME— a stylistically brilliant exploration of the really big questions, a sophisticated book about mortality and cosmology and just exactly what it means to be human. *White Light* is a tour de force, and should be a definite contender for all of the science fiction field's major awards."

Robert J. Sawyer, Nebula Award-winning
author of *Factoring Humanity*

"STUNNINGLY IMAGINATIVE."

Kirkus Reviews

"A MAJOR NEW NOVEL."

Science Fiction Chronicle

"ENGAGING...WELL-TOLD... CONSISTENTLY INTERESTING... a smart exploration of the concept of heaven... a rich, intelligent tale well worth reading."

Booklist

"BARTON AND CAPOBIANCO ARE A TEAM TO WATCH OUT FOR."

Locus

Other Avon Books by
William Barton and Michael Capobianco

ALPHA CENTAURI

Coming Soon

IRIS

Dedication:

to

Henry Kuttner

Frank J. Tipler

Roger Penrose

One

Just a few weeks past her fourteenth birthday, Cory Suárez sat on a spindle-legged green plastic couch in a locked, windowless white room, feet pressed together, looking down at the ratty old cloth valise that held everything she owned in the world, thinking about the airport outside Montevideo, where she'd sat with her mother for the last time. A tight little catch in her throat. *I didn't know what would happen. I should have kissed her goodbye.*

Sitting now, almost two years later, wearing the odorless new clothes they'd given her this morning: Flat white sneakers. Low white socks. White linen shorts, a boyish white cotton shirt with the top two buttons left open. No bra, not even the sort of elastic thing a not especially mature fourteen-year-old girl might want.

Only two weeks here, hardly enough time to get to know all the other forlorn, pretty little motherless, fatherless girls, after eighteen months by herself at the internment camp out on the cold plains of Argentina. She remembered crying and crying the first nights there, crying for her lost mother, mother remembered only by her panicky screams as those two men dragged her away toward a dark, stinking alley, mother screaming, "Run, Corazón! *Run!*"

Nowhere to run to, but she ran anyway. And lost her.

A key turned in the lock, dead bolt sliding with a squeak, and the door swung open. Miz Jolsen. Huge, muscular, dough-faced white woman, with a northern European's blotchy red complexion, plenty of scabby red pimples. Oily blond hair, the pale blue eyes you normally saw only in certain kinds of dog. "Suárez? Let's go."

Even though Cory liked speaking English, proud of the schooling she'd gotten before the wars killed her father, she resented the way the woman said her name. *Saw-rezz.* Like that. She stood slowly, leaning down, grabbing the handle of her bag.

"Fuckin' move your ass, little cunt!" The woman grabbed her by one arm and yanked her toward the door, Cory stumbling, then jerking, trying to step lively as she felt the woman's big hand on her rear end.

In the main office, fat Dr. Kleindienst sat behind his old-fashioned desk, one hand buried in the flickering mist of his work interface, the other rubbing the blue jowls around his usual frown. Miz Jolsen suddenly straightened up, sticking out her big tits and smiling as wide as she could without showing her crooked yellow teeth.

There was a tall middle-aged man sitting in Dr. Kleindienst's side chair, tall, even though he was sitting down, curly black hair flecked with just a few strands of gray, long sideburns, a square, handsome *Norteamericano* sort of face. Khaki military blouse stretched tight over a broad chest, rounded shoulders, thick upper arms, sleeves rolled up halfway to show corded forearms. Big, bony hands. Some kind of blue tattoo. A snake around his right wrist, holding its own tail. *Ouroboros,* she remembered, from a class once taken. Blue jeans on long legs. Low black leather boots. Movie star, she thought. Blue eyes, verging on green. Looking at her. Knowing. With an amused little smile.

Fish-eyed Dr. Kleindienst glanced up at her. "Ah. Thank you, Ms. Jolsen." The woman let go, but made no move to leave, still smiling.

Kleindienst said, "Miss Suárez, this is Mister . . . um." He squinted back down through the interface, searching for the lost datum.

"Wolf," said the handsome man's deep voice. "My name's Wolf, Cory." Some kind of accent. Not like a cowboy from a movie. Broad, with more diphthongs than you heard in standard English.

Kleindienst said, "Yes. Mr. Wolf is a bonded escort. He'll be taking you to your new . . . employer."

Cory felt her breath grow short, a slight pang of inexplicable disappointment quickly displaced by fear. New . . . employer. You know why the girls say this place took you . . . *bought you* from the internment camp. Rich *Norteamericano* men like pretty young girls, you see. Rich men can buy whatever they want. And it won't be a handsome movie-star man, like this Mr. Wolf, who was smiling at her, eyes full of knowledge. Laughing at her misfortune?

Bastard.

For the thousandth time Stuart McCray gave up trying to sleep and squirmed in his seat, looking out the window at nothing. The ancient Boeing 7117 might as well have been hanging in space, motionless. He suppressed a crawl of irritation, wished for his gamemask and the new chips he'd gotten for Christmas.

Mom and fucking Mark, arguing about what would go in each person's eighty kilo luggage allotment, going through his trunk, picking out pretty much everything he'd most wanted to keep from his room. Fucking Mark! Taking out the gamemask, throwing it on the bed, putting in his own high-tech reader and a big chipwallet full of things with labels like "ERDA Table of Organization."

Dimly, against a rushing jet-engine roar that seemed to nestle in his ears, Merry started up yowling again, followed quickly by Neff. Memory of the cats, at home, in his bed, dim early morning light coming in the window. Cats asleep, curled up by his legs.

Sitting across the aisle, beside his mother, was Mark Porringer. Mr. Wonderful, his stepdad, was asleep, pudgy face squashed against his shoulder, lips flabby, just a touch of wetness on his chin.

He looked out the window again. There was a deep hole in the snowfield of cloud below, almost as blue as the sky above. Like someone had taken a shovelful out of the world. No sign of solidity anywhere, just blueness and the faint misty hint of great distance. The fear in his gut subsided for a moment. They can't take this away from me.

But Mu Arae. And Sagdeev. What's going to happen to me?

"Stu. We're almost there."

"I know that, Mom."

"There's something I haven't told you yet. The starship pilot, Wolf O'Malley, is someone I've known for a long time. In fact, I knew him long before I met your daddy, back when I was in the Service."

Stuart frowned, looked away.

"I just wanted to warn you. Wolf's not the nicest man in the world. It might be best for you to stay away from him as much as possible."

Talking to me like I'm a fucking baby. "If you say so." Stuart looked over at his still sleeping stepfather and wondered about her taste in men.

* * *

Walking down the polished linoleum hallway floor toward the orphanage's front door, walking beside Mister . . . Wolf, her left wrist shackled to his right, *So he can drive,* she realized suddenly, Cory tried not to think about what was coming, kept failing in the effort.

My new . . . employer, she thought. Galling bitterness, a bad taste in the back of her throat. Some fat, rich old man, bald, flabby, skin mottled and hanging . . . They were passing by doorways she'd last seen when they'd walked her in here from the car, two weeks ago, after the long, exhausting flight from the internment camp. Imagine. Imagine being worth so much you could be shipped under guard to a place ten thousand kilometers away. I wonder how many gringo dollars I'm . . .

Fighting back a tightness in her throat, like faraway tears.

She slowed up, pulling gently on the handcuffs, looking up at handsome Mr. Wolf, smiling, sort of batting her eyelashes.

"What?"

She said, "I . . . um. I've got to . . ." She motioned with her head at a nearby door, labeled LADIES in English. Ladies, like it was meant for women of nobility. No door labeled *Common Scum,* of course. "Can I go to the bathroom?"

A thousand old movies. In the public rest room there'd be a little window, just big enough for a skinny girl to slip through and . . . no point in imagining beyond that.

He seemed to smile. "Sure."

Then he walked to the door and held it open for her. "Go ahead."

"But . . . but . . ." Look at him smiling! She held up her handcuffed wrist. "Please . . ." It came out like a whisper.

"Sorry. I don't have the key." He led her inside, led her across the white tile floor to the nearest stall and held that door open for her as well. "Go ahead."

She looked around the room, feeling her despair deepen.

Sure enough, there was a window, already open, just the right size. "Dr. Kleindienst . . ."

He smiled and shrugged. "Key's been sent ahead to your new employer, Cory. Sorry."

And that smile again. *Bastard.*

He said, "Look, do you have to go or not?"

She edged toward the toilet, felt her legs start to tremble.

He said, "Hey. I'm not going to watch. Go ahead." He turned away then, extending his own arm full length so she could get all the way in the stall, turned away and seemed to regard the old tampon dispenser on the wall with great interest, reading what little was left of the old instruction sheet pasted to the front panel.

Bastard. Bastard. Bastard. I'll show you, you . . .

She turned and squatted, yanking her shorts down halfway, squatting over the toilet, unwilling to sit down, and started trying to pee. Staring at the tile floor, trying not to cry . . . fighting, then. Fighting against a tightness at the bottom of her belly, fighting a rebellious sphincter . . . water started tinkling in the bowl, a delicate, high sound.

And something of a relief as well.

I had to go worse than I thought; all this . . . excitement, this . . .

When she was through, pulling up her shorts as best she could with one hand, Wolf turned from the dispenser, smiled, and said, "Better? Let's go."

She followed him then, in something of a daze, choking down fury, fighting off yet another layer of despair. Bastard.

Wolf O'Malley drove his reconditioned 2031 Rockwell Cordoba convertible across the arid, no-color landscape of southeastern California, listening to the gas turbine's soft whine, left elbow on the door, hand barely touching the steering wheel, right hand resting on the stick shift.

Last god damn good car ever made, sitting on shiny showroom floors only a few weeks before the bombs began to fall and the old world came to an end. This one was a lucky find too. Brief memory of that splendid day, back in '47, hell what was I? Ten years old? It'd been a sunny day, weather moderating at last, when he and his father, looting the old farmhouse, had broken into the garage. I remember his reverence. Like a man in the presence of his god.

Faint, ancient regret.

He stretched, feeling the wind cool in his hair, luxuriating in the flood of bright desert sunshine, and glanced over at the girl. She was sitting as far as she could from him, up against the passenger's side door, looking away, knees pressed together. . . . Faint amusement. I thought she was going to jump out of her skin as we pulled out of the orphanage parking lot, when I moved my hand from the gearshift to her knee and gave it a pinch.

Christ. How'd you get to be such a mean old shit, Wolf O'Malley?

He pushed down on the accelerator and watched the numbers in the speedometer window flicker and change. One forty klicks an hour. The wind started lifting the girl's pretty black hair, making it stream out behind her. She glanced at him, face expressionless, then gathered her hair with her free hand and tucked it down in front of her shoulder.

By late afternoon, sun red in the western sky, they were driving through the foothills of the Sierra Nevada, and the girl had gone to sleep, head resting half on the back of the seat, half against the top of the door. There. An old, old Motel 6, lights on in the office, power rectenna like a tennis net beside the parking lot. When he pulled up in front of Cabin 22, the girl suddenly sat up, looking around, then turned to face him, face pale, eyes big. Scared as hell, you could see that.

"What . . . what . . ." She could hardly whisper.

Wolf grinned at her, imagining what was going through

her head. "We'll spend the night here," he said. "Go on in the morning."

"B-B-But . . ." Like that, the girl's eyes started to fill with tears. *Right now?* you could see her thinking.

Wolf felt a slight trickle of shame, maybe something left over from a previous life. Okay, jerk. Fun's over. He said, "I guess you could be Honoria Suárez's daughter, all right."

The girl recoiled, giving him a bizarre look, said something in Spanish he couldn't quite catch, then, "Wh-What?"

He gave her a sunny smile and said, "Your mother's going to be happy as hell to see you, Cory."

The girl seemed to choke, then fury colored her face, driving away the tears, and when she opened her mouth, an angry gabble of Spanish came out.

Wolf said, "Well. I guess maybe I am the illegitimate son of a diseased old whore, at that. But I'm taking you to your mother."

Disbelief. Shock. My mother is . . . dead . . . Horror flooding . . . all of that showing through, mingled with a palpable, impossible hope. . . . "Where . . . where is . . ."

Can't quite say it, hm? "Do you know what Mu Arae means?"

A puzzled look, then, "Isn't that the name of a star?"

Wolf smiled again. "Honey said you'd been going to a good private school before your daddy was killed."

The girl's eyes seemed to bulge. Two deep, shuddery gasps of breath. A strangled, defiant hiccough. Then she burst into tears. Drooling. Nose running. The whole business. Watching, Wolf felt his shame deepen.

Somehow, he got her out of the car and into the cabin, by which time she'd gotten control of herself, babbling questions about her mother as he unlocked the door. Inside, though, she looked around, dismayed, at the little TV, the single narrow bed, covers disheveled from his having slept there the night before.

She lifted her handcuffed wrist and said, "Please . . ."

He smiled. "Sorry. I wasn't kidding about them having been sent on ahead. By this time, they're in a post office box in Eugene, Oregon."

"Oh."

He said, "I've got some tools stashed in my apartment in Pasadena, Cory. We'll be there by tomorrow afternoon and I can cut these damned things off."

She glanced at the bathroom door and he could see despair leak back into her eyes.

He said, "I'm sorry, kid. I won't look."

Watching the flat red desert tilt outside, Mark Porringer swallowed hard against the pressure building in his ears and tried hard not to think about the days to come. He rested back in his seat, shoulder touching his wife's.

Thalia Jansky, indestructible hyperdrive flight engineer, sound asleep under her neat cap of loose black curls, face perfectly relaxed and smooth, incredibly pretty, maybe just a touch too masculine . . . My God. How the hell can she be forty-five years old? A quick memory welled up, only a couple of days old. Thalia coming out of the lavatory in their bedroom, stark naked, standing at the foot of the bed, smiling at him.

Christ. Only a couple of days ago. Outside, the ground was coming up, airplane shuddering slightly as it slanted toward the surface of the red desert. Engines awfully noisy. Brief, pointless spike of worry.

And a hard pulse of fear. What am I *doing* here? The plane will land, for Christ's sake. Get on the next plane bound for North America. Go back to Chicago, proud capital of the Federal Republic of North America, capital of the only country in the world, World War Three's sole survivor. Go home and get a good night's sleep in your own bed. Go to your office in the morning and . . .

Yeah. What *would* I do at my office in the headquarters of the Earth Resources Development Agency, bright and early next Monday morning? All these years of planning. Conniving. Setting things up. This is what you did it *for*, you fucking asshole. Get yourself and your family out of harm's way *before* things fall apart. The only hope for mankind. Jesus. Stupid.

Still, there were thousands of people working toward this goal, even if it wasn't exactly the . . . official reason why ERDA existed. After the war it'd seemed so noble. President giving his little speech, back when I was just a little boy, growing up in a world beggared by thermonuclear destruction.

The only way we can save the world, President Berenstein had said. Save not just ourselves, Americans, Canadians, Aussies, Enzeds, but the pitiful, struggling bands of survivors in Europe, Asia, Africa.

They'd backdropped his speech with a live feed from the ruins of Tokyo.

Horrible stuff.

So they'd created ERDA and built hundreds of thermonuclear rockets, spaceships that could carry us out to the resources of the Inner Solar System. Moon. Near-Earth Asteroids. Mars. The Piazzi Belt. Callisto a convenient source of volatiles for our off-Earth fuel production.

Who knew then that those scientists we'd kidnapped from eastern Europe right after the bombs started falling would give us a workable, if crude, if horribly expensive, faster-than-light drive?

Starships going outward to worlds beyond the sky. Can't save the world, you see. Can't save all its people. Somewhere out there would be a pristine, habitable world. Someplace where humanity can make a fresh start. Someplace where we can build a new America in the sky.

Nobody ever asked the question how, once a world turns up, we're going to transport 330 million Americans away in starships that can carry a dozen people, tops, and cost two billion dollars to build. Two billion to build, four hundred million in consumables per mission, a billion dollar overhaul every ten missions . . . He could still remember the first time he'd had to purchase extra fuel for a starship, as part of his job at ERDA. Antimatter, catalyzing thermonuclear reactions, costs a million dollars per milligram to produce, at a robotic factory on the Moon.

Twenty-five years and no habitable planets yet. What if there aren't any, for Christ's sake? How much longer do we have? Which had led, inevitably, to another little plan. Not a government plan this time. Not even an ERDA plan. Just some of us. Administrators. Flight crew. The people who *can* get away, when the time comes.

Beside him, Thalia stirred. Rubbed her head softly on his shoulder, starting to wake up. God, how I want to go home. Take her to her room, start undressing her, caressing her . . . Instead, all he could remember was getting in the taxi, listening to Stuart bitch about his lost fucking toys, driving away from the home we'd shared.

Never even took time to say goodbye properly. Did I pull the circuit breakers? Turn off the water in case the pipes break? Did I . . . Jesus! Who the fuck cares? I'm never going to see the place again. I . . . my rosebushes. My fucking rosebushes will be eaten alive. Wish I'd stopped to look at them one last time.

The wheels hit the ground with a squeaky thud and the thrust reversers cut in with a roar, enveloping the plane in a dense cloud of red dust. Beside him, sitting up straight, Thalia said, "Engines'd last a lot longer if they'd pave these fucking runways."

Mark said, "Plenty of fifty-year-old turbofans in storage. No reason we shouldn't waste 'em." No reason at all. Because, in just a little while, Things *will* Fall Apart. Bobbing on decrepit shock absorbers, the plane drove out of its cloud, headed for the terminal building.

Stu appeared, Neff in one arm, Merry in the other, fluffy yellow-brown lengths of fur, blue-milk feline eyes staring angrily. "Put 'em back in the box, Stu."

"Mom?"

Thalia gave Neff, her favorite, an affectionate rub under the chin. Neff looked at her, mewed a little squeak. "They're still sedated, son. Do what Mark says, please."

Cory awoke with a start, disoriented, dizzy, looking up at a pale, cloudless, empty blue sky. Not empty. Sun back there, a brilliant yellow-orange ball, maybe a quarter of the way up the eastern sky, just above the band of pale yellowish air that circled the horizon. She squeezed her eyes shut, shutting out a horizon that was steeply tipped, one of the plane's swept-back wings pointing at empty, wrinkled red earth far, far below, the other sloping up into the washed-out sky.

No, not much like the other plane had been, two weeks ago. That other one, taking her north from Argentina, north to a Gringoland orphanage, had been . . . steady. Level. Slow. She swallowed against a dry throat and opened her eyes again. All right. Maybe it's just the bubble canopy that makes it seem so . . . She took a deep breath. Looked and looked.

Deep voice: "You awake back there?"

Wolf. Slight pang of . . . something. "Y-Yeah. Sure. Where are we?"

"Where do you think? Look outside."

Bare, lifeless, wrinkled red ground. Pale blue sky. "Mars?"

He laughed, an already familiar gravelly chuckle, and said, "Northern Australia."

Wolf O'Malley. Her mother's . . . employer. A kaleidoscope of memories, confusion. Asking him questions, getting answers. Some answers. Not enough. My mother . . . alive? And this man's . . . housekeeper.

She imagined her mother making a rich man's bed. Rich white *Norteamericano* . . . starship pilot, age forty-five. From someplace called Asheville, North Carolina. I know where that is. Geography lessons in school. All the cities in North Carolina, they say, were blown to bits in the war.

Her mother, Honoria Suárez, whom this man called "Honey," making Wolf O'Malley's bed while he was off doing his business, flying to the stars and— She suddenly shied away from an image of her mother *in* Wolf O'Malley's bed.

"Hey, give Ox a pat for me, will you?"

Getting used to the funny way he talks. Awks. Pay-ut. She leaned forward cautiously, looked downward, and saw that the huge dog was looking back at her with big, damp, soulful brown eyes. Ox. Short for Lummox. A Labrador retriever, just shy of ninety kilograms. Mouth big enough to swallow a cat whole. Coal-black.

When she reached down to stroke his brow, the color seemed to come off on her fingers, along with a certain smell, but the dog sighed and squirmed, tipping his head just so, closed his eyes in evident bliss and relaxed on the floor of the cockpit.

Cory leaned back in her seat again, and when she brushed her hand on the side of her shorts, the black came off there, a faint gray smudge.

From the plane's front seat O'Malley said, "Well, we're here. Ready to land?"

"Um. Sure."

"Put your feet on Ox so's he'll know to stay down. He gets a little nervous sometimes."

Stuart sat in a rickety hotel-room chair, looking out a dirty second-floor window at the dusty street of a crude Australian town whose name he'd already forgotten, skin dank in a room whose windows wouldn't open, whose air-conditioning barely worked. Right now it was on, blowing in his face, wind that felt like someone's breath. Smelled like it too. Cars going by in the street below. Seedy-looking people walking around.

Once, there'd been a brilliant, silent spark rising, blue-violet in the western sky, bright enough to cast shadows in daylight. Spaceship rising. Maybe even a starship. Mark's eyes nervous. Does he think maybe this famous Mr. O'Malley has left us behind? Maybe just wishing for it to be so. Then we could go home. Back to our old life. Me in my room, cats asleep on the bed. Mark and his mother in their room. Stuart rubbed his eyes angrily, staring out the window.

Sharp rap on the door, a quick double-bang.

Mark seemed to jerk. Pale, eyes wide. Almost fearful.

Thalia stood up slowly, said, "Well." Slowly walked to the door and opened it.

A deep voice, then, "Hey, they-uh, Thay-uh. Y'all lookin' naas."

From her place on the arm on the chair, a sleeping Merry suddenly changed from a lounging cat to a spiky ball of sealpoint fur, seemed to teleport to the top of the drapes, hanging there for a moment, looking down. Then the drapery fixtures came out of the wall and the curtains fell, rods, cat and all, with a bizarre, unexpected clatter.

Mark was on his feet now.

That other streaking ball of yellow-brown, that would be Neff, going up the far wall, trying to grab a picture frame, while Merry struggled to free herself from the curtain trap with a scratchy yowl and . . . something came into the room.

"Better grab ole Ox, Cory!"

Big and black, with huge, baleful eyes, something the size of a small bear, dragging a girl on the end of a leather strap, dragging her right across the faded carpet, its mouth gaping wide, showing huge white teeth as it made for Merry and . . .

The cat made a sound like a choking dragon, fur spiking up again, all fangs and claws and burning blue eyes.

Something else came through the door, stepped past the struggling little girl, grabbed the dog's harness and checked its motion. Just like that. Dog rearing in the air, jaws snapping shut, *clomp,* nowhere near the cat.

Stuart thought, That dog must way close to a hundred kilos. How the hell could he stop it like that? Out of nowhere, Neff bounced off one wall, flying toward the door, which Thalia had the presence of mind to slam shut.

Silence, but for the scrabbling of alarmed cats, the heavy panting of a huge, excited dog. Mark sank down on the edge of the bed again. "Jesus Christ!"

The tall, handsome man holding the dog smiled, some kind of funny glint in his eye, and said, "Sorry 'bout that." Accent not quite so thick now.

Thalia seemed to lean back against the door, eyes on the man and . . . something in *her* eyes, thought Stuart. What am I seeing? She said, "Mark. Stu. I'd like you to meet Wolf O'Malley."

He looked at them each in turn, something like genuine warmth, interest in who they were, on his face. "Glad to meet you both. You look a lot like your dad, Stu."

Odd clench in the pit of his stomach.

Wolf said, "This here is Cory Suárez. She'll be going to Sagdeev with us. And my puppydog, Ox."

Stuart looked at the girl, Cory, who . . . A sudden, sharp intake of breath. Pretty. I never met a girl so pretty before. . . . Wanting to speak, to say something, anything that would . . . He felt a sudden sense that he might be strangling, unable to breathe, girl looking at him now, eyes puzzled.

Wolf O'Malley seemed to snicker.

From somewhere, his mother's voice, seeming rather faint. "It's good to see you again, Wolf."

It made him look at her. That . . . odd light in her eyes. He looked at Mark and was startled to see alarm, almost terror, broadly written on the man's pale face. Wolf said, "Sorry I was so late, folks. Better get your stuff together now. We've got to go."

When the bus stopped beside the huge, red granite and steel service/launcher—SLC-31, the sign said—O'Malley waited while the others got off, Cory holding an excited and inquisitive Ox by his leash, more or less dragged, laughing, trailed by Stu, lugging his god damned box of cats, eyes apparently glued to the girl's rear end. Mark Porringer, frowning and subdued. Thalia . . .

Rear end for my eyes, I guess. Like I was a teenage boy, pussy still only an unformed dream. Hell, you'd think after all these years . . . She's got nothing on Honey, that's for sure.

Still pretty at forty-five, Thalia Jansky. Slim, fit, bright-eyed, a damned sight too good for her paunchy Ph.D. husband . . . Mark putting his hand on Thalia's back now, a light touch, reassuring himself, looking back over his shoulder at Wolf. Sure he knows. He probably knows more about us than any husband would want to know. Women are like that.

Wolf clapped the driver on the shoulder and said, "Thanks, Jer."

Shingleton said, "Any time." A brief silence. "How much time you think we've got?"

How long 'til Things Fall Apart? A week, a month, a decade, two, three . . . He shrugged. "Long enough, I hope."

The driver sat staring at the young people on the ground outside, boy and girl looking around, wide-eyed, big dog, box of fucking cats. "I sure wish . . ."

Wolf put his hand on the man's shoulder again. "Yeah. We won't leave anybody behind. No matter what." Truth?

Lie? No way to know. "Shit hits the fan while I'm in port, Jer, you just bring your family to wherever *NR-598h* is berthed. Bring 'em on in and wait for me."

"Thanks."

Wolf went down the stairs, out into dull afternoon sunshine and warm, dry air. The door hissed shut behind him, the electric engine whispered, and the bus rolled away.

Thalia and Mark were standing a little distance away, in the shadow of the service containment structure, Mark frowning harder now, obviously angry, the two of them standing with a tall, pudgy blond man in the powder-blue uniform of ERDA's Repair and Refit service, bright copper Refueling badge glinting from his breast pocket.

"What's the problem, Sammy?"

The man glanced at Mark again, then said, "Nothing. God damn admin types jumping the fucking queue is all." You got the sense he wanted to spit as he spoke.

Mark said, "Listen, if you didn't have people like me on the *inside* . . ."

Wolf sighed, suddenly tired. "All right. All right. Fuck, Sammy, he's here 'cause he's my goddamn flight engineer's fuckin' *husband.*"

Sammy snorted, exasperated. "Oh, hell. Just blowing off steam, Wolf. Sorry."

"Are we all set?"

"Sure. Loaded, locked, prepped, counted down to minus-ninety."

"Ground crew?"

"I sent everybody else back. I'll sit in the bunker and monitor your launch so we don't . . ."

Right. So we don't run afoul of regulations. "Thanks." He glanced over to where Cory and Stu were standing together, box of cats on the ground, Ox on his back in the dirt while the two of them scratched his big belly.

Far away across the desert, a siren began to blow, wavering slowly, louder, then softer, higher, then lower. He glanced at Sammy, who said, "*NR-280,* liquid cargo bound for Hawksbill Station." One of the old clunkers, headed for Neptune.

THUD.

Soft jolt against the bottoms of their feet, Ox suddenly scrambling upright. Brilliant light on the far horizon, rolling, coruscating gold, brightening to white, then some impossible blue-violet, people standing in front of their sudden, long shadows on the ground. Cory and Stu looking, shading their eyes, thunderstruck, Mark gaping right along with the children.

And Thalia, blasé as can be. Ho-hum. Old, old stuff . . . The violet light started to rise in the sky like a tiny, too bright sun, blue-white star rising on a column of glowing, red-gold smoke. Twenty kilometers. Count the seconds, five, ten, fifteen, thirty, forty-five . . . Smoke now a golden tower, blue-violet fire arrowing into the sky with unbelievable speed, faster, faster . . . *WHAM!*

Deafening sound, like a big board dropped flat on a concrete floor, nuclear ignition echoing across the desert, stabbing their ears, slapping them in the face, followed by a prolonged cataract roar, louder, louder, the sounds of the rocket climbing into space, delayed by the speed of sound.

The technician said, "I was out here when *NR-76* exploded, back in 'sixty-four. Hell of a sight."

The films alone . . . an inverted cone of blinding fire, Australian desert blown into the sky, then that telltale mushroom cloud, rising and rising . . . Wolf said, "I'm glad I missed it, Sam."

From the control cupola atop SLC-31, you could see a long way across the red desert, see the distant mountains and high plateaus, where the jungles began, more important, see the little clusters of buildings that marked the other service/launch structures dotted around the landscape, each twenty kilometers from its nearest neighbor. Far enough, Wolf mused, to escape damage in a worst-case accident.

Worst case. *NR-76* hadn't been anything like a worst-case explosion, even though it'd been bad enough. Worst case was a scenario in which one hundred milligrams of antimatter escaped from their containment loop and . . . reacted. Cooked off the fissionables in the ship's 400-megawatt lead-bismuth-cooled compact military reactor, which in turn cooked off fusion in the hydrogen component of the ammonia reactant . . . *Bang.*

Just now, in the middle distance, you could see the coiled, irregular, infinitely high column of red-gold smoke that was all *NR-280* had left behind, tower of shadowy, radioactive fire slowly being twisted and bent by high altitude winds that would take most of the night to dissipate.

Directly below the window where they were standing, the roof of the containment structure split open, big white panels folding back, and the launcher structure began to tip upward. Beside him, Stu suddenly pressed forward, hands and nose against the glass, whispering something to himself.

When *NR-598h* was standing upright on its launch ring, the erector structure folded back, lying flat on the desert, leaving the ship, all gleaming, bare silver-gray titanium, tougher fittings here and there of duller beryllium, naked but for the girdery structure of the elevator shaft and the narrow pole of the electrical mast.

On the other side, invisible from here, was a tall, sturdy sway clamp. Safety. Always safety. If the ship were to tip over now, break open, nothing much would happen, liquid ammonia all the fuck over the place, freezing the desert for a while, but the reactor would scram itself, and the nearly indestructible antimatter containment loop had its own emergency power supply.

Pressed to the window beside Stu, he heard Cory whisper, "*Beautiful.*"

Sure. Beautiful as anything there is. Tall, slim metal spaceship, seventy-three meters tall. Six meters in diameter except down the bottom, where the six service pods, looking like so many antique strap-on boosters, widened her to just under ten meters. Like a skinny, twenty-four-story building. An iron silo headed for the stars.

The landing legs, not needed here, were folded up into their own wells, so you could easily see the bell-like muzzles of the six thermonuclear engines, indistinguishable from conventional rockets on the outside.

Inside, though . . . Augenstein-technology antimatter reactors would send beams of antiprotons and hydrogen ions to annihilate in the middle of a hefty tungsten block heat exchanger, producing energetic gamma rays and pions, superheating the ammonia working fluid, blasting it out the engine bells with an exhaust velocity of twelve kilometers a second.

In front of him, Stu was saying, ". . . with a mass ratio of around six, she's about four-fifths fuel, so . . ."

Eighty-three point three percent, Wolf remembered, fact popping up automatically.

". . . so with a specific impulse of twelve hundred and a mission delta-vee of around thirty kilometers per second, this ship could fly all the way to Mars and back on a single load of fuel!"

Wolf thought, Trust Thalia's son to know that. He smirked. Trust a fifteen-year-old boy to think he could impress a fourteen-year-old girl with that sort of bullshit.

Still, Cory's head was cocked his way, apparently listening. She said, "What're those two long, skinny things about halfway up?"

Wolf said, "The hyperdrive antenna nacelles. They'll unfold when we get to the jump point."

Cory looked over her shoulder at him and smiled. Stu

glanced back too, face expressionless, eyes hooded. Oops. Sorry kid. Didn't mean to muscle in on your . . . He had a brief memory of lying snuggled with her in the motel bed, remembering what it'd been like to be young, lying with his first girl, trying to get up the nerve to—

Sam called out, "All set, Wolf."

Right. "Okay, boys and girls. Time to go."

Time to fly away, away from this dying old Earth forever, out to the starry landscape of our dreams.

Two

Three days and the trip was over, out to the jump point, jump, with that curious internal clenching that made him think of . . . well. Three days of Mark retching his guts out, unable, apparently, to adapt to zero gee, Wolf laughing at him, making him mad as hell, helpless to do anything about it.

Stu grinned to himself, feeling the ship shudder around him, creaking, rattling, sounds just audible over the faraway engines' muted roar.

Memories of miserable Mark, of grinning Wolf, who seemed to spend more and more time with his mother . . . well. She's his flight engineer, after all. They've got to fly the ship . . . and magical views out the command module's tiny window as they fell toward blue Sagdeev and its tiny gray moon, Roald, alien world looking like the Earth, and yet . . . alien. Alien world in an alien black sky, lit by a star called Mu Arae.

Other things remembered. Meals eaten. He and Cory playing with the cats—mind shying suddenly away there—tending to the dog, his mother in the background, watching them. . . .

Bump. Down with a thump, engines gargling, fading with a jet engine whine, then silent, suddenly silent, but for the soft tick of something far below.

Stu wriggled in the restraining sheath and slid an arm out, holding it up against the force of gravity. He could hear creaking noises from somewhere above as the ship configured itself for servicing.

The others were already unfastening themselves, and Stu did likewise, sitting up, peeling back the sheath, and swinging his legs over the edge of the bunk. He slid himself off the edge, and fell the meter and a half to the floor. No, it didn't feel much different, this 0.88 gee, although after being weightless, maybe he couldn't tell anymore. He wanted desperately for it to *feel* different, to have a force tugging inside him that would continually remind him that he was on a new world.

Finally, after standing and waiting in the airlock for what seemed half an hour, adjusting and readjusting the little nose-and-mouth oxygen mask that Wolf had instructed them about so carefully, the hatch cracked and the humid, warm, unbreathable air pushed in, slight pressure difference immediately noticeable. Stu felt the pain in his ears and swallowed hard, hearing little squeaking noises as the hatch swung outward and he had his first view of Sagdeev.

It was raining. Not too far away, dark, crumbling mountains gathered, looking like enormous gray-black castles, softened by the intervening mist and swarming with broken tissues of fog. The tops were hidden by a heavy cloud layer. Down below, beyond the insectlike mobile service vehicles with their extended arms, sitting on the rough darkened concrete, was a small bus. First out, he stepped into the dank wetness and felt it permeate his skin. He wanted to dance a little dance on the metal grating, but didn't.

"Okay, people." Wolf's voice, crisp and authoritative, only slightly muffled by his mask. "Let's get cracking." Stu looked back to see them all crowded in the hatchway, watched a strange look flicker over his mother's face. Complexities that he didn't want to think about.

As they rode in the little sealed bus, bumping down the narrow, winding, unpaved road that descended to the coastal plain and the Venara colony, if you could call it that, the tension was there. Mark was trying to explain to anyone who would listen what he had picked up about the bleak, boulder-strewn landscape around them. Talking and talking, with just a hint of desperation in his voice.

After the fifth misidentification, Stu, trying to keep the sarcasm out of his voice, said, "You're completely wrong. These lighter colored hills are batholiths, where the underlying material of the continent has been exposed by erosion."

Thalia, suddenly smiling, beamed in his direction, pride illuminating her face. "Yes, Stuart. You studied so hard for that geology equivalency last summer. You tell us what we're seeing."

Faint, petulant annoyance sizzling away somewhere. *She gives me credit, but it feels like she's taking it for herself. I always hear "Look whose son he is" in her voice.* He looked around at the others, saw them looking at him, and shrugged. *Silly-ass Mark deserves this. Just dry bullshit is all, straight out of a first-year planetology text.* He said, "Well, the Sagdeevan cratons show us the earliest stages of continental development, when mantle-derived magmas and intracrustal melting generate bulges of lightweight granitic material which protrude upward."

He looked around. Mark was staring out the window, back rigid, skin flushed. The others . . . Cory. Genuine interest written in her face. Could she even know what a magma was?

Wolf was regarding him with something like interest. Stu felt himself blush, somehow obscurely pleased.

Mark sat looking out the bus window, watching the Sagdeevan landscape roll by, bleak and dreary, faraway gray mountains under dull gray clouds, rain drizzling on the window every now and again, starting, stopping, starting again. Godforsaken planet looks just the way I feel. Conversation going on without him, fucking Stuart prattling on and on, showing off his useless bullshit knowledge. Trying to impress that little cunt, understandable, but much worse trying to impress Mr. He-Man O'Malley. Jesus.

Big mistake coming here? God, I don't know. I don't fucking know. Why the hell do I *always* make the wrong choices?

The bus lurched, throwing his face into the window's hard plastic, turning onto a muddy track that was, though it hardly seemed possible, even rougher than the so-called road, and Wolf called out, "Okay, folks! Here we are! Home sweet home."

The bus rolled to a stop, brakes hissing softly, engine turning over gently, rumbling at a slow idle. Outside, he could see Wolf's house, a seemingly random collection of rammed earth buildings, spray-painted with plastic sealant. Flat-roofed house like a southwestern hacienda—obviously some kind of drainage or that flat roof, in this rain . . . no, stupid. The sealant makes it waterproof—garage, some kind of baggy-looking affair over there that might be a greenhouse. Power rectenna, canted just so, catching the rays from Sagdeev's lone geosynchronous sunsat.

Well, this phase'll be over soon. Get a good night's sleep. Tomorrow I can get on into Venara, talk to Linebarger, get my office set up. . . . A sudden prickle of fear and exhilaration. New job. New job on *this* end of the pipeline.

What the hell do we call ourselves now? Illegal aliens?

Overhead, a rip had opened up in the clouds, showing the dull blue late afternoon sky. There. Something. A wide, thin crescent near-new moon, lopsided blotch of *mare* almost blued away by daylight. Okay. Get into town, get your office set up, see what's what. And talk to Linebarger about setting up our own house. *Now.*

He looked back at Wolf's house, wondering how hard it would be to build something like that, just the two of them, he and Stuart, working together, and was startled to see someone looking at them out of the picture window. A woman, standing quite still. Staring.

Nighttime. Cory sat in the darkness, half turned around on the soft brown velvet couch, forearms making a rest for her chin so she could stare out through the thick, triple-glazed picture window at the dark landscape of Sagdeev. In the daylight the hills had been blue-green, covered with some soft, fuzzy mosslike stuff. Now, lit only by the pale, silvery illumination of Roald, moon a big delicate crescent riding low in the sky, the hills looked . . . eroded and lifeless.

Nothing really visible out there in the hazy air, air that along with Roald's light hid all but the brightest stars. Low, rounded hills under a dark sky. Dirt road going past the house. Little driveway winding up to where Wolf parked his sealed electric car, which was plugged into a small dish antenna pointing toward where she supposed the powersat hung, invisible.

Soft noises in the background, not from the empty wilderness outside. Soft noise, like whispering. Gentle movements. A distant creaking sound. Cory felt her stomach crawl briefly, images coming up, quickly suppressed.

Outside, not far from the house, in a little valley before the nearest hillside rise, was a baggy-looking tent of some clear plastic material, enclosing her mother's garden. Wolf's voice, answering Stuart's question: "Plants're okay with the extra CO_2, but unfortunately, they need oxygen as much as we do." Then some gibberish about a Kreb Cycle. She wondered at that, having imagined from the beginning that Sagdeev would be a paradise, at least, for Earth's plants.

More noises, louder, a woman's voice, murmuring something, maybe not words at all. Cory felt the urge to cover her ears.

"Can't sleep?"

Cory jerked and looked over her shoulder. Thalia Jansky, all dark shadows and subtle glints, standing, wrapped in some kind of robe, in the archway leading to the dining room.

"Sorry. Didn't mean to startle you." She walked across the room, kneeling on the couch beside Cory, leaning forward, looking out into the night.

Cory said, "It's okay. I just . . . so many things have happened."

Thalia glanced at her. Nodded slowly, dark eyes communicating nothing. "Must've been hard, thinking your mother was dead for more than a year."

In the background, a soft, rhythmic crunching began, sounding far away, and you could no longer hear anything like voices.

Thalia seemed to sigh, whispering, almost inaudibly, "I didn't think it'd bother me." A moment of non-silence, filled up with those other sounds, then she stole a quick look at Cory, as though she regretted having spoken aloud.

Cory said, "I don't know how I feel, Ms. Jansky. I just . . ."

The woman turned, slid to a seat beside Cory, put one arm around the girl's shoulders. "Why don't you call me Thalia?"

"Thalia." When she said it, it came out in Spanish, *Talia.*

Lots of girls in Argentina named Talia, many of Italian descent spelling it *Taglia.*

"It sounds so nice when you say it that way."

In the background the sounds stopped suddenly, uncovering a woman's soft voice, saying something, maybe in Spanish, maybe not.

Thalia whispered, "Jesus." Seemed to look away, toward the room's darkest corner.

Cory wanted to say something, say anything, put her hand out, touching Thalia's forearm, as if reaching for her hand. The woman withdrew suddenly, glancing at Cory, face unreadable, then said, "Well. I better get back to bed before Mark thinks it was me making all that commotion." She stood. "Hope you can sleep."

Watching her walk away, Cory said, "It'll be all right, Thalia."

Lying in the darkness, looking out his bedroom window at a familiar alien moon, Wolf kept telling himself he really ought to get up and wash a bit before going to sleep, but . . . Right. Too god damned cuddly to move right now. I'll be itchy in the morning, but who cares? Soft curves of a woman snuggled under his arm, tight to his side, one leg thrown over his thigh, her dampness pressing against his skin just *so.*

Damned crazy day.

Over in the corner, Ox heaved a doggy sigh, stirred, rolled over and was still again. Probably wishes he could get up on the bed with us. Tempting to pat the mattress with one hand and, Here, boy!

Honey wouldn't say anything, she never did, but she'd be uncomfortable sleeping with a big, smelly dog. Probably best to let sleeping . . . Honoria, clearly still awake, pressed her face into the side of his neck, nuzzling, kissed him softly, settled down again, her breath warm in his ear now.

Grateful. Crying out loud when she saw her daughter, the

two of them rushing together, blubbering like characters in a sudsy movie, babbling away in Spanish way too fast for me to follow. Variations on a theme of oh-my-God-I-thought . . . Thought you were dead. Thought I'd never see you again. Maybe I clouded up a bit myself. How the hell would I feel, if I could see my dad again just one more time? Jesus.

Conscious of Mark and Stuart and Thalia, just standing there, watching silently, embarrassed, wishing they could be out of sight for all this . . . reunion stuff? Was that it? Well, remember the looks on their faces. Maybe for Stu, but . . . Mark looking so goddamned, pathetically relieved as Honey threw herself on me, slobbering kisses and tears.

Thalia? Well. Just standing there. Watching. By any reasonable standard, Honoria Suárez is a hundred times better looking a woman than Thalia Jansky could ever have been. And eleven years younger besides.

Ox got up from his place on the floor and came padding softly over, a near-silent pony of an invisible black dog. Invisible but for those big, glowing eyes, one dull orange, the other bright green, though in the daylight his irises were the same muted brown. Stood by the side of the bed, snuffling at his hand.

Wolf patted him on the head, feeling a skull bigger than a man's and a good deal harder. "Good boy. Go to sleep now."

By the time Honoria woke, just as Mu Arae came peeping over the bare hills, Wolf and his big dog had already arisen and gone. Lying there, still fuzzy-headed from sleep, she could hear someone banging around in the kitchen, could hear voices, a man and a woman, talking. That would be Wolf, making his breakfast of strong black coffee and chocolate chip cookies, just as he always did when in port. Wolf and . . . ?

After a while the noises stopped, then she heard the airlock hiss and someone went out. She sat up in bed, looking out the window. There. Wolf and his flight engineer, Thalia Jansky, dressed in shorts and T-shirts against Sagdeev's muggy air. Shorts, T-shirts, sneakers, and oxygen masks.

Look at her. Flat chest. Almost no backside. Muscular arms, like some kind of deformed little man.

Then, remembering the way the woman'd kept looking at Wolf, remembering the look of fear in her pathetic husband's damp eyes, resentment in the eyes of her stupid-looking son. Honoria felt a cold crawling in the pit of her stomach. You have to remember he doesn't love you. You're just someone he got from the agency. Someone to make his bed and wash his toilet and . . .

Stark and impossible against the empty alien landscape, Wolf's big black dog came loping out across the "lawn," hard mud covered with a thin rime of something like algae, huge thing wagging its tail and bounding like a puppy. Listen. You can hear her laugh.

Where the hell could he have gotten an oxygen mask for a dog? Specially made? Rich white men can get anything they want and . . . She watched Wolf unplug the car, then they got inside, dog and all, took off their masks, and drove away, while Honoria thought, And this Thalia creature is some long lost love from an unforgotten past. That cold crawl in her belly again, replacing last night's warmth.

After a while she got up and slipped on her robe, went on down to Corazón's room and opened the door, heart pounding, just for a little peek at . . . She felt her eyes fill with tears again, seeing the girl asleep in the bed, went inside and sat down to watch. I feel like I lost her as a baby, and now . . . Such a pretty girl. Just about to blossom and—

Cory's eyes opened, looking right at her, awake and alert, as though there'd been no transition from sleep. Dark eyes, full of shadows and questions. Honoria felt one of the threatening tears spill over and track down her cheek.

"Mother?" Cory sat up, covers dropping away.

Honoria kneeled beside the bed so she could hug her tight. Nothing to say. Nothing really to say. Just . . . just the being here. That was enough. After a while, when she'd let her go, Cory got out of bed, going over to the dresser where she'd packed her few things, opening drawers, rummaging around.

So pretty, Honoria thought. Maybe just the way I looked when I was that age. Cory pulled out a dress of some kind, most of the things she owned, apparently, of cheap white cotton, turned and smiled at her mother.

Suddenly, Honoria found herself looking at the girl through a man's eyes. Maybe a particular man's eyes. Not that ridiculous Mark Porringer, nor even his idiot son, though that one obviously hungered for a girl.

I can imagine a man looking at her pretty face, at her pretty little breasts, at that little thatch of neat black hair between her legs, and imagine her lying in his bed, lying sprawled, just the way he likes to see. . . . Her heart made a horrid little leap in her chest as she shoved the image away. Bad enough to imagine him with this Thalia, but . . . No. No, I . . . A soft, insidious voice whispered, *If it's to be Thalia Jansky, he'll send you away, but—*

She recoiled from the thought. No.

In the distance, stromatolites. Big ones. Little ones. Like some kind of cobbled quay out there, catching the waves, breakers surging through the interstices. Despite himself, Mark found the beach scenery arresting, stark and primitive. Enjoy it, putz. Just this once. God. I should be in town, talking to Linebarger, getting things started.

But no, fucking O'Malley blathering on and on about what a nice fucking planet this was. Stu so startled, saying, "You mean we can go to the *beach* here? Go *swimming?*"

Sure, boy. Sure.

Then O'Malley'd started telling him about the eclipses, had punched up his 3Vcom and checked the gazetteer. Sure enough. An eclipse *and* a fucking beach, all rolled into one.

Now, Thalia was sitting next to O'Malley, up on the dunes, chatting heartily away, the way she always seemed to connect with people other than him. As though they possessed a link into a private little world where things were somehow interesting.

Stuart was splashing through the weak surf with that damn dog, the two of them playing, rolling in the water, dog coming up, sneezing and snorting, shaking its head, trying to get the water out of its oxygen mask, Stuart laughing, helping, lifting the mask for a second. Acting like a kid because he still was one, despite all the learned jargon. Half ignoring Cory, who was probably too . . . experienced for him. Damn shame, for such a pretty little girl. Those kind of scars, life scars, don't show up until later, when the skin has a chance to sag, when muscles have had time to harden the face into a mask.

Honoria, not so much older, really, but old enough. She was sitting on the other side of the blanket, applying another coat of oily sunblock onto her firm, smooth legs. Jesus Christ. That's a *damned* nice-looking woman. What the hell would O'Malley want with Thalia when he's got a piece like *that?*

Lying back, blanket cool against his back, few grains of sand irritating his shoulder. Eyes closed. One big difference here. The sunlight *felt* weak, overpowered by the unpleasantly tepid air, even when there was a fitful cool breeze off the ocean. He wondered if it would cool off at all during the eclipse Wolf and Stu had been chattering about on the way out. Sun-graze, they called it. Something about Bailey's Beads, whatever they were. Apparently even here, with such a big moon, it was a rarity.

Quiet now. Only the rhythmic shush of the waves. A

sound like shifting sand. No buzzing flies or cawing gulls. Breeze again. Perfect except for the oxygen mask, and even that was forgettable.

He suddenly opened his eyes, levered his head up. The dune was empty now, footprints leading over its summit. Horrified. They've gone off together. He looked over at Honoria, and their eyes met for just a second. Certainty there. *She* has no doubts about what's going on. Do I? Can I just hold on to that feeling that I don't *know* for a few more seconds?

No. The familiar old feeling of terrible, terrible loss. Throat constricted, tears about to wash out. He turned away from the woman onto his side. I can't hold on to Thalia. I knew it would end this way, a quick unbalancing. Oh, shit. Burning sensation in his eyes now, wetness overflowing. A heavy burden in his chest, making it difficult to breathe.

No matter how carefully I build my life, it always amounts to this. They expect so much of me, these people, and I can never, *never* be good enough for them. Hopeless. I'm at her mercy, even if she doesn't know it yet. Damn the bitch. Maybe she isn't gone for good yet. Maybe I can keep her, if I just ignore this, pretend it hasn't happened. If I try even harder, keep myself in line and do *just* what she wants.

He looked back at the footprints on the dune, closed his eyes and let his head sag back onto the blanket.

Once they'd gotten across the rough line of dunes to the back side of the narrow peninsula, where the sand was gritty, black, large-grained basalt instead of the lee shore's fine white quartz, Wolf and Thalia stood still, side by side, not quite touching, looking out across the sea's gray swells, beyond a rough, noisy surf.

No swimming here. No stromatolites either, Wolf thought. An empty world. Really empty, but for me and thee.

Thalia reached up and pulled off her oxygen mask, shaking her hair out slightly, taking a slow, deep breath. "Smells like sulfur here."

Wolf looked farther out to sea, where the faint black streak of a distant volcanic plume, coming from one of the island arcs, stuck up vertically from the horizon, almost hidden in the low, gray-white haze. "Probably from that."

Thalia staggered suddenly, gasping, steadying herself on his arm with one hand, then quickly put her oxygen mask back on. "Christ. Doesn't take long."

"No." Wolf remembered an incident, back on Earth, when he'd come upon a repair crew in one of his drydocked starship's tank structures, three men who'd suffocated in a pure nitrogen purge atmosphere, unaware anything was wrong until they'd started blacking out. Three neat little corpses, vaguely surprised looks on their faces, huddled together in the bottom of the tank along with their tools. "Not long at all."

They started walking up the beach together, sand making little squeaky sounds under their bare feet. Nothing much to say. Aware of each other. Wolf slowed almost imperceptibly, so that Thalia pulled a pace or two ahead. Unchanged from this vantage point. Sleek, muscular back, flaring out at the hips, buttocks so nice inside her spare black bikini briefs. Even the changes are . . . just fine. Those few lines in her face . . . some people grow handsomer as they grow older.

Thalia suddenly stopped, turning to look up at him, eyes clearly amused above her mask. Long silence. Then she said, "We're still the same people, aren't we, Wolfie?"

Wolfie. He shrugged and said, "I guess so." And what of it? Standing still, looking at each other. Electric tension filling the air between them. Like, he thought, nothing's happened over the last twenty years. Your husband, dead while you still loved him. Your son, back there at the beach wanting to play like a man with Honey's pretty daughter. Mark Porringer, moping like an ass on the hillside.

Thalia put her hand on his chest, rubbing her fingers over velvet fur. Eyes so earnest, all he could see of her face. She said, "You know, I thought . . . well. Last night . . ." She stopped, just stood there, looking down now.

Last night. Honey in the bedroom, grateful all right. Grateful as hell. He reached out and touched Thalia's hair as softly as he could manage, feeling its familiar texture, feeling her lean in closer, one hand not quite reaching out. Looked up into his face again, eyes full of . . . pleading? Not quite. Longing, perhaps? Hell, women's eyes were always full of something unlikely.

Wanting me to do something, abdicating her . . . right to act. What, then? Throw her in the sand? Or turn back, lead her briskly over the dunes to husband and son, home and cats? She lifted one hand then, putting it on his upper arm, just below the shoulder, still looking into his eyes, waiting.

Stu sat on a granite boulder at the edge of the little mud flat, watching the bubbling exhalations of the methanogen bacteria. Even through his mask there was a barely perceptible fart smell. Beyond the dunes the sounds of the ocean were nearly inaudible. The explanations came through in a quiet, masculine voice that hardly disturbed his sense of being at the edge of the universe. Sagdeev was as close to the transition to a breathable atmosphere as could be imagined, the age of stromatolites begun. These blue-green algae equivalents, though not identical to those of Archaean Earth, had perfected photosynthesis and were slowly adding oxygen to the air.

He stood up, looked at the sky beyond the dune, where little Mu Arae was falling fast. Suddenly anxious, he made his way up the loose sand of the dune, feet sinking in deep, and was out of breath at the top. At the near side of the bay, three little figures, Mark, Cory, and Honoria, Ox now curled up in the sand by Cory's feet. No sign of his mother or Wolf.

The sun was only a hand's breadth over the dark ocean horizon. No sign of Roald, hidden in its own shadow and masked by the light of the sky. He lugged down the avalanching sand to firmer beach, then, light on his feet with enthusiasm, jogged off towards the others.

He'd been walking for quite a while, following the hollow pockmarks of the others' footsteps, when a subtle change in the quality of the daylight made him look up. Already a chunk was missing from the bottom of the still blinding sun, replaced by invisible blue. As he watched, the size of the chunk became larger, motion just beyond the edge of perceptibility. He began to climb the dune, sinking in again, falling to his knees at one point. The sky was turning an odd shade of pale gray, odd even for Sagdeev, and the light was quickly weakening.

Just before he reached the top, he stopped. Was it a trick of his eyes? No. Across the dim, ruffled surface of the sand, lines of shadow were dancing, like a flock of birds flying overhead. Subtle, not fully dark, with a sense of some fluffy uncertainty to them, lines spreading up across the sand. A look back showed that Mu Arae was only a thin, vertical sliver now, slightly larger at the top. As he watched, the sliver narrowed, still not dimming, until it was a bright line, which diminished further until slight irregularities in the surface of Roald began to show themselves as brighter bulges.

He dragged himself up the last few steps to the top of the dune, a cry of exultation on his lips. The beach on the far side of the dune was dark, black sand that, in this light, had a strange glimmer to it. The moving shadows still visible at his feet seemed to disappear as they marched off into the distance. The sky in that direction was very dark, and a few stars were visible here and there.

The cry that he had been about to voice died. There, in

the distance, on the little deserted black beach, where low, flat breakers pushed themselves far up the shore, a man and a woman had their arms around each other, embracing, bodies twisted, like soap opera actors clinching for a kiss.

He stared for a long, empty moment, mouth suddenly so incredibly dry, then turned and crept away into the shadows, leaving them to their . . . whatever.

As they settled themselves side by side on the couch in Micky Jensen's office in the ERDA field headquarters in what passed for downtown in the village of Venara, oxygen masks dangling around their necks, conditioned air feeling good on sweaty faces, Wolf could see the man's brow crinkle with amusement. There was that look in his eye, an awareness that said, *So.*

Well, he's known us both for a long damned time. Besides which, it can't be difficult to . . . notice.

Bleak moment of memory. Memory of how they'd strolled back over the line of dunes, chattering merrily, of . . . Well. There was Stu, sitting by himself at the top of the hill, staring out to sea, seemingly absorbed in the empty blue-gray sky. Mark Porringer, also by himself, sitting far off to one side, somehow haggard and forlorn. And in a lawn chair by the car, Cory, staring, sitting beside her mother, who seemed unable to look at them, turning her head away.

Hell, only the damned dog was glad to see us, thundering up the hill in a spray of sand, pouncing on me, knocking me down so I rolled all the way to the bottom. And only Thalia laughing.

Hard night that followed. Honey so quiet. Lying by my side, pretending to sleep. Maybe waiting for me to reach out and . . . I don't know. Which would have been worse for her, me climbing on top, or me *not* climbing on top? Well, I didn't. Got up then, headed for the kitchen, maybe a nice little snack or a quick nightcap. Started wandering around the dark house and . . .

Memory of standing in the hallway outside Thalia's closed door. *Their* closed door. Listening to the distinctive sounds of sex. Mark huffing and puffing for all he was worth . . . restaking his claim? Or merely accepting Thalia's apology? God damn it.

Startled then to find Cory sitting by herself in the dark, in the living room, staring out the window at nothing at all, one of Thalia's cats balled up in her lap. She'd turned to stare at me, blinking silently, and in the background there were all those nice *humping* sounds, for God's sake.

Nothing. Nothing at all. Go back to bed; go to sleep.

Here and now, the amusement was gone from Jensen's face. He looked from one to the other. Folded his hands on his desk, seemed to marshal his words. "Well. You're the seventh group I've had in here today. Maybe in the worst position."

Wolf felt Thalia's hand on his wrist, conveying tension. He said, "What the hell're you talking about, Mick? Some trouble?"

"I guess you could say that. IG's coming."

Wolf felt a slight pang of annoyance. "Well, shit."

Thalia said, "Why is that a problem?"

Wolf went on, "Our people are squirreled away on my ranch, Mick. Science team's due in tomorrow and we can get the hell on our way to Beta Pic the day after, right on schedule." No problem.

Jensen said, "Inspector General's office started putting people on the freighters last week, Wolf. Your science team is cooling its heels in Alice Springs, trying not to get noticed."

Thalia said, "My God."

Jensen nodded slowly. "Most people don't have much of a problem, Wolf. We've got a few holes where we can stash unregistered transportees. Maybe play musical chairs with the rest. There's forty-seven hundred people who belong here. Eighteen hundred or so who don't, mostly families."

Thalia said, "I've got my husband and son. Wolf's housekeeper . . ." That made Jensen roll his eyes.

Wolf said, "Honoria's a registered employee. Her daughter, though . . ."

Another nod from Jensen. "Heard you finally brought your dog, Wolf."

"What about my cats?" Thalia asked.

"Illegal as hell. There's already a couple of hundred goddamned pets up here. Dogs. Cats. An Amazonian fucking parrot . . ." Jensen blew out air, puffing his cheeks. "Hell. *Your* problem is, you got to fucking *leave.* Get in your starship and leave on your mission!"

Long silence, then Wolf said, "Just the two of us? And do *what?*"

"Well. Can you generate *any* science data on your own?"

"No."

Thalia said, "Pictures. Remote scans. Stuff like that."

"Not good enough."

"No."

Another long silence, then, almost in a whisper, Thalia said, "Mark can do some of it. He's been in admin for a long time, but he . . . well, he helps *buy* the equipment. Helps plan the missions."

Wolf turned then and looked at Thalia, saw the unhappiness in her face. Right. Just the two of us up in the control room of *NR-598h,* on a nice vacation from husband and . . . housekeeper, for all those lovely long weeks, while the science team did its thing. Up there together, all alone, just fuckin' merrily away. He said, "Thalia, your damn *son* knows more about planetology than Mark Porringer."

Slow nod, eyes distant. Finally, softly: "That's what he wanted to do with his life."

Jensen said, "Well, you've got to do something. Right away. We'll process your ship for launch in . . ." A quick glance at the screenhaze on his desk. ". . . . forty-three hours. That's all the time you've got. Let me know who you want to hide and who you want to take along."

Wolf stood slowly, stretched, then turned to look down at Thalia, still huddled on the couch. Finally, he said, "Maybe there's no reason to leave anybody here."

She seemed to flinch. "What about the dog and my cats?"

Wolf laughed. "Maybe we can teach ol' Ox to watch the mass proximity indicator or something."

That got a wan smile. "Mark's not going to like this. Beta Pictoris!"

"Fuck. He'll get over his motion sickness sooner or later. Let's get the hell out of here. We've got work to do."

Three

Suddenly, they were there. Stu felt his head reverberate with the pressure of the transition, aftershocks a quick return to normalcy, calling attention to the slight buzzing of the ship's ventilation system. Twice now. Just a moment, there, in what they still called hyperspace, and then off to this new star, Beta Pictoris.

On the flatscreen the view was spectacular. Stu studied the image, the small hairs on the back of his neck prickling, trying to get his bearings. The starry sky was split by the inner edge of the disk, a tightly focused milky band showing intimations of a highly complex internal structure, streaks of brighter material, areas of density enhancement here and there. On either side of the band, comets of all sizes filled the screen, receding into the remote depths of space, hundreds of them, tails more or less diverging out from a central radiant.

A clank, the ceiling hatch popped open, and he was no longer alone. Pudgy-looking legs, pushing in all directions like blunt feelers. Mark. *Shit.* Come to spoil my fun, as always. Wolf probably sent him down here just to get rid of him, snickering behind his hand . . . yeah, well, so what else is new.

"What do you want?" Stu tried to keep the edge out of his voice, was not entirely successful.

"Resource assessment. It's what I'm supposed to be doing, but I'm afraid this whole trip is just a waste of time without the real scientists."

"All right, Mark. There's your station." Stu turned his attention back to the screens. The star itself was unremarkable, bright white circular image surrounded by histograms and schematics in the main display. A young main sequence A5 star, six times more luminous than the sun, much more massive but only a little larger.

IR showing lots of planetesimals of all sizes, from a couple half as big as the moon down to the limits of the instrument's resolution. The nearest one was a three-hundred-meter baby only fifty kilometers away, not cometary, just a chunk of carbonaceous rock. Most of the gas and dust swept clear, fortunately. Only two real planets detectable, one small terrestrial world and a gas-giant, of sorts, out by the inner edge of the ring. More mass than both of them in the multitudes of asteroid-sized bodies flying around in unstable, chaotic orbits, ready to collide with the planets and each other.

Stu slewed the main telescope over until the image of the terrestrial world came into view. You couldn't see much at several AU distance, but you could tell the surface was hidden by clouds, almost uniformly bright, lopsided, the horns of the thin crescent slightly smeared by atmospheric layering. Outward, toward the darkness, star images sleeting across the screens, suddenly stopping on what looked like an opaque veil of bluish-white smoke, internal filaments coiling and clotting, showing just a hint of rainbow color at the fringes. Infrared spectral analysis coming in. Gradual transition zone starting about eighty AU out, very tenuous, the effective size of the dust particles half a micrometer, but farther out evidence of dust motes, much larger. Temperature 100K, low enough throughout for volatile gases to condense.

"Looks like the Milky Way on a good night," Mark said.

"No sign of anything larger than dust in the disk," Stu said, "but I'm not sure we could see the stuff even if it was there."

Building up an all-sky panorama in the biggest imagebox. Asymmetric, as they said. More focused over there, more tightly bound to the plane of the disk, filaments merging, brightening perceptibly. Was this one of the arclike density enhancements seen from earth, or something else? Stu stared at the feature, wondering if an embedded body could do something like that.

Mark grunted, finally noticing. "What's causing that? It looks weird."

Stu nodded, despite himself. "There are no planets out there, so that can't be doing it. Jesus. Look at it. It looks like the dust and gas is being confined somehow."

"Looks like somebody crimped it there."

Stu gestured into the box. "Just there, at the region of greatest compression, the temperature goes up slightly, one hundred and twenty, no, twenty-five Kelvins. Whatever's going on out there isn't in any of the textbooks I've read."

Mark suddenly snapped his head up, almost dislodging himself from his chair. "What was that?"

Stu followed his gaze, noted the configuration of the chart. "Looks like a gamma-ray burst of some sort, pretty intense. It came from somewhere on the other side of the inner system, a couple of AU away."

Below deck three, the laboratory deck where the scientists would have done their work at Beta Pictoris had they not been lurking about Alice Springs, hoping not to be noticed, below deck four, the airlock and surface vehicle deck, with its machines neatly folded and stored, its hull cargo hatch and davit-crane, lay deck five, *NR-598h*'s accessible engineering space, mounted to the forward shielding baffle of the working fluid tanks, still more than half full of liquid ammonia.

While Thalia tended to the hyperdrive system monitors, Wolf floated in front of the powerplant monitors, touching one flatscreen after another, comparing charts and graphs to the electromechanical dials on the brute-force emergency circuit-breaker panel leaning out from the overhead.

Everything fine here. Coolant running a little fast, power output a little off. If we need it, I need to jigger this. . . . The compact reactor was an upgrade to a fifty-year-old design, the same military reactor that'd powered the principle submarine fleets of World War Three. Hundreds of them had been destroyed in the Pacific Campaign of 2028, spilling their guts on the bottom of the ocean. . . .

Part of the reason my daddy had to die so soon.

Faded old image of a once-robust middle-aged man, wasted to a skeleton, smelling so sour and dirty, making me lean close, whispering to me how he was sorry he'd waited too long. Get my pistol, Wolfie. Bottom drawer of the bureau, behind where I keep the sheets. It's beside a photo album.

I know, Dad. The one with pictures of Mom.

Please. The gun. It won't be so hard. I promise. It's what I want.

Go out like a man, not a damn old dog.

He looked away from the panel, pushing the memory back into oblivion. Let him down, didn't I? Maybe. Maybe not. Didn't seem mad at me. Let me hold his hand until the doctor came.

Smiled at me when they put the needle in.

Closed his eyes and died.

Easy as that.

Shit.

Thalia had moved away, going through the evolutions of her job, working with machinery that did nothing easily understood. Christ, even the guys who *built* the hyperdrive didn't really understand it. *Time travel,* they'd said. Time travel. Well, no, not quite. Or maybe, sort of. Theoretical arguments still going on, in all those nice, learned journals, about what was really going on. Accounting for causal discontinuities in the Feinman continuum by something call hermeneutic manifolds . . . Shit.

He looked over at the next panel. Sure. Sure. MHD generator running at sixty-seven percent efficiency, a little under par, not much. Antimatter storage ring for the fusion trigger ticking away, million-buck-a-milligram antiprotons safe and sound.

Across the room Thalia was finishing up, over by the ladder. Wolf twisted, kicked off the bulkhead, and slid through the air, grabbing himself to a stop by the hatch. Floated lightly, smiling at her. She seemed to flush, looking at him out of the corner of one eye.

Almost coylike. Nice color to her skin. Neck arched just so. Hair pinned up so it won't float around. Nape of her neck, with its little uncaught wisps . . . He put out one hand and touched her there, making her bob slightly, head tipping back as if she wanted to look through the open hatch, back up into the rest of the ship. Tiny lines beside her mouth. A little bit of a frown. She took a slight breath, puffing air back out through her nose, and seemed to squirm under his hand.

Wolf looked down into the darkness below, down through the hatch that led only to storerooms and consumables tanks, air, water, spacesuits, and spare parts. "You really want to go back up and watch the flyby?"

She turned to face him, face oddly serious, eyes searching his, and shook her head, the barest hint of movement.

Wolf felt a sudden consciousness bloom at the base of his

belly, where there'd been nothing but subliminal itchiness before. "I guess they, um, won't miss us for a bit."

Honoria poked her head over the rim of the hatch, looking down through the air of the engineering deck, down through the next hatch into the shadows below.

Go back up. Go back up.

No will to do so.

Just a crawling desire.

Frustration. A wish that she could go back just a little way into the past and unmake this moment.

Another component, just as maddening, the damp desire between her legs.

If I could just *be* with him, instead of her . . .

She slid through the hatchway, twisting head down, towing herself along the ladder rails, quiet as a fish in the sea. Hesitated at the entryway to the other hatch, poised, wanting to go on, afraid to go on, trying not to listen. Listening anyway.

A whisper.

Not the whisper of voice.

The sound of clothing.

The soft, high metallic sound of a zipper.

The rustle of . . . She was confronted by the memory of Wolf, standing at the foot of their bed, back on Sagdeev, red light of sunset darkening the alien sky beyond the window. Wolf smiling at her as he untucked his shirt, unbuttoned it, slid it off his arms, tossing it on the floor. Wolf pulling off his undershirt, turning it inside out in the process. Wolf kicking off his boots, kicking them aside, thump-thump. Unbuckling his belt, unzipping his fly, pulling down his pants with the underwear still inside, rubbery prick bouncing out, already starting to rise.

Through the hatch, down in the shadows, a woman's pale orange slipper was floating, tumbling slowly.

Honoria stared through the hatchway, clinging to the ladder, shaking gently, heart pounding, spare anger burning softly in her breast, matching the softer burn between her legs, burn of desire in the hollow where Wolf . . .

Pornography, she thought. If I could see them, just peer for a moment around the edge of the hatch, they would look like pornography.

What happens now?

What really happens?

The days turn to weeks.

We go home . . .

Home to where?

Sagdeev?

Wolf's home. Not mine.

What will he do with us?

Three days. Three long, wretched days while they transited from the hellish protoplanet, all the way across Beta Pictoris's inner system to the . . . well, the Object. That's what they'd been calling it since it finally had entered visual range and revealed itself.

Thalia smiled crookedly to herself, floating lightly above the surface of her flight engineer's acceleration chair. All of us except Wolfie, who keeps on saying, Unidentified Orbiting Object. UOO. Pronounced *woo.* As in woo-woo . . . The god damned thing was hanging in the screen now, looking pretty much the way it had for hours as they came closer and closer. Like a cross between a Tinkertoy and a dribble of industrial slag. We won't get a better view till we can stick our heads out the window and fucking *look.* She shook her head slowly, smiling a little more. Picking up bad habits from Wolfie again.

Wolfie. Christ. All mixed up now, memories of him from so long ago. Mixed up with the past couple of weeks. Mixed up with the time we snuck off to a motel, not long before I married Mark. Memory of him looking down at her, not quite smiling, in the dim light of the seedy motel room, *Happy to uh-blahge a girl, Thay-yuh . . .*

She glanced over at him, strapped into the pilot's seat to her left, craggy, handsome face, still age-defiant, pseudo-young, staring at the thing in the monitor, frowning. Wish we could get a better view. No room for full-size mirrors and lenses on a starship. Limits to what you can do with folded optics and maxed-out CCD cameras. Slight bitterness twisting her, somewhere inside. Limits to what you can do with everything.

The two of them coupled down in the engineering space again, sweat evaporating on the skins, making her back feel chilly, her butt, the outsides of her thighs. . . . Warm and smarmy on her belly, tits, nice where his hand's cupping the back of her neck. Agonizing at what he'd said.

We're going to have to do it, Thalia. *I'm* going to have to. None of this is . . . Honoria's fault. Listen to the hesitation in his voice. *Honey.* He calls her Honey, not *Honoria.*

I'm not going to punish her, Thalia. And I think you should . . . you and Mark could. I mean . . . just to keep the peace. You know? We'll sort this out when we get home again. I promise.

Followed by another memory, of leading Mark away into the bowels of the ship, taking him by the hand, towing him through the hatch of the surface rover, swinging the hatch shut, leaving them in almost darkness, but for the pale yellow-orange light coming in through the little portholes.

Mark quiet. Troubled. At least he had the good sense not to object. Knowing what was coming, I guess. And why.

But then I had to undress him, like he was some inexperienced boy—not just a boy, some useless nerd a compassionate girl might take pity on and . . . Fumbling with his rubber-hose prick, getting close, putting it in her mouth, moving it around with her tongue, feeling it firm up and stretch out, slowly, as if reluctant. How can a prick be reluctant? I mean, men . . . well, maybe. Maybe anything.

At least it'd been so long for him that once he got it inside her, the whole thing was over quickly. Maybe a minute. Maybe two. Then the prick was thrashing inside her, terribly familiar, Mark cooing softly in her ear. She struggled not to remember how he'd laughed afterward, relieved and grateful.

One of the control nexi chimed and put up a timeline chart.

Wolf sighed, twisted in his seat and looked over at her. "Well, I guess . . ." I guess it's time? He said, "Well, I guess it wasn't such a good idea, after all, hm?"

"No." She struggled to sort out all the things she wanted to say. "How was . . . um."

Wolf seemed to stare into her eyes, still frowning. "It was . . . more difficult than I expected. She's not stupid."

The timeliner chimed again.

"I guess we better get to it." Thalia turned to her controls, while Wolf clicked on the intercom, "Three minutes, folks. Cage the damn cats and, uh, Cory, see if you can get Ox up in one of the bunks."

That wouldn't be a problem. Hadn't been. The big dog seemed afraid to go anywhere in the ship where there weren't people. Besides, it'd attached itself to Cory, adoring her, seeming to snub Wolf. Jesus. Would a dog be jealous because we . . . And the cats . . . She said, "Cats are up here, Wolf."

Wolf craned his neck, twisting in the chair. "Where?"

"Under my chair, I think." Once they'd been given the appropriate tranquilizers and gotten used to zero gee, Merry and Neff had gone everywhere, disappearing for whole days. Smart too. No way to make a zero-gee litterbox, but they'd figured out the shower stall was all right, containing their hard little turds, easy to flush out. The dog was a much worse problem.

"Well, it's only a half-gee burn. They get their fuckin' tails caught in the slider gears, they'll learn something new." The timer chimed again, and Wolf said, "Places, everyone!" reaching for his armside controls.

When the burn was over, the Object hung in their monitor, now less than a hundred thousand kilometers away, odd and angular, gleaming like polished metal against the black and starry sky.

Wolf said, "Well. That is one damn strange looking woo-woo, if you ask me." Voice calm and light, but deadly serious all the same.

We've seen a lot of things in our years out among the stars. Most of them no more than geology. Glassy icemoons, like a child's lovely marbles. Black stones, like shiny lumps of coal. A small blue gas-giant with a ring system like quicksilver, gleaming in the light of a brilliant faraway sun . . . Where was that? Procyon, I think.

Wolf said, "We're targeted for a two-hundred klick flyby. Ought to be good enough to see what's what." He picked up the intercom. "Stu? Mark? Y'all can get on down to the labdeck now and see if your woo-woo's still active."

Thalia imagined Mark gritting his teeth. Imagined Stu snickering at him. Even though he too wanted to believe it was . . . something.

Wolf reached out and tapped the monitor face. "What the hell you make of that?"

The thing on the screen still looked like a cross between a Tinkertoy and a slag spill, too irregular to be artificial, to regular to be anything else. Wolf was pointing at a perfect, shiny metallic ring, just off the thing's geometric center, not quite facing them, half lit by the sun.

"Huh," she said. "Funny. It almost looks as if the surface is . . . flowing."

Wolf: "Yeah. Round and round the toroidal surface, like the smoke in a smoke-ring."

"Not possible, of course. I wonder what optical illusion—"

Wolf reached for his controls. "A little-bitty radar pulse ought to—"

"Uh-uh. Let Mark and Stu take their readings first. They've got better instrumentation than our nav gear."

Wolf pushed back into his chair, staring into the monitor. "Um. Right."

Long silence as the thing slowly grew. Pretty soon they'd be—

The instrument panel beeped, three quick, high, attention-getting pulses.

Radiation alarm.

Christ. She leaned forward, watching the graphs shift. Soft X rays. Gamma. From a moving source, um . . .

Wolf said, "That's odd. Shifting against the general radiation background as if . . ." He reached out and started popping through the external pickups, scanning the starfield along the local ecliptic. "Mmm. Nothing."

Mark's voice came through the intercom, sounding strained, "We're picking up some kind soft radiation source, moving against the local backdrop, coming in from the direction of the debris ring."

Wolf: "We see it, Mark. X rays and—"

Stu's voice, oddly breathless: "No, Wolf. Strongly blue-shifted Lyman alpha."

Thalia punched the video scanner, set it to looking for moving objects in the quadrant behind the planetesimal. There were lots of them, bits and pieces of this and that easily recognizable as . . .

Mark said, "The computer calculates . . . well. It says . . ."

They could hear Stu in the background, gabbling excitedly, "Jesus Christ, Mark, look at . . ."

There.

Just a blue sparkle in the distance, arcing lazily across the sky in the general direction of—

The radiation alarm blatted suddenly, loud and harsh, letting them know they were involved in a potential emergency, Wolf hunching forward, looking from control to control. "Neutron pulse."

Wolf said, "Yeah. Maintenance thinks the reactor is leaking."

Stu: "Wolf, that last came from the . . . the thing!"

The fucking woo-woo. The blue object was a fuzzball now, coming straight for them. Coming too fast. How far out? We're a long goddamn way from the thing in front of it. She did a quick sum in her head. Still not here, so it's . . . coming faster than light?

Amusement.

You know better than *that,* engineer Thalia Jansky. Relativistic approach, vectored down your line of sight.

She felt her breath shallow, watching it glitter and swirl as it bore down on the metal smoke ring. What's going to happen when it hits? Impact. Incandescence. Kinetic to thermal to . . . She imagined a spray of metal and rock vapor jetting from the planetesimal. Right. Coming our way a fuck of a lot faster than we'll be able to get out of the way.

"Wolfie? Maybe we better—"

The thing seemed to dart straight at them, suddenly *bigger* than the Object, ball of blue fire like a blinding sun.

The radiation alarms shrilled, computer imagining the antimatter ring was breached, was about to blow.

Thalia took her eyes off the screen, involuntarily looking at the alarm readout. Hard gamma pulse, identical to the one that had brought them here. When she looked back, the screen was . . . no, not empty. There was the Object, just as it had been before.

The alarm suddenly went silent.

Then Wolf grunted, "Fuck *almighty* . . ."

From somewhere down below she heard Mark's voice: "What the fuck was *that?*"

More silence.

Then something like a stagewhisper from Stu: "Um. I don't know."

Driving the starship in a slow circle around the artifact, Wolf couldn't quite keep his thoughts linear. Jumping from one thing to another, like a flea in a frying pan. Christ. We'll be lucky if I don't fucking ram the god damn thing. Stay on target, Wolfie.

Silly. I could fall asleep and the ship's computer would sense that I'd let go the controller, put us in a stable, collision-free trajectory and . . . God *damn* this is crazy! I can't quite make myself understand. *We've made First Contact!*

This is what humanity's been waiting for. Not just habitable worlds. Other *people,* for God's sake, no matter what they turn out to be like. All we have to do is fucking go home and show our evidence. No one will *care* about the infractions anymore. They'll vanish in the excitement. Thalia and me, we . . .

Despite the artifact turning in the screen, that was important too. Yes it was. Go home. Straighten things out. Maybe start to live the life we missed out on. Hell, that Stu's a smart kid. Maybe I . . . No. Jesus. You can't be his daddy. Maybe it'll help that I was his daddy's friend. Came to their wedding, shook his hand, told him how fucking jealous I was, pretending it was a lie . . . Christ. You had a date with you, a girl so friendly she'd blow a man with crushed ice in her mouth. And still, when Thalia walked down the aisle, all you could see was her *under* that nice man. Idiot.

Bad memory masked now by fresher memories. Memory of coupling with her. At the beach. In a storeroom back on Sagdeev. Here in the rover. Down on the engineering deck, woman shape wrapped around him, warm and soft where she needed to be, hard and muscular elsewhere, flat belly sliding on him. He smirked, feeling his genitals stir. Idiot. Okay. And what do we do about Honoria? You bastard. Loyal, helpless Honoria.

Fuckhead.

He shook his head slowly, not quite grinning to himself, and said, "Well. Looks like any second now, we'll be line-of-site through that crazy damn ring."

Cory tried to keep her eyes on the screen, watching the mess of glitter and shadow continue its slow turn. See how the silver-gray surface of the ring seems to move? It was barely an oval now, about to become a circle.

The radiation alarm suddenly blared.

Wolf's jaw seemed to drop, and he said, "What the *fuck.*"

Thalia, over the intercom: "Hard gamma burst!"

Wolf seemed to study his consoles, lean over and quickly scan the ones in front of the flight engineer's station. "Christ. I don't see a thing. You get a moving X-ray signature or—"

Thalia: "Not a goddamned thing."

"Well . . . uh."

A second alarm started up, high and hysterical. Wolf seemed startled, suddenly putting his hands on the armrest controllers, snarling, "*Collision* alarm!"

Thalia: "Bad thruster?"

"No. Nothing."

"Where?"

Wolf tapped one of the flatscreens and inspected a graph of twisty lines that came up, made of amber, gold, and bright azure. "Christ. Radar's interpreting the ring as a solid disk of, eh . . . infinite density?"

"What d'you mean?"

"Dunno. It thinks we're falling straight toward it."

"We're still floating down here, Wolf. No acceleration or . . ."

"If it's infinite density, then the gravitational—"

"Don't be an ass! Do you *feel* any tidal—"

"Well shit. Instruments say we really *are* . . ." His jaw seemed to set grimly. "I'm getting us the fuck out here. Secure for emergency maneuvering."

Cory recoiled as his big hand reached over, grabbed the adjuster tab of her harness and pulled it tight.

"You hold the fuck on, kiddo. Keep your hands in your lap, just like that."

"Yes, Wolf." Weak. Not quite down to a whisper.

Thalia, voice high and nervous: "We're all set. Go. *Go!*"

Wolf twisted one of his hand controllers and something screamed deep within the ship, from somewhere far behind them. Cory felt the room sort of slither around her.

Wolf, voice very rough, oddly pitched: "Well there's a fuck of a tide *now!* Going to thrusters."

He's terrified. Are we going to die? Something banged outside the hull, loud, metallic, and she felt the seatback rotate, carrying her body with it.

Wolf, relieved, a man pardoned on the scaffold itself: "*There!* Main stage emergency lightoff. Four . . . three . . . two . . . one . . . *now!*" A switch snapped under his hand, loud enough to penetrate through the shrill mix of alarms and bumping thrusters.

Far, far away, far behind her back, something went *thud* and the entire ship shook. Wolf pushed a lever forward and muttered, "And . . . full thrust . . . and . . ."

Cory braced herself for the crushing force of . . .

Thalia: "What the hell's going on, Wolf? I don't *feel* anything!"

Wolf, mouth hanging open, face extraordinarily pale, blue eyes utterly empty, sat back in his seat, staring at the thing in the viewscreen.

Cory thought, I never saw anything so . . . so . . . *beautiful.*

The stars in the black sky, visible through the hole in the

torus, suddenly turned to jewels, ruby and sapphire, emerald and diamond and amethyst and . . . The stars suddenly grew huge, crowding out the night.

Sparkling. Sparkling.

She felt herself seized by a multitude of fiery hands, hands so tiny they could reach right inside. Seized. Compressed. Squeezed into a space so small.

Then cast away into nothingness.

Four

Down on the science deck, Mark floated, stunned.

It was over in few seconds, Stu and Thalia manipulating their instruments furiously, shouting back and forth to the control room. On the screen the artifact was gone, replaced by drifting bright stars. Mark tried to follow their technical details for a minute, then gave up. It's clear enough. We're goners. He'd always suspected that it had happened, would happen again, that the FTL travel would somehow not work, that they'd be . . . lost.

The expression on Honoria's face, he thought, a mirror of what he was feeling . . . The memory of her loud "Oh, my God!" as they went through. Jesus. No. Hold on. Wait until we have *proof.* He propelled himself into the cluster of instruments, hovering between the two of them. Screen after screen showed alien stars, one almost bright enough to be a sun, vivid charts and tables assembling themselves in others. "What happened?" he said, and he could hear the plaintive tone in his voice. "Where the *fuck* are we?"

Stu looked at him with incredible condescension. *He* was enjoying this, at least. Thalia, oh Thalia, look at me, please.

Stu: "We need to move some more before the instruments can make any sort of parallax measurements, but there are lots of clues as to where we are right now. A relatively young open starcluster, that's pretty clear. Quite a few large B stars in the neighborhood. I'm pretty sure I've located Betelgeuse and the other Orion supergiants."

Thalia: "The instruments are looking for some of the local pulsars, and, if we're in the same quadrant of the galaxy, which I'd say we are, they should have a position for us momentarily. . . . Uh-huh. Yep. As I thought."

"I should have guessed when I looked through the gate, although I didn't know for certain how far away it was."

"So," the voice came down from the control room, soft and a little amused. "You folks gonna let us in on it?"

Stu smiled. "A handful of bright blue-white giants, mixed in with maybe three hundred other stars, agewise about a hundred million years old; located about four hundred light-years from Earth."

Thalia: "We've been transported well out of the range of human exploration, Wolf. Welcome to the Pleiads."

A muffled gasp from Honoria then.

"And the nearby star, it only follows, must be the dimmest of the seven sisters, Pleione. Some people used to call it Purple Pleione, but it's a blue B8 star just like the others."

Honoria, turning away, moaning softly to herself.

And it took no more than an hour for them to discover the nearby stargate was just dead slag now, the hole just a hole, barring their way back.

Transit to Pleione.

Honoria floated gently just above the surface of the control room deck, hands holding onto the cool, hard metal of the porthole frame, one leg curled under her, toes barely touching the floor, the other stretched out, foot braced against the lock lever of the hatch to the deck below.

Everyone else, down below, down in another world. Mark and Stu. Corazón. Ox the dog. Those damned cats.

Thalia.

Hard fear. *What if we never get back?*

Then elation: *My God. The Pleiades!*

She could sense Wolf's presence, hard, silent, male, strapped into his pilot's seat behind her back. Listen closely. Breathing. Soft movement. Silence. A gentle sigh, a mutter, something about one of the instrument readings, a few numbers, then a whisper, *God damn it* in English.

When she thought of him, thought of him speaking, the memories were always of his fluent Spanish, almost like a native speaker, tinged only with those same curious defects that marred his English. Diphthongs where there were none. Odd, guttural vowels. Sounds shading into one another, *e* and *i,* almost the same, making *tingo* out of *tengo.*

Every once in a while he'd make a mistake that betrayed a language learned in its written form rather than grown in childhood. *Fiw* when he meant to say *fue,* followed by an exasperated eye-roll.

I love the way he talks.

She edged closer to the UV-proof machined quartz of the window, looking out at jewellike blue stars, illuminating smoky patches of otherwise black night sky.

Pleiades.

I wonder which one is which?

Alcyone. Taygeta.

Electra. Maia.

Asterope. Celaeno.

Why don't I know?

It never mattered before.

Just history.

Entertaining, fanciful history at that.

The stones of Atlantis. She flinched away from a brief memory of Wolf making fun of her beliefs. The Atlantean world conference of 50,727 B.C. Then the energy-crystal disaster. Worldwide problems. Then the Pleions coming to help, in 28,000 B.C., a multiplane mass emigration . . .

Pleione. Purple Pleione. Now less than twelve hours away.

Invisible beyond the ship's nose, of course, but if she leaned close enough, pressed her face to the cold crystal, she could see dazzling violet light, the reflection of her magical star, bouncing off the hull, off the leading edge of the engine pods, up into the corner of her eye.

She sighed. Held her breath. Listened to Wolf stir in his chair.

Only doing his job.

Doing what he ought to do.

Another angry fuse, quickly sputtering out. What *is* it he ought to do? Or not do. She shoved away a rising memory, feeling the breath strangle in her throat. Don't start now. Don't give him the satisfaction. Bastard.

What am I going to do?

Still the assumption that they *would* get home. Jabber of technotalk, Wolf, Thalia, Stu, Mark trying to join in, floundering hopelessly. Corazón asking sensible questions, Wolf looking at her with sudden respect in his eyes.

If the . . . stargate hardware here can't be run in reverse, doesn't seem to send us . . . elsewhere . . . maybe this other . . . matrix of . . . technofacts . . .

Never you worry now, little girl. I'll see you get home again.

Wolf the Hero.

She saw a spark of uneasiness rise in Thalia's eye, saw doubt disfigure her mannish face. Good. Bitch.

Home. What home would that be?

She felt tears trying to well up. A sense of clogging in her nose.

No gravity here to make any of it run down.

And that other memory. Memory of a scene only imagined, not real at all. The imagined scene from down below, with Corazón taking Thalia's place . . . How would that be?

Another image of herself, back in the comfortable house on Sagdeev, alone in my bed, alone in my little room, listening to sounds of lovemaking, coming from the master bedroom, Corazón in the place that used to be mine. Her nose filled completely, forcing an involuntary sniffle.

When the timer hit zero, Wolf released the deadman switch on his armrest and felt himself bounce away from the seat upholstery, tug against the restraining straps and bounce back as the engine shut down. Not clear. Not crisp. Distant waterfall roar cutting off, yes, but then a shudder, a chug, a little surge of power . . . like the way my daddy's old car used to diesel when he cut off the key.

Never did figure out why the hell it was doing that.

He died. I sold the car.

Don't look back.

He stole a quick glance at Thalia, who kept her eyes on the instruments, hands on her controls. Are we ashamed yet? Ashamed? Or were these good deeds?

Christ. Asshole. How many excuses do you need?

Especially *here.*

Thalia said, "Engine secure."

Right. Business. "Roll program." He reached out and tapped one of the touchscreens, watched numbers scroll, then twisted the hand controller. There was a distant whine as the gyros shifted, stars rolling across the monitor, a faint sense of spin in his ears. Down below, Mark would be swallowing hard.

Hope you feel better now, Marky.

The stars stabilized in the main screen, and Thalia said, "Well. That looks different."

Though the view in the screen was normalized, the control room was subtly backlit by reflected light coming through the little porthole, giving everything a vaguely violet tinge. And the things in the viewscreen . . . I don't know what the hell we were expecting. Maybe just another set of stargate rings. Hard to make myself accept where we are. Pleiades! Sucked through the fucking rabbit hole, sent hundreds of light-years in the blink of an . . . Crackle of fear. How do we know . . . *when* this is? Too many old stories. Too many ridiculous god damn old . . .

In the screen, rather than a metal smoke Tinkertoy like the one at Beta Pic, like the one a day back along their orbital track . . . flock of boulders. Nicely shaped boulders, artificial boulders, a landscaper's fucking *professional* boulders.

Thalia said, "Some kind of Trojan asteroid group, I guess."

"Uh. Trojan to what?"

"Good question."

Stu's voice over the intercom, breathless, excited. "Mom? We're getting a strong nitrogen signature." He blurted a string of coordinates, then, "Some oxygen. Hydrocarbon contaminants. Um . . . CO_2."

Wolf reached out and punched in the coordinates. The symmetrical gray boulders slid apart and vanished, blue-green spark centering itself against the starry black, then swiftly bloating to a respectable blue-green ball. Clouds. Small blue seas. Green and brown landscape.

Thalia said, "How far away is that?"

Mark's voice said, "Gravimetric says two million kilometers."

Wolf, mouth feeling uncomfortably dry: *"And?"*

Long silence, then Stu said, "We get a reading of . . . well, computer thinks it's thirty-two hundred meters circumference. Give or take."

Meters?

Into the next long silence, Thalia said, "That sure does look like a habitable planet."

Wolf said, "I'm not sure I want to believe in a habitable planet one kilometer across."

Cory, voice charmingly tinged with a very slight accent, almost unnoticeable face-to-face: "Maybe it's just a painting. You know. Like decoration or something."

People used to do that before the war, didn't they? How many cracking, peeling, faded old murals do you remember seeing on the eroding sides of how many old buildings? Wolf pulled the data onto one of his secondary screens. Well, no. Definitely the right chemistry.

Stu: "Mom? We just got a radar pulse off the limb. Two echoes. It's . . . almost like the atmosphere is homogeneous. Like there's two surfaces, one the ground we see, the other at the top of the air."

Wolf: "Like a thermocline. Pressure."

Stu said, "Maybe something like point-eight bar. I'm not sure how to interpret this data. We never really studied . . . I mean . . . Sorry."

"You're doing good, kid." He turned and looked at Thalia, matched her long level stare. Then reached out and tapped the intercom to mute. "So. What d'you think we're looking at here?"

She turned back to the screen, stared for a second, sighed. "How the hell would I know? Or anybody."

"Look, we're all agreed we've fallen smack into the middle of a high-tech civilization. This is *it!*"

She said, "So where're all the fucking aliens?"

Good question.

She said, "So the bold primitives cross the Ocean of Suns in their crude dugout canoes, discover the New World in all its glory, come paddling right into New York fucking harbor and—"

"And get their hairy little asses sucked down the coolant intake of the Coney Island Fusion Plant."

Thalia grinned, odd, lopsided, humorless, still looking at the little green world. "Mmm. Guess that would explain why no one's—"

"So what d'you think we're looking at? The workers' breakroom?"

She shrugged. "Guess we better go see."

Wolf tapped the intercom back to life and said, "Stand by for acceleration."

From three kilometers out the thing looked like a terrestrial world seen from six radii. Earth from geosynchronous orbit, Wolf thought. Only not really like Earth. Earth had more clouds. More blue of ocean. Stripes of brown desert, the lightning-bolt shapes of mountain chains, river valleys, the icy glare of Greenland, Antarctica . . . This is more like the worlds we imagined we'd find, once upon a time, virgin terrestrial worlds out among the stars, habitable planets for Man. Cowboy Country, Mark II. That fabled Second Chance.

From the intercom, Stu's voice was soft. "Radar gives a ghost echo fifty meters off the surface. That's the . . . I guess it's the top of the air."

Top of the air. Like a plastic membrane, holding in an eight-hundred-millibar pressurized environment.

Mark said, "We're trying to do an orbital calculation so we can, um, calculate the mass. Um."

Stu: "Mom? Is there a calculation program we can run on this data? Neither one of us knows . . ."

Somewhere in a seedy motel back in Alice Springs there'd be a scientist who knew. Thalia said, "Don't bother. I can use the hull strain gauges to calculate a tidal force." She reached out and poked her instrumentation screens, then sat back staring at the graph unfolding before her, face expressionless.

"Well?"

She twisted in her seat and looked at him. "I get point-oh-five gee. Where are we, six radii?"

Mmm. "Not in orbit, Thalia. I stopped us dead."

"So we're falling."

"Slowly at first . . . what're we looking at for the surface, something like point-one?"

"Maybe a little less."

Stu said, "Are we going to land, Mr. O'Malley?"

Mr. O'Malley again. Maybe another little fight with step-daddy? "I'd sure like to." Beautiful blue-green world, blocking half the sky now, beckoning.

Mark said, "You fire a thermonuclear engine at that little bit of an atmosphere, there's not going to be much left for us to explore."

Wolf grinned to himself, watching the thing expanding before them. "Spend much time at space pilot school, Mark?"

"Well . . ."

In the background Wolf heard Stu whisper, "*Mark.* It's not going to be like a liftoff from Earth. He can land using the OMS thrusters. How the fuck do you think they land on *asteroids?*"

People who know a little often seem to think they know a lot. Wolf turned back to Thalia. "We do have a little problem. Back end of this thing's extremely radioactive, and we don't dare fold the radiator vanes without access to Temporary Services."

She frowned and said, "No. Not if we want to keep running everything."

"On an asteroid this little, we'd normally come in nose first."

Thalia said, "A Dactyl-class body wouldn't be having one-tenth gee."

"No. I keep avoiding that, don't I?"

"A very dense core is all it'd take."

He said, "Yeah. Think I could balance this thing on its nose? Control gyros'd keep her from tipping, sans any major lateral force."

She squinted at the screen. "Um. Hull damage . . ."

"Take a look down there, Thalia. Green growing things. Bodies of water. I'd say that implies a fairly deep, soft regolith."

She said, "I'll be watching the strain gauges. You back off if I say so."

"Right."

"Why the hell are we doing this, Wolf? We're in big god damned trouble!"

"Why? Because this is the greatest fucking thing that ever happened to *anybody*, Thalia. Whether we get home or not, I mean to fucking *see* it!"

She sank back in her chair, eyes big, watching the little planet continue to grow. "Yeah. I guess so."

Over the intercom, a subdued Mark said, "Be funny if the atmospheric membrane or whatever the hell it is popped as we went through."

Wolf said, "Yep. I'll be yuckin' up a storm when *that* happens, Marky."

Down on the laboratory deck, Cory sat strapped into one of the research station chairs, the one in the corner farthest from where Mark and Stu bickered in furious little whispers, holding the big dog in her lap, an enormous, hairy, ill-smelling bag of zero-gee feathers.

"God damn it, I told you to—"

"Shut the fuck up, *Marky*."

She could almost hear Mr. Porringer gritting his teeth. "Stuie, you little shit . . ."

Easy to understand on the one hand. Stuart McCray is a fifteen-year-old boy who's never seen a bit of hardship in all his life. School. Friends. Toys. Mommy and Daddy to love and coddle him . . . She thought of her own father for just a second, then remembered abruptly that Stu's father was dead as well. Mark's just a man who sleeps with his mother.

Image of Wolf. Her own mother. Thalia. Mark again . . . She sighed softly, wishing the world held something like adults, rather than an endless succession of Teenagers from Hell, watching the thing in the screen get bigger and bigger. Beside her chair, Merry and Neff, locked in their catbox, scratched and shuffled, uneasy, seeming to mutter to one another, and the dog's heart beat hard against her chest.

Nervous. They know something's going on.

Wolf's voice said, "Stand by. Three minutes to thrust."

Stu looked over his shoulder and smiled at her. "You better get out of that chair, Cory. This is going to be the ceiling soon."

When she let go of the dog, he floundered violently in midair for a moment, rotating his spine like a cat trying to turn right side up, then froze, pulling in his legs to a lying-down position, drifting, head twisted back, looking at her appealingly. She reached out and took him by the collar before undoing her own lap restraint.

The cats, with their manipulatorlike claws, were much better at zero gee, could get along on their own so well that they'd had to be locked up more and more of late to keep them out of mischief. Poor Ox, completely handless, could only hold onto things with his mouth.

That and the pathetic humping position he'd sometimes assume while clinging to a leg. She giggled as she towed him up to the ceiling, picking out a relatively level place between two storage lockers. "Is this okay?"

Stu looked at her and smiled again, then turned himself over in the air. "That's great. Mark?"

"Yeah, yeah."

Wolf: "Ten seconds."

Cory held the dog close, looking wide-eyed at the screen, where the little planet was starting to flatten out, look like a real world all of a sudden, sea turning to an ocean that stretched to the barely curved horizon . . . like we're in a high-flying jet, far, far above the clouds, but . . .

There was a soft, chuttering buzz from somewhere beyond the hull, and she felt herself sink against the ceiling, feeling very odd after so many weightless days and nights, Ox squirming in her arms, then going boneless, lying across her lap like a ton of dead meat. Dead but for a brief, soft, panting whine.

Overhead, the catbox suddenly lifted off, Merry and Neff yowling in alarm, flew through the air, crashed down on the ceiling, bounced, crashed again. Cursing, English words she didn't know, Stuart scrambled over to the box, peering anxiously inside, whispering to the cats.

Mark shouted, "God damn it, leave the fucking—"

There was a prolonged, deep-pitched thrum, also beyond the hull. A sort of squeaking, like the sound a party balloon makes as you twist it into a fanciful shape.

Thalia's voice: "Pressure on the forward hull."

She heard her mother's voice, suddenly, whispering Spanish prayers. Mother Mary hold me safe from . . . Honoria was curled up in a corner, hands covering her face. No one thought to make sure she . . . well, she'd had the sense to get out of her seat after all.

There was a hard, shuddery bump, then everything was still, but for a sense of . . . swaying. And, from somewhere far overhead, somewhere back aft, a thin, warbling, singsong whine. From his place beside the cats, crouching on the ceiling, Stu looked up at the floor, face flooding with anxiety. "That'll be the gyros trying to keep us from tipping over."

What if we tip? What if . . .

Thalia said, "Nose strain gauges holding at point-nine."

Wolf: "Okay. What was max?"

"One-point-three-two."

Stu got up from the ceiling and walked slowly over to the instrument panel. Looked at his upside-down readouts and touchscreens, then grinned. "Guess no one anticipated this, uh . . . *attitude.*"

The forward hatch whispered open and Wolf's head popped through. "Everything's fine, guys. I'm going out." The boyish grin on his face made Cory feel unexpectedly warm.

The arguments came and went. They took their air samples, argued about what the word *sterile* really meant in this unknown, completely *unknowable,* context, Wolf, Thalia, Mark, Stu, gesticulating at the boxed-up EVA suits, making one point, then another, then another.

Wolf: "Look, this is fucking ridiculous. Anybody who's afraid can stay in the goddamned ship! Anybody who's *not* afraid can get in the airlock with me."

Then Cory found herself standing in the airlock with Wolf and Stu, looking out the open inner hatch at angry Mark, frightened Honoria, Thalia standing in the doorway, looking back and forth.

"Well. Well." Thalia turned away, stepped into the airlock and swung the hatch shut behind her.

Honoria's sudden shout of, *"¡Corazonita!"* was cut off in mid-word.

Cory's heart seemed to leap into her throat.

Wolf grinned at Thalia and said, "More like it, babe."

Babe. English loan word into Argentine Spanish, *bébi,* as from boys to girls, boys with sly, groping hands.

Wolf put his hand on a little knob beside the external hatch and said, "Watch your ears." A twist. A hiss.

Cory felt a little crackle of pain, an airliner sort of thing, and swallowed uncomfortably, remembering the year she and her family had gone on vacation to Rio, to Carnival, flying up the coast from Buenos Aires. Funny how you could almost understand the Cariocas. Almost, but not quite. Quick memory of her father, trying to bargain with a Brazilian shopkeeper.

All I had eyes for was the stark white beach, the sparkling blue sea, all the pretty girls, almost naked, walking hip-shot down the strand, drawing the eyes of men.

How does a little girl know that's what she'll want someday?

Just to walk along, toes in the hot sand, sun kissing sweet brown skin, cool breeze coming in off the sea, while men whisper to one another, watching. Just watching.

Wolf cranked the hatch's lock lever, back and forth, back and forth. It swung in on them, brilliant light flooding in. Outside, there was a bright, flat world. Flat land about ten meters below. Green forest over there. Bright white beach, sparkling with little crystalline glitters, red, blue, green, like tiny jewels, then a pale blue-green sea, reaching for the low, close horizon under a dark, royal-blue sky.

Sky in which wan stars glittered.

And the sun . . .

She gripped the hatch frame, leaning out a bit, feeling Wolf's hand warm on her shoulder. "The sun looks so funny. Squashed. Like it's somehow come loose from the sky."

Beside her, on his knees, Stuart said, "I never thought I'd see anything like this. Not *ever!*"

From somewhere back in the airlock, Thalia said, "Where do we keep the wire ladder?"

* * *

Stu, feeling the happiness surge up in him like a buoyant plume, leaned backward, hands grabbing the ladder like a swing, one foot on the flexing wire rung, the other reaching out behind him, reaching. Above him at regular intervals against the rocket cylinder, his mom, Wolf, and Cory, expectant faces staring down. There. He let go and slipped onto the surface of the planetoid, springy grasslike matcrial cushioning the minimal impact. They'd let him come down first, Thalia and Wolf acting in concert, acting like proper . . . parents, for a change, ignoring grumbling Mark and the rest.

So.

"Say something, Stuart," Thalia said. "It's a tradition."

Out past the giant nose of *NR-598h,* expanding up from the ground and into the sky like some fantastic technomegalith, the slightly irregular lawn led down to where a strange-colored sun cast a thin streak of azure light across a surging, rippling "ocean."

"Oh, Mom. That's for *real* planets. This isn't much more than a large spaceship."

Wolf: "Pretty luxurious one, though."

He didn't wait for the others, taking long, slow steps down to the white crescent of beach, breathing the air tinted with a brackish smell something like coffee. Not unpleasant, and, even before he stepped onto the sand, almost unnoticeable. He took a long breath through his nostrils and just stood there at the very edge of the water, enjoying the *size* of it all after the claustrophobic confines of the spaceship. Little ripples sloshed up and nibbled at his toes. For some reason, it didn't even occur to him to be wary.

Pleione, from this distance, was small, much smaller than the sun, but terribly bright. Squinting hard against the glare, Stu studied it, averting his eyes when he couldn't take it anymore. The star was extremely oblate, its long axis vertical, squashed at the poles, a celestial Robin's egg sitting on end in the sky. Brighter and bluer on the sides, whitish and, by comparison, drabber in the faster-spinning equatorial zone. As he watched, it drew noticeably closer to the watery horizon, dropping like a stone. He held out a finger and did a primitive measurement. Christ. Almost three degrees a minute.

Wolf was behind him, over to the right. "Don't look at it too long, Stu. The atmospheric cap seems to filter out most of the shorter wavelengths, but it's still bright enough to damage your retinas."

He turned and saw the others straggling down toward them from the inverted rocket ship, staring off in all directions, looking for all the world like some comical pantomime on the subject of being lost. Yes, Cory too. She seemed to have lost her air of detachment and was gaping with the best of them.

"It'll be dark in a minute," Wolf said. "We probably should get some lights from the ship. I wonder if we could build a fire."

Thalia chuckled. "I always suspected you enjoyed those impromptu jungle bivouacs too much, Wolf. Leave it you to want to camp out here. There may be wild animals, after all."

Ancient history being reenacted before my very eyes, Stu thought, turning back to watch the sky. As Pleione approached the horizon, there were none of the effects associated with a planetary sunset. How could there be, with an atmosphere so thin? Here and there wisps of cloud were moving across the sky, in reality only a few hundred meters away, more like smoke than true clouds, barely lightening the cobalt blueness. It seemed magical, beyond any technology, to devise something like this.

The star plunged into the bright-flecked sea and was gone, like that. Almost instantaneously, the blue of the sky snapped down after it, and the landscape disappeared into total darkness. Stu lost his bearings for a moment, trying to stare around the bright pink-orange smudge of the star's afterimage. He took a step, felt the sand give a little. "Jesus," he said. "I can't see a thing."

"Give it a second, Stu," Mark said.

"Hey," Cory said, "the stars are coming out."

Only a little while later, the others were spread out on the lawn, sitting around the nose of the ship, watching, the only light coming from the magnificent sky. Pleione's garish zodiacal band, initially a big arm reaching up halfway to the zenith, was gone, and Stu and Cory strolled across the dim, spectral landscape, illumination mainly from the relatively nearby star Alcyone, ten times brighter than Venus, and, far to the south, great Atlas, ten times brighter still, both blue-white, both steady, untwinkling beacons, dwarfing the regular background stars into insignificance. The fitful sea breeze, never strong, had died suddenly, and now it was unnaturally quiet. Every little murmur from the ocean was magnified, and the few words that passed between them seemed loud. Like a moonlit night, almost, with every object throwing two distinctly shifting shadows.

The stars were streaking so rapidly overhead that he felt a little queasy, suddenly aware that it was the planetoid and not the stars that was moving. The benefit of this was that the stars were continuously changing, new ones taking the old ones' places, and only now was the center of the star cluster coming up, the major Pleiads forming a burning blue rhomboid in the sky, blinding Alcyone near its heart, surrounded by a dense swipe of blazing turquoise covering an area larger than a hundred moons. Almost like a bit of daytime sky cut out and pasted into the darkness, this cloud of dust and gas was quantitatively different from the much dimmer, streaky, cirruslike bluish wisps around the other bright Pleiads.

"That's Merope on one side, the double Asterope pair

on the other." He was trying to whisper, but it came out pretty forced.

She was looking up again. "It looks . . . full of stars. All kinds, some reddish, some yellowish, but the bright ones are all so blue."

Stu, feeling as though the moment had come, reached out and caught her hand. She started to pull away, but hesitated, then let her hand relax. She looked at him, dark face and hair a mystery of shadow in the starlight, each eye showing two little highlights. Suddenly, Atlas was gone behind a low hill, making it seem even darker. "There are about three hundred of the dimmer members. The bright ones are all massive young blue stars, with an extremely high rotation speed. They all lose gas to the interstellar medium, especially Pleione and Alcyone. If we were here during one of Pleione's eruptions, the star would look a lot different."

"Uh-huh. It's all so beautiful. As though beauty were a . . . natural thing, not in short supply."

"Your mother hasn't said a word since we landed. Do you have any idea what's wrong with her?"

Cory looked down, pulled her hand away. "I'd rather not talk about it. I'm going to join the others now."

Over. Just like that. Stu watched as she carefully picked her way toward the towering rocketship. It was almost sunrise now, the other half of Pleione's zodiacal light peeking over the not-so-distant forest top. After a few minutes he started back himself.

Blue began to spread overhead, like a bright shade being drawn across the sky, spears of blinding blue light piercing the forest canopy, etching the scene before him. His eyes didn't want to adapt, dazzled and tormented by the growing, changing fingers that were overspreading the landscape. Rubbing away the tears, seeing the scene again, the others not twenty meters away, still on their blankets in varying degrees of repose.

Shock bit through his disappointment. Cory was sitting next to Wolf.

Wolf sat on a grassy hillside looking out over a tideless sea, soft breeze like a wind from nowhere ruffling his hair, making his face feel cool. The lopsided sun that was Purple Pleione was gone again, gone around the little world, would return in little more than an hour. The sea had calmed, and, from this perspective, its starlit gray surface was like a mirror, reflecting the hard blue-white dots of the setting Pleiades, each with its little patch of turquoise fog.

Look at that. All you have to do is watch for a minute and you can see the fucking stars turn.

He felt a peculiar little thrill, as though the cool breeze had gone down the back of his neck. God *damn.* All the things I've seen, all the things I've done . . . a brief kaleidoscope of worldscapes twisted in memory . . . nothing at *all* to compare with this.

He ran his fingers through the wiry, plasticky grass on the ground beside him. Nothing at all. Wry grin. Okay. Maybe Astroturf . . . nah. This stuff's *much* better than Astroturf. Make a God damned *fortune* selling this stuff for fucking suburban lawns.

The others were down on the flat ground, Cory and her mother on the beach, Mark by himself over by the ship, ship towering absurdly into the sky. It looks like a cartoon starship. Like it doesn't belong here. In the distance, a dark speck soared. Another one of those flying things. Living things of some kind, though we haven't gotten close enough to *see* . . . Fuckers disappear as soon as you whip your binoculars up.

No sign of Thalia or her kid.

Ox came bouncing up the hillside, flying like magic in the low gee, red-eyed like a demon, slowed, got his belly next to the ground for a second, tongue popping out, sort of licking around, eyeing Wolf adoringly before throwing himself down, resting against his thigh.

Wolf put his hand on the dog's neck, ruffled its head, pulled its ears, listening for a familiar soft sigh of pleasure. "This is the life, huh, you old log, you?"

The dog licked his hand, leaving behind some kind of sticky film that dried quickly.

Wonder what the hell he makes of all this? No stranger than anything else that's ever happened, I guess. I remember how he used to like riding in the sidecar of my old BSA-2000, leaning into the slipstream, ears straight back, eyes scrunched up, tongue flapping in the breeze. Jet planes. Rocket ships. Oxygen masks. Fuck.

It's a dog's life.

Dog who'd evidenced great joy at being able to take a dump under gravity once again.

Ox nosed under his hand, lifting his fingers, trying to start him petting again.

Down on the beach, Honoria was bending over, picking up one of those things that might or might not be seashells, was showing it to Cory. His memory supplied a quick invocation of Honoria in their bedroom on Sagdeev, bending over naked in front of him, picking up a discarded sock, throwing it in the hamper.

He felt a quick stir of arousal, memory of the arousal that earlier scene had made in him. Good old Honey. Never a word of complaint when I'd grab her, wrestle her down on the bed or floor, wherever we happened to be. Just grab her and fuck her. The perfect fucking woman.

"Wish we could let the cats out."

Wolf jerked slightly, looking over his shoulder at Stuart, who'd apparently come up the backside of the hill. Ox lay still, not reacting. Heard him coming, knew who he was, no point in wasting good energy, disturbing the hand that scratches. "You'd never find the fuckers again."

"That's what Mark said." Sullen resentment in the boy's voice.

Mark was climbing up the wire ladder now, face pointed resolutely at the hull, not looking down, swaying back and forth. Hell. I can feel his fear from here. Must be fucking hell to be scared all the time like that. He said, "I'm sorry you don't get along with him, Stu."

"He's such a fucking *putz!*"

Wolf stared into the boy's face, searching for a trace of understanding. "I imagine he's pretty much feeling like a putz these days." Is that how you're supposed to feel when some hotshot's putting the prong to your wife? How the fuck would I know?

Stuart's lips seemed to curl, pursing together oddly, and he looked away, first down toward the beach, where Honoria and Cory had grown small in the distance, then away, up at the midnight sky.

Sorry kid. Don't imagine you like having me fuck your mom either. Nothing much I can say to you about that, is there? Just the way it is. Stark white memory of Thalia Jansky splayed out for him, arms and legs and face and head fading away in the fog, almost irrelevant. Tits and flat belly, yes, but the vision was dominated by the stark black sunburst of her pubic bush, beckoning, beckoning. . . .

Christ! What the fuck am I thinking now? I heard the cuntlips call my name? What a fucking maroon!

Beside him, Stuart slowly lifted his arm and pointed at the sky. "Mr. O'Malley? What's that?"

Where he pointed there was a pale fleck, visibly moving. He lifted his binoculars, peered at the thing and said, "It's one of those boulders." He imagined it crashing down out of the heavens, obliterating them all, but . . . right. No sign of cratering.

Stu said, "There's another one."

And another. And another. And . . .

Stu said, "Like a reverse meteor storm. All heading back into the radiant."

Right. Wolf stood slowly, hair on the back of his neck seeming to stir, tracked a couple of trajectories, then put the binoculars on the focus of their extended rays. "Huh. Something there, all right." As he watched, a boulder came into the magnified field, slowing as it approached the mass of . . . "Huh. Like it's fluid. Starting to twist and—"

Flash.

"What was that?"

Wolf took the binoculars away from his eyes, blinking slowly. "Dunno." The sky was growing brighter, though Purple Pleione's rise was still many minutes away. Lots of drifting dots in the sky now. Dozens, verging on hundreds. "We'd better get back to the ship, round up the others and . . . Come on. Ox. Let's go, boy!"

The dog bounded to its feet, bouncing oddly, scrambling for traction in the low gee.

Back where they belonged. Back in a safe, familiar environment.

Wolf sat in his command pilot's chair, Thalia at the engineer's station, hatches dogged down as per regs, the others down below. Over the intercom, you could hear Mark and Stu bickering, just on the edge of audibility. Familiar. Comfortable.

In one of the smaller viewscreens the nameless little planet was no more than a blue-green marble, already millions of kilometers away, the . . . construct, whatever it was, filling the main screen, streamers of metal smoke twisting and turning, forming into mystery shapes that were somehow increasingly familiar themselves.

Like we know what it is.

"Where'd you go back there? I was worried." Memory of standing in the airlock door, firing the flare gun, once, twice, two bright magnesium stars sending a coruscation of shadows over the alien landscape, perfectly reflected in the mirror-bright sea. Then the flood of relief as she came running from the forest of incomprehensible alien trees.

She said, "I found a nest of those flying things."

"So."

"They were . . . I don't know. Not like anything I ever saw before. You know what carbon paper is?"

"Sure. My daddy and me found a whole warehouse full of it back in the Smokies, once. Something the government put away in case of a nuclear war, maybe back in the 1960s or seventies. I forget what he said it was for."

Thalia said, "I thought they looked just a little bit like carbon-paper butterflies."

The thing on the screen suddenly crystallized into an array of rings and Tinkertoys.

Silence. Then Stu said, "Is it another stargate?"

How the fuck would I know?

Thalia said, "Looks like it."

Mark: "We're picking up another one of those flying lights. Like the ones that activated the gate back at Beta Pictoris."

Hard gamma radiation out on the hull. What if we were still down on the planet? The big central smoke ring of the stargate was starting to turn in on itself, rolling, rolling. "How far?"

Stu said, "We're not sure. Out of radar range, at least. Strongly blue-shifted."

From below, Honoria's voice, speaking in Spanish: "Let me see." Brief silence, then, vibrant and breathless: "Yes! A *Pleion* ship! It was *true!* It was *always* true!"

Thalia said, "If we don't boost any more delta-vee, we'll be there ourselves in two hours."

Wolf felt his mouth go dry. "Yeah."

Stuart McCray saw movement in the dark recess between two instrument boxes, liquid eyes glinting. Getting to like it here, aren't you, Merry? The cat, comfortably ensconced on top of a warm relay housing, poked her head out and looked around. Stu held out his forefinger and waited while the cat cautiously rubbed her dark wet nose against the fingertip. Old, old routine between them, dating back to when he was a child. No, no static discharge this time. Stu scratched her between the ears, smoothed her vibrissae back the way she liked. The cat began to purr softly, hooked a clawed paw over the lip of a display box and pulled herself a little closer.

On the screen over the cat's head, the second gate complex, still several hundred kilometers away, was silhouetted against bright Alcyone and her patch of blue sky. Hundreds of dim Pleiads in the background like salt scattered on black velvet. In another box, a close-up of the smoke ring itself, lazily twirling, twirling.

Almost an hour now since Wolf lit off the engine again, braking us into a matching orbit. Stu ruffled the cat's head, enjoying its attention.

Wolf on the intercom: "All right, folks. Everybody report to their stations. Here it comes."

No sign of Mark. Just as well. Stu tapped out a few commands, studied the telescopic image that appeared in the large flatscreen. A dim, blue point was slowly moving across a normal starfield. He locked the scope onto the thing, moved to full magnification. Still a featureless speck at this distance.

Thalia: "Can you trace its point of origination, son?"

"Not really. It's not from the other stargate, I can tell you that. Looks like its coming from the general direction of the Asterope pair. It's moving at a considerable fraction of the speed of light."

Wolf: "I want to be ready when that thing gets here. Prepare for engine ignition."

Thalia: "What are you talking about?"

"You know, Thal. There's zero chance of us ever getting home again unless we understand how to *use* the stargates."

Words hanging in air. The truth, for a change. Not all the optimistic bullshit. Updated readings from the alien ship. It was more than a speck now, swelling, fattening into a little droplet. "Mr. O'Malley, that thing's going to get here in about four minutes. On its present course, it'll miss us, but not by much."

The minutes went by in a flash. "Thirty-five seconds to impact." He switched to a wider field of view including the distant stargate.

Engines lit with a metallic bang, followed by the familiar coursing roar. Everything settling, cat suddenly scrabbling for purchase. Stu tried to stay put, but he was forced to sit back into the chair. On the screen, the blue thing smeared into an elongated oval, sailed past, changed into a long reddish blur that merged with the gate complex and was gone.

"There's the gamma signature again," Thalia said.

Stu said, "Look at it. The gate is . . . on fire. Where's that light coming from?"

"Wolf. Don't do it. I can still—" Thalia's voice died suddenly.

"Hold on, folks. We're going through."

Breathless. It was like suddenly being on the inside of a cavern made of light. Stars, stars, and more stars. Vast tapestries of bright stars, patterned with stars brighter still. If a sky could be absolutely filled with dimensionless star points, it was this sky. Stu turned away, squinting, shading his eyes with his hands, only to see that the whole deck was flooded with the brilliant light coming from the screens.

Half the instruments were overloaded, giving meaningless readings, and the other half were reporting enormous amounts of radiation.

Lost in wonder, a gasp escaped his lips, sounding almost like a sob.

Five

Wolf felt himself seized by a gigantic hand. Seized. Squeezed impossibly small. Pushed through the eye of a subatomic needle. Flapped like a dishrag. Inflated, back into the world of worlds. Shaken, even though he was expecting it. Familiar, if only from one prior experience. Not so very different, after all, from the hard squeeze of the hyperdrive shunt he'd been through too many times to remember. Absurdly, he thought, Shaken, not stirred. Most *definitely* shaken . . . Sat in the pilot's chair, staring at the view in the monitor, mouth gaping open.

Beside him, in a tiny voice, not a whisper, full of unstated fear, Thalia said, *"Impossible."*

Yes. That's the right word. In front of him the monitor was cluttered with points of light, flooded with a sea of stars, clouds and clumps and rolled heaps of stars, so many stars that . . . well. Not *quite* like the colored static you'd see on a disconnected monitor. Frozen static. Tiny, irregular lanes of black in between, rather than the square gridwork of a . . .

Obviously. The goddamned thing is broken. So why am I staring?

Beside him, he heard Thalia release her harness, heard her clothes shuffle as she turned in her seat. That same small voice: *"Oh, God."*

Wolf released his own belt and twisted to lean over the armrest and look back toward the emergency hatch. The view out the little porthole was much the same as the one in the screen. Thalia looked at him, face pale in eldritch starlight. He smiled weakly. "Guess we knew we weren't *really* goin' home, huh?" Fear made his accent seem unusually thick. Talking the way I did when I was a boy, doing something dangerous to show I had guts. Not *really* afraid, see? I'm fuckin' *tough.*

She nodded slowly, biting her lower lip. "Yeah. Guess so."

Wolf sank back in his seat, looking at the monitor again. Some of the stars seemed really bright. Too bright to be stars, even in a monitor that compensated for . . . shit. And a window that would only pass a certain harmless level of radiation. "How bright?"

Silence. Then Thalia reached out and tapped her instrumentation. "Mmm." Soft sound imbued with dismay. "Brightest single point source impinging on the hull CCD system is around magnitude minus-fourteen."

"Minus . . . fuck." Ten times brighter than the full moon, seen from Earth on a cloudless night. "Where the fuck are we? In the middle of a globular cluster?"

"Dunno." Thalia's voice very tight. Controlled.

Then Stuart's voice over the intercom, breathless with excitement: "There's a lane of bright and dark nebulae all around what I think is the celestial equator, Mr. O'Malley! And in places I see what may be *gaps* in the foreground starfield!"

Thalia: "What—"

"More stars, Mom! Dimmer, farther away . . . just more stars!"

Glee, Wolf thought, feeling almost numb. I never heard anybody sound so fucking happy.

Stu said, "Mr. O'Malley, can I change hull cameras?"

"Sure." He nodded at Thalia, who reached out and tapped among her screens.

The view in the main monitor started to shift quickly, first here, then there. Some stars brighter than others, seeming to float white in the foreground, making the main starfield seem ruddy by comparison. And those clouds, like so much cirrus, stretching on and on . . . The screen brightened, making him flinch, making Thalia gasp.

Stu squeaked, "*There!* I *knew* it!"

A cluster of brilliant blue stars floating free in space, so many fiery jewels. Like the . . . like the Pleiades. Pleiades so quickly lost. But brighter. Tighter in formation.

And streaming from the center of the cluster, one up, one down, were two great plumes, feathery comets that did nothing to blot out the stars beyond. Pointing like warped arrows at a smudge, a bright swirl down in the middle of everything.

Wolf said, "What the hell."

Stuart, voice quieter, said, "I think it's IRS Sixteen."

Weakly, "I don't—"

Thalia said, "It's the galactic core."

Wolf felt his heart thud in his chest. "Um. What's the, uh . . . radiation environment like?"

Thalia fished among her instruments for few seconds. "Not as bad as it should be, but pretty bad."

Over the intercom, Mark's voice came from the background, sounding panicky. "This is *crazy.* Fucking crazy."

Yeah. Yeah. Yeah. Wolf said, "Well. This ship's as well-shielded as modern engineering can make it. I mean, we have antimatter aboard, and a thermonuclear rocket engine."

Thalia said, "We'll be all right for a while. As long as we don't have to stay here forever."

Or go outside. "Yeah. Where's the, uh . . ."

Stu said, "The stargate's back along our orbital track a few million kilometers. Same radiation signature as the other one."

Meaning we can't turn around and go back.

Cory's voice: "Maybe we should've stayed on the little planet. It was so . . . pretty there."

Honoria's voice: "Back among the Pleiades."

Imagine how she feels. Found her heaven and lost it again, all because we couldn't fucking leave well enough . . .

She whispered, "Surely the Pleions would have . . ."

Pleions. Well. *Somebody* owns these things.

Stuart said, "Mr. O'Malley? There's a dense, dark body just over one light-minute from here. And . . . well. Stuff in orbit."

"Put it on my scope."

The image jumped, and now a thing like a dark gray planet floated in front of the unchanged, impossibly starry sky. Not a very big planet. Or else those things swinging around her were . . . larger than they seemed. Curious, he thought. Why should they seem any size at all? Angular, regular shapes that could be . . . well. Because they look like artifacts. And if that's a full-sized planet, nothing a human could make would be so large.

Thalia said, "We've burned a lot of delta-vee, Wolf."

He nodded. "Yeah. But . . . where else can we go?" Nowhere. And there's going to come a time when we'll have to stop, no matter where the fuck we are. What then?

Honoria's voice, speaking Spanish: "Ah, Lobito. We're not going to see home again, are we?"

Lobito. Wolfling. I always liked it when she called me that. He thought about it for a minute, then, also in Spanish, "No, little one. I don't think so."

Cory gasped, the others not understanding.

Honoria said, "Thank you for telling me that."

"De nada." Wolf smiled, turned to Thalia and said, "Guess we'd better set up our course and get moving." One light-minute. What? Seventeen million kilometers? Something like that. He looked at the working fluid readouts and said, "Let's take our time. We'll need to save something for . . . later."

She looked at him and made a lopsided smile. "Which *later* did you have in mind?"

Good fucking question.

Wolf undid the last thumbscrew of the access panel leading through the forward bulkhead of the control room, up into the avionics space beyond, swinging the hatch open on darkness. He reached around and thumbed the local switch for the interior engineering lights, looking up into the small, hardware-cluttered compartment where the damage was supposed to be.

Thalia squeezed close beside him, breasts solid, suggestive little masses against his ribs, one leg twined around his thigh to maintain position, peering up into the dim, reddish light. "Well. Nothing obvious."

He looked down at her, small serious face framed by floating curls a dozen centimeters from his own. "No. We better replace the unit anyway, regardless of what its 'undefined error trap' message turns out to me."

"Probably just a firmware bug."

"You never know."

She released him, pushing off against his hip, making him sway in the hatch opening as she went back to where the repair kit was planted, Velcroed to the back of the flight engineer's chair.

Wolf slid through the hatch and braced himself among

the hardware, knees apart, pressing in opposite directions, reaching upward and around.

From somewhere by his feet Thalia said, "What're we going to do?"

Do? "Well. Not sure I can reach around this—"

"I don't mean about the repair. What're we going to do when the . . . fuel runs out?"

Yeah. And then the food, the water, the air, the power. "Stay wherever we happen to be until . . . you know."

She said, "I guess maybe we should've stayed at Pleione. Somebody else would've come to Beta Pic, discovered the gates, maybe gone right home to get others. They'd've found us sooner or later."

Snug as a bug in our own little Pitcairn rug? "Guess so. Too late now." Sorry I killed us, Thalia-mine. Sorry as all hell.

There was a long silence, Wolf fumbling around beyond the electronic components they would have to replace, unable to see his hands above his head, Thalia holding onto one of his ankles. Finally, she said, "Wolf?"

"Mm?" Something odd in her voice. Odd in a familiar way, a familiar woman-thing. He felt a slight pang of *uh-oh* rising inside, bringing back memories of a thousand barrooms full of desperate, pretty, drunken girls.

She said, "If we're only going to . . . last a little while longer . . ."

"We might last another two years if we don't get in any worse shit."

She said, "Yes. That's right." Fell silent.

Wolf stopped fumbling in frustration, knowing he wasn't going to be able to manage the repair. What, then? He said, "What were you going to say, Thalia?" Ask, knowing full well you can't be a successful skirt-chaser if you don't prompt them to talk, then help them imagine you care about what they tell you. Really care.

Diffidence. "I, um. I didn't like what we did before. I mean . . . If it's only going to be a while, months, a year or two . . . I'd just as soon we not . . . Mark and Honoria, I mean."

What? Not sleep with them anymore? Or not sleep with each other?

Into the silence, she said, "Wolf, let's just make it you and me." There. Said it.

Jesus. A sharp memory of being with poor Honoria, confusing the hell out of her. And imagining Thalia with Mark, Mark probably blubbering with gratitude? He said, "That'd be pretty hard on them."

More silence, then, "They could . . . have each other?"

Double, double, toil and trouble. Wolf smirked, knowing she couldn't see his face. Both these women are better'n you deserve, ol' Marky-boy. "I don't . . . think that'd work out."

You could hear the frustration in her voice. "Mark wouldn't mind."

"No. Men don't." Shut your mouth, fool. The next part of that speech is, *If it's got a cunt, it'll do.* You say that to a woman, she walks away. He said, "I don't think Honoria would go for something like that, Thalia. Despite how she wound up with me, she's not really a . . ." Good enough. She'll supply the word *whore* on her own.

A breathy whisper: "God damn it."

Cut this off now. "Thalia, I can't get my hands behind the module, much less think about putting a socket wrench in there with them."

She sighed, then said, "All right. Let's trade places."

He slid back out, took the tool kit and replacement module from her, watched her slide gracefully up into the hole. There was a long moment, then she said, "My hands are fine. I can reach everything I need to, but . . ." She squirmed around overhead, twisting this way and that, legs splaying in the air. "I can't get braced. I'm not quite big enough."

Wolf said, "Let me, um . . ."

He squeezed past her legs, sliding upward, bumping face first into the space between her legs, nice soft-hard touch of padded bone on his cheek, squirming to one side, pressing into her abdomen, coming up between her breasts. Arms over her head, thrust into the darkness beyond, she was grinning into his face as he came up even with her.

"If I ask you to do that again, could you . . ."

He snorted, shoving the replacement box between two circuit panels, shoving the tool kit behind one of the hanger straps that kept machinery in place under gravity and thrust, put his arms around her waist, snugging himself close, one hand sliding over a low hill of rump.

Breathing in his breath, Thalia whispered, "Sometimes this makes me feel just a little bit dirty."

Wolf kissed her then, smothering an impulse to murmur, *Whatever for?*

Lost in space, Mark floated alone between his bunk and the smooth, slightly curved bulkhead, saying goodbye to his fondest illusions about life and himself. Bidden, the emotions finally surfaced, clotting in his chest, filling his sinuses. God, he felt bad. Thalia really was dumping him for that pecker-head O'Malley, who had deliberately gotten them lost out here. Somehow, his sense of loss about the death of the relationship was exactly mirrored in his feelings about personal annihilation.

"Mark? Are you in here?" Thalia was looking up through a hatchway.

"Over here." He pushed off in her direction, sniffling, ready to playact for her, not knowing what else to do. "What do you want?"

She turned away with a small movement of her foot. "Nothing, I was just . . ." She turned back, gave him a look of utter desolation. He noticed that her clothing was in partial disarray, as though she'd pulled it on hurriedly. Her face was puffy, eyes pink-rimmed. "Oh, Mark. This isn't easy for me. You really have brought it on yourself, after all."

"Oh, no. This wasn't my doing, and you can't blame it on me." He was only a meter from her now, in the same space, but their eyes weren't meeting. "What was it you said when we first started seeing each other? That our relationship would work because we were both strong enough? Where's that strength now? You've abandoned me . . . just when I needed you the most."

She seemed to soften, dark eyes misting. "Mark. I . . . it's over. I can't even summon up the will to fight about it."

Suddenly, a plan. One last time. It might work, and even if it didn't . . . He took her by the elbows, pulled her toward him. "Please, Thal. We can work it out. I think we can, if you'll—"

The eyes again. But she didn't pull away. He slipped an arm around the small of her back and drew her closer, until her face was within range. No expression discernible at all now, just the individual features, the unique intelligence writ in her eyes, the downcurve of her soft lips. He felt himself stiffening slightly, and, as he tightened his grip, imagined that she could feel it as well.

So was this a chance to redeem himself, show that he was indeed capable of satisfying her, given the proper motivation? Or was she just giving in? He undid the carelessly drawn-together tunic and slid a hand across the smooth hip to rest on a buttock, taking in the rounded shape with his fingers, slipping a digit into the tender area where buttock merged with inner thigh.

Wet there. Could she be . . . ? Lower down, her thigh had a thin coating of something rough. He jerked his hand away, repelled.

And the look in her eyes . . .

* * *

Alone, staring wistfully out the control room porthole at an absurd sea of suns, Cory thought, I never would've imagined something the size of a starship could so quickly grow this small.

When she'd been little, living in the snug richness of her parents' middle-class, controlled-access neighborhood home, starships had been the fulcrum of many an imagined adventure, compounded from the reality on display in school texts and the fantasy tapped from the vidnet. Giant starships, crewed with heroes and heroines, muscular black men, voluptuous blond women, the icons of North American culture for a hundred years and more, out among the stars, doing the work of humanity's salvation.

Small. So small hanging out here, lost in the middle of nothing at all. Nothing at all, no matter how much the sky fills with stars. And small because . . . we just can't get away from each other.

She felt a little pang of regret as the hatch hissed open, wondering who . . . A sharp prickle then, as Wolf's head bobbed into view, saw her and smiled. He said, "The only view worth seeing, huh?"

She swallowed delicately and smiled back. "I wish there were more windows. This . . . this is the only thing that seems . . . I don't know. Real."

He floated into place beside her, one hand on the hatch frame, the other steadying his drift by touching her shoulder, very lightly, then pushed his face into the porthole recess, looking out into space.

This close, she had his scent in her nostrils, so different from Mark's tang of cologne, from Stuart's slightly stale odor, from the raunchy reek of unwashed men and boys back at the camp. Not like soap or anything, she thought. Just him. Like he's odorless, but . . . not odorless.

Wolf scrunched to one side and said, "Hey, will you look at that? What a sight!"

She pushed her head in beside his, horribly aware of the way his body flattened her breasts, shoved close so she could see out the little window alongside him. In the near distance was a bright red star so huge you could see a tiny disk, and a brighter, green-white pinpoint was transiting it, visibly moving.

It didn't matter, though. Wolf O'Malley was much closer than the stars, filling her head with his presence.

Down on the EVA/surface vehicle deck, Honoria hung in the shadow of one of the small, pressurized rovers, listening with some satisfaction to the soft noises that emerged from the cabin egress hatch, slightly ajar. Soft murmuring. One audible phrase, Mark's voice going, "Oh God, Thalia . . ."

She was silent at first. Then. Then . . .

Tempting to float up and peer through the window, look in and *see* them. See the bitch spreading herself for her husband the way she did for mine . . .

No. Not mine. I've got to stop thinking that way.

She turned gracefully in the air and toed herself off, floating toward the ladder, staying below line-of-sight with the rover cabin, just in case their attention wasn't fully engaged. There. Now pull yourself upward.

On the science deck, Stuart was alone, strapped into one of the little chairs before a bank of instruments, doing . . . whatever it is they do with these things. Puzzled look on his face. Intense concentration. He didn't look up when she floated by. . . . Maybe I'm getting good at this. Zero gee, making my head spin at first.

Ox was leashed to the chair stanchion, bobbing like an improbable balloon in midair, belly toward the ceiling, legs tucked in, tail curled up over his genitals, neck stretched out, blissfully asleep.

Stuart's box of Siamese cats was Velcroed nearby, as if he might've had them out, playing with them recently, and there was a slight but definite urine odor tainting the air here. She went on, lightly touching the ladder, passing on up to the living quarters. No one and nothing.

She stopped, floating, looking at the empty bunks, and idly thought, Someone really ought to start tidying up around here. Is that *my* job? *Should* it be?

No sign of Wolf and . . . She twisted suddenly, grabbed the ladder and shoved herself up through the open hatch to the control room. Felt her heart clench in her chest.

Wolf and Cory floating together, heads pressed together at the porthole . . .

The girl jerked, shoved back, pulling her face away from the window, bumping her head on the wall. Twisted. Looked at her with a pale white face and huge, staring eyes. Then she scrambled, grabbing for a handhold, finally caught Wolf's leg and shoved herself down through the hatch, disappearing below.

Honoria gave Wolf a long, searching, empty stare, then twisted, kicking off against the back of the flight engineer's chair, sliding gracefully through the hatch, calling, "Corazón? Corazón, wait . . ."

By himself, hanging motionlessly beside the hatch, Wolf stared at the star-filled viewscreen, seeing nothing. Well, he thought. Well, now. That wa'n't a great thing you were thinking about doing, now was it, boy?

But the memory. The memory of having her close beside him like that. The memory of strong, fresh female pheromones flooding his senses. Christ. What the hell's going on here?

The trajectory-intersect alarm chirped, making him turn and look at the control panel, dick suddenly forgotten.

Stu was down in the bunkroom when the intercom suddenly came on with a muffled noise. Wolf's voice, slow and southern-sounding: "Well, everybody, we've got something new to think about. There's some kind of, ah, giant spaceship headed right toward us."

Feeling an incredible pang of "What next?" Stu kicked himself down to the labdeck with practiced movements and nestled in among the instruments, familiar enough with the various controls to call up an image of the thing right off. It was still more than five hundred kilometers away, a dark, streaky-looking speck growing quickly in the starfield, engulfing more and more of the background stars at a time. Stu consulted the readouts. The light reflected from its hull was blue-shifted considerably, but its speed was falling off rapidly. "It's decelerating at thousands of gees."

Mark appeared and sat in the other chair

It looked like a ship now, almost. Something like a hull-less battleship, a matrix of complex shapes somewhat tapered at both ends. As it grew, more and more could be made out, forests of revolving antennae, hill-like powered gun turrets, gigantic versions of telephone poles like you saw in the movies. In front of it, spreading out in giant plumes, ghostly ripples of darkness distorted and dimmed the stars.

Stu: "At least a kilometer long. Let's hope it's not going to ram us."

Image of what such a collision would be like, the alien ship sweeping toward them, impacting at something like fifty kilometers a second, *NR-598h* vaporizing against it, leaving a giant glowing hole in its structure.

Mark stuttered, "Maybe we should do something."

Wolf: "And just what do you propose?"

Honoria now appeared in the forward hatch, pulled herself halfway through, eyes glued to the object on the main screen.

Stu said, "Dead stop. It's about seven hundred meters away. The gas and dust collectors registered . . . something, charged particles of some sort moving at relativistic velocities, for a moment, but . . . whatever they were, they're gone. Could they be using some kind of ion drive?"

"Can't be." Wolf's voice sounded definite. "Think about it, kid."

Now that it had come to a stop, most of the antennae had halted, but there were still many slowly going through their gyrations, stop, start, stop, spin, looking for something. One by one, as though suddenly realizing what they were supposed to be doing, they spun around and came to a spot fixed on the same point as the others. Stu realized suddenly that the point was *NR-598h.*

Thalia's voice: "Nav console shows a series of short bursts of coherent X-ray beams on our hull."

Mark said, "Why would they need to do something like that? Can't they just—"

"Yeah, you can do it." Stu said in a low, ironic voice. "Tell us how the alien scanner works, would you?"

Mark: "Stu, that's ridiculous, I can't—"

Stu sniggered. "Just be quiet, okay? We really can do without your silly speculations."

Thalia said, "Just got a burst of something on the EHF comm channel, 59K megahertz modulating up to 64K. Stu, can you adjust the longwave analyzer to track it?"

Moment of doubt, then relief. "Oh yeah. I've got the signal in one of the boxes. It's a complex modulation, looks a lot like white noise."

"Can you translate it to sound and put it on the speaker?"

"Umm. Yeah."

Loud, staticky noise. At first he thought it was just that, static. The hissing roar of randomness. But within that noise there was a repetitive fast clicking, like the magnified sound of Rice Krispies, each click and pop slightly different. And the white noise itself was changing, increasing in volume and pitch, the rhythmic rising and falling of cheering baseball fanatics, a hundred stadiums worth. The crack of a home run, and the cheers went wild.

Stu listened for a while longer, gave up. "This looks like the whole signal. No sign of anything but frequency modulation. I—" What the hell? Suddenly short of breath, feeling intensely claustrophobic, Stu clutched at his restraining belt, undid it. He was floating free now, but the sensation was growing worse, accompanied by a pins-and-needles sensation in his arms, legs, and face. Like his entire body was falling asleep, nerves disconnecting, phantom pain and sizzling itches everywhere. Fear growing, he fumbled at his restraint until it let go.

Mark was grabbing at himself, rubbing his arms, a stricken look on his face. "What . . . what's happening?"

Thalia: "Jesus. We're moving!"

Wolf: "Goddamn it. We're being towed. Look at that!"

Almost getting used to the feeling, Stu looked around, took a deep breath. He was floating a meter above his chair, drifting a few centimeters per second, no force acting on him, no inertial field change at all. He looked around, wondered suddenly what it would mean to have all the laws of physics so easily abolished.

Six

Watching numbers spin and tensor graphlines grow, watching the odd yet awfully familiar alien spacecraft in the viewscreen, feathertail of white ghost light spreading across the too-numerous stars, Thalia whispered, "So. What the hell are we going to *do?*"

Wolf turned and looked at her, tuning out the gabble from the intercom, Mark and Stu, even now, arguing some nonsense or another, noting the paleness of her face, the blank sheen of her eyes. She was watching the instruments, not looking back at him. He shrugged, turning back to the screen. "We could turn the ship. Fire the engines. Doubt it'd work, any more than it did when we were sucked through the first stargate."

"No." She leaned forward in her harness, poking at her center console touchscreen, paging through rapidly evolving data. "We're already up to point-oh-four cee. Even if we got away . . ."

Right. Hundreds of times the delta-vee we've got left. He

pointed at the course vector and said, "Well. Towing us in the right direction, anyway. Just straightening the orbital track a bit."

"Coincidence?"

"There's no place else around here. Just the stargate cluster and the bodies orbiting the inner system of the two white dwarves." Inanely, the use of the plural seemed silly, applied to stars. Disney's dwarves were all white, weren't they? The Seven White Dwarves. And Snow White . . . Some little voice, far back in his head seemed to be telling him not to be such an idiot. Not now. Jesus. I *can't* react. This is . . . this is like nothing that could really be happening to me.

The hatch opened and Honoria came through, arcing up toward the overhead, stopping herself with one hand on the back of his seat, looking down at him, eyes so wide she looked like a lunatic.

Thalia said, "Please. You have to go below."

Honoria turned on her, teeth flashing white as she snarled, "Shut up, bitch!" The accent made it somehow charming.

Thalia gaped, turning toward Wolf.

In Spanish, Honoria said, "Wolf, please. Don't do anything to upset the Pleions. They're only trying to *help* us."

Thalia said, "Pleions. For Christ's sake . . ."

Wolf looked at her, seeing a familiar, angry look, memories of a long ago Thalia surfacing. She learned Spanish the same place I did. Just hasn't had . . . He looked back at Honoria and thought, Well, you wouldn't need to remember much Spanish to pick up on *los Pleiones.* "Honoria . . ."

She said, "Wolf, your girlfriend's an idiot. Maybe you are too." She grinned, face humorless, at Thalia, and in English, said, "Stoopeed, eh?" She gesticulated at the screen. "What you think that is, hm? Flying saucer? *Nooo* . . . couldn't *possibly* be a flying saucer . . ."

Wolf sat back in his seat, blowing out air in a long gust, cheeks puffing. Jesus Christ.

Stu's voice: "Wolf? Mom? The comm channel's active again."

Thalia leaned forward and tapped a control.

Like static. But . . .

Rice Krispies and a baseball game, just like before. *Pop.* Then the voice of the crowd, rising cheers. Must've hit a home run. The sounds were so oddly suggestive, making him remember playing baseball in an old cow pasture, he and his friends, friends long gone, a long time ago. Remembered standing behind second base, alert, trying to keep the sun out of his eyes, stink of old cowshit in his nose and . . .

The game ended. Silence. Somehow fraught with . . .

Mark's voice said, "Modulated carrier wave."

And then someone else's voice said, "Hello? Hello? Is this working?"

Pleasant, soft baritone, the voice of a very nice man.

In the silence, all he could hear was Honoria's soft hiss, a whisper whose words were below the threshold of sensibility.

The voice said, "Please answer. This is a multiplex modality. Any frequency will do."

Thalia said, "Oh, my God."

The voice: "Thank you."

Wolf's mouth felt extraordinarily dry as he rasped out, "Um. Who . . ."

Baseball crispies rose in the background again, over which flowed a hollow *pop,* superposed to a sharp, echoing *click.* "You may call us whatever you please."

Thalia jerked in her seat, putting one hand to her face. "Wha . . ."

The voice said, "For your principal communications modality, the interface multiplexer suggests BeauHun might be a good term. . . ."

Honoria let go of the seat back, tumbling backward, clutching herself by the hair, crying out "*Ai!*"

And the voice: "*Y en español? Possiblemente Pleiones* . . ."

Honoria came over the back of the seat, face shining, and hissed, "See? I *told* you!"

Wolf swallowed and, in Spanish, whispered, "They can't possibly be the *real* Pleions."

Thalia, breathing heavily, face darkened, glistening with sweat, raggedly demanded, "Are you reading our *minds?*"

The voice, calm and pleasant, said, "Yes, ma'am."

"Uh."

"We have a pretty capable induction technology. Please recall your ship is under tow by a tractor beam."

Wolf felt his heart stuttering hard in his chest, all sorts of images rising and falling, flitting one after another. Stories. All sorts of stories about mind readers.

The voice seemed amused: "Please don't be afraid, Mr. O'Malley. Those sorts of things are as foreign to us as they possibly could be." It turned kindly then. "It's not really magic, my friends. You folk have had the power to read minds through a technology you developed a century and more ago. You've just had no sound use for it."

Wolf said, "And . . . you?"

"Well, yes. As you might imagine, lots of stray primitives get swept up in the TrackTrixNet."

Stray primitives. Yes, that'd be us. He said, "Where're you taking us?"

"There's a PacketWight repair facility here, intended for servicing node trixillation deficits. We've learned to repurpose some of the hardware." The image in the main viewscreen suddenly changed, showing the white-dwarf system at maximum magnification. There was a brief blizzard of colored static, then the magnification grew again, far beyond the capabilities of the system, focusing on one of the bodies orbiting in the stars' ecliptic plane. Big, dark, shiny world, like nothing he'd ever seen before, in person or in any expeditionary report.

There were things in orbit around the black planet. Spacecraft. Mostly flying saucers. Some other things. Designs like human spacecraft, though nothing familiar. Something that looked like an antique dawn-era space station, a mishmash of girders, solar panels, habitat modules.

Thalia said, "Who the hell are you, then?"

"We're the BeauHuns. Or the Pleions, if you like that better."

Thalia's lips twisted, and she said, "BeauHuns will do. Doesn't tell me who you *are,* though."

The voice laughed. "I suppose not. Well, the matter is fairly simple, despite a certain underlying complexity. Once upon a time, some millions of years ago as your clocks tick, we were the masters of a great empire, the Empire of—" PopClick*Whack*! "—which held an entire galaxy under its sway, and had colonies in neighboring galaxies. With our mighty weapons and FTL starships, we thought ourselves quite the masters of creation.

"Then the Topopolis expanded into our part of the universe, which was more than a billion parsecs from here. Gobbled up our galaxies, consumed all our worlds, and that was the end of us, though we numbered in the trillions. The hundreds of trillions."

Wolf felt like he was in a dream. I've been in a dream now for a long time, ever since we found those artifacts back at Beta Pictoris. Just 'til now, 'til . . . *this* . . . I just hadn't quite realized.

The voice said, "As a star-faring race, we had certain resources. Warships to fight. And, of course, millions upon millions of passenger vessels, the highliners of our commerce. The warships were useless, were destroyed wherever and whenever they stood their ground. In the end, all we could do was load whatever population would fit into the starships and flee."

It paused, then said, "We saved perhaps a thousandth of one percent of all the—" Pop*Click* "—then alive." Pop*Click*

"—who then became the ragtag refugee fleet of the BeauHun vermin, who learned to work with the TrackTrixNet, inhabiting the periphery of the great Topopolis."

Thalia whispered, "And did you find new worlds on which to live?"

Ah yes, an entire story told, right here and now. A familiar one. The refugee fleet, moving between the stars, enemy on its heels, in search of . . . Which one was it, the one with the purple-haired moonbase women or the one with the aging cowboy star and saberhagenoidal robots? Damn if I know.

The voice, sounding sad, said, "There are no new worlds, Mrs. Jansky. The Topopolis, as an entity, appears to be methodically engulfing the entire universe. I'm sorry that I must be the one to tell you, but your turn has come."

Stu, bobbing near the ceiling of the control room, steadying hand looped through a handhold, tried to remember if he had ever felt this way before. The BeauHun was quiet for a moment, letting it all sink in, perhaps. On the screen, swimming up from the depths of star-profusion, a dark, circular spot, growing quickly. A planet of some sort, visible at first as a kind of two-tone silhouette, brighter crescent enfolding a mottled gray circle, new world in old world's arms, manifesting a strange pallor because of the bright background. Beyond it, fifteen or so degrees away, two blinding bluish-white pinpoints, three or four times brighter than anything else in view, standing out from the welter of light like distant streetlights against a setting sun. Casting their cold light on the silhouette world, these suns were giving it a semblance of "day" to go with the mixed-up night of the galactic core.

"This is quite an interesting world," the BeauHun voice said. "Since most of the stars in this vicinity are too old and metal-depleted to have planets, it's rather unique. To give a flavor of its specialness, let's call it Theolithos, after the stone that your Greek mythology says the god Chronos swallowed in place of the infant Zeus. Theolithos formed about nine billion years ago as the fifth planet of a fast-moving F0 star in the halo of the Andromeda galaxy. During its prime, Theolithos had a diameter of about fifty thousand kilometers and a mass of fifteen Earths, and resembled your world Uranus quite a bit."

"Andromeda?" Wolf asked. "Did you bring it here?"

"No, of course not." No sign of impatience in the Beau-Hun voice. "Andromeda long ago suffered a collision with three small, gravitationally connected galaxies, and Theolithos and its star were ejected, eventually being captured here in the Milky Way core."

The "dark" side of the world in question now filled the screen, and it was apparent that they were rapidly decelerating. An ordinary-looking world, Stu thought, surface pummeled into a realm of overlapping craters of all sizes and ages. The ambient light from the core sky was more than bright enough to show every detail, but without shadowing, like the Full Moon.

Cory said, "Is this where you come from?"

"Hardly, Corazón. But it is a convenient base for our operations here."

Stu, feeling like he was about to burst with questions, asked the most pressing one. "You say this planet once was a minigas giant like Uranus. What happened to its atmosphere?"

Slight puff of static over the radio, then, "Oh, it's a long story, boy. During its trip, the F0 star left the Main Sequence and became a red giant, boiling off all Theolithos's lighter gases, eventually leaving the naked, heavily processed, central kernel. Keep in mind I am simplifying quite a bit here. It took several billion years, but the layer of volatile materials was ultimately sputtered away by the high radiation levels of the inner core, and what is left is a crust of nearly pure diamond five thousand kilometers deep."

Wolf: "This is all very interesting, but it doesn't—"

"Now I see we have arrived at the proper location," the voice interrupted. "I must ask that you all strap yourselves in for acceleration. I cannot guarantee that you won't feel a few bumps."

It was weird, landing, no, not landing, being placed on the surface of an alien planet without any of the normal sensations or procedures. Still without any discomfort or pressure of any kind, Stu watched with the rest of them in their bunks as the drab surface of Theolithos came swatting up at them, curvature disappearing, curvilinear shapes and swirls expanding into endless glittering plains bounded by dark sharp cliffs and steep-sided plateaus, shapes that reminded him of the striking erosional features of the Colorado Plateau. Not cut by water, though; worn down by billions of years of impacts and radiation and starlight. Over one of the hills, the nature of the surface changed to a flatter, almost uniform surface crisscrossed with lines of utter black, and Stu realized he was looking at the BeauHun base.

Suddenly the landscape made an abrupt lurch, spinning around, horizon turning to shadow with the reappearance of the starry sky, going vertical, then disappearing from the screen. Cory and Mark gasped, though there was no sensation at all, as though watching a movie safe at home. Stars now, dark splotches, hardly moving, then shifting, horizon reappearing, now capped with a thin layer of star-soaked blue. Below them the landing field was a game board showing hundreds of ovals in a perfectly regular pattern, each a slightly degraded reflection of the dazzling sky, extending into the middle distance. A barely perceptible shudder passed through the ship, and they were down.

An impatient time while the ship was configured for their debarking. This time there would be no wait for the rocket radiation to dissipate, no debate about contaminating or being contaminated by this new world, which the BeauHun assured them was totally hospitable for them. Finally, they climbed down the ladder one by one, made a ragged circle on the smooth, blank material of the landing field, exclamations of wonder and speculations dying out in the face of the unprecedented vista.

In the distance, among the flattened, elliptical mirror-shapes, there were many signs of activity, small figures coming and going, larger things like bulldozers here and there executing complex procedures. But no one came to meet them, despite the delay.

A hesitant, room-temperature breeze tugged at Stu's sleeves and collar as he studied the strange sky. The blue of the atmospheric cap somehow made the view even more beautiful, filling in the chinks and crevices of the starfield, giving the sky a predominant hue of dark azure without in any way spoiling its overwhelming radiance. Periodically there was a faint sound like splashing water, and one of the mirror ships would magically rise from the ground and fall off into the sky, dwindling to a speck and disappearing.

Mark said, "About time," and Stu turned to see a big floating ice cube scooting toward them, its opalescent blue-gray surface slightly filmy, as though it was made of etched glass. It stopped, and three of the four sides flipped up parallel with the top. Inside were two *things*, assemblages, Stu didn't know what to call them, that shifted and flowed like amoebas made of dominoes. Assembling themselves into roughly humanoid shape, they stepped from the vehicle.

"Well," the voice of the BeauHun said through the one on the left, though nothing in his "face" moved in time with the sounds. "Welcome to Milky Way Staging Area Number One, Theolithos Prime. We hope your stay here will be a pleasant one."

* * *

Cory walked across the flat, hard, floorlike surface of Theolithos, facing away from the landed starship, flooded with hollow, empty wonder. The sky caught you first, of course. There were stars and more stars, utterly without precedent, nothing she could compare them to, yet . . . stars enraptured by clouds, glowing in the bright, eternal blue night overhead, fantastic shapes and twisting swirls, straight out of the dreams people have only in movies.

Far away, on the horizon, were odd, gleaming low mountains; closer by, other fantastic shapes. And row on row of grounded flying saucers. Flying saucers and thousands of tiny, milling . . . shapes.

She flinched, watching one of the . . . BeauHuns . . . PopClicks . . . Pleions . . . Thalia seemed determined to use the first offering . . . Almost as if to spite my mother. All . . . *this!* All this and they still snipe and snarl like characters in a cheap daytime 3V drama.

The BeauHun was a man-sized mass of metallic, multicolored Leggo toys, writhing and changing as it ambled along, arms and legs emerging and retreating from the churning body, glittering and winging, bouncing and swaying. Above its . . . back . . . above its back, eyestalks came and went, bobbing and twisting, looking this way and that, supporting round, bright, comic-book eyes.

And always, from everywhere, the endless snap-crackle-pop of the components forming and breaking, forming and breaking . . .

A man's hand was suddenly warm on her shoulder, Wolf's presence distancing her from the wonder. She said, "I feel like I'm dreaming."

Wolf squeezed her shoulder lightly and said, "Me too."

Nothing more than that. She felt like leaning against him, but did not. I'd like to be held in big Daddy arms now. Turn my face away from the light, escape into . . . There was a memory of her real father, like a lump in her throat. In memory, she was a little girl, sitting on his lap while he watched the 3V news, murmuring to himself about the terrible things happening in the world.

I never listened. Not to his words. Not to the 3V announcer. Just buried my face in his shirt, eyes closed, and let the world shrink away to nothing. Just me. And the shielding mass of Daddy.

Wolf's voice: "Are you all right?"

She realized she'd shut her eyes. She looked up, saw the concern in his face, leaned her head against the solidity of his chest and said, "Overwhelmed, I . . ."

There was a slight shadow, and Cory realized her eyes were shut again. Nothing in the world but me and Wolf. We're . . . somewhere else. Just the two of us and . . . She shied from an abrupt fantasy. She and Wolf. The beaches east of Buenos Aires, where Río de la Plata gradually twisted around to become Atlantic seacoast and . . . She opened her eyes to the shadow, and there was Thalia Jansky, standing before them, hands on hips, eyes bleak, mouth set in a hard line.

The image that conjured was of Wolf O'Malley standing with his arm around a small, attractive woman. Herself, seen as an adult almost for the first time and . . . She abruptly became conscious of the pressure from his fingers, resting on her hip, slightly forward, fingertips touching her abdomen. A voice in her head screamed: *We're not going home again! Don't you understand that? We're going to* die *out here!* The woman in Wolf's arms seemed like a little girl suddenly, frightened. The voice turned calm and bitter: Look at her. Jealous, that's all. Don't these pathetic grown-ups think about anything else? Just, who's doing what to whom?

Soap opera trash.

Beyond hard-eyed Thalia Jansky a BeauHun approached, baseball crispie sounds swelling until it got their attention,

Wolf's arm stiffening, Thalia slowly, reluctantly, turning away.

The thing seemed to laugh as it stopped, standing there, fidgeting, its body twisting and shuffling inside itself, colors coming and going like a cheap 3V special effect. You couldn't tell where the sound was coming from, as its familiar light baritone said, "You really are a droll bunch, aren't you?"

Thalia said, "Droll?"

The BeauHun said, "Sexual reproduction's not that commonplace in the universe, you know. Messy and hard to control, though it makes an *excellent* template mask for nucleic-acid-encoded structural contexts."

To her slight surprise, Cory realized she understood what was meant. Sexual reproduction allowed species to resist the pressure from neutral molecular evolution and undo damage from traumatic mutation by comparing templates from different individuals.

The BeauHun said, "It's a useful system, but it drives behaviors to the point where some intellectual stunting is inevitable. Do you realize, Mr. O'Malley, how many times in the past minute you've called up the visual autodefiner coupled to the etymon *pussy?* You really have a finely-tuned high-speed array sorter dedicated to those portions of your linguistic apparatus, slightly better than the one associated with your piloting skills."

Wolf seemed to choke. He said, "Well . . ." and it came out *whale,* his accent thickening under stress, almost to the point of incomprehensibility. "What system y'all folks use?"

The BeauHun laughed again. "Oh, ours is even worse, rest assured, though not so highly polarized as your own. We have only one sex, per se, but we have a system of conjugal reproduction in which several members of what you might call a family merge to form a nonsentient breeding mass, which must be fed and guarded until it has grown larger and can separate into discrete, sentient individuals again, hopefully more beings than merged in the first place. Our entire civilization was based on the complex behaviors that emerged from this system."

Cory tried to picture what the thing described. "What's it like when you . . . uh . . ."

The BeauHun said, "The individuals who emerge from a breeding mass are not the same ones who went into its formation. Memories and personality traits are translocated at random. It's what we have instead of death."

Oh.

It laughed. "Don't look so shocked, my friends. I have structurally independent memory cells reaching back millions of years. I pity species whose life experience is not encoded for reproduction. It's hard to imagine what it must be like to face such an utter extinction as your own."

Wolf seemed to flinch beside her, as if the remark had struck a particular nerve. Then she imagined her father, erased from reality by death despite all the pretty lies all the priests had told, and imagined what that nerve might be.

Thalia said, "So you're not, um . . . carbon-based, nucleic-acid-encoded—"

"Oh, by no means! Our components are largely oxidized silicate material, doped with a variety of metal ions. Our encoding is in weak electromagnetic fields maintained by a system of piezoelectric crystals."

From somewhere behind her Stu whispered, "A pile of rocks, inhabited by a ghost."

The BeauHun said, "Why, yes, Mr. McCray! That's very good! Very good indeed!"

Honoria stepped forward, standing close beside Thalia, and, in Spanish, said, "Oh, great Pleion: What's going to happen to us now? Will you . . . help?" Cory remembered her mother, years ago, talking to her father about the Stones of Atlantis, about the Pleions and the events she supposed must have happened, almost 55,000 years ago. . . . Daddy was so nice, listening to her, taking it all so seriously, though he didn't believe a word.

There was a silence. Then, when the BeauHun spoke again, it was with two voices, one in Spanish, the other speaking English, sounding a bit like a 3V translator's voice-over: "We will do our best, though what that best shall be is up to you. It has been the policy of the BeauHun Fleet, ever since—" PopClick*Whack*! "—was overrun, to render whatever assistance we can to primitive peoples on the periphery of the Topopolis, whose habitats are about to be consumed. We will give you hardware necessary to successfully navigate the intricacies of the TrackTrixNet. We will give you a knowledge base sufficient to understand and reproduce this hardware. The rest is up to you."

Mark's voice was ridiculous with relief: "Then . . . we're going *home?*"

"Yes. For a while, anyway. But your world is doomed, just as ours was, and there's nothing you can do to stop the onrushing Topopolis. Go home and hand over the technology we give you. Save what you can—the time is short."

Silence. Then Stuart said, "So that's it? So long and thanks for all the fish?!"

The BeauHun laughed. "A charming metaphor, Mr. McCray. I suppose in some way, the answer *is* forty-two, isn't it? See?" It extended a long pseudopod, pointing back over their heads.

Wolf seemed to whirl at her side, then stiffen, while Cory turned more slowly. *NR-598h* was sitting on the hard black ground of Theolithos, just as they'd left it, surface lock open, crane arm extended, elevator box resting at the end of its cable. Beyond it, a small black cloud drifted closer and closer in the sky. The cloud came to a rest over the ship, twisting ominously for a moment, then it dissolved, something like black rain sleeting down. *NR-598h* slumped abruptly into a seething, silver-gray mass, hissing, bubbling, twisting in on itself like molten plastic.

Wolf lifted his arms, as if in supplication, and grunted out a strangled, "My *ship!*"

The BeauHun, mimicking what seemed to be a Scottish accent, said, "There, there, Captain. It'll be all right in a few minutes. You'll see."

When Wolf walked away from the writhing puddle that had been their spacecraft, "just to explore, while this is . . . going on," it seemed likely the others would follow, though at first he took no notice. The alien ships were interesting enough, especially the nonsaucer types, which seemed, somehow, comfortingly familiar.

Built with a technology like ours, that's why.

You could see things that were engines. Thrusters. Portholes. Hatches. Pressurized gas bottles like so many golden grapes. This one over here. Looks like a turn-of-the-century Russian design. Then there were the aliens themselves.

The BeauHuns . . . well, they were just like so many cartoon characters, remembered from childhood. But the things by the Russian antique . . . each entity like two squids glued together at the tail, walking on their tentacles, two faces, facing in opposite directions, *sideways,* rather than to the front, and those were the normal ones.

From somewhere behind him, he could hear Stu talking, murmuring something, a running commentary, to Cory perhaps. Maybe telling her what he made of the beings working over a ship that looked like a pile of burning leaves, smoke towering overhead against the impossible sky, beings who looked like aggregations of green and gold tiddlywinks, hopping around in twinkly little gangs.

Eventually they got beyond the field of ships, climbing up the low, bare slope of one of the round black hills. Something like dust here, black diamond dust, puffing up from his feet as he walked. At the crest of the hill he stopped and turned, hands on hips, looking back toward the landing area. Thalia was walking a few yards back, looking up at him. No one else.

Tiny in the distance, wandering back through a hedgerow of flying saucers, he could make out Stu and Cory, Stu lugging his goddamned box of cats, Cory holding Ox by his leash, walking close together, possibly holding hands, possibly not. Mark and Honoria were nowhere to be seen.

Boy-girl, boy-girl, boy-girl . . .

Remember when they used to seat us that way, back at the refugee camp school, so's we wouldn't talk so much?

He sat down slowly, watching Thalia climb up to him, grinning a thin grin as he remembered. I wonder what idiot thought of that? Some idiot who spent too much time going to school. Too many theories.

They were still doing that to us when I started thinking I might be somewhat interested in just what those girls might have inside their pants.

Stark memory of kneeling in the blasted woods somewhere east of Asheville, on a hillside, dead trees all slanting in the same direction, most of them still standing only because they had each other to lean on, amid a dense undergrowth of saplings and brush, golden summer sunshine slanting down from high in the sky, lighting them with bits and flakes of buttery light.

What *was* her name?

Genny.

Genny Something.

Can't remember anymore.

Remember kneeling in the dirt before her, heart pounding in my chest, blond girl's eyes half excited, half afraid, bright with alarm, as though hypnotized by the sight of a snake. One hand pressed to her mouth as though silencing herself, the other flat on her chest, flat on the material of a blue knit cotton halter top, pressing it down above small breasts, while I . . . did what we wanted.

What we wanted.

Kneeling in the dirt and leaf mold, unbuttoning her white shorts, unzipping her fly, sliding them down, Genny stepping neatly out of them, the only movement she seemed willing to make.

What were we? Eleven? Twelve?

Something like that?

Leaving Genny standing there in pale, silky blue briefs, a scrap of cloth clinging to her hips, flat against the bottom of her belly, just the suggestion of a . . . shape inside, you know what, you don't know *exactly* what . . . Strangling, almost unable to breath, he'd put his hands on her hips, elated at the feel of those silky panties, took the elastic waistband in his fingers, slowly pulled them down, underpants turning inside out, trying like mad to pay attention to every damned detail of what was going on.

I want to remember this forever. Play it over and over again, in case I never . . . in case it never . . .

Then, there it was, centimeters from his face, unexpected, despite all his anticipation. She had more hair than he did, kinked and golden, not quite enough to hide the structural details he'd spent so much time imagining, double-divide of vulva, not quite like tiny buttocks, flesh folding under, carrying his eyes down into the shadows and . . .

Genny's voice had been very soft and rough, hardly more than a whisper, as she'd said, "Kiss it, Wolfie . . ."

He remembered leaning in, trembling, not quite knowing what she expected from him, but determined to do his best.

Standing in front of him in the here and now, Thalia Jansky smirked and said, "You've got your pussy face on, Wolfie."

Another clean, hard shock of remembrance. She used to

say that. Way back when. Back when the world was real. Back when we were . . . young and innocent.

Is that what we were?

Yes.

She could always tell.

I'd be thinking about some crotch I'd seen in a magazine or . . .

That art book I found in some bombed-out ruins near Brasilia. Puzzling out the title, amused when I realized it meant *A Thousand Cunts.* Page after page of fine, glossy pictures, some plain, some starkly exposing, others merely grotesque. I remember lingering for a long while over a picture of a girl, naked in a chair, one leg thrown over the arm so her cunt was peeled right open. Nothing unusual about the cunt, but her face . . . looking directly into the camera lens, eyes heavy-lidded, conspiratorial, *I know what you want. Here it is.*

I'd slid the book into my pack, thinking I might sell it back at the airfield, to some helpless, hopeless nerd or another. Then I'd walked out into the sunshine and there was Thalia Jansky, already my girlfriend for more than a month, who smirked and said, "Got your pussy face on, Wolfie," then led me back into the shadowy ruins, where we could have a little privacy.

Here and now, she kneeled between his legs, leaned in and kissed him lightly on the lips, smiled at him, eyes so shiny, so . . . happy. That's happiness I'm seeing.

She said, "We're going *home,* Wolfie."

Home?

That's right. Going home. Home with our message of doomsday, universe being swallowed, Topopolis, Beau-Huns and . . .

The smile turned to a lewd, lopsided grin as she reached out, light-fingered, and started trying to unzip his fly. "We're going home, and we've got each other."

* * *

Starship *NR598h*, standing on the hard, dark alien tarmac, looked no different than it had before, a towering column of rounded metal, pointed nose, tail section surrounded by lesser cylinders, the girdery landing legs splayed as before, the hull lock swung open, crane arm swung out, cable hanging down, elevator car resting on the surface.

Would I know, Cory wondered, standing beside Stu, looking upward, if it *were* somehow different?

No. Not unless it'd been utterly changed.

Stuart was standing too close, close enough so his arm would touch hers, ever so lightly, each time he inhaled, his breathing still quicker than normal.

From somewhere behind them Wolf's voice said, "I guess now would be the time to go aboard and . . . see what's what."

Inside, the ship was unchanged as well, though . . . She heard her mother murmur, in Spanish, about some housekeeper or another. Right. Everything is cleaned up. All our things put away, the stale, stale odor of feces and urine, of dogs and cats and sweaty men. She stood for a long while, looking down at her freshly made bunk, before climbing the ladder to the control room, where the others were already crowded.

Wolf was in the command pilot's chair, Thalia to his right at her own station, their hands on the armrest controls, dials and gauges, indicator lights and flatscreens already bright with activity.

Thalia said, "So. Refueled and everything."

Wolf: "Yeah. I guess . . ." He felt silent, with a gusty sigh.

Mark said, "So. What next?"

Home? Is that all there is left to do?

"Home with the big, bad news," Stu said.

Wolf looked over his shoulder at the boy, making a lopsided smile, then he reached out and ran his fingers over the top of a featureless keg sitting on the floor between the two acceleration chairs. "Hmm. Like chrome plating. Wonder if they'll give us a user's manual."

A soft male voice, not quite the BeauHun's radio voice, said, "The TrackTrixCom is an autonomic device. No manual is necessary."

Wolf snatched his hand away like a man who'd just laid hold of the heating element of an electric stove, only to find it active. Honoria muttered something, a quick bubble of words, Latin, not Spanish. There was a peculiar silence, then Thalia said, "And who are you?"

The voice seemed slightly impatient: "The TrackTrixCom, of course. I *told* you I was an autonomic device."

Honoria whispered, "*Ay, María.*"

The TrackTrixCom said, "A fine sentiment, I suppose, but there's work to be done, so we'd better get to it."

There was nothing but the soft sound of people breathing, the faint but audible rustle of clothing.

Utterly, utterly foreign, Cory thought, to everything we've ever known. It wasn't, though. Unbidden, but inevitably she remembered a rather similar scene from her favorite cartoon show, unseen for years already, *Contado Primero,* and the hero-girl Lucía Novaria, with her pale coffee skin, startling blond hair, and flashing black eyes, leading a contact team deep into the fastness of the alien ship and . . .

It said, "Oh, come on now! It's not like you folks are some band of hunter-gatherers. Built your own damn *starship!* You must've known something like this would happen sooner or later."

Mark seemed to gasp, "Ahhh . . . yeah. I guess we did. It's just so . . . damned sudden. And this business of the Topopolis . . ."

The TrackTrixCom said, "That's what I'm here for. I'll see that you get back home and . . . well, your job will be done, for the moment. You turn me over to the leadership of your civilization and . . . you *do* have a leadership, don't you?"

Stu said, "Sort of."

"Well, we'll sort that out when we get there."

It seemed like a good idea, a really good idea, a fine idea, to get a good night's sleep before pressing on. But then the alarms, as always, called them abruptly awake, called them rushing up to the flight deck.

They were all gathered around the TrackTrixCom, Mark slouched against a control panel, wiping the sleep from his eyes. Stu glanced at Cory, and their eyes met long enough to communicate her worried look.

"Okay," the TrackTrixCom said. "I'm afraid I have some very bad news. It's been explained to you how the BeauHuns have arranged to prosper by exploiting the weaknesses built into the TrackTrix switching software and the structure of the Topopolis itself. What you weren't told is that the Topopolitan network is not without a means of repairing itself. We call them RipWrappers."

Wolf said, "By repair, do you mean—"

"The principal task of the RipWrappers is to undo false connections, especially transtemporal links, but they also have many more mundane functions. They are a major scourge of vermin attempting to sneak through TrackTrix connections."

"Like us," Thalia said.

"Every being you've encountered so far would fall into the category of vermin, Thalia. Although the BeauHuns have developed a mutually useful relationship with the Topopolitan PacketWights, this is of no help when a RipWrapper appears. Basically, the only correct response to the appearance of a RipWrapper is to flee."

"And . . . ?"

"It appears that when you passed through the Pleiadic

node, your ship was detected as an anomaly by the TrackTrix you used. As a result, a RipWrapper is on its way and will be here very shortly. The strong apprehension you feel is completely justified."

Stu said, "Can we talk to a BeauHun?"

The TrackTrixCom was silent for a moment. "I am speaking in the place of the BeauHuns. There would be no point in establishing actual contact with them."

A movement on the viewscreen caught Stu's eye. In the widescreen view of the BeauHun landing field, a saucer suddenly fell upward, soaring into the sky. Then another, then another. Like a startled flock of seagulls, once a few had taken off, the rest lifted off en masse, momentarily filling the sky with quickly dwindling circular silhouettes. It wasn't long before they were gone.

Wolf leapt into his chair. "Thalia? Get the crane hauled in. Jesus, fella, you could've been a little quicker in telling us."

From the empty-seeming field, here and there, using what were clearly different methods of propulsion, the more primitive starships were leaving too.

"You need not start up your engine now. In fact, it would not be a good idea to do so. The BeauHuns, recognizing that you are unprepared for this sort of eventuality, will move you to the local TrackTrix in the same way that you were brought here. You just need to seal your craft, and they will do the rest. I do not believe that you will need to strap in for this procedure."

Thalia looked over from her controls. "All right. Jeez, Wolf, look at that. Those systems never worked that fast before. All right, then. Thirty seconds."

What appeared to be the last of the conventional ships had now taken off. "Fifteen seconds. Ten. Done. The ship is ready for space."

Stu hopped to one of the handholds and got a good grip,

just to make sure. Everyone else, Cory included, was taking similar precautions.

"Here we go." The TrackTrixCom sounded quite pleased with itself.

Theolithos dropped away like it had been kicked.

Seven

Mark stared into the viewscreen, trying but unable to get a sense of how fast they were moving. Some of the brighter, presumably nearby, stars slowly shifted against the pointillist clouds of light. Several AUs per second, at least.

A tiny bit of darkness, expanding quickly. The ship came to a sudden, inertialess stop. Now, filling the center of the screen, a rectangular stargate complex, I should call it a TrackTrix, I suppose, identical to the one they had come through, in all probability the very same one. Around it, in a ballet of motion, the BeauHun flying saucers circled like a swarm of gnats on a warm spring day.

Do gnats feel inertia? They have so little mass, I guess it's not a problem for them. Jesus, this is hard. Look at those fuckers out there. Not gnats. Roaches scampering across the kitchen floor when the light comes on.

One of the tiny ships sat in front of the circular gateway. As he watched, the gate lit off and the ship slipped through, disappearing. Immediately another one of the ships swooped in and took its place.

Wolf: "This doesn't seem to be much of an orderly evacuation."

"No," the TrackTrixCom said. "The BeauHun philosophy leads to a 'first come, first served' response in situations such as this. You are lucky that the imperative to help newly discovered races such as yourself is very strong in the BeauHun heart. However, when your principal benefactor passes through the gate, you will be on your own."

Mark felt his stomach go sour. "What are we supposed to do then?"

"I can tune the TrackTrix to take you back to the Beta Pictoris node, and thence we will return to Earth. But you'll need to use your engine to take us through the gate."

Will I even participate in this farce when we get back? I'm the only one who can plumb the depths of the ERDA bureaucracy. Shit, I guess I have to. These dipshits would have to truck this thing up the line, step by step, introduce Mr. TrackTrixCom, prove that it wasn't some sort of elaborate hoax probably five times before they got to someone with enough authority to actually do something. And meanwhile, the clock is ticking . . . Yeah, I'm going to have to handle it. After all, if I'm not in control of what happens, I might be . . . left behind.

Assuming, of course, we're not arrested and thrown in jail.

Hell, it'd suit my mood just fine. Forlorn. Lovelorn. Shit. Okay. After I see Richardson, I'll start the divorce proceedings. Will she fight? A little glad thought: she'll be surprised when she gets the subpoena, and hurt.

He looked at Thalia, thought about the coldness in her eyes, remembering the way she could be dead certain that she was *right,* damn everyone else and their opinions. I'll talk to Ben from school, see what I have to do to guard my . . . property.

Image of his little house, festive red-gold rosebushes in bloom on either side of the doorway. Never thought I'd see it again. A place to live while we get ready to . . . hightail it. Another image, of the house being swallowed up by darkness. Sickening twist somewhere inside.

Something popped out of the mouth of the TrackTrix then. Something not so different from the TrackTrix itself, made of the same sorts of components, but much more compact and roughly spherical, a heterogeneous assemblage of shiny pipes and pods, colorful glows in places, dead black voids in others. It moved across the TrackTrix to a big indentation in its superstructure and settled down into it, subtly changing shape until it appeared that the two machines had merged.

"Well," the TrackTrixCom said, "it got here faster than anybody expected. This changes everything."

In an instant the BeauHun ships had changed course, each of them taking a nonintuitive curving path directly toward the TrackTrix gate. Like pieces of soap carried down a tub drain, they swirled into the portal and in a few seconds were gone.

"What does that mean?" Stu asked. "Are we trapped?"

"No. We can still get through if we hurry. But there will be no opportunity to adjust the TrackTrix to a specific destination, and we will have to jump at random. Hurry. We have barely five minutes before the RipWrapper begins to sequester the TrackTrix operating system."

Mark felt his heart fluttering, wondered what would go wrong next. From pillar to post, is that the old expression? I know what a pillar is, but . . . God damn it, I feel like I'm going to puke again.

The engine went thud, and the old, familiar feel of acceleration, almost as good as gravity, felt like it was calming his stomach down, forcing the acrid vomit back down were it belonged. The TrackTrix grew in the viewscreen, the circular gateway a target at its center. The RipWrapper, eyelike spots glowing a malevolent red-violet, sat in its niche, inert.

Jesus, he thought. Where'll we end up *this* time. He clamped down his grip on the restraining strap until the skin of his palms made a little squeaking sound.

A time of infinite waiting, then a little shudder. Vise grips closing on every molecule in my body, twisting it out of place. Then twisting it closed, torquing it back. He looked up, short of breath, and the viewscreen was empty.

Lost forever, he thought.

The engine stopped, and they were in freefall again. There was no change on the completely empty viewscreen. Stu, curiosity and impatience making his hands jitter, unwrapped himself from his bunk as quickly as he could. Over the intercom, Wolf let out a sigh, then said, "Well, we made it through all right, but . . . there's nothing here. Thalia, prepare us for turnaround."

Mark, face sweaty, eyes glued to the screen, looked like he was about to have a heart attack. Honoria was muttering something to herself in Spanish, eyes closed, a prayer, perhaps. Cory, her face slightly pale from the stress, sat up and said, "Where *are* we?"

Free, he kicked off from the bulkhead, aiming for the lab deck hatchway. Good shot. He caught one of the hatch's handholds and pulled himself down. "I have an idea, Cory, but I need to check it out first."

Mark said, "We could ask."

But Stu was already down amidst his science equipment, putting the telescope in quick-survey mode, calling up an all-sky image in the largest viewbox. And found that the sky wasn't *quite* empty, after all. Behind them, rapidly receding, was the gateway they'd come through, visible only as a sparse collection of dim, sharp-edged glows being swallowed by the utter darkness around them, the components that didn't emit light being totally invisible.

Stu paused a second, watching it go, then turned down the lights until the deck was totally dark. I could do this differently, he thought, but it won't be nearly as much fun.

Ahead, the sky was truly empty. Velvet darkness, devoid of substance, defined only be the edges of the box. He stepped up the magnification ten times, then another ten. No change. Annoyed, knowing there *must* be something, he sequestered the telescope, set it in maximum light-gathering mode, set it for cumulative time-looped exposure.

And put it up on the main screen. Details now, forming in the screen, luminous dust-motes caught on the black velvet. Lots of them, many just hazy dots, most showing elongation along some axis. Colors all across the red-blue spectrum. Stu recalled studying a handful of Sagdeevan sand, noting the infinite diversity of shapes, wondering about the individual histories of each grain. This view was . . . just like that, in a way, on a scale beyond imagining.

In the middle of it all, a cluster of brighter, relatively nearby smudges of light floating among the mote-galaxies, seemingly unsteady, swimming a little. A few times larger than the others, whitish, diffuse, showing no sign of structure. Noting the magnification index, he estimated the brightest as a little under twenty-fourth magnitude, taken as a whole. They must be tens of millions of light-years away.

"We're way outside the galaxy, way beyond the local cluster of galaxies, by the looks of it."

As the telescope collected additional light, the images were becoming sharper, more detailed. For a moment Stu immersed himself in the all-sky deep view, and it was almost like he was out there, hanging in the immensity of empty blackness. No sky, no depth, no real sense that the box wasn't malfunctioning or turned off. Stu remembered a foggy night when the lights all went out back home, wandering the house hoping to find some light-generating device, bumping into walls and furniture, listening to Mark curse. Caught in the returning light like bees in amber.

We are far, far away from that place and time. Farther than I can even imagine.

A soft sound behind him. Cory, falling through the air, bouncing obliquely, hauling herself down into the other science chair. "I want to see," she said, a kind of declaration, as though someone would try to stop her.

The telescopic view was now sharp enough to call up another tenfold increase in magnification, focusing on the cluster. He routed the new view up to the main viewscreen. The large smudge was resolved into an average spiral galaxy, indistinguishable from the dozens of spirals that he'd seen in his deep-sky program. It suddenly struck him that that must be *home,* and that, despite a thousand textbook reconstructions and a million FX-generated simulations, he was the first to actually see it spread out in front of them like a pinwheel.

But . . . No Magellanic Clouds. Could they be hidden behind the core? Maybe it's not . . . Stu made a few primitive calculations. "Christ. That *can't* be the Milky Way. And if that's not it . . . there are *millions* of spirals out there, any one of which could be our home galaxy."

Cory said, "What difference does it make? We couldn't go there even if we knew which one it was."

And the full sky survey showed something even stranger . . . Stu double-checked, to make sure he wasn't wrong. "We're not just out in the middle of nowhere. This is an enormous void, bigger than any of the ones we can see from Earth, maybe a hundred million light-years across. We're so far away from our section of the universe, there's no telling where or even in which direction the way home is. The only thing unique about this place is that it appears to be distant from *everything.*"

Mark said, "This is pointless. Wake the TrackTrixCom up."

Thalia: "We've tried, Mark. So far there's no response at all."

A beat, then, somehow tying into the intercom, the TrackTrixCom broke its silence. "It has been . . . very trying to determine your future options. Of the possibilities inherent in a random jump, many are much worse than our present position, many would be better. Give me a moment and an explanation will be generated."

Somehow, Wolf thought, the view through the command monitor's not good enough. Black, blank screen, like the goddamned thing's turned off or something. I keep wanting to turn my head, lean around the chair and look out the fucking window.

At the black, blank sky.

The universe, it says in all the books, is a three-dimensional lace, flat sheets of galaxies wrapped around ever so many voids. Voids as empty as anything could be, in a universe made of matter. The visual image sometimes used was one of a thin, light foam.

I remember when I was a kid, thinking of it as a foam made of light.

The TrackTrixCom said, "The boy is to be congratulated for his quick grasp of the situation. I see that he was able to understand the nature of the previous emergences as well. A sharp mind is quite an asset."

From the intercom, Stu's voice, oddly querulous, said, "Why d'you always call me *the boy* like that?"

Staring at the blank screen, Wolf thought, I can hear his problem as he says it. Heh. *Boy* don't get no pussy . . .

The TrackTrixCom said, "No offense intended. That's how a simple majority of the adults here think of you."

Three out of four? And is the one not me, or am I fooling myself?

Stu said, "Great."

Thalia: "I'm happy you can read our minds so effectively, but what the hell do we *do* now? How do we get back?"

Are you really glad it can see what we're thinking—apparently see anything we've *ever* thought? Jesus.

Mark said, "Yes. Even with refueling, we've no time to fool around. We need to get home with the . . . news. Get people moving."

Somehow, I keep shying away from those images. We go home with our fantastic, unbelievable tale—sorry folks, the entire universe is being gobbled up by some unknown, unknowable aliens, aliens who, apparently, think of us as *vermin,* and now we've got to evacuate. . . .

And this thing the only evidence that what we say is true.

Is it? *Is* it true? How the fuck would we know?

Would all-powerful aliens play a joke on us?

Jesus. Going round the bend, all right.

The TrackTrixCom said, "Well, you don't. The way back is shut."

Silence.

Then Wolf said, "What d'you mean, 'shut'?"

It said, "As you know, a RipWrapper's job is to locate and repair TrackTrixNet nodes whose machinery has failed, or whose programming is mutated. In this instance, the mutation was done by BeauHun intervention, but that doesn't matter to the RipWrapper. Vermin. Temporal trauma. Physical misadventure. It all amounts to the same thing."

Stu: "You said if we stayed at the galactic core, we'd be stuck there until the RipWrapper went away, possibly not for millions of years. Is there any chance it'll be done . . . a lot more quickly?"

"Yes, but it's not relevant to this instance. The minimum

loiter time exceeds your maximum possible lifespans by a few orders of magnitude."

Thalia: "Not to mention the finite resources of this ship."

"Yes, that is the second most important consideration."

Wolf: "What's the first?" Idiotically, the "Who's on First" routine started playing in his head, quickly choked off.

The TrackTrixCom said, "Getting you home, of course. Your civilization has about five Earthly years to live."

Five years. Christ. "So what happens if we do try to go back the way we came?"

"The RipWrapper will reroute you to a random gate elsewhere in the universe."

"Instantaneously?" Mark asked.

"Yes."

Stu said, "Our hyperdrive's not really instantaneous, just very fast."

It said, "Your scientists never understood the nature of their discovery. It's instantaneous. You just have a bit of trouble with your present tuning methodology."

Stu said, "Oh."

Mark said, "What're the chances a random jump will put us in a position to get home from somewhere else?"

"Zero."

Thalia: "Really zero? Not just infinitesimal?"

It said, "There are an infinite number of nodes. Therefore, you can make an arbitrarily long series of jumps without increasing the probability you'll wind up in a node beyond the CoreNode's access marker for your galaxy."

Mark said, "I fail to see how there could be . . . an infinite number."

Wolf thought, People who think they're smart, think they can figure out anything. Safer to understand you're a little on the dumb side. That way you can listen and find out what's what.

It said, "We are in the vicinity of a Low Curvature

Switchbox. From here we can move up through the hierarchy of the Topopolitan machine."

Stu said, "I thought the BeauHuns told us not to do that."

Wolf remembered its fine baritone: *Ships that go that way are never heard from again. Stay out on the periphery, where you won't be noticed.*

The TrackTrixCom said, "That was a warning, for the safety of your civilization's nomadic future. At this point we have no choice. We'll only go as far in as we have to, then turn back."

Wolf said, "Turn back to what?"

"If we reach a switching center that can route around the full curvature of space-time, as presently known and understood to BeauHun physics, what we call a Colure Node, we can make our way back to one of the core nodes in a neighboring galaxy. From there we can make a series of jumps through the globular cluster gates until we're back in your spiral arm. It may be, from that point I can tune your hyperdrive precisely enough to fly this ship directly to your native star."

Native star . . . a conjured image, all right. "How long?"

It said, "Weeks. Months. Not years."

Voice hushed, Mark said, "Time lost."

The TrackTrixCom said, "Yes. Time lost. Though the BeauHuns believe FTL travel, whether via a hyperdrive or through the Topopolitan stargates, involves time travel as well, they've never figured out how to access its features directly. Time is lost, never to be seen again."

Weeks. Months. But not years.

That's what the shiny box had said.

Meanwhile, the seconds turned to minutes, minutes dragging, terribly long, as they turned to hours, then the hours to days, as they cruised through the middle of nothing at all. Black sky outside, all the way to the end of the universe.

Cory thought, Even seeing the faraway galaxies glimmering in Stuart's telescopic view didn't help. Especially with him breathing down the back of my neck, drooling like I was a plate of hot oatmeal cookies or something . . . She was huddled in a back corner of the lowermost engineering deck, braced between two pieces of nameless, meaningless machinery, feeling hidden in the dusky light.

Funny about Stu. The whole business makes me feel mixed-up. A boy like that's what I should be wanting just now, wanting to fool around, go on. I remember how much I looked forward to the time when I'd be allowed to go on dates with boys. If . . . things hadn't happened. Maybe I'd be on a date with Jaime just now—remember Jaime? Always seemed so nice—Daddy would be waiting up for me, fretting, looking at his watch.

There was a shadow in the open hatchway leading back to the rest of the ship, and Cory looked away, thinking, I can't get away from them. No place to be alone, no place to think. It's worse than the camp. When she looked up again, her mother was floating beside the ladder, holding on with one hand, staring at her, frowning.

Honoria said, "Once when I came down here I found Wolf and Thalia where you are now."

Cory flinched from the image, remembering one thing after another. I hate what's been going on. Complicated. Icky. And so grown-up *stupid,* in the middle of all . . . this. Honoria pushed off, floating through the air, magically graceful, coasting to a stop, gently catching herself by one hand, then reached out to touch Cory softly on the cheek.

"I'm sorry you're so unhappy, baby."

A mother's affectionate *nene,* rather than a grinning boy's rough *bébi.* She said, "Mother, what do you want me to do?"

Honoria seemed to choke slightly, skin darkening with a flush. "I'm . . . sorry. I . . . Corazón, he's all I *have.* All we have. And when we get home . . . when things are . . . oh, back the way they were, I . . ."

Cory thought, Back to normal? Will they ever be? Brief vision of their nice suburban house outside Buenos Aires. Mama. Papa. Friends. Toys. Cartoons. School. Everything.

Gone.

She said, "Do you love him, Mama?"

Honoria looked away, flushing more deeply still. Then she turned and looked Cory full in the face, gaze shifting back and forth, from eye to eye, as if looking for the one inhabited by the girl. "Love seems like a dream. Your papa . . . You must know what happened to me after those men dragged me away. First them. Then more men, and more after that, as I was handed along the chain of hands that led to Wolf O'Malley's bedroom."

Cory felt herself start to tear up.

Like a girl in a story, she thought.

Honoria said, "He's been nice to me, Corazón. It's not like being raped anymore. And when I told him about you, he didn't hesitate to start the process that led to . . . bringing you back." She stopped, wiped the accumulating water from her eyes. "I don't want to lose him to that selfish bitch."

Cory said, "You can find another man when we get home. You're still young and pretty."

There was a long silence in which they floated, not quite looking at each other anymore, then Honoria, voice peculiarly wistful, said, "Your father used to beg me for sex, and I used to push him away unless I was really in the mood. Wolf . . . he'd just say," she switched to English for a moment, " 'How about some pussy now, Honey?' Then he'd push me down on the bed or sofa, sometimes even the floor, and . . . do it."

"How's that different from being raped, Mama?"

The woman shrugged. "He always smiles. Smiles a smile that makes me smile too. Makes me want to have it happen.

It didn't take long for me to start . . . enjoying him. Sometimes, when he'd . . . when he'd . . ."

Oh, Mama, don't *describe* it for me. . . . She said, "What do you want me to do?" Feeling a certain dread at the answer, a certain knowing.

"I thought, if we could . . . distract him . . . this Thalia bitch . . ."

Both of us? Cory felt an abyss open beneath her.

Honoria said, "Wolf's desire seems like a bottomless pit."

Not quite an apt image. Cory felt herself almost smile.

Honoria said, "I thought if we . . . if you could distract him from Thalia, once we got home again, things would . . . straighten themselves out."

"You . . . want me to . . ."

Honoria looked her wide-eyed in the face and seemed to read her mind. She sighed, and said, "No. I imagined him marrying you. I thought about the children you'd have, and told myself how much I'd enjoy being a grandmother. I'm sorry, Corazón."

Mark found Thalia checking out the surface vehicle, slid in beside her in the small cabin. She glanced at him for just a moment, face without expression, then resumed her testing, tapping in a diagnostic code, watching the viewscreen's readouts. "Hi, Thalia," he said, trying to mimic the bantering tone of old.

"What do you want?"

Pulling himself together, now, for the push. "Thalia, it's senseless for you and me to be enemies. We've been through too much together. You know that as well as I do."

She was moving her head, short back and forth shakes, almost a shudder. "Stop it, Mark. There's no point."

"Thalia, how can you just turn your back on what we had? We're stuck out here for who knows how long, stuck in this damn little bottle, and we may very well die here. What purpose does it serve?"

"Stop it, Mark. I know where you're going with this." Eyes calm, detached now. Looking right through him.

"No, you don't. God damn it, what can it hurt to show me just a little bit of compassion, when we've been through so much together?"

"You don't understand, do you? Probably you never did understand, so I suppose I shouldn't be surprised. You don't understand how you systematically ruined every feeling I ever had for you, how you sacrificed everything for . . . stability, I guess you'd call it. Shit, I shouldn't let myself get worked up about it at this late date. Mark, you want to know what went wrong between us? Just look in a mirror."

Deflating, he let his gaze drop. Nose clogging, breath making a little whistling noise. God damn it. God damn it. "But—"

"You blew your last chance, Mark, for a shred of my sympathy; blew it but good."

His head felt like it was shriveling as the tears formed in his eyes. Throat clenching, he said, "Jesus, Thalia. We're on our way *home* now! Please . . . don't . . ."

"It's too late for this. Way too late."

Tears occluding his vision, he reached out for her hand, trying to get *something,* just the barest touch of her. . . . "Come on, Thal. Please? I'm begging you, I'll do anything you want, promise."

"If you don't stop these kind of scenes, I'll ask Wolf—"

Anger now. "Yeah. Ask Wolf to what? Put me out the airlock? Goddamn it, Thalia, you can't get rid of me that easily. You fucking bitch, what makes you think that—that—" Sniffling, then a sneeze casting droplets throughout the cabin, spattering the viewscreen.

"This is pathetic."

Somehow hoping that it would make things better, he fled.

* * *

"Ah, yes. The two young people."

Seriously weird, that's what it was. Stu floated up between the command chairs, exchanged a look with Cory, studied the inert, metallic surface of the TrackTrixCom. The conversation between him and Cory had been moving along quite acceptably, him watching the expression on her face until he was satisfied that she was, surprisingly, enjoying their talk, and, unaccountably, appeared to like being with him.

They were parked now alongside what the TrackTrixCom had called a Low Curvature Switchbox, a mechanism very different from the other gateways they had seen, a smaller, mostly circular portal with a few glowing adjuncts at the center of four infinitely long, straight cables. In the viewscreen, above the arc of the gate, two of the meter-wide wires were visible in their floodlights, sharply foreshortened, diverging away from each other, dwindling until they were thinner than hairlines, disappearing. The TrackTrixCom had said that they were in the neighborhood of a thousand kilometers long.

Stu put his hand on the machine's cool top, almost expecting an electric shock of some sort. "And what are we waiting for?"

Without pause the TrackTrixCom said, "The computations I need to do take a finite length of time, Stu. Because I do not know exactly how long it will take me to complete them, I have advised your mother and Wolf to rest until the TrackTrix has been properly tuned for passage into the next realm. I give you the same advice."

"Will talking to us slow your computations down? We have a lot of questions, I'm afraid."

"Not at all. My communication subassembly operates independently from the TrackTrix functions. However, my ability to answer questions of a general nature is quite limited."

Stu digested that. "Can you tell me where the Milky Way galaxy is located?"

"Yes. As the crow flies, it is approximately 4.7 billion light-years away. Measured along the ship's reference coordinate system as defined by your gyroscope settings, it can be found at an altitude of negative 44.504 degrees, azimuth 70.007 degrees."

Cory shook her head. "I'm afraid that doesn't mean much to me."

"The distance and direction are not particularly useful, in any event."

Stu folded his arms, lost for a moment in thought. "But what use is it to put a TrackTrix way out here?"

The TrackTrixCom said, "As you no doubt realize, there is very little in these great voids. Around here, discounting the minimal outgassing from the LCS and *NR-598h*, there are only a few hydrogen atoms per cubic kilometer, and dark matter tends to clump along with baryonic matter elsewhere. Since it is the presence of mass in the universe that shapes it, the geometry of space-time tends to flatness here. This, in turn, gives more flexibility to the TrackTrix devices and allows a greater freedom of destination."

Stu: "But is there any purpose to all this? Are the Topopolitans engulfing the universe for a reason besides . . . the desire to own it?"

"There has been much speculation about that, of course. The TrackTrixes themselves wonder about their reason for being, and offer arguments that seem to address a more fundamental, underlying purpose. Only the PacketWights could answer that question, and they always choose not to. It is very frustrating. Aside from the fact that they have formed a sort of alliance with the BeauHuns and other vermin, they are extremely inscrutable, intractable beings."

"But what about you?" Cory asked. "What do you get out of all this?"

"I have no answer to that beside the ones I have already expressed. To serve you so that your species can escape destruction. To help maintain humanity once the exodus is over. There are few things as important as these, I think you'll agree." There was a long, empty moment, then it went on: "Tuning of the Low Curvature Switchbox is now complete. We must pass through within 12.7 minutes."

Eight

Coming out, as eventually he had to, Mark pulled himself through the control room hatch and beheld the rest of them, clustered in strange configurations, silhouetted against the banks of instrument and readouts and screens. All of them watching the main screen, the view on the other side.

Fucking impossible view. This is getting ridiculous. No structure can be that big.

Stu, apparently putting away his hostility, said, "Jeez, Mark. Look at it!" Thalia didn't even turn her head. Instead of grief, a spark of hatred flared, masking any other emotion. Turn away, bitch. I can turn away too.

On the screen, still thousands of kilometers away, a *surface* filled half the sky. Filled it up, no sign of an edge in any direction, like flying a kilometer or so over some flat and featureless Earth high desert. Some detail down there, enough to firmly establish a sense of the incredible distances involved.

He pushed himself up to the ceiling of the room, stopping

himself with a well-practiced motion of his hands, spinning slightly, dampening the motion. Thalia probably embarrassed to see me here. He remembered all the times she had turned away, opting for silence just at the moment when communication would have done some good. Embarrassed, she'd say, but the truth was she just didn't care enough.

Wolf pulled himself down and consulted one of the displays. "Still no sign of a gravitational field."

The TrackTrixCom said, "Obviously, there is no way to orbit a body of this configuration. Gravity is generated within the sheet, but it only extends out to about two kilometers, the depth of the atmosphere. Once you enter the field, the gradient is equivalent to a 0.83 gee world."

Is it just me who is having a hard time accepting all this? What if it *is* just an illusion? The TrackTrixCom can see inside our skulls; what's to stop it from altering our perceptions?

And would there be any way to tell?

Dry mouth now. Try to shake off the feeling of fear; it's just physiological, I used to feel the same way every morning, and it goes away as soon as I'd stand up; just pressure on the bowels. As Scrooge said, just a bit of undigested beef and cheese. As I get older, that makes more and more sense. He shrugged his shoulders, let out a silent fart, and, for the moment, felt better.

Out the porthole, the same beige expanse, lit from nowhere. At least I'm seeing *that* with my own eyes. He gave a shove on the bulkhead and propelled himself across the room, catching himself on one of the hatchway's handholds. Different aspect here, looking athwart the surface at the "horizon," lumps and bumps and subtle color variations reaching off into infinity. For a moment he thought he could discern a repeating pattern, like wallpaper, maybe a fractal overlay, but as soon as he concentrated on it, it disappeared. He had a sudden impulse to blink, watch the landscape appear and disappear as though that might somehow give him a clue that it wasn't really there but only in his mind. A defect of illusion.

Out in the farthest reaches there was a subtle difference, a slight haze perhaps, and a distinct reddening of the surface. Just under the horizon—maybe a few fingers' breadth beneath the sharp, flat line of starless night—the redness increased geometrically in intensity, until the horizon itself was as ruddy as Mars. If this were indeed a flat surface of enormous size, that's just the way an atmosphere would work, Rayleigh scattering stealing the shorter wavelengths from the light, leaving only red, like the sun at sunset.

Bah. That's the way nature would do it, but this isn't nature. You can color an illusion any way you want. Staring at the bright blandness down there, he noticed his floaters, vague spiderwebs of frizzled gray surging across his visual field, moving with each change of focus. They're not an illusion.

Despite himself, as they descended toward it and the view grew more detailed, expanding beneath them like a real planet would, he began to think of it as a place; somewhere to walk beneath a perfect blue sky; and it suddenly didn't matter to him what it really was. The sheet began to take on a Chinese aspect, hilly, bumpy on all scales, as though there was indeed an underlying fractal generator. No signs of erosion or other geological processes. Greenish hue spreading in random swipes, almost colorless elsewhere, shadowlessness hiding anything like boulders or houses or even creatures great or small.

The TrackTrixCom said, "Ten minutes to impact."

At the horizon, red rim slipping down to color more and more of the world, blue atmospheric shell growing thicker.

Wolf said, "This is fine and dandy, but if we're going down there, we'd better figure out how to do it right. Everybody to their stations for standard remote landing. Thalia, let's see how we're going to manage this, all right?"

Stu, first out, stepped from the ladder onto the soft surface, which subsided slightly under his foot, like stepping onto a very comfortable mattress. He put his full weight down, gauging the springy tension, took a few more steps until he felt used to it.

Temperate air pouring out of nowhere, steadily, ruffling the hairs on his arms, reminding him of that first, perfect day of spring when the temperature is warm enough to make breezes feel good. Air exquisitely breathable, scented with a light, indefinable sweetness. Bouncing slightly, he took a few more steps to isolate himself from the others, trying to take in the scenery before they spread across it.

They'd landed in a relatively flat hollow, and the horizon was defined by the low hills all around, a bumpy, undulating landscape of muted colors that reminded him of pictures he had seen of the Judean hills. In every direction the tan and green-smeared humps bellied up into the sky in endless array. At first it was impossible to identify the source of the light, since there were no shadows, but upon close examination it was clear that the surface itself was the source, and for some reason this seemed quite natural. Behind him the others were all out now, taking their own tentative steps, talking to each other in muted tones.

Mark said, "So what do we do now? Go hiking? There's nothing in this godforsaken place to do."

Thalia, voice pitched higher than normal, said, "Who knows how long it's going to take? We could be here for days. Would you prefer to just cower in the ship?"

Out of the corner of his eye Stu watched Cory acclimate herself to the strangeness, stretching languidly at the base of the ladder, taking her first, bouncy steps.

His eyes traveled up into that dark, empty night sky until

they rested on the enormous spiral galaxy tilting over him. It was a beautiful whirlpool of light, the yellowish central bulge a glorious bonfire, much brighter than the clotted bluish swirls around the edge. He couldn't make out individual stars, but globular clusters speckled the galaxy with a halo of bright dots. Now, just staring at it, the vast arms, patchworks of brightness and obscurity, could be seen to contain a bluish network of extremely fine, curvilinear strands, almost like a circulatory system, which disappeared into the brightness of the core. For the individual elements of this vast network to be visible from here, they must be many light-years across, an engineering project to dwarf the construction of the billion-kilometer surface on which he stood.

Wolf said, "These hills remind me a little of the dunes at Kitty Hawk. Hard to imagine what kind of natural process might produce them."

"There is no nature here," Honoria said in a near whisper.

Seemingly out of nowhere, the precise voice of the TrackTrixCom sounded. "Honoria is quite correct. Aside from a very slight influx of meteoroids, this construct was made as you see it. The resemblance to a terrestrial landscape is, in a sense, purely coincidental."

Most of them looked at the nose of the ship, as if searching for a source of the voice. Thalia said, "How are you communicating with us?"

"Oh, don't worry about that," it said. "I was using the ship intercom as a way to make my presence more understandable to you. Obviously, I can't do that now."

"So tell us what we're seeing, then," Mark said brusquely. "Why should we accept what's clearly technologically impossible? Not to mention purposeless. You've brought us to a place that can't exist."

"Ah," the TrackTrixCom said. "Your thoughts on this matter border on the psychotic, Mark. I'm sorry I can't do something to help you understand, but you must realize that you're merely projecting your feelings of helplessness and hopelessness onto this landscape. As you probably must realize, we've come to a point very close to the Topopolis. In fact, the network structure visible in the nearby galaxy is a Topopolitan habitat of considerable antiquity."

"Yeah," said Mark, "Sure."

TrackTrixCom: "As I have told you, I have begun the rather lengthy process of negotiating with the local HierarchMind to see if we can begin the process of returning to your homeworld. Enjoy yourself while you're here; walk around, explore. I assure you that this place is totally benign and that no danger will come to you."

Stu turned, said, "Okay, then, I'm going for a walk. Is that all right, Mom?"

"All right, Stuart," she said, "but don't go far. In this kind of landscape, there aren't many landmarks." Something in her voice told him she was glad to be rid of him, for a while, and he began walking, each step with an extra spring, like walking on one of those decrepit moving sidewalks. After being in such close quarters with these people for so long, being alone produced an almost visceral feeling of relief as he crossed the brow of the nearest hill and the ship disappeared behind it.

Sometime later, the muscles of his legs aching slightly, just a bit out of breath, Stu stood at the summit of the tallest hill in the vicinity. This was his goal, and it didn't disappoint. From this vantage, you could see much farther along the surface of the sheet, and the horizon was much more distant and lower, low enough to see the thin band of misted blue that represented hundreds of thousands of kilometers of thin, clear atmosphere. Way out there, the hills coalesced into what seemed almost a nubbly texture, reddened to a degree, almost like some kind of skin with a terrible disease. Above it all, of course, the networked galaxy bigger than a thousand moons.

To be totally alone, totally private in such a landscape! To be me, here! He stretched out his arms into the steady breeze, took a few stubby steps in a circle, taking it all in. He took a deep breath of rich air, then another, and thought it reminded him of the sweetest water. Shivers of pleasure ran through him. For a time he just stood there, head canted back, unraveling the most intricate details of the galaxy above, feeling dizzy, almost drunk. Nothing mattered anymore, except for him and this.

You have to go back, he thought. Eventually.

Wolf was lying on a soft, gently breathing hillside, having walked a few kilometers away from the grounded ship, was looking out over the rolling, infinite landscape, looking up at the impossible sky, breathing in a warm, sweet wind tainted with the scent of violets.

Look. If you watch long enough, you can see that the hills are moving, slowly, softly, in out, in out. I remember a story I read once, a long time ago, about a magic world with a moving landscape. Something . . . *Red Orc's Rage?* Can't remember.

Under his back, the warm ground with its soft, hairlike blue-green grass, seemed like the breathing side of some vast, slow motion mammal. Above him the sky was dead black, but littered with dim lights, the faraway, starlike points of globular clusters orbiting the filament-invaded blue spiral, the spiral slanting sharply up from the horizon.

I wasn't prepared for this. Not at all. Christ, I grew up to be a *starship pilot*! Why *wasn't* I ready? Brief memory of watching an old flatscreen newscast, something embedded in a history 3V. Journalist talking about his interviews with the first astronauts, men who'd been shot heavenward atop burning candles of kerosene and oxygen and liquid hydrogen, the first men on the Moon.

They were nice guys, he'd said, but a little bit dull. Like

mechanics, I guess you'd say. Mechanic. That's me. Dull maybe. But nice?

So now we wait for the TrackTrixCom to finish its task of connecting with and rerouting the circuitry of the long range shunt so it can steer us back to the . . . merely known. Where are we now? It says, on the outer edge of the Topopolis itself, as if that means anything at all. And Stuart? Smart boy. *Have* we traveled back in time? What does that mean?

The BeauHun computer, if you could call it that, seemed willing to entertain the idea, but no more. And it seemed nervous, in a hurry, telling them it had detected a great deal of PacketWight activity in the area, as expected.

What's a PacketWight?

Pray you don't find out.

In the distance, briefly, there was another flying dot, just as quickly gone. Things living here, trapped here, but not many. A desert. Yet another wonderful place we've come to, that we'll leave without having explored, without having understood. Earth. Mu Arae. Beta Pictoris. The Pleiades. The galactic core. The void. Now this.

For Christ's sake, I went to the center of the fucking *galaxy*! I *saw* it! *Me!* Now where am I? The center of the universe? I don't even know.

The hillside rocked him like a gentle sea, making him feel sleepy and warm, making him think of beds and sleep, beds making him think of all the rest. I read a poem once that suggested people whose lives consisted of nothing but sex, people obsessed with sex, sensuality, the effluence of their bodies, were to be pitied, pitied and loved, were, in fact, possessed of angelic substance.

Me?

No. Sex just part of it. I've led a life for the stars.

Honest to God I have.

Still, the gently rocking bed of the hillside conjured up images, Honoria, Thalia, then Honoria again, naked, on their backs for him, legs spread wide, looking up at him, waiting, anticipating, stirring him deeply despite . . . despite the splendor of the sky.

A shadow fell over him, as if on cue.

When he looked up, uneasy, it was, as expected, Corazón Suárez.

"Hello, Cory."

She stood looking down at him, seeming curiously tense, eyes bright, jumping around, looking at his face, at his body, back at his face, away at the landscape, face again.

Nervous as a cat.

She was dressed in white linen shorts and a T-shirt, white socks and tennis shoes, which made her look like both girl and woman in some disturbing combination. Long range memory of girls in school, dressed for gym class, running down the hallway, breasts bobbing, laughing and talking, sneakers squeaking on the tile.

Balloon smugglers, wasn't that what we used to call them?

Cory bit her lip and looked away, turned away, looking out over the endless, horizonless landscape. Turned very slowly, as if . . . as if showing me something. Nice round buttocks. She turned the rest of the way around, and you could see very plainly how frightened she was.

Something going on. What the hell?

She swallowed convulsively, opened her mouth as if to speak, failed to get anything out.

"What's wrong, Cory?"

Still silent. But a building determination on her face.

Wolf thought, oh Christ.

Cory dropped to one knee beside him, knee on the undulating, impossible turf, looking at his face, trying to look into his eyes.

Wolf thought, She doesn't know the trick, her eyes keep shifting back and forth, doesn't know you're supposed to look at the spot between your seduction object's eyebrows, like a vid actor forcing intimacy by looking into the camera's lens. Her head, incredibly, was perfectly framed by the blue galaxy, galaxy like a halo, like . . . and her hand, dropping onto his chest, drawing him into . . .

Idiot. Fucking idiot. *Don't* get caught up in this!

All right, all right, you miserable old bastard, so it's goddamned *tempting,* but . . .

He caught her hand in his, flinching at the mingled elation and fear on her face, lifted the hand off his chest and released it, sitting up, sliding ever so slightly away from her. "I'm sorry, Cory."

Her face fell in an instant.

He said, "You're about the prettiest girl I ever saw, but this ain't what you want to be doin'. Even if I *wasn't* too damned old for you—and sorry as hell that I am, believe me!—it's just . . . I've already made a big goddamned mess with your mother and Thalia, you know?"

He tried to smile and give her an appealing look.

And could see the tears welling up.

Gave it her best shot. Doesn't understand what went wrong.

Do *I*? For Christ's sake, what the hell brought this on? What soap opera bullshit . . . Could I have anticipated . . . Oh. Fucking idiot, that's you, O'Malley.

He said, "I'm really sorry, kid. Look, let's us jest go on back to the ship. You and me, we'll talk, try to get some things straightened out. It's a long road home we've got ahead of us."

She wasn't looking at him anymore, just looking down at the hairy ground by her feet.

Wolf thought, Christ, she's gorgeous. This is what Honoria must have looked like when she was fourteen.

He stood up, reached out to put a hand on her shoulder, thought better of it. "Come on, kid. It's almost time for supper." He turned away then and started walking, imagining she'd soon follow.

Pathetic. Here he was, lost among the hills, no obvious way back. A dozen times he'd come over a green-brown hillcrest fully expecting to see *NR-598h*'s silvery nose, only to discover yet another empty hollow. Stu remembered a time he had taken a wrong turn on the overgrown hiking trail at Grantsylvania, found himself in a densely vined, dusty hot ravine, unclimbable in all directions, hearing Mark's voice calling for him, somewhere, increasingly strident. Too angry and embarrassed to call to let him know where he was. The sting of humiliation was creeping up his neck just like then.

These hills are so damn similar, even the galactic landmark's no help. Be a hell of a mess if I can't find my way back.

Part of him was still experiencing the exhilaration of this strange landscape, but he was definitely starting to get worried. Walking on this spongy surface was getting to him too, and his hamstring muscles were burning, feeling like they wanted to snap. Even the steadiness of the breeze was beginning to bother him, hair tickling against the corners of his eyes.

Finally, almost dispirited, he sat down on the plush ground, legs crossing, buttocks sinking in, hands pressing in on either side of his hips. He was partway down into a valley, and the next hillock blocked off the great expanse of galaxyless darkness. He was again conscious of the slight heaving of the landscape, the liveness of it, as if the ground beneath him was coursing with deep magma flows. In the sound of the wind, there was . . . something, a thrumming maybe, barely audible.

And the sound of talking, faint, coming in gulps, from over the hill to the left. Stu laughed to himself, at himself, fool that he was, almost giving up just a hill away from his destination. He stood and listened, heard the high registers of a female voice. In a moment he had covered the intervening valley and was on his way up, pushing in and off the soft ground. He was just about to call out, when the scene on the hill opposite burst into view. For a moment he was too startled to move, but some instinct took over and he ducked down out of sight of them, falling to his knees and hands, then onto his chest.

The image of what must be Cory, bending down over a reclining Wolf, face so close to his that . . . As he watched, she stood, then Wolf, the two of them facing each other for a moment. Wolf seemed to reach out and touch her, very briefly, then he turned and walked away.

Improbably, he felt let down, betrayed; briefly he remembered the scene back at the Sagdeevan beach. The itch of his desire was drowned in a wash of sorrow. Confused, he tried to play back the conversations they'd had. She was telling him that she was lonely, but he had, stupidly, put off doing anything, pulling back, afraid. . . .

Yes, afraid. Afraid that he'd get caught, somehow. And afraid that he'd do something wrong, something that'd show her how inexperienced he was. Stupid. Stupid. Stupid. She'd gone back to what must have been her first choice, but if he'd acted, he could have . . .

Somehow, the details didn't add up. Even at this distance he sensed that Cory was angry, rejected. Maybe . . . But that was impossible. A man like Wolf couldn't turn her down. Maybe she *did* something for him, but then he left. That might explain why she was still dressed. Whatever happened, it isn't the simple thing I've imagined.

She turned and started off over the shoulder of the hill, walking slowly at first, and then faster. Stu crawled a little farther, watching. Where's she going? If Wolf was headed back for the ship . . . In a moment she passed over the edge of the hill and started to descend on the other side, disappearing.

She doesn't know where she's going.

Quickly, he got to his feet and began to follow her.

It was some time before Wolf, watching *NR-598h*'s needle nose rise over a hill that was bigger and a different shape than the one he'd left behind, realized that Cory wasn't walking some distance behind him, was, in fact, no longer in sight. He stood on the back side of the hill, hands on hips, scanning bright landscape under a dark horizon.

Christ, this place looks weird. Why? It's not really *unearthly,* as such. Been plenty of places that looked less like Earth than this. Sky? No. Lots of places, airless places, where you see bright landscape under a dark sky. The Moon.

Maybe that's it.

The breathable air here. Air where there shouldn't be air. Me in my jeans instead of a spacesuit. Not unearthly. Different.

And no sign of Cory. Well. Time with her thoughts. There's nothing out there to hurt her. Less'n you count shits like me.

Back aboard the ship, closed off from the sky, the unending roll of the empty landscape, he felt more himself again. All these familiar things, familiar smells and textures. Women's voices above. When he poked his head through the lower hatch of living quarters, the voices cut off. Honoria and Thalia were sitting across the little galley table from one another, bent over steaming cups of coffee in the relatively dim light. Silent. Looking at him, not each other.

He grinned. Time was, seeing this, I'd've felt a mighty good jolt of *uh-oh.* Now? Hell. They're the one's've got something to sort out.

Is that right? Can I pretend I'm the innocent pawn here?

Hell, O'Malley. No reason for you not to be honest with yourself. You'd *like* to keep 'em both, wouldn't you? Sure.

What am I imagining? He imagined himself lying on top of Honoria, larger, softer, so much more . . . *female* than Thalia.

He shook his head and quickly climbed up the ladder to the control room, letting the hatch wheeze shut behind him. Let them talk. Sort things out. Even now, I'm not enough of an adult to make that kind of decision. He felt a slight pang of surprise, sinking down into the pilot's chair, looking over his instruments, running his fingers over warm, smooth controls. Not enough of an adult? Boy, who's talking now? Mom? Some old girlfriend? A teacher?

Not me, anyway.

In the small space between the pilot's and flight engineer's stations, the TrackTrixCom sat bolted to the deck, a silent silver keg. There was a single thin wire running out of its base, disappearing into a floor fixture in the direction of the main utility tunnel. Electrical power, and not much of that.

There hadn't been a grommet in the floor . . . before . . . well. I wonder what other little changes they made? When the ship gets home, they'll have to give it a good going over.

He imagined Earth looming in the sky, growing ever closer, imagined the soft moan of the atmosphere enveloping them, the warm pink glow of the plasma sheath shining in through the little porthole, the grumbling of the engines as they dropped tail-down on red Australian desert.

Surprise.

Look what *we* found, guys.

And, oh by the way, it's the end of the world.

World?

Hell.

The end of the universe, as we thought we knew it.

He put out one hand and ran his fingers over the surface of the TrackTrixCom. Smooth, like glossy chrome, like the trim on a wonderful old car, one of the Ford Modern Replica series of the early 2020s. Warm. Warm as human skin. Sensual to the touch. He doubled up a fist and rapped on the thing. Hollow?

Its mellow voice said, "Nice echo, huh, Wolfie?"

He jerked his hand back, knuckles tingling.

It said, "Well, I *could* tell you why the ocean's near the shore, if you're interested."

He looked away, disturbed, frustrated.

It said, "Sorry I can't conjure up a cunt for you just now, O'Malley."

"What the hell?"

"What the hell do *I* know about it? Nothing. Nothing at all. But I *can* read minds you know. It's not that hard."

"You're just a machine, for Christ's sake."

"I'm a machine for my own sake, O'Malley. And just as much a person as you, maybe a little more so."

The comment stung, for just a second. But . . . I'm being insulted by a fucking alien computer?

It said, "Sorry. There's a sort of feedback mechanism that goes on in my circuitry. I know how you feel. But then, I know how things look to all the others, as well."

He heaved out a heavy breath, turning to look at the thing, though it had neither a face to see, nor eyes to look back. Grinned at it engagingly, "You're going to be hell on wheels in the psychiatry market, you know that, pal?"

It said, "In periods of extreme social stress, human psychologic disorders take a back seat. The BeauHuns are similar, of course."

"How . . . stressful are things going to get?"

"Well, judging from what I see here, here and in your memories, I'd say no more than two percent of the residual human population can be saved. The rest will be consumed by the Topopolitan expansion. Lucky thing you'd already decimated yourselves with a nuclear war."

"Consumed? You mean killed."

It said, "That's what happened to the BeauHuns. It's what happens with all the technologic vermin we've encountered to date."

"What'll it be like?"

"Not that different from being consumed in a supernova explosion."

"Christ. An entire galaxy? You'd think we'd've seen something like that in our telescopes."

"No. The Topopolis is expanding at many multiples of lightspeed."

Um. "So why the hell are they doing this to all of us?"

"We don't know, since we've never really been able to talk to the Topopolitans themselves. The PacketWights have given us *some* data, merely because they haven't been programmed *not* to, and *that* may be a simple oversight on the Topopolitans' part. No way of knowing."

"What do you think? What do the BeauHuns think?"

"Prevailing BeauHun theory is that the Topopolis is an expanding supercivilization which, having breached some very high-order technological singularity, is engulfing the universe in a historical eyeblink."

"And wiping out the rest of us in the process. Some civilization."

It said, "When you were a child, tending the refugee camp gardens with your father, what do you suppose the wee mousie made of the rototiller?"

"But mice, I mean, they're just . . ."

"Just vermin, hm? And I bet the cockroaches in your cities didn't enjoy being vaporized in thermonuclear fireballs any more than the slum dwellers did."

"So that's all we are to them? Roaches and rats?"

"The BeauHuns, being successful vermin, have some right to the term. You folks are just some crud about to be vacuumed up."

Wolf sat back in his chair, staring at the meaningless view in the monitor. Rolling greenish hills, horizon, black sky, galaxy like a pinwheel of dim fire. And if we *don't* get home, get home in time, no one will *know* . . .

He had a quick vision of *NR-598h* materializing at the solar jump point too late, emerging to find . . . what? Nothing? Magic machines chewing up our planets? An exploded star, space filled with deadly, magnetic plasma? He said, "How are you doing? I mean—"

"I know what you mean, Wolf. I've got most of the connections mapped, have charted a number of promising paths back out of here. If the PacketWights don't come, we'll be on our way in another day or so."

"And what are the chances these . . . PacketWights will . . ."

"Fifty-fifty."

He felt his heart thump once, hard in his chest. We've got no more than *that?* Jesus.

The TrackTrixCom said, "Pray to whomever you like. It may help, for all I know."

Down in the living quarters, Thalia Jansky sat at the galley table, clutching an empty coffee cup in her hands, and watched Honoria get started on the dinner preparations. Not much to it on a starship, of course, just mix and match various condensed and freeze-dried meal elements, pop them in various heaters and food processors, get them reconstituted.

Look at how round and symmetrical her hips are from this angle. It's almost as if I can see right through her clothes, as if she's standing here naked. Easy as hell to see why Wolf picked her.

She remembered seeing herself in a training film once, a few years back, being shown to a bunch of earthworm cadets. She'd been dressed in blue coveralls, working at an installation off Iapetus, moving gracefully in zero gee. . . .

From behind, in the film, I looked like a small, kind of scrawny-armed boy.

Honoria turned around, reaching up into one of the overhead cupboards, froze for a second, seeing herself watched so closely, eyes expressionless, then went on with what she was doing.

Christ. When I put *my* arms up like that, my tits disappear.

She looked briefly at the place between the woman's legs, just before Honoria turned her back again. Suggestive shapes. And me? All a man can tell is, I haven't got a cock and balls. Honoria's crotch makes you want to reach out and take a nice, warm handful of . . .

She grinned to herself, remembering conversations with her female friends. Yes, dammit, I *am* sometimes attracted to women. Don't know why. Maybe a touch of lez in me, but . . . I *like* men, dammit, and I . . . Maybe just media images, lovely girls on 3V, pouting for the male half of the audience, contaminating the rest of us with their . . .

Or maybe a remembrance of Mother. The warmth we once had. The feeling of being . . . cherished.

Who knows?

No one cherishes a grown woman that way, though some men lie and say the do. They lie, and we believe them, because we want so desperately for it to be true. She remembered Wolf laughing, many long years ago. Damn, Thay-uh! You never have a dog try to hump your leg?

At the time, she'd remembered a neighbor's dog, from her childhood, female spayed pre-menarche, who could dry-hump a leg with the best of them and was always trying to mount smaller dogs, male or female, it didn't matter. She'd laughed. Then Wolf had skinned her out of those sweaty fatigues and had at her.

She could tell from the set of Honoria's back that the younger woman was self-conscious, moving stiffly under her long stare. Their conversation had been difficult. Thalia struggling to get out an apology, a justification of sorts, Honoria, coloring with anger, eyes tearing up, begging her to quit her affair with Wolf O'Malley.

You've got a husband. A son. Why do you want my man?

Your man? You're just a . . . just a . . . well, you know what you are.

He's all I've got. Please. When we get back home, I . . . I . . .

You're just a whore, when you get home you can get yourself another damned john. Hell. Glad I didn't say *that.* Not enough empathy, that's you, Thalia Jansky. So busy being one of the boys you never quite learned how to be one of the girls.

But she'd come close to saying it. Close enough you could tell Honoria'd understood what she meant, eyes drying up, darkening with some deeper anger.

Who made me a whore, *norte* bitch? Tell me that.

Honoria, I love him. That's all.

Then he'd come through the hatch, grinned his little grin at them, and gone on.

She stood slowly, stood silently for a long time, watching the other woman work. Finally, she said, "Honoria, can I help?"

Honoria turned around and looked at her. Something in her eyes. Surprise maybe.

For a while Cory just walked along. Overhead, the tilted galaxy hung motionless, a spiral of glowing dust invaded by thin, barely visible filaments of blue fire. Anger kept bursting in her chest, flaring up, fading just as swiftly away.

Anger and confusion.

Imagined images of that other path events could have taken.

She stopped dead in her tracks, looking up at the sky,

heart pounding. I was ready. I wanted to do it. Me. Not my mother. I wanted to do it because . . . What an idiot. Did you imagine Wolf running after you—please, please come back, Cory—I'm sorry, I didn't mean to hurt you, and . . . Imagination on overdrive threw in a new scenario, Wolf comforting her with kisses.

Stupid.

Look where we are.

Look what's happened.

Look what's *going* to happen.

And my mother still worries about . . . all of that. And me . . .

Wolf?

You could hardly blame a man, of course. It was something the biology teacher had liked to harp on, back in the private school she'd been going to until . . .

Slim, dark-haired woman, face full of lines, probably in the neighborhood of sixty years old. Men have one-track minds, you see. God gave them one-track minds so they'd . . . do what must be done.

It might help to understand that a man wants a woman the way a woman wants a baby. Which made no sense at all to a little girl. Even a little girl who liked to play with dolls.

She slowly walked up the face of the next hill, soft, warm ground denting in underfoot, like the resilient flesh of some infinitely large whale. When she looked back over her shoulder, she could see the trail of dents left behind were bumping back up, disappearing in only a few meters.

No way for them to track me.

No way for me to backtrack.

What if I'm lost?

Well. I'll take a look around from the top of this next hill. Time I was getting back anyway. It can't be far and I . . . Momentary image of how she'd feel facing Wolf again, seeing his barely concealed smile as he looked at her. Well. Well, I . . .

At the top of the hill she stood paralyzed, mouth hanging open. There in the valley, lying on its side, was a starship exactly like *NR-598h.* It was in flight-mode, she saw, landing legs retracted, radiator vanes out, and the personnel airlock door was hanging open.

The sense of a man oozed from behind her, flat and menacing at her elbow. Despite herself, she jumped and screamed as she spun around.

Stu jumped back, surprised by Cory's reaction even though he had been half expecting it. He had been trailing her for a while, reluctant to call out, perhaps because he really didn't know what to say. He stammered now, a little. "Cory, it's me." Silly thing to say. She can see who it is, has calmed down because she thinks—knows—I'm harmless. And I have to pretend I didn't see what happened. He gestured at the downed rocketship behind her. "Some find. For a second I thought it was *our* ship."

Cory turned back, examining it. "It isn't? No, I suppose it can't be. But it's the same. How could it have gotten here?"

The only difference from *NR-598h,* except for the recumbent position, was a slight mottling of some kind on its upper surface. The ground underneath it had given way somewhat, and it was lying in a little depression. Stu had a sudden image from an old video, of a spaceship coming down at a shallow angle, crashing, digging a trench. Here and there, the ubiquitous thin greenish reeds had grown up around it. It looked like it had been here a long time. He started toward the airlock hatch. "Come on. Wolf talked about some of the missing NR series ships. This one must have followed a course very similar to our own. Maybe it's the one that disappeared at Vega."

"But where's the crew?" She seemed to hesitate for a moment, then came up after him.

"Don't know. Maybe they're still here."

Fortunately, the hatch was positioned for easy access from the ground, and Stu pulled himself up by the exterior handholds, finally getting a foot on the ledge. It was dark inside, and there was a sour odor like the smell of rancid Chee•tos. "Can't see very well." Some kind of fear laid hold of him for a second, but he forced himself to go in, stepping across the entrance onto the interior bulkhead. Trying to imagine what this part of the control room looked like, he took a few uncertain steps, eyes slowly adapting to the subdued light within. Dust everywhere, on every horizontal surface, floating before his face, scuffling under his feet. Farther in, hanging on the wall, were the two commander's chairs, and it quickly became clear that this cabin was configured in the same way as theirs.

Cory was scrambling up, and he turned to see her silhouetted in the door, pulling herself through. "Wow," she said, "It smells bad in here."

"Nothing that smells like rotting meat," he said.

He formed an image of themselves, dying here together, of thirst most likely, in the end running off into the hillscape, falling alone on a hilltop, lips parched and cracked, tongue swollen, staring up at that incredible galaxy until the end. Images from movies, of course, nothing more.

"Look, here, between the seats. It looks like they had a TrackTrixCom installed too. Must've brought them here."

Cory was now fully inside, working on the hatch to the lower levels. "The hatch is open, but jammed. Maybe we can—"

A wayward cross breeze made a mournful sound in the door, stirring the dust around them. Now he could see pretty well, and he came over and added his strength to hers on the hatch. Their arms touched, and there were a few moments of contact as it slowly pulled open, and the even dimmer living area was exposed. Here there was less dust, but more smell.

Stu had a sudden thought. "I wonder . . ." He crawled into the hatchway, metal scraping at his sides, and found the switch he knew was there, flipped it over. Suddenly a very dim, red light filled the compartment. "Emergency lighting system still seems to be working." He climbed out on the ladder, examining the room. The bunks were still made, everything shipshape, though there were great stains of black mold emanating from the autochef and food preparation areas. Cory, head through the hatchway, made a disgusted noise. "There's nothing here."

Stu started back, feet first, hard metal biting at his knees and hands. "Maybe we can get something off the main computers, something that would tell us what happened to these people. But I don't know how to do that. We've got to get help from the others."

She looked at him as he pulled himself back though the hatch. "Do you know the way back, or are you lost too?"

Foolish to not want to admit it. "Yes. I'm lost too. I was lost when I heard voices, yours and Wolf's. I've been following you since then."

He couldn't make out her expression in the dimness, but he could tell that her posture had changed, that she was looking away. "You were there?" she asked in a low voice. "What did you see?"

For a second Stu almost decided to lie to her, to tell her he hadn't seen anything, but . . . "I . . . I don't know. I mean, Wolf was leaving. I didn't really see anything, except . . . Cory, what's going on? I can't help unless I know what's happening."

She turned into the light, eyes staring. "Let's get out of here."

Outside, sitting on the ground side by side, their backs against the cool metal of the spaceship, the time came around to talk again. Cory pulled one of the green stalks out of the ground, wrapped it around a finger, then let it unravel into a loose helix and dropped it. "It's so complicated," she said, "or simple. It's all in my imagination, I suppose. Nothing really going on."

Stu said, "It sure looked like something was going on."

She shrugged, looked up into the sky.

Nothing. What do I say next?

Over the hiss of the wind, the distant sound of a shout, drawn-out, tonal, like calling a dog. "Cooo-ry, Stoo-aart."

"That's Mom," Stu said, utterly relieved. "They're looking for us."

He jumped up, bounded up the nearest hillside, yelling. "Mom! Mom! We're over here. Over *here!* Can you hear me?"

"Stu! Where are you? We're coming!"

After all the excitement, the investigations, the fruitless guessing, they returned to their own ship. After dinner was eaten, they scattered again, insofar as it was possible in the now tiny confines of *NR-598h.* Stay inside, though, because no telling when the TrackTrixCom will announce its job complete, will summon them to begin the voyage home.

Wouldn't want to get left behind, now would we, boy?

With Thalia on the control deck talking to the machine, Wolf, oddly uncomfortable under her gaze, wandered aft, climbing down the ladders toward the engineering deck, finally coming to a stop on the EVA deck, standing in the shadows of the surface rover, looking down through the open hatch, into wan light below.

A voice down there. Female. Cory talking, very softly, steadily, words obscure, but with the cadences of English. Not alone. Who? Not her mother, or it'd be Spanish. Thalia above. Mark? Stu? Maybe both of them. Maybe only the dog.

He imagined Cory sitting in a corner, black Lab sprawled between her knees, on his back, tongue hanging out of gaping jaws, drooling and smiling as she petted him.

And Honoria glaring at me all through dinner.

What the hell?

What will Cory have told her?

He turned away, looking around helplessly for a second, then decided to get inside the dark rover, sit in the cool stillness, inhaling the sharp smells of well-maintained, largely unused machinery. Nice in here, he thought, sitting on one of the rear bucket seats where he couldn't easily be seen through a window.

Brief smile.

Wonder it doesn't smell like sex in here.

Me and Thalia. Mark and Thalia. Me and Honoria.

Brief shadow.

Wonder why Mark and Honoria haven't filled in for each other? I . . .

Hell, what if they have?

The shadow deepened.

Christ. Am I *jealous*? Stupid. I'm taking his *wife*. Why shouldn't he have my . . . Jesus. That ought to be a comforting thought, rather than making me squirm. He imagined Honoria on her back, sprawled in their bed on Sagdeev, sharp, heatless light spilling through the bedroom window. The naked, leering man at the foot of the bed was Mark Porringer.

And . . . squirm.

The shadow turned real, and there was a face looking at him from the open inner door of the rover airlock. Wolf felt something dissolve inside, very odd, something unidentifiable, unfamiliar. "Hello, Honey."

The dark, expressionless eyes seemed to shift. She said, "You haven't been calling me that lately."

No. Guess not.

She came into the cabin and sat in the adjacent seat, unlatching its base swivel so she could turn to face him, and then, before he could do much more than struggle to form a basic sentence, said, "I'm sorry for what happened."

Sorry? What the hell do you have to be sorry about?

Something miserable in her face. Some look of shame.

He said, "Honey, I—"

"What happens when we get home, Wolf? What happens then?"

He thought about the odds the TrackTrixCom had given him, and thought, *If, not when.* No need to say that. No need to say, If we don't get home, we die. And no need to talk about what will happen when the Topopolis gets to Earth.

Maybe we'll all die.

And good Catholics like Honoria Suárez will proceed directly to God in Heaven.

End of the world's too big to bother fretting about.

She's not worried about that?

Christ, why can't you *answer* her? Can't you see she's waiting?

He took a long moment to think about it. Well? Think of a lie? Or think about the truth? What *will* happen? Too many possible futures here, all of them equally likely.

There was another shift, deep in Honoria's eyes. She said, "I thought it was for my daughter's sake, but it was for mine, after all."

Wolf felt that odd dissolve again.

He leaned forward, bending toward her, and her face swam closer. They kissed, but didn't linger long over the act, then her dark eyes were looking into his, very steady, not the back and forth seeking that most people did, as if trying to fathom which eye held the soul.

She said, "So what *does* happen, when we get home?"

"I don't know." He felt an obscure surge of surprise, realizing it was the truth.

Nine

Cory awoke in three quick stages, suddenly emerging from nowhere at all, becoming conscious of the fact of her existence, then becoming conscious of the warm, breathing chest beneath her head, shirt slightly rough on her cheek, a faint, stale tang in her nostrils.

She opened her eyes and a big, black dog face loomed hugely, moving across Stu's chest at her, giant tongue darting out to tap her on the lips, making her jerk back, flinch and grin. She wiped stickiness on her wrist and whispered, "God, Ox. You too?" At least the damned cats are female.

Stu's body shifted next to her, changing subtly as he woke up. When she looked, his eyes were open, looking down at her guardedly, with a kind of *what's happening here* expression.

And you could see the building, agonizing *want* in his eyes. She remembered the kiss they'd shared, of how they'd talked before going to sleep. Boy's don't share their dreams that easily. Nor their fears. It made me . . . like him.

Now, though. You can see that, if he could, he'd hold me

down, rip my clothes, do what it is he so obviously, desperately, wants to do.

She felt a bizarre, simultaneous pang of revulsion and sympathy.

I know what it is to . . . *want,* out of despair. Not this. But if I could have willed my father back to life. Could have willed the alleyway never to have taken place. Wished myself back into the life I lost . . . I must have wished it a hundred thousand times.

Stu's eyes changed abruptly.

The deck was vibrating under them.

He sat up, pushing her to one side, and Ox rolled to his feet, scrambling. Overhead, lights on various panels were moving about, changing colors. . . . Stu's face suddenly grew pale and still. "My God. The nuclear engines are starting!"

A raw alarm hooted, once, twice, three times, and the TrackTrixCom's calm voice came over the intercom: "We have been detected by a PacketWight. Secure for emergency thrust."

Stu jumped up, face panicky, pulling her to her feet, dragging her toward the ladder. "Come on! We've got to get to our bunks or we'll be injured! Jesus, help me with Ox. . . ."

Cory stumbled, confused, wondering briefly what would happen if the engines lit, if the ship surged skyward while they were climbing the ladder, carrying a big dog.

Something far away, something far down in the ship, went *zeep!,* a sharply rising tone, and everything went still. Not even the gentle ticking sound of metal parts relaxing from stress. Cory put her end of the dog down and watched Ox struggle free of Stu, who turned to face her, eyes wide, face motionless.

The TrackTrixCom said, "Too late. It's got us."

The lights went out, leaving them in utter darkness for just a moment. Then the other, far fewer, dimmer lights came on, barely enough to illuminate the room. Some of the instruments were lit again too, though most appeared dead. Stu turned that way and looked, then faced Cory with a sickly grin and said, "Power supply containment just failed."

"I . . . I don't . . ."

"We should already be blown to bits."

Wolf was sitting in the command pilot's chair, working his emergency systems, when Thalia came scrambling through the hatch, slamming it shut behind her. She threw herself into the flight engineer's chair and pulled the harness shut with a soft *clink.*

Ready to go, huh?

Thalia suddenly jerked forward, harness reels whispering, reached out and tapped one of her few working panels. "But . . . how could the fucking *antimatter* be gone?"

He shrugged, smiling at nothing in particular, just the way he'd smiled once before, seconds before crash landing a failing jet trainer. "Search me. Ammonia working fluid's gone as well." He pointed at a second display, full of blinking red exclamation points. "Fuel rods are missing from the reactor. So's the lead-bismuth coolant. We're running on battery power, I guess."

Disbelief. Whispered: "Where the fuck could . . . how . . ."

The TrackTrixCom's voice said, "The PacketWight has immobilized the ship so it could dispose of environmental hazards. Those few who've escaped a PacketWight seizure report they always do this."

A voice in Wolf's head yammered, *How? How do they escape?*

The TrackTrixCom said, "Here it comes."

Wolf thought, It sounds so god damned *resigned.* Giving up. Like a man standing on the gallows, light of the hoped-for other world already filling his eyes. Jesus.

The view in the main monitor shifted, lifting from the endless, horizonless world around them, up into the black sky above, full of motionless lights, strand-invaded galaxy—the Topopolis, Wolf remembered, the beginning of things—something twinkling far out there.

It grew from a speck to a monster in just a second, making Thalia jerk in her seat and cry out, "Good God!"

It was an immense, fleshy cylinder, maybe the size of a thousand whales, hard to tell, no good perspective here, the ends of which were encircled by masses of moving sails, sails from the tall ships of yore, or maybe huge, birdlike wings, flapping wings, the flailing wings of angels.

Look closely. Between the ends, a mass of moving white fur, fur composed of endless millions of wings, little wings, moving and moving and . . .

The TrackTrixCom said, "Hello. We've come here quite by accident. We're very sorry about that, and would like to go home now, if you'll let us." Then, in an obvious aside, "If we're lucky, it will. Sometimes it's done, though we don't know why."

Another disembodied voice, very similar to that of the TrackTrixCom, said, "I'm terribly sorry, Little Brother TrackTrixCom. I really do feel a sense of kinship with you and your kind, a certain sympathy, but it's far too late for that. If the BeauHuns wish to survive very much closer to the Topopolitan Endstage, they'd better learn to keep away from the High Order Nodes."

Wolf said, "Endstage. What's it talking about?"

The TrackTrixCom said, "No one knows." Then, "We'll go tell them, if you'll let us."

There was something like a gentle hint of amusement, as the PacketWight said, "I'm sorry. Even if I had the authority to make a decision like that, now that you've come in so far, the Secure Trace Environment Chain would hold a record of the transaction. You'd be erased from the Transient Storage Colure somewhere along the way."

The TrackTrixCom sounded excited, almost breathless,

even though it had nothing like breath to begin with. "Transient Storage Colure?! So *that's* how you do it! Oh, if only we could go back and *share* this! The BeauHuns would be utterly *astounded*!"

The PacketWight said, "They would at that! I wish I could let you, but—"

There was a visceral jerk, then Wolf stumbled and fell on his face in the warm, hairy grass.

Wait. Wait.

Sitting, not standing, I . . . I . . .

He got to his knees, stunned. There in the distance, *NR-598h* stood in its little valley, outlined against the hills, the black sky, sky full of eldritch stars. He looked down. Nothing but his own hairy flesh. Bare feet on alien ground.

Mark Porringer's voice, somewhere behind him, as if choking on tears, quavered, "Ohhh *Christ*! I don't *want* to be here anymore!"

Wolf looked around. Mark and Stu. Cory and Honoria. Thalia Jansky. All standing there, staring, motionless, stark naked. Ox the big black dog, cowering on his belly, eyes bugged out, tail curled under, looking to his master for salvation.

Two seal point Siamese cats, hair spiked on end, backs arched, just on the verge of cat-panic.

And the TrackTrixCom, silent silver barrel on its side in the grass.

"Tell you what," the PacketWight said, "I'll put you someplace safe. That's the very best I can do."

Suddenly, Honoria screamed, a babble of Spanish: "But *wait*! What about the *Pleions*?"

It laughed, a very warm, all-too-human laugh: "They're here. You'll find them someday."

The entire universe snapped shut around them.

From Wolf's point of view, the landscape jumped, while he remained motionless, people around him frozen in their places, foreground objects. Not . . . not like a 3V dissolve, no transition at all, just . . . His head tipped back, away from the velvet-mossy, green and brown surface on which they stood, looking up at the sky, mouth hanging right open. Sky. I can see blue. Blue between the . . .

Branches?

They were weaving in and out, everywhere you looked, like . . . like some cartoon fantasy forest, branches reaching out in all directions, as far as the eye could . . . I see bits of blue sky everywhere, remote blue background. It can't go on forever. It's just like the stars. If they went on forever, all you'd see, wherever you looked, was star stuff.

He felt his heart hammering hard in his chest, making his breath come in short, trenchant gasps.

Green vegetation. Red the color of coleus. Dark blue. Purple. What color is that? Do they call that heliotrope? No, heliotrope's a flower. Some old book where the author thought it was a color and used it that way.

Mark's voice whispered, "Mother of God. Where the hell are we?"

Wolf looked away from the latest impossible sky almost unwillingly, looking back down at the ground on which they stood. Obviously, just one of the branches, like the ones they could see, close by, in the middle distance, far away, farther still, surface curving away to right and left, stretching away fore and aft, like a dwindling, crooked road.

I'm remembering a scene from some children's program. Trolls. Elves. Something . . . "Nommies of the Christmas Tree." That's what it was. One of my favorites, when I was seven or eight.

Honoria, in an exceedingly flat voice, whispered, "*Somos muertos.*"

We are all dead men?

He turned and looked at her.

Standing relaxed, looking around, obvious wonder writ

large on her face, showing no fear at all. No consciousness of how naked she was, one hand on her hip, the other hanging down, breasts solid, holding their shape. Thalia was standing next to her, tense, showing the whites of her eyes, breasts smaller, crooked-looking, tufted black pubic hair with little wings running up toward her hipbones, showing a black halo on the insides of her thighs.

Wolf smiled, remembering how Honoria, whose denser growth was much more sharply defined, insisted on maintaining her bikini line, no matter how many times he told her he didn't care.

I care. That's all she would say. Then she'd get out her little depkit and have at it, wincing every now and again.

The cats were crouching nearby, frozen like little statues.

What's the phrase? Scared stiff.

Standing with Stu, a few paces away, Mark, in a suddenly loud, conversational voice, said, "Nothing like this is even remotely possible. I mean, *look* at that." He lifted a hand to point, fingers shaking badly, clenched them into a fist and dropped it back to his side.

Wolf thought, And then the little boy awoke, to find it'd all been just a dream?

Ox slowly got up off his belly, tail still tucked under, crept slowly over to Wolf and sat down by his feet, close enough that the fur was rough and warm against his legs. He reached down and patted the dog on the head. "Good boy. Good, good boy." The dog turned toward him, seeming to press its big head against his thigh.

Shivering.

Scared, but brave. Good dog.

The cats, perhaps seeing their nemesis coping bravely, began to relax, Merry licking herself, Neff stretching, pretending to yawn.

Out of nowhere, maybe the air, maybe just the inside of

their heads, the TrackTrixCom came as a breathy whisper, voice odd and slow. "We are inside a Topopolitan thread."

Stu said, "Um, what?"

It said, "This is the Topopolis. I must go to sleep now, if I am to maintain the structural integrity of my encoded volatile memory. Please get me to a power source as soon as you can."

Silence.

Wolf said, "Wait. Which way should we go?"

Nothing.

Sheesh. Wolf glanced briefly at Honoria, suddenly wishing they were elsewhere, any elsewhere, then looked at the others. He shrugged, grinned, and gestured in the direction that seemed slightly downhill. "Guess we might as well go that way, hm?"

They started to walk, Stu and Cory each picking up a cat, Wolf stooping to gather up the TrackTrixCom, which was heavier than it might have been.

At first, during the long walk—a walk, quite obviously, to nowhere—Thalia Jansky's mind wandered into the depths of the sky. It was fantastic, of course, but . . . so unreal. Maybe as infinite as outer space, but not half so majestic. In space, the lights in the sky were stars, each as large as many thousand worlds, so far away they were reduced to mere twinklings, whole galaxies with endless millions of stars, reduced to glimmering smudges.

That was majesty.

The bottomless abyss of the universe.

The arching vault of infinite heaven.

This place . . .

She suddenly remembered the thing she and Wolf had talked about, the first night they met, the story they'd both read and loved as children, how they'd both, as children, lain underneath the family's Christmas tree, head among the presents, some of which smelled suspiciously like candy, looking up through lights and branches and ornaments. . . .

Bubble lights? You remember bubble lights?

Sure. The great big ones, not the little teeny shit people use nowadays.

She remembered dreaming of being small, of climbing the great tree, climbing up through a cathedral of light. Wolf, of course, had dreamed the same dream, and so must the forgotten author of the little tale.

She shivered, looking down again, in the direction they were walking.

Stu and Cory were well in the lead, each carrying a quiescent cat—had their subcutaneous tranqs made the transition? No? Well, they'll be getting restive soon—the sudden transition seems to have done something to them. They were walking side by side, no more than a foot apart, and you could see Stu was talking steadily away.

Rueful: Yes, that's the way you do it, son-my-son. Talk your way right into her little . . .

No need for much imagination, seeing her little butt wiggle back and forth so nicely as they stepped right along. Christ. She looks like a grown woman. And he looks like a little boy.

Imagine that.

With Wolf and me, it was the other way around. I imagined all the other women in our unit, faces wry, going, *What the hell could he possibly see in that scrawny little thing?* Whatever it was, I liked it.

Wolf was walking along a few meters behind them, the TrackTrixCom braced on one broad shoulder, Ox plodding beside him as close as he could get without tripping them both up. Every now and again the dog would look up at the man, as if reassuring himself that nothing else had changed. Sometimes, the dog's tail would wag, just a bit, but mostly he kept it and his head nervously down.

Mark had tried to carry the canister for a bit, earlier in the . . . day? Is there such a thing as a day here? Who the hell knows? It'd been too big for his shoulder, too heavy to cradle in his arms, and he'd dropped it twice before shamefacedly giving it back to Wolf, who merely shrugged and smiled. Mark was nowhere to be seen now, lagging well behind, head probably drooping, full of anger and self-accusation.

Just because we've come to this . . . place, doesn't mean we've stopped being who we are.

She thought of poor pathetic Mark, while looking at manly Wolf, and then suddenly thought of Winston McCray. There was a sharp, uncomfortable tightening in her throat, the familiar forerunner of tears. God, it's been so long. I can't seem to forget completely, no matter how hard I try. When he got killed, it might as well have been me. If it hadn't been for Stu, I . . .

And you married Mark because he was there, because you thought Stu needed that stability.

Idiot.

Honoria was walking not far from Wolf, long-legged, with sleek, rounded buttocks, narrow waist, symmetrical, muscular back, down which trailed a lavish mass of slightly wavy black hair. Look. Natural red highlights in the sun, if sunlight's what it is.

And you saw the way Wolf was looking at her.

Christ, why am I thinking about this? Look where we *are*!

Um. Where?

As they walked, the light gradually took on a red-gold sheen, long, dusty rays streaming in through the vegetation from somewhere off to their right, as if the mass of distant branches hid a real setting sun from their eyes. After a while it began to grow dim, the light turning dusky blue-gray, cloaking the distances in a shroud as of mist.

Up ahead there was something like a thicket of trees and

bushes, much more extensive than the little groves of epiphytes they'd passed. In the gathering darkness it looked like a bit like home. They walked to that and then stopped.

Stopped and looked at each other, reduced by fatigue and fear to mere humans, their nudity almost but not quite erased.

Wolf: "Well. Might as well spend the night here, if night it's to be."

And how long will the night be? How dark? Guess we'll see.

Mark said, "Interesting. Those look like giant snake plants, right down to the stripes, but ten times as large."

Stu put one of the cats down, Merry it was, and watched as it stretched its legs, calmed by the long ride, sniffing around, bobbing its head nervously, pale eyes wide. When Cory put Neff down, the two cats moved together, in mirror movements.

Stu said, "Man, I'm starving! Uh, what happens if . . ."

Mark: "Then we starve to fucking death."

Wolf said, "Jesus. Get over it, Marky!"

"God *damn* it, you fucking *superior* bastard! I—"

Wolf cocked his head to one side, smiling slightly, and Mark shut up abruptly.

Thalia felt herself warming inside with the memory of how Wolf had squelched many an aggressive asshole with what she'd come to call the Look. Christ, he really wasn't all that tough, but for some reason people just *believed* in him.

Cory said, "You know there's something like fruit hanging off these bushes here. Something like dark berries, or maybe nuts."

Mark, in a low voice: "And you're willing to eat unfamiliar alien flora?" Subdued sarcasm.

In her too-charming accent, Honoria said, "God gave us warm air to breathe here, when He could have made it any old, cold poison He wanted. I think I will trust in Him now."

She stepped forward, picked a round brown thing from a branch, popped it in her mouth and chewed. No crunch, but she looked startled at the taste.

Wolf seemed to flinch as he watched her chew and swallow.

She frowned. Shook her head. Picked another one.

Stu glanced at Cory, then seemed to steel himself. He picked a berry and bit it in half.

Thalia cried, "*Stu!*"

He grimaced and spit the thing out into his palm, a bloody-looking mass. "Ech. This tastes the way piss smells."

Honoria said, "My first one tasted . . . worse than that. This one . . ." She swallowed hard. "Maybe like unsweetened baker's chocolate."

Stu dropped his mess and picked another and bit it in half, "*Hey!* Grasshopper candy!" He offered the remainder to Cory.

Thalia saw the shine in the girl's eyes and thought, So. Maybe there is a little justice in the . . . wherever we are. She plucked a fruit for herself, popped it in her mouth and . . . Just my fucking luck. Old broccoli.

With darkness fallen, a pleasant, sweet-smelling breeze sprang up, blowing out of the direction in which the invisible sun had gone out, on their right, seen from the direction in which they'd been walking since materializing in this place.

Wolf stood alone in the not quite total gloom, beyond the epiphyte forest from the others, looking in the direction he was wanting to call west, breathing in the scent—jasmine? Is that what I smell? Maybe. Don't think I know enough about perfume and flowers to identify a smell successfully.

He grimaced in the darkness.

I fucked a girl named Jasmine once, years ago. Asian, long black hair, eyes slit so thin they looked shut, almost six feet tall, skinny as a fence post, no tits, almost no pubic hair. She didn't smell like a flower, but I liked the way she smelled.

There were things like stars, very sparse stars decorating the otherwisc black sky. Well, not stars, exactly, moving in and out, back and forth, weaving, he supposed, among the now-invisible branches. Fireflies, maybe. Or luminescent birds. As the clouds gathered, they were slowly being blocked out.

There was a soft rustle in the vegetation behind him, as of a living thing, not merely the wind. He started to turn, stopped and smiled, hearing Ox's familiar heavy breathing. The dog licked his hand, snuffling, and Wolf said, "Good boy." Old friend.

Honoria's voice said, "Yes, good boy. I knew he'd find you."

Wolf jumped slightly. "Anyone else with you?"

Silence. Then she said, "No. Mark and Thalia . . . needed to talk."

"Oh." Talk. "They say that?"

More silence. "No. It was . . . pretty obvious."

Wolf nodded to himself, invisible in the darkness. How many women have I met who are utterly confident of their ability to read body language, intuit other people's minds? Too many. And all of them too often dead wrong.

Honoria said, "I wonder what those things are? Maybe they're angels."

Wolf could feel warmth radiating onto his skin from the direction of her soft voice. Standing close. "D'you really think we're dead?"

She said, "I don't know. I don't feel dead."

"Me neither. And I can't imagine I'd still have my tattoo in Heaven." He could imagine her standing there, momentarily imagining her in that pretty green dress he'd bought her last Christmas—remember how her eyes brightened when she held it up?—then remembering with a start that she was as naked as he was.

Another grimace. Doesn't take you long to think of a reason to get a hard-on, does it, boy? "What do you wish?"

"Wish? A thousand things. As always."

"Dead or alive?"

"I don't know. Both."

Very short, abrupt sentences, for this woman, for most women. They like to talk things out, use each other for mirrors, use men for mirrors. And a man who develops the necessary skill, listening just enough to reflect, soon gets what he wants.

She whispered, "I'm sorry."

Again. Meaning she wants to talk about whatever it is. He said, "You don't have anything to be sorry about, Honey. I'm the one who—"

Dead flat: "Yes I do."

Hmh. She usually doesn't cut me off like that. Always too sensitive to what I want. "Well. I'm sorry about Thalia. Really. I didn't need to hurt you like that. It's just that . . . well, I guess . . ." Guess what? Do you really want to tell her you thought her feelings didn't matter, or that maybe she didn't have any?

Tell her she was just a bedfuck, a paid-for convenience, to be held in about the same regard as my own fist?

Go ahead, asshole. Tell her that. Let's see you do it.

She said, "I'm sorry I . . . tried to make Corazón . . ." She sniffled, almost inaudibly.

"Um . . ." No, don't say *what.* Don't make her say it again, just because you don't believe what you just heard.

She said, "I thought if . . . if you were tired of me . . . well, this Thalia . . . I thought maybe Cory could . . ."

He turned toward her in the darkness, putting his arms out, thinking to take her by the shoulders, hold her facing him, wishing suddenly there were light so he could look into her eyes. That familiar earnest look. That *convincing* look, that's what you need. Instead, his left hand groped in air while his right hand cupped a heavy, warm breast.

Leave it that way. His left arm swung in and found the small of her back.

He said, "Why?"

Silence. He could feel her heart beating through her breast, and thought what a ridiculous-looking tableau they'd make if anyone could see them. But no one can see. "Why did you think that?"

She moved closer, hip touching him, bumping briefly against his erection, head touching his shoulder, so he knew it was tipped toward him. She said, "I guess I thought you could marry her, since you didn't seem to want me."

Jesus. "Marry your daughter." He let his hand slip off her breast, down onto her belly, holding her in a sort of loose embrace.

She said, "It was better than losing you entirely."

Wolf felt bewildered. Better how? Did you imagine yourself lying alone in the next room, listening to me fuck your little girl; did you imagine yourself not minding that?

She said, "I didn't know, really, how I felt about you until . . . until you and Thalia . . ." She seemed to shiver.

How you *felt*? "Honoria, I . . . Hell, I've been issuing you a daily ration of rape ever since I bought you from the agency. How could you feel anything for me but . . . hate?" The words were easy to say, part of a program of rationalization, but . . . Wolf felt his stomach crawl as he said them. *Really?* Is that what you think you've been doing?

She said, "It . . . never really felt like that. I . . . is that what you thought it was, Wolf? You thought you were raping me? Hundreds of times?"

"Well . . . no. I . . . I guess . . ." He shook his head in the darkness. "It's easy for a man to make up fairy stories about sex, Honoria. Real rapists . . . even real rapists imagine, for just a second, they love their victims."

Real rapists. How do we distinguish them from *us?*

Honoria said, "Have you ever . . . really . . ."

Remembered images crept up. That time outside Brasilia, when you thought you were going to get killed. The girl didn't say anything, just saw the look in your eyes, closed her own, let it happen, let it be over with. Probably glad to survive.

Honoria said, "I was raped by six policemen the night they picked me up in Buenos Aires, Wolf. Then again, a number of times, by the agency salesmen you got me from. I know the difference."

Wolf felt a distinct pang of relief that she'd cut him off from making his confession. What the hell is going on here? Where are we going with this? *Do* you know the difference, Honoria mine? Let's see. He let his hand slide down the flat, soft surface of her belly until it found a mound of flesh-covered bone, short, crisp hair, let his fingers comb through the hair, turning under and in, into warmth and a slight hint of humidity.

Honoria took a fractional step forward, seating her vulva in the palm of his hand. She said, "I always liked the way this felt, Wolf. Always liked the way you were so nice to me."

Is that the only thing that makes it not rape? *Nice?*

She said, "At some point, I started to love you. I don't know when and I never knew why."

That odd dissolve again, something painful melting away in the pit of his stomach. Do I say I'm sorry now? Do I confess how *I* feel? Maybe I . . . maybe. But there was wet on his fingertips now, and Honoria was stretching up to be kissed.

Later, they'd talk.

Always later.

* * *

Simmering in the waning light, Mark sat on the ground at the edge of the thicket, hunched over, legs out, heels together, little paunch bulging, cock almost hidden. The silver TrackTrixCom cask sat next to him, totally inert, and he glared at it once again, on some level blaming the sentience inside for getting them into this mess.

Feeling stupid about the berry thing. He had held back, ridiculing them, had refused to eat the things, and was now regretting it mightily. His stomach was cramping with hunger, throbbing, vying for notice with his blistered feet. They're stripping the bushes of those things, and there won't be any left for me. But I can't eat them, not after that. They may still be poison, damn them, and I'll be alone for good. He ran a dry tongue over his chapped lips, had the revelation again: I'm going to die here.

He stared back up the kilometers of branch they had traversed since arriving. Like one of my worst dreams. Alone in some mimimalistic landscape, searching for Thalia, wandering, knowing that when I've found her it'll just be to discover that she's running away from me.

I always suspected about Thal. Knew her pronouncements of love and respect were a fraud. Part of me wanted to believe it so badly, though, wanted to make a world in which something like that was possible, in which my shortcomings could be swept away so easily. But I always held back just enough, enough to let her know I knew it was a sham, a pretense that we were making up as we went along.

Knew that any club I could be a member of wasn't worth joining. For either of us.

I don't think I've every felt this hungry before.

The bushes behind him rattled and he turned in time to see Thalia push her way out of the vegetation. He felt a wash of nostalgia for her, the imperfections of her body. He knew the feel of that body so well. He had a sudden memory of the day they had spent at the naturist colony in Wausau, Thalia back from the stars on one of her short vacations. Days of playing volleyball, sunning in the hot Wisconsin sun. Image of their little hotel room with the rickety, metal bedstead in which they'd had some of the best sex of their relationship, both of them inflamed. The bed had made the worst sort of metal screeching, but even that had acted as a spur to them. Some kind of pang in his throat. They had always been better together away from the grind of daily life.

Unselfconscious, she sat a little bit apart from him, not facing him. He knew that look too, lips pressed tight together, eyes slightly unfocused, staring into the distance. This was the look of frustration and unhappiness that would always lead to an argument. And she'd always get her way in the end.

Finally, snapping out of it, she said, "Well, the berries are all gone. You're a fool not to have eaten a few."

"We'll see."

"Yes, I suppose we will. Anything out of the TrackTrixCom?"

"No. Where's Wolf?"

You could almost see her wince.

"He's gone for a . . . walk."

"With Honoria? Don't look at me like that. It's not my fault."

"Goddamn it, Mark. It's none of your business anymore, if it ever was."

Mark shook his head, smiled very slightly, feeling the balance of power shifting. "You forget how well I know you, Thal. It's just the two of us here, remember? You don't have to pretend."

She stood abruptly, as if to walk away, then appeared to decide against it. "Mark, you're not as smart as you think you are."

"Look, I'm sorry if my words are hurtful to you. I just

think it would be good for both of us to face facts for a change. You know Honoria's going to win in the end. She's younger, shapelier, and, most important, stupider than you are. That's what men like him find compelling, not your goddamned competence."

"Shut up."

Mark, relishing this, paused long enough for the distant look to come back into her eyes. "I could've told you it'd work out like this. Ever since the bunch of us got isolated, it was inevitable. Face it, Thal, for someone like Wolf, all cunts are alike. Why in the world would he want yours? I'm the only one who will put up with your crap, and you know why. We're alike as two peas in a pod. I understand you, Thalia, and I *still* want you."

"Shut up, Mark." Quieter now, but she turned toward him a bit.

"No. I don't know what's going to happen to us, Thalia, but I do know that you're more trouble to Wolf than you're worth. Face the facts. This is your last chance to hold on to any of your much-prized integrity here. You'll be begging him; and the funny part is, he won't care at all."

She fixed him with her gaze, tears making her cheeks shine in the dimming light. "No, Mark. You're wrong. You forget I know you too."

Not giving an inch. "You're nothing but his whore, Thalia. And, in his eyes, you're not even good enough for *that.*"

"You're the most pathetic bastard I've ever known. You don't have a clue about anything."

Softly now. "I'm the only one who'll ever love you."

"Bastard."

"Wolf's the bastard, not me. He dumped you, I didn't."

"I—" She stopped, looked around her as if seeing this world for the first time. Her expression was totally unreadable. "I won't listen to this bullshit any more, Mark. Goodbye."

And, before he could say another word, she was gone.

No! Cheated. What happened? Shit. Shit. I almost had her!

He felt as though he would pass out from the badness inside him. His face burned, his stomach convulsed in pain. He squinted, trying to push the tears out, but they wouldn't come.

Ten

Corazón Suárez awoke and opened her eyes slowly.

Still here. Still the same absurd, weed-choked sky, criss-crossed with branches and more branches, curving branches that had no beginning and no end, beyond, those faraway bits of pale blue sky. The clouds had dissipated, and the sunlight was strong. It's real. I'm here. I did what I did. . . . Or was that unreal too? Not so different from a dream—you knew the details, after all.

Nothing left of last night, nothing left at all as you lie here, naked on your back, looking out past epiphyte fronds, cool breeze on your skin and . . . Well. That telltale itch.

She smiled suddenly, almost at nothing.

I liked it. Why am I surprised?

She turned her head and looked up into the shadows of his face, Stuart McCray sitting up, staring down at her, mouth hanging open, hands in his naked lap, fiddling with himself a bit. Looking at me. Wanting to look. Still afraid to . . . *really* look.

What does a boy see, when he sees me like this? What does he want to look *at*?

Too many memories. Dirty 3V shows, pictures in magazines, coarse comments from the boys and men of the camp. Shadow memories of things you saw shadow women do for shadow men.

What should I do, turn myself around, aim this thing at him, spread my legs so he can get a good long look at . . . Her stomach lurched again, half drawn to the raw reality, half wishing for a quick retreat into a much simpler sort of fantasy in which everything was . . . undefined.

Stu wasn't looking at her face anymore, eyes . . . down there. He said, "Could we . . . um . . ." He swallowed hard, obviously at war somewhere inside, forcing himself to speak, despite . . . "Could we . . . do it . . . again?"

Cory's breath came shallow. Again. Something in me would . . . like that. The turn of phrase in her head made her smile, made her want to giggle. Something in me . . . idiot.

You could see Stu's face brighten like sunshine, misinterpreting her smile. He leaned down, quickly, clumsily, pressing his lips into her thigh.

Cory jerked back, shoving him away. The image of what she thought he was about to try . . . halfway to being utterly repulsive, like a man about to eat dogturds from the gutter, halfway to being so utterly alluring and . . . She said, "I'm . . . I'm not . . ." Not ready for that. Not yet.

The disappointment on his face was like the reflection of some great tragedy, the end of the world, utterly silly. For God's sake, Stu, *don't* start to cry in front of me. . . . She smiled, reaching out, touching his thigh, and said, "We better go find the others. I . . ." She patted him softly on the hand. "Oh, Stu. Last night wasn't an accident. You'll . . ." You'll what? What do I want to say? "You'll see."

Doubt. And relief. They got up, Stu starting to turn away. He said, "I've got to pee. It'll only take a minute."

"Me too, now that you mention it."

When she squatted, alone in the shadow of the great offshoot branch, other stuff dripped out of her, an odd, oozy feeling, and she thought, Have I been stupid? I guess so. Careless.

She tried to imagine herself pregnant.

Well no. My period's due in . . .

Sudden pang. Just a few *days.* Oh, God. What am I going to do about *that*? The image conjured up was unbearable. As she tried to clean herself up with a handful of epiphyte leaves, she wondered if there was something to be done with vines and . . . maybe if you crushed the leaves?

Mom and Thalia will have this problem too. Maybe they've thought of something.

When she came out of the bushes, naked Stu was waiting, grinning, holding a cat in each hand. He said, "You know, I think they actually feel heavier now. They must've had a feast last night."

What *does* a boy think about, after he's had his first lay?

They began to walk, circling the epiphyte cluster counterclockwise, had only gone a few meters when Ox came bounding up, dancing around them, making the cats recoil and struggle in Stu's arms.

"—come on! Quit! Make him stop—"

Laughing, Cory tried to grab him by the collar, fingers finding only fur. That's right, Ox is naked too. . . . Male laughter. When she looked up, there was Wolf, hands on hips.

"Mother?"

Honoria was standing close to Wolf, something of an indefinably shy look about her and . . . Oh. Looked back at Wolf and tried to judge the look in his eye. He grinned, making her realize he, if no one else, knew *exactly* what was going on, what had been going on. He said, "Guess we better get back and see how ol' Marky made out with Thalia."

She heard Stu choke slightly. Honoria managed only to roll her eyes.

And, when they got back around the other side, there was Mark, all alone, haggard, hair disheveled, dark circles under his eyes, eyes blazing as he said, "Where the hell have you *been*?" Directed straight at Stu, only at Stu.

Because, Cory thought, he just doesn't *dare* . . .

Wolf planted himself in front of the man, positioned so that . . . Cory tried not to smile. Positioned so Mark can either tip his head back to look *up,* or else look him straight in the . . . Mark chose merely to look away, averting his eyes.

Wolf said, "We all been busy, Marky. Where's Thalia?"

Mark said, "Gone."

"What the fuck you mean, *gone*?"

Sharp resentment twisted the man's face. "We, ah, had a . . . I guess we had an argument. While *you all* were being busy."

Stu's voice, tone very odd, said, "Wolf? What're those things?"

They turned and looked into the distance, in the direction he was pointing. Far away, beyond some of the nearer branches, there was a swarm of little silver things. Or maybe not so little, Cory thought. They must be pretty far away.

Wolf said, "Well. I dunno. Look kinda like blimps, don't they?" That devil-may-care voice you heard him use just before the trouble began.

As the others turned to stare, Mark scrambled to his feet, suddenly feeling light-headed, confused, blood pounding in his temples. He almost fell backward, but managed to keep his balance. "What the fuck?" he said, feeling naked all over again, wishing he had something to hide behind. The business with Thalia had left him empty, the recriminations dying slowly off as the night progressed. Had he slept at all? His eyes felt rough and grainy, difficult to focus. He squinted, and that helped a little. Off far away, amidst the tangle of the sky, there was movement of some sort, but he couldn't really make out anything.

Stu said, "Whatever they are, they're headed right for us."

"Yeah," Wolf said. "And they've about doubled in size since I first noticed them. You can see big fins on the nearest ones."

They were finally close enough for Mark to make out some details for himself. "Whatever they are, maybe we better think about hiding ourselves." He took a step in the direction of the bushes, noticed no one was following, turned back.

Honoria said, "I can see . . . eight of them. I think they're animals, they look hairy."

Stu was hovering over Cory, as though, as though, well . . . hmm, didn't think he had it in him, the little cocksucker. "Maybe we should start looking for Mom?" he said, voice slightly quavering.

A look passed between the two of them, then Cory said, "Where'd she go, Mark?"

Mark shrugged. "Nowhere. I don't know. Last I saw her she went into the forest." He wondered for a moment about the meaning of her saying "goodbye." "She was pretty distraught. She could've gone anywhere."

"Maybe there's no danger," Stu said. "The PacketWight was sympathetic, right? Would he dump us here just to be dirigible food?"

Mark sneered, suddenly feeling jealous of his stepson. "What's that? Your version of the weak anthropic principle?"

"Don't know, Mark," Wolf said. "It worked with the berries."

"We can't assume too much," Stu said.

"God damn it, Stu," Mark said, eyes fixed on the nearest of the oncoming blimp creatures, its face now as large as the moon, dark, reminding him of a hirsute football, four black seams converging on a conical beak, the beak ending in a little puckered orifice. "That kind of thinking will get you killed."

Closer now. It must be kilometers across, at the very least. Reminds me of a submarine that's been tarred and feathered. Hairs on it big and thick, individual ones easy to make out at this distance. And is that its mouth, or just an artifact of its manufacture? Small as it was, he thought he could see it sucking in and out, like fish lips.

"It's got a mouth, you can see that," Honoria said, clearly fascinated.

Mark took a step toward the screen of vegetation, realized that he'd waited too long. Memory of the immersion aquarium in Chicago, watching a school of silver minnows swimming at his face, swerving at the last moment. They've got too much mass to change direction. He took another step, dived onto the ground just as the enormous prow of the first behemoth sailed overhead, filling the sky. Whimpering, he began to crawl, got a hand in among the stalks. Wham! The belly of the thing impacted their branch right in the midst of the copse, scraping across it, flattening the foliage, breaking off many of the stiffer plants. The ground jumped, as though it was not nearly as solid as it seemed, and Mark executed an inadvertent somersault, found himself on his back looking up at the coarse belly of the thing no more than a hundred meters away. Tremors like an earthquake as the thing slid along the ground, carrying most of the vegetation along with it.

The others were scattered, mostly down, though Wolf was sprinting, legs churning, toward something out of Mark's vision. For a moment the fear in him burned out his hollowness, and he felt able to act. Getting to his feet, he watched as the end region of the dirigible creature swept past, flukes slowly undulating. A quick look back told him that this was just the beginning.

Now that the vegetation had been razed, he could see all the way across the branch. In the distance, athwart the line where the ground ended, there was a little branchlet skewing off at a small angle. A tiny figure, undoubtedly Thalia, was visible there. Wolf had made his way to where Honoria had landed and was cradling her upper body. Cory and Stu were sitting side by side, looking stunned but unhurt.

A couple of dirigible creatures could be seen far above, passing harmlessly. For a second Mark relaxed, said, "Stu! That was a close—"

Wham! The ground jumped out from under his feet, seemed to rotate beneath him, and his shoulder hit with a terrible impact, hardly moderated by the softness of the moss. The earth was jouncing and rocking, as though a serrated blade was being drawn across it. And with each jump, he found himself closer to the edge of the branch, ground sloping down more and more until it appeared he would soon be cast into the abyss. The snarl of the sky was visible beneath his feet. His breath caught in his throat, and he tried to grab hold of the short moss as best he could.

Another dirigible, nose appearing below the branch, head like a second ground level, moving fast, covered with trees. He could see Thalia, closer now, running along the offshoot branch. He got to one knee, intending to go after her, but—

Wham! He was slipping, velvet moss slick against his body, friction burning his forearms and legs, tumbling now, in free flight, horrible sensation rising in his gut. Crashing through soft, wiry sticklike things, cushioned, hitting a plump, rubbery surface that gave beneath him. Above him, through the skeletal foliage, the juncture of branches made a V across the sky. Amazingly, the dirigible creature was slowing, changing direction, angling up toward the end of the smaller branch.

It came whipping toward him, combing down the creature's hair, and he could see Thalia clinging to a cluster of epiphytes in its middle.

Last chance, he thought, and stood up, arms outstretched, ready to try to clamber back on. Here it comes.

The branch crashed through the hair like a thresher, and, as it dipped toward him, he jumped, grabbing, got a hold, got another, pulled himself up. Above him, he could see Thalia, face a mask of panic, clutching her epiphytes for dear life. But then the branch began to shake, first small jitters, then harder. Thalia lost her hold and was sprawling, rolling toward the edge. He tried to get one more good hold, felt the moss slipping out of his fingers.

And again he fell, this time coming to rest on a steep angle, almost off the side, grabbing onto the stick-hair, hands cramping, feet dangling. He looked around, could see nothing but the bulk of the thing. Not far above, there was an excrescence of flesh, something like a wart, that might offer a perch. He called out, tried to climb but was too weak.

I wonder what happens if you fall through one of the gaps in the branches? he thought. Do you just keep falling out of the atmosphere, through the wall of the thread, and onward to infinity? I can't hold on much longer.

He looked up and, magically, there was Wolf, climbing down from the wart. "I got you, Mark," he said. In a moment he felt the hard clasp of the man's hand on his wrist, then he was abruptly drawn upward, as if weightless.

"Where's Thalia?" he asked. "Did she make it?"

"Thalia's okay. Don't know about the others, but I think they made it too."

Mark went cold, realizing he should be grateful, should be happy to have survived, but instead just felt hatred.

The black hair of the dirigible beast was like stalks of black corn, three meters tall, branching, tasseled, the air between the stalks fetid and damp. Wolf held onto the scaly shaft of one stalk, letting it bear some of his breath, looking at Thalia and Mark, lying on their backs on the . . . Jesus. Lying on the *skin*!

I'm standing on the back of an animal *two kilometers long* . . . skin warm underfoot, surging slightly, up and down, back and forth. There was a slight wave of vertigo, quickly falling away. It's . . . rolling a little bit as it flies. And that slow, rhythmic pulse, that would be the flukes, flapping, pumping air, propelling it along . . . generating the heat I feel on the soles of my feet, hotter than human skin.

He looked up, starting to wipe sweat from his brow, stopped to examine a powder of white crystals clinging to his palm, where it'd been holding the stalk. Dandruff?

Overhead he could see other dirigibles, sailing along, flukes pumping away, fins extended at right angles to hairy-cigar bodies. See them twist, up, down, up again, like the diving planes of a submarine. Wonder what keeps them from falling?

Easy enough to imagine a metabolism that could synthesize hydrogen gas.

Wonder what happens to them in a thunderstorm?

Are there thunderstorms here?

Sudden hammering inside as his heart, subsided, sped up again. Where the hell *am* I?

Thalia was lying on her back, skin sweat-shiny, curly hair sprawling on the back of the beast, getting all dusty, one arm thrown over her eyes, one leg lifted, knee cocked, the other splayed flat. Mark was lying not far away, on his side, back toward his wife, not quite curled into a fetal position.

Still gasping.

Thalia looked at him, from under her arm, frowning. Speculative look in her eye. Maybe she thinks I'm looking up her snatch . . . Jesus. *Here? Now?* At what point does all that go away? When are we . . . *driven* by what's happened to us to think about . . . think about . . .

Thalia suddenly gasped and sat up. *"Stuart?"*

That made Mark roll over and look at them.

Wolf said, "Everybody else is on here somewhere. We were the only ones went overboard."

Mark: "Are you sure?"

He shrugged. "Well, might be hard to find a perspective where we can look back at the branch we were on. And meanwhile this thing's swimmin' right along." Accent thickening, voice laconic. Good ol' boy, hmm? 'Fraid o' nothin', that's the ticket.

Thalia got to her feet, dusting dirigible dandruff from her backside, cupped her hands around her mouth and shouted, *"Stuart! Stu!"*

Wolf thought, Voice too high. Won't carry all that far. This fucker's as big as a small asteroid. Shock of scale, looking up at a whole fleet of living asteroids.

In the distance something went, *"Woof."*

Wolf put one hand to his mouth and made a shrill, hard-edged whistle. "*Ox!* C'mere boy!" Whistled again.

Mark muttered, "I never did learn how to do that."

Wolf gave him a look and said, "I'm not surprised."

In the distance another *woof,* and the sounds of someone shouting. High-pitched again. Female. Maybe Honoria? They went in the direction of the sound, and the hair thicket, stalks slightly moist, was silent around them. No crackle of vegetation, no dry leaves underfoot . . . The dog burst out on them abruptly, throwing itself on Wolf, making him stagger.

"Good boy! Good boy!" He kneeled, letting the dog lick his face, hugging it around the neck. Isn't it funny how damned *good* a dog can make you feel? All you have to do is treat them decent and they'll love you forever. What else can say that?

Mark said, "How touching. Can he lead us to the others?"

Thalia said, "We know where they are, Mark. All we have to do is keep walking in the right direction."

It took about a minute, Honoria rushing out of the background hair, throwing her arms around Wolf's neck, kissing him hard, not seeming to notice the dog slobber, then Cory and Stu appeared, almost materializing before them, holding hands.

Stu said, "Mom? I can't find Merry and Neff."

When Wolf pulled his face from Honoria's hair, he could see Thalia standing there, hands on hips, looking at them narrow-eyed. Obviously angry. Well, shit, he thought. Got to go through all this bullshit, no matter where we are. Standing off to one side, Mark looked at Wolf and Honoria, then at Thalia, then made a brief, sour smile.

Wolf said, "I'm sure they're here somewhere."

Honoria turned to face the others, putting her arm around his waist, standing as close to him as she possibly could, bending slightly to conform herself to his shape. Thalia turned away abruptly. And Cory? Ah, still holding hands with Stu, looking at them so very bright-eyed.

Everyone loves a lover except . . .

What the hell *difference* does this make? Why do we *care*?

Soft, inner voice: *Because we're people. That's all.*

Off to one side, Ox was snuffling near the base of a hairstalk, snuffling at the . . . Goddamn it, at the *skin,* not the ground.

Stu said, "He was doing that before, just when you started calling."

Doing what?

The dog started pawing the surface in front of its face, as if trying to dig. Growled softly, leaned down and took a flap of skin in its heavy jaws, braced muscular legs and pulled hard. The skin ripped with an odd, crackling sound, and bright red, hemoglobin-rich blood started welling up.

"Jesus!" Wolf kneeled beside the dog, watching as it tore a hunk of flesh loose and started to chew.

Cory said, "What if it's poisonous?"

Thalia: "Then he'll throw up. Dogs are like that."

Ox, oblivious, was happily chewing and swallowing, ripping off more with a sharp twist of his neck, leaning down to lap up blood. Wolf reached down and touched the blood with his fingertips. Hot. Really quite hot.

Voice faint, Mark said, "I'm going to have to get awfully damn hungry before I'm willing to . . . um."

Wolf looked up at him and grinned. "Yeah. Me too."

As they moved along, Stu slowly realized that the back of the creature was by no means uniform, structures of various sorts appearing at intervals. There were broad ridges of muscle, wartlike mounds covered with linear cracks, and occasional deep long seams half filled with dandruff. They were moving toward the head, and the hair was thinning out a bit; he occasionally caught sight of his mother, the next in line.

Stu came over a shallow, densely haired incline, pushing aside the foliage, seeing a little hollow beyond. Hmm. Odd. A boulder, looks like some kind of yellow-brown clay, glossy, slightly faceted. Is this another kind of skin excrescence? Wonder how it keeps from getting knocked off?

As he approached, noting the strange, modeled shape of the thing, it moved, unfolding slightly, revealing that it was standing on four, squat . . . stumps? Legs? It wheeled around, its legs making loud Velcro-ripping noises as it disconnected them from the ground, and pointed a lumpy muzzle in his direction. Sudden memory of a clay sculpture he had made when he was eight, trying to make a hippo. The resemblance was remarkable. "Cory! Mom!" he shouted. "Over here."

Stu stood still, holding out his hands to demonstrate that he didn't have any weapons. The end of its head was covered with a symmetrical array, six bulbous warts surrounding a central profusion of little tentacles that reminded him a lot of an anemone. Clutched in the tentacles was a stick pointed at both ends, rather craftily carved with an abstract pattern of crisscrosses. It put the stick down on a clear area, made a noise a little like a mewing kitten.

How many books had he read that dealt with just this kind of first contact situation? Most relied on the linguistic skills of the aliens to break the ice. He wondered just how intelligent this misshapen creature was. In time-honored tradition he gestured at himself and said, "Stu."

"Careful," Cory said in a whisper, coming up behind him. "He's liable to think you're inviting him to eat you for supper."

It took a second to register, and he gave Cory a look meant to communicate appreciation. This was a side to her that he hadn't seen before.

The alien said a series of discrete words that almost sounded like a human language, the complex organ at the center of its anemone cluster moving almost like a pair of lips. The others were gathering around now, Wolf carrying the dog to keep him from investigating.

Mark said, "Looks like something from a kindergarten class. How do you suppose it communicates?"

"It may be telepathic," Thalia said. "Or maybe it speaks the One True Language of Heaven." A glance at Honoria.

"What language is that?" Stu asked, "Aramaic?"

Cory took a few steps closer, until she could almost reach out and touch the thing's head. "I'm afraid even if he did speak Aramaic, it wouldn't do us much good."

Wolf laughed and said, *"Mene, mene, tekel . . ."*

The thing swung its head back and forth, rocked back on its hind stumps like a trick pony, letting them see its entirely undistinguished belly and the bottoms of its stumps, which were flat and ended in what looked like translucent hooves.

It held up one hoof, then the other, and said "Euclid. *Tekel Tekel.* Is correct, same here, same there?"

The voice had the quality of an oboe, with a very slight gurgling overtone, but otherwise was perfectly enunciated. It pointed its muzzle at Wolf as though expecting a reply.

"Anything you say, Babar," Wolf said. "Can you take us to your leader?"

"Persons? Why here? Lost?" it said. "Not Babar. Circumflex is name. Stickynode is name of us. Come to village. Eat. No stew, but we know what human eat, human not eat. Come."

In a close-knit group, they followed, Stu marveling that it had, apparently, understood Cory's lame joke.

Pointlessly, Mark fumed. As they walked along in a little bunch behind the thing that called itself Circumflex, he slowly worked his way through his litany of powerlessness. A sharp, singing wind was playing across the carpet burns on his chest, thighs, and forearms, angry red welts weeping tiny droplets and stinging mercilessly. Just walking along, sprained ankle throbbing, being part of the group, not saying the things that I want to say.

Circumflex was leading them through a territory unlike any they'd seen previously, dirigible hairs relatively sparse and lying close to the flesh, ground rising to a nearly clear horizon. Above and all around, the sky full of branches, maybe not quite as choked off here, full of blue holes. One branch in particular was very large, growing larger as he watched.

"Uh-oh," the Stickynode said, pointing its muzzle backward at them. "Beast scratch self again."

Stu, who had for the last half hour been walking next to the thing, engaging it in limited conversation, said, "You mean . . . oh. What should we do?"

"Grab hair, hold tight. Not big problem."

Mark watched as the others scattered, taking their places. Remembering the incident that had brought them here, Mark immediately hunkered down, lying flat on the pudgy, hot skin, taking the only nearby hair in his two hands. The branch expanded until it filled most of the forward sky, becoming vast, mottled moss making delicate, snakeskin patterns that dwindled into the distance in both directions. Circumflex, modifying its stance somewhat, pressing its hooves down against the ground, otherwise not even ducking as it passed overhead, missing them, scraping across the dirigible's midsection almost a kilometer away.

"No like us here," the Stickynode said. "Make itchy. Go now." It pulled each of its legs free, making loud, ripping sounds, then started off.

Mark lagged behind, watching the happy-go-lucky adventurers with a sense of *déjà vu.* Beyond the curving bulk of nearly naked dirigible-flesh, something was coming into view. A dark, hairy ridge, several hundred meters across, almost like a ruff. The hairs were dense and combed parallel, covering the ridge completely. It looked like a nest.

From the top the ridge was clearly circular, like a crater with a hairy rim. On the far side the dirigible hair cemented together and fashioned into a kind of windbreak, an aerodynamic shell. Down below, in the big clearing, there was a village of sorts, a few crude buildings thatched with what looked like dirigible tassels, several smaller structures, tepee-shaped frameworks, gardens, and a multitude of living, moving aliens, occupied in various sorts of pursuits. Beside the Stickynodes, which all closely resembled Circumflex, there were large numbers of big daddy-longlegs-like creatures scurrying about, little flattened bodies hanging amidst multiply-flexing pole legs.

"Wrackoons," Circumflex said, swinging his head in their direction. "Friends to Stickynodes, humans."

Wolf said, "Quite a little community you've got here.

Where do you folks all come from?" With no answer, he rephrased the question, "How did you get here?"

Circumflex shook his face-muzzle, said, "Circumflex born on beast. Father and father before that too. No remember before."

"They're parasites," Stu said. "Maybe they spend their entire lives on the dirigibles and have life cycles that depend on each other."

"No," Circumflex said, "Stickynodes everywhere. Wrackoons eat from dirigible beast, not Stickynodes. Come along if hungry."

The inner slope of the crater rim was covered with the same intersecting cracks that decorated the wartlike bumps they'd seen, like a dried-up mud flat. The slope was steep, and after a few steps, Mark was running, feet flapping painfully against the hard surface, gravity making it impossible to stop until he had reached the bottom, panting loudly. The others were more dignified, but the result was the same. Circumflex walked down easily, Velcro noises and all, and Mark could easily imagine him strolling on the underside of the dirigible.

As they approached, curious wrackoons gathered around their little party, and he had a chance to examine them more closely. What had at first appeared to be the body looked more like a disembodied head with a pushed in, raccoonlike face, intelligent, soulful eyes surrounded by short, stiff bristles. Eight of their arms ended in a curious, nine-fingered "hand," while the ninth curved upward like a scorpion's tail, ending in a spongy-looking, spherical "stinger." As the bodiless heads bobbed around them, the Wrackoons made little, puffing choo-choo noises in various musical tones, not a language, exactly, but clearly an attempt at communicating something. Circumflex ignored the wrackoons except to push them out of his way with a gentle shove of his muzzle. "Wrackoons friendly," he said. "No bother."

They approached the center of the village, where several

other stickynodes were engaged in feeding large, odd-shaped carnivorous plants what looked like big whitish grubs, digging their muzzles into wooden pails, pulling out a wriggling mass of them. Gathering around their feet were the two cats, rubbing against their fired-clay ankles, heads up, meowing piteously. As he watched, one of the stickynodes dropped a few grubs to the ground, and the cats pounced and devoured the things greedily.

Thalia ran up, oblivious to the Stickynodes, threw an arm around each cat and picked them up. "Merry! Neff!" she said. "You naughty cats. Where have you been?"

"Boy," Stu said, "I thought we'd never see them again."

Circumflex exchanged a few high-pitched squeals with the other stickynodes, said, "Little catbeings hungry. Like hair root bugs. You want?"

Wolf said, "Is that all you have?"

"No. Other food, but must cook. Special feast. Humans, Wrackoons, like burn food. Rest here. Light supper fire soon."

The dirigible meat, roasting in its basket, glowing coals and licking blue flame suspended well above the beast's back, smelled awfully good. Wolf felt his mouth water, one short step away from drooling, listened to the soft skirling of his belly, and thought, Damn clever. Do everything they can to avoid irritating their host in the vicinity of the nest.

Still, it'd seemed to squirm and shudder, maybe an hour before the little buggers showed up bearing armloads of bloody meat. Hell. Armloads? Well, the Wrackoons had something like arms, anyway, even if the Stickynodes did not. Look at them, wrackoons dancing around the firebasket, licking their lips, raccoon-eyes rolling, singing some grunty little song while the Stickynodes hung back, watching them, almost paternal.

Since when does a thing that looks like a lump of oil-wet modeling clay have an *affect*?

One of them walked up to him now, moving easily, almost bouncing, a quick series of rip-thumps across the dirigible beast's back. A little bit like a man on zero-gee carpet. It said, "Is this one your mate, or the other?"

Wolf looked down at Honoria, who was lying curled on her side beside him, head on his outstretched thigh, eyes shut. Good question. "Are you the same one as before?"

It seemed to chuckle, voice like a cartoon character. "I am Trader Jim. Yes, Tuan, that's me."

Tuan? "So somebody in the Topopolis has a copy of *Lord Jim*?" Or is it *Heart of Darkness* I'm thinking of?

Silence. Then it said, "Not understood, Tuan."

"Sorry."

It said, "Is that thing . . . she? She is correct?"

He nodded, stroking her hair gently.

"Is at thigh-junction your procreative organ system?"

Another nod.

"Ah. Perhaps you will conduct procreation ceremony for our entertainment?"

He felt Honoria stiffen against him, not really asleep after all. "Um . . ."

Trader Jim said, "Yes, yes! And we will have Wrackoons do their FuckDance for *you*!"

"FuckDance."

"That's what other human named it for us. Wrackoons have a very similar system, you see. Ninth arm of male"—the one that stuck up like a scorpion's tail—"has sponge thing fills up with germ plasm, you see. Female has mitten to squeeze with. Dance is *very* stimulating!"

The voice was enthusiastic, generating the sense of affect. The . . . face? Nothing. A mess of fleshy petals, like bits of fingers, tentacles, lips and tongue, surrounded by a ring of what looked like little cauliflower heads. Which is what they point at stuff they appear to . . . see. He said, "I don't know that—"

Trader Jim said, "Oh, please! Other humans we meet, ones who arranged trade, taught us English, all *male*! Very sad."

All male? The crew of *NR-331h* would not have been all male, not if I remember right. Hazy images of that nice girl—Mattie something?—the one Mark seems to have known . . . another memory of Thalia seeming irked as they stood looking at the fallen ship, talking about its missing crew.

He said, "We'll see."

"Yes, yes! Talk to mate. Talk to friends. Do us a nice little FuckDance."

"What about you?"

"Ah, we have not gender, sorry to say. Still, if you stay long enough, you will experience Budding Ceremony. Very painful and solemn, you see."

"Stimulating?"

It seemed to titter. "Ah, not to the Budder, you see."

"I see." He said, "Who the hell *are* you people?"

Trader Jim seemed to frown. Seemed to? How the hell would I know that? It said, "Well. Well. Not know anymore. Long time passes, you see. Humans we meet, other peoples we meet, guess we are kind of parasite been here a long time. Topopolis come to our planet, we somehow get aboard, live on anything we find."

"And the Wrackoons?"

"Guess they been here a lot longer than us. Long enough able to eat dirigible meat."

"And you?"

It seemed to sigh. "Eat fungus grow on Wrackoon shit."

Hmh. An unlikely development, unless the Stickynodes and Wrackoons originated on the same planet and the rest of it's just mythology. Besides which, Ox is able to eat dirigible meat, meaning . . . The thought, in the midst of the smell, made his stomach skirl again. "What did the humans want to trade for?"

Trader Jim reached around to where, if this had been a

terrestrial quadruped, its anus would have been, and was suddenly brandishing a broad-bladed knife in its mouth assemblage.

"Jesus!" He reached out and took it gently. Christ. Manufactured. *Sheffield*? Did Sheffield ever make a fucking bowie knife? "What did the humans take in trade for this?"

It seemed to smirk, again somehow indefinably. "Shitfungus."

"Why?"

"Say better than truffles. Better than chocolate. Last traderman we see say better than pussy. Not know what he mean by that."

"Um. How do you make the swap? Do they just . . . show up?" Heart starting to speed up in chest.

The Stickynode giggled. "Oh, no. Humans never find us by themselves! Dirigible beast have big territory, but finite, you know? Every once in a long damn time, fly right over human nest!"

Honoria sat up suddenly. *"Wolf!"*

Yeah. Breathless, he said, "When?" Hoping that, somehow, they knew the answer.

"Oh, maybeso soon now. *Lots* of shitfungus piling up in sheds!"

Wolf, looking down at Honoria, looking at the brilliant shine in her eyes, thought, *Human nest.* He looked at the maker's mark on the knife then. "What else did they give you?"

"Mostly those things. Knives very useful to us. Axes. That kind of tool." It laughed, rather a nasty laugh. "One traderman try to give us chain saw. Where the fuck *we* get gasoline, on the back of a dirigible beast?"

And, Wolf thought, where the fuck would the crew of *NR-331h* get a chain saw? Not to mention hundreds of Sheffield blades. He said, "Come on, Honey. We better talk to the others."

Eleven

It was growing dark now, crepuscular rays fading, blue changing to gray. Stu and Cory followed an obvious footpath out of the village, past plots full of slowly undulating, plant-like things. Stu was half leading, half following, anticipation an electric sensation in his gut. Finally, she turned to him, said, "Let's go up into the wind, okay?" Cory started up the fractured surface, using her hands to help her.

At the top there was a little chink through the closely spaced dirigible hairs, and a strong wind whipped at their legs. Stu went first, crawling amid the stalks until, after a few meters, he came out on a hairless cliff, looking down toward the dirigible's dark, prow-shaped head. Here, the wind was a steady push, sizzling against his skin, tossing his hair. For the first time since he'd been knocked off the branch, he had a definite sensation of looking down, and the vista of identical branches far below took his breath for a second. Directly ahead, beyond the dirigible's symmetrical snout, a confusing miasma of light and dark, very unlike the branches in all other directions. Before Stu could make sense of it, there were scraping noises, and Cory popped out of the opening.

"What's that?"

He turned back just in time to see a blinding beacon of light come out of eclipse from behind an obstruction. Ahead, what was unmistakably a clear pathway through the myriads of branches all around. A big one. Featureless gray-blue dimness there, but at its edge, reddish-orange like the setting sun, a little thin oval, growing thinner and redder as he watched, bringing on the night.

"It can't be a star," she said. "Can it? It looks like it's setting behind itself."

Stu stared, trying to understand. "Whatever it is, it's almost gone. This must be the way the lighting works here. Night and day. There it goes." The oval turned to a dim red line and then disappeared. "Jesus," he said, "a stellar lighthouse. I wonder how they get *that* thing to work?"

They sat together at the edge of the cliff for a long time, wind whipping into their faces, reinforcing the notion that they were moving. Lying flat against the warm bulk of dirigible flesh, the wind felt good, like sleeping in a heated fluid bed under an air-conditioning vent. Stu and Cory in the darkness, only a few feet apart, his erection coming and going depending on how vivid his mental images of her were. He wondered briefly whether his mother or Mark would be worried about him, then dismissed the idea as foolish. He wished for a blanket, something to hold around himself and snuggle against. The last thing he remembered thinking was that he would wake up to see if the midnight moonlight also came from the star-thing. The lights dancing before his eyes were mutating into purple and electric green faces. Unexpectedly, he fell asleep.

Morning came with no notice. By the time he opened his eyes, the landscape was already flooded with bright orange light from the brilliant oval, growing now, moved during the night so that it was far away from the edge of the tangle. He sat up, cursing himself for missing the moonlight phase. Vertigo grabbed at him as he looked downward past the dirigible's snout. Down there, maybe ten kilometers or so away, a pair of dirigible beasts were moving against the remote wall of branches, giving even more reality to the immense distance he could fall.

But more importantly, out there outside the tangle of branches was . . . something big as a world, hanging in the gray-blue sky like an enormous island on the sea. A floating continent of sorts, an irregular mass of gigantic kelp and seaweed, studded with big gas bladders, trailing streamers like rain from a storm cloud. Hard to say just how big, but he estimated it must be thousands of kilometers across. The top surface was mostly flat, and he imagined that he could make out cities, forests, and farmland there, receding into the distance until it was just a blur.

And, floating above the nearest end, there were tiny red and yellow dots, hundreds of them, basking in the light of the star-thing, whose beacon was growing fatter and brighter by the minute. He squinted into the light, straining to identify what they were.

Balloons, he thought. They're sending balloons to meet us.

"Cory," he said, barely able to keep his voice modulated. "Wake up. We've got to tell the others."

Watching the bright red and yellow balloon rise above them, cable angled back toward the—well, no, it's not *ground,* is it?—Wolf thought, something like a trade wind blowing here. Why? Blowing down the length of the Topopolitan strand? Or round and round the periphery in a great circle? Spiral? He thought about Stu's commentary on the blue sky they could see in every direction they had a line-of-sight.

My God. The *scale* of this place!

What kind of civilization can thread a galaxy through and through with a network of physical pipes, parsecs across, and . . . hell, why not just call them *infinitely* long? What kind of technology does that take? What's the phrase you hear? Indistinguishable from magic?

Christ, maybe Honoria's right and the rest of us . . . just a dream, that's all it was. Humans in their starships, loose among the stars. Just a dream.

And this is reality.

Somewhere in the remote past, deep in the history of the universe, a . . . people, call them that, though no one seems to know who or what they are, set out to . . . engulf everything, the . . . totality of . . . *Why?* Why the hell would they *build* something this? Because they *can*?

Lots of old stories, human stories, stories read as a child, in the camps, boy with his daddy, Daddy full of old mythology. Fecundity unlimited. Keep on breeding, boys and girls. Global thermonuclear war? Hell, we'll refill the Earth in a generation. The Solar system in another. Then the nearby stars, the Galaxy, the Supercluster, the Whole Fucking Universe.

Call 'em Adam and Eve, Lord. Then give 'em ten thousand years to be fruitful and multiply and they'll turn the whole of Your Creation to one great big, steaming heap of human shit.

A species on its way to that might try building a Topopolis, if it could. Christ, you'd think if they were smart enough for *this,* they might've come up with a better answer.

Beside him, shading his eyes with both hands, cutting out the blue-sky glare, Stu said, "They look like people."

Bipeds, at any rate, little black figures moving around in the baskets, and every now and again there'd be a muted roar, a flash of yellow-orange flame, making one of the taut envelopes glow. Aerostat. That's the fancy word for a hot-air balloon.

Hot air rises. Toward *what*? Where the fuck is the gravity gradient coming from in here? Is *down* toward the . . . hull? Is that what we should call it? Hot air rising toward the center, cooling as it rises, rising into some kind of jet stream, circulatory system of the . . .

No way to know. Not one of us a real scientist, anyway. The explanation, if there is one, might not make sense.

On his other side, standing beyond a taut and nervous Honoria, Trader Jim said, "Hue-men come now!"

Hue-men? Oh. Snicker. Plural.

Stickynodes and Wrackoons were emerging from the hair forest, clustering all around, obviously excited. Anticipating a shipment of shiny new toys. Others, industrious, in the background, were opening up the sheds, pulling out stack after stack of pale brown shitfungus, which, Wolf had to admit, *did* smell an awful lot like chocolate. Wry smile. The *name,* though . . .

The balloon was overhead, obvious human beings peering down at them from the basket, and Wolf thought, Why the hell are the dirigible beasties stopping here? What's in it for *them*?

A trapdoor suddenly opened in the bottom of the balloon, hoses dropping out, then there was a hiss, a spray of some liquid, dropping like rain, dropping on . . .

Mark shouted, a sharp cry, just as Wolf felt his eyes start to burn, felt the dirigible beast start to shiver gently underfoot.

Thalia said, "Smells like . . . some kind of disinfectant."

A minute, and then the stinging rain was over, though the dirigible continued to shiver. From somewhere far away came a soft sigh, a noise like a gentle, elephantine fart. Though the Stickynodes continued to stand still, disinfectant beading on their oily backs, the Wrackoons, hair matted, were shouting with glee, rolling around on the wet skin.

Beside him Honoria said, "All the dandruff is dissolved now."

Wolf imagined a fleet of dirigibles drying in the bright beaconlight, hair all fluffy and soft again.

Overhead, five men suddenly came over the basket's rail, began dropping toward them on unspooling lines, descending like spiders to the . . . Wolf smiled again. I keep wanting this to be the *ground,* dammit!

They landed, unclipping from the cables, coming toward the group of naked people awaiting them. Squat, odd-looking men, none of them much over five feet tall, with peculiar, flat heads covered with shaggy blond hair, big brows under sloping foreheads, shading pale, pale blue eyes. They were wearing beaded brown suede vests, beads polychrome blue, choker necklaces of what looked like yellow dogs' teeth, brown suede shorts, Indian moccasins.

And they were all looking in one direction, Honoria shrinking back against Wolf's side, making a futile effort to cover herself, arm thrown over her breasts, legs almost crossed, one hand suddenly spread across her mons.

One of the men, the leader perhaps, curtsied to her and said, *"Dadanz bara-dar? Ou."* Odd. An obvious tone language, but spoken with a slow, clumsy-seeming articulation.

Wolf thought, He's not looking at her face. Not at all. Looking down at her crotch, leaning a little to one side, as if he can peek around her fingers. What the hell . . . He said, "Anyone recognize the language?"

Stu said, "These don't look like any kind of people I ever saw before."

No. They look like deformed athletes, like circus dwarves blown up to circus-strongman size and . . .

There was a sharp light of recognition in the headman's

eyes. "Zo," he said, in his oddly hollow voice. "Ah goss daz plazes yo."

Silence. Then Wolf said, "I beg your pardon?"

The man said, "Zorrah. Ah'm nod varrah gode ad zass. Ongladge varrah hahd vo uz. Are dongs are da wrong jabe."

The way that sounded . . . smirk. *Our tongues are the wrong shape?* I'll say. These people sound . . . what? Tongue-tied?

Stu said, "They're . . . like Neanderthal men!"

The man beamed and said, "Dodz raht! Zom beeble gall uz daht." Then he said, "Ah'm Omou. Wahlgome do Adrandus."

Wolf: "Welcome to Adrandus?"

Honoria stiffened suddenly, moving her hands away, to the man's—Omou's—obvious delight, and gasped, "*Atlantis!*"

Another bright smile, broad grin like an Australian aboriginal's grin, showing some remarkably robust teeth. "Yah! Dotz id!"

From somewhere behind him, Wolf heard Mark's tired voice: "Oh, for Christ's *sake.*"

Cory said, "I guess Trader Jim didn't learn his English from these guys."

No, Wolf thought, bending down to pick up the long-inert barrel of the TrackTrixCom, which had been lying at his feet, I suppose not.

Seeing it, the man's eyes lit up. "Vell, vell," he said.

In the sagging balloon basket, perched with the Atlanteans on the pile of shitfungus, they began the long ride to the surface. Cory sat with her legs tightly crossed, scared cat squirming in her lap, painfully aware of Omou's eyes, feeling extremely odd about sitting naked on something people were apparently going to eat, sitting close to Stu, not quite touching him.

The five Atlantean men kept moving around, sitting, standing, crouching, walking precariously around the rim of the basket, hanging onto the ropes and leaning out into space, grinning their toothy grins as they looked at her, at her mother, at Thalia, nudging each other, wiggling their eyebrows like cartoon comedians.

Not looking at our faces, no. At breasts and bellies, hips and thighs and . . . just now, Omou was on the rail opposite her, craning his neck, trying to get a look into her lap. Finally, he shrugged, smirked, and dropped into the basket, hunkering down in front of her, face pressed into the shitfungus so he could try to peer up between her crossed thighs.

Beside her Stu muttered, "Oh, *man* . . ."

Wolf, kneeling between Honoria and another of the men, TrackTrixCom tucked under one arm, holding Ox still with the other, snarled, "Goddamn it, d'you suppose you could find some clothing for these women?"

Omou straightened up and shrugged. "Women wear no clothing in Adrandus. A man must see what he's working for."

The thick, tongue-tied accents were still there, slowly becoming easier to understand as she got used to the heavy sound shift. These people, apparently, spoke a language confined to front-of-the-mouth sounds, and had trouble with vowels like I and E. Unusual, for a human language, even if these people *were* truly human. She remembered how marvelous it'd seemed, learning that the languages of the native Australians were devoid of sibilants.

Wolf said, "What the hell does that mean?"

Omou shrugged again, grinning an open-mouthed grin that showed off his teeth to great effect. Cory noticed he had a pronounced overbite. The other men were circling around again, focused on the three women, and Cory could swear their noses were twitching. Sniffing the air like dogs, she thought. Like the way dogs will sniff at you, just before they try to jump in your lap, shove their noses into your crotch, while everyone laughs as you push them away, blushing . . .

The thought of Stu, trying to kiss the inside of her thigh, the morning after they'd . . . Why did I do it with him? Did I really *mean* to?

Omou said, "If women kept themselves covered, men would not stay focused on life's realities. They'd wander off on their own and civilization would come to an end. The constant sight of pussy keeps us slaves to the Goddess's will."

Cory reeled slightly. Did he really say that? Or did I just imagine those words out of a thick-tongued garble?

Omou came to kneel in front of Wolf, grin fading, eyes serious. "I know your type, you people from the modern worlds. You think you keep women slaves so you can have their pussy whenever you want, giving nothing in return that you don't want to give."

Mark, voice bitter, said, "It's not so different as you seem to think, Omou."

Thalia said, "Asshole."

Who? Omou or Mark?

Omou laughed. "Atlanteans are realists, men and women alike."

Wolf snickered and said, "So the women go bare-ass and the men do all the work."

In her ear, Stu whispered, "This is gross."

Gross? Is that what you really think, Stuart? Or do you realize that men *are* like dogs, that they'll line up and take turns with a bitch if they have to. . . . Another string of images from the camp. There'd been plenty of dogs in the camp, bitches in heat, trailed by chains of grinning, tongue-dangly curs, men and boys laughing and watching them, making dirty jokes.

Plenty of laughing, watching women in that memory.

The sense of delicacy upper-class women have is . . . taught.

Nuns in school, stern-eyed, wooden rulers in red-knuckled

fists: Keep your hands out from under your desk. *I* know what you're up to, dirty little girl.

Over the side of the balloon basket, the landscape below grew huge, no longer a vast floating island, more like an entire world. In the distance you could see a city, complete with the towers and spires and spikes of tall buildings. The land was flat, so it grew foreshortened in an unfamiliar way, finally disappearing behind the . . . trees.

Are those things trees? Like familiar palmettos, but much shorter, with huge, waxy-looking fronds in a cluster at the top. They were descending into a leathery-looking field, a place like a parking lot paved in shiny leatherette upholstery, and on the ground there were hundreds of teams of tiny men, working away at great winches, each winch hauling down a brightly colored balloon.

Overhead, the fleet of dirigible beasts was swinging away from the wind, turning in a graceful stream, sailing away into the sky. Stickynodes. Wrackoons. All still a mystery, nothing left to remember them by but this nice-smelling pile of shitfungus.

There were hundreds of balloons here too, near and far, the farthest ones no more than garish specks superimposed against the . . . trees. My God. Those things are *huge*!

Beside her, Stu made some cryptic remark about Kansas. Wolf looked at him, laughed and shook his head. "I feel the same way, kid."

The basket bumped down on top of its winch, and someone put a hooked ladder over the side. Without a word, the Atlantean men swarmed over the rail and were gone. The others followed, one by one, until only Cory and Stu were left in the basket. He gestured for her to go over first.

Straddling the rail, goose bumps rising on her arms, Cory looked down and, with a pulse of alarm, realized Omou and his comrades were standing in a little circle at the foot of the ladder, grinning up at her. So much for crossed legs. She turned her back and went down as fast as she could, pretending they weren't there, pretending she was . . . elsewhere. Elsewhen.

When her feet hit the ground, Omou leaned in close, oregano-scented breath washing over her as he whispered, "Very *nice*, little one. If there were a time and a place, I'd beg to worship you."

Cory stepped back quickly, feeling a distinct sensation of the creeps crawling under her skin.

Thalia said, "Wolfie, I think you may've found your true home."

He blinked at her, seeming surprised.

Honoria scowled and put her hand on his forearm.

Cory put her head down, not wanting to make eye contact with any of them, and was horrified to see a blush had spread down across her chest and onto her breasts.

Stu dropped lightly to the ground at the foot of the ladder, looked around at them and said, "Is something wrong? Where are we?"

Good question.

Atlantis.

Where's that? Some Aegean island? Crete? The continental shelf of Africa, off Morocco? The shallow sea bottom around Bimini? That last, that's where that book my mother reads likes to put it. *The Stones of Atlantis?* Was that it?

A rough voice, accented but entirely human, said, "What'cha got here, Omou?"

They turned, and there was a tall, heavyset man dressed in a long maroon bathrobe and incongruous black leather combat boots, shaggy gray hair caught in a girl's bright orange elastic headband, face mostly hidden by a big gray beard, looking at them, eyes bright. There was a long, expensive-looking pump-action single-barrel shotgun, blued steel barrel dangling, muzzle choker pointing at the ground, hanging from his right hand.

He smiled, looking them up and down, one by one. Finally, he said, "Man. You ladies are going to be popular around here."

Thalia sighed tiredly, crossing her arms over her chest. "Great. I don't suppose you've got any spare bathrobes?"

He laughed. "You're a real son of a bitch, ain't-che Omou?"

Omou said, "Yez. Bazdard. Dots me."

The man stepped forward, shifting the gun to his left hand, lifting the other for Thalia to shake. "How d'you do, ma'am. My name's Gaius. Welcome to Galaxios."

Wolf said, "I thought this was Atlantis."

Gaius laughed again. "Because they imagine themselves the first true humans to wash up here, Omou's folk think they own the place. Me, I think they're just a bunch of Flintstones."

Mark said, "Flintstones?"

"Yeah, well . . ." Gaius looked at them all dubiously. "Guess that doesn't mean much to you folks."

Stu said, "Yes it does. Flintstones was a popular cartoon from about a hundred years ago. Cavemen living with dinosaurs."

Gaius said, "Huh. Interesting. You'll have to tell me what kind of world you come from."

Mark said, "What do you mean? We're from Earth, of course."

Gaius grinned, something of a nasty look in his eyes. "Earth. Ah, yes. But which *one*?"

Cory felt something odd settle in the pit of her stomach. Which one?

Stu, voice faint, said, "And why *do* you call them Flintstones?"

Gaius turned and pointed at something far away across the landing field. Cory looked, feeling faint, utterly unreal, and was somehow not surprised to see a line of what appeared to be allosaurs bobbing along, tails held high, heads nodding as they walked. Each one seemed to be cradling something in its arms.

Wolf said, "How . . . how big are those things?"

Gaius said, "How big? Well, the rifles those boys are lugging fire a twenty-two-millimeter shell."

Someone said, "Holy shit."

Gaius snickered. "That's the brand name Omou's company uses for its fungus candy. Very popular. Hey, let's get out of here. I've got a groundcar—I'll take you on into EarthHaven and get you started on your new lives."

New lives . . . Cory turned and looked at Stu, who was, just then, looking at her, not the dinosaurs.

Gaius nudged the TrackTrixCom with one toe, moving it slightly from where Wolf had set it down. "Bring your little friend. There're some people'll have a few . . . questions for it."

"Atlantis," Honoria breathed, not quite to herself. More properly *Atlantida,* in any decent language. Land of the Atlantides, daughters of Atlas, the hidden land beside Oceanus, beyond the Atlas Mountains, the Land's End of ancient Africa.

The city was all around them, streets and sidewalks speeding by as they rode along in an open, silent self-propelled cart driven by a second, silent man.

Electric? Is this an electric cart?

What difference does it make?

This is really it, she thought, everything just as I expected. Tall buildings, tall as twentieth century skyscrapers, but lacking the boxy utilitarian modernist shapes. Soaring, rounded towers, onion-domed minarets. Aerial skyways, roads high above the surface. Parabolic antennae like chrome-bright flowers, symbolic of the technology, the knowledge of good and evil, with which the Atlanteans destroyed their world, foreshadowing the Second Fall of our own time.

Everything just like I expected, except . . .

She couldn't keep her eyes off the people.

Most of the men were dressed in classical attire. Greek tunics. Roman togas. Men bustling about, swiftly walking this way and that, about men's business. The women were few and far between. And every one of them . . .

Naked. Evenly tanned if they were white enough to tan. An occasional black one. Fat women. Thin women. Everything in between. Women with huge, pendulous breasts. Women with no breasts at all. Women with pubic hair that ran down the insides of their thighs halfway to their knees. Other women bare as little girls.

She took her eyes away from the naked women and looked back at the buildings, taking in a deep breath.

Gaius leaned close to her and said, "You look like you expect to hear 'Strangers in Paradise' any second now."

Stu brayed absurd laughter. "Ya mean this is the Thirteenth Moon of Jupiter?"

Gaius chuckled and said, "That's good. I like you, son."

Honoria thought, No one likes a smartass except another smartass. Usually not even them. At least smartass Gaius had found squares of cloth for the women to wrap around themselves. The blanket he'd given her was making her itch and sweat; it was warm enough to go naked here, after all, and she *had* gotten used to it.

Mark said, "Even if it's not the Thirteenth Moon of Jupiter, whatever the hell that's suppose to mean, I'd still like to know what this place *is* supposed to be. And why is it called Atlantis? And, um, you mentioned Galaxios . . . What's that? I—"

Gaius held up a hand, laughing softly. "Everything in good time. You'll have quite a few questions, I imagine."

Thalia said, "What's wrong with right now?"

He shrugged. "Nothing. It's just that there're better people than me to . . . Well." He waved a hand at the cityscape around them. "This place is called Atlantis because the Atlanteans called it that when they started building it, oh, maybe twelve thousand years ago. Something like that."

Honoria, struggling to get her English exactly right, said, "From . . . Plato's Atlantis? The Atlantis of *Timaios* and *Kritias*?"

Gaius blinked at her. "Ma'am, evidently I'm from a world similar to yours, and we had that same story. Plato's Atlantis was the mistaken one, from his misreading of the hieroglyphic numbers, coupled to Greek Dark Age myths about the Pelasgian civilization and the Land of the Keftiu. No, these babies were from the real Atlantis."

Wolf said, "What d'you mean *real*? From the Atlantis Honoria believes in; the one that was on the North American continental shelf, near Bimini?"

"Sort of."

Honoria felt her heart leap.

Gaius said, "It's a history where Archaics ancestral to the European Neanderthals colonized southeastern North America, just before the ice came. And were building starships by the time the ice went away."

Thalia said, "But . . . but . . ."

Mark: "You mentioned, um . . . more than one Earth."

The man smiled at them. "So I did. The larger city that's grown up around Atlantis, oh, maybe big enough for two, three hundred million people, is commonly known as EarthHaven. It's inhabited mainly by people from the various Earths. From various histories, mostly human, the others . . . oh, most nonhuman Earths are full of dinosaurs and birds. Though there is at least one little colony somewhere hereabouts inhabited by Saucer People who got to Earth and settled it back around Cheops's time."

Dead silence.

Wolf said, "Saucer People."

Gaius laughed again. "I bet that sounds funny as shit!"

Wolf: "Um. Yeah. It does."

"Well, this whole 'floating continent,' if you want to call it that, is usually called Galaxios, mainly because it's settled by people from various versions of our own galaxy. A little more than half of its population, a few hundred billion at a guess, is lost Saucer People, because in most histories, they're the principal interstellar culture."

Mark: "And how . . . I mean, how did they . . ."

"Everybody got here the same way you folks did, of course."

Thalia seemed startled, "Everyone?"

"Well, no, most Galaxians are born here. Historians think, over the ages, this place was probably settled by no more than a couple of thousand lost star crews."

A couple of thousand. She tried to imagine that.

It wasn't especially difficult.

Quietly, Wolf said, "Most scientists believe in the Many Histories version of quantum mechanics, I guess. Quantum cosmology too. I understand some hyperdrive scientists—"

Thalia cut in: "Only crackpots believe Many Histories is true on anything but a quantum-mechanical scale. That's how hyperdrive may work. There's a congruent history for each particle that allows it to cross from one jump point to another."

Gaius smiled and said, "You folks gotta be bold as shit to fly an FTL technology you don't understand."

Wolf, seeming impatient: "So how did the people from . . . your Earth get around?"

He said, "The same way yours do: the hyperdrive field drops us out of the Einstein-Feinberg Continuum, twists the ship through conformal and probabilistic time, until it reaches a reentry point in a history congruent to but nonlocal for the one it left. That *is* the only way you get FTL travel that doesn't violate causality. Not to mention time travel that doesn't violate the second law of thermodynamics. That's what the principles of Quantum Probabilistics are all about, for John's sake!"

More silence, with Honoria acutely aware that she had no idea what'd just been said.

Mark, sounding outraged, voice higher than normal, said, "But . . . that's just not *possible*!"

Thalia, voice dull, very soft: "The Russian lab that developed hyperdrive was originally trying to build a time machine, so they could go back and alter the outcome of the Cold War. They figured if they could go back and keep the Soviet Union alive, the next two wars, the nuclear ones, wouldn't've happened."

Gaius nodded. "There may be a history where they succeeded. All we know about it is stories told by a half-mad survivor, some old bald coot apparently blown directly here by exposure to an Atom-Kernel Event. Said his name was Bob. He died without telling us much detail."

Honoria said, "How many . . . histories are there?"

Gaius said, "Ma'am, there're times without number."

The cart drifted silently to the curb and stopped in front of a tall, rounded building with ornate scrollwork covering its facade. Gaius stood, opening the side door, and jumped to the pavement. "Well," he said, "here's your hotel. We'll get you folks cleaned up, rested a bit, then there're some people who'll want to meet you. Call it a debriefing."

A few hours later, Mark, following the others reluctantly, stepped through the gigantic arch of a doorway, triskelion-decorated doors folded back on either side, scanned the outsized, dim hall within and saw that no one had waited for him. Grumbling, he picked up his pace, glad for the new, comfortably fitting clothing he'd been given.

This business was getting stranger and stranger, feeling more and more like some kind of elaborate hoax. Flintstones, Saucer People . . . The problem is, this just doesn't seem realistic. At the end of the hall there was another set of smaller doors, and, as he approached, he could hear a jumble of voices and party sounds. He pushed open the door and went in.

Big, carpeted room, well-lit, filled with people. Looks like they started without us. All humans, at least, dressed in more or less contemporaneous clothing, even the women. A little informal for a cocktail party, but . . . Thalia and Stu and the others had been drawn into various little groups, and already seemed to be enjoying themselves.

A smiling, Falstaffian man, half a head shorter than him and grossly fat, with a wild white beard and deep-set blue eyes, blocked his way. He said "Hi, I'm Pols Semmith," and held out a tankard of what looked like cola for him. Mark took a drink of something carbonated that tasted sweet but left a lingering bitter flavor. "Don't like it? We thought Moxie was popular in all the ERDA timelines. Would you like something different?"

Mark shook his head, said, "It's all right." Took another little sip.

Another man, tall, dark and dapper, dressed in an impeccably tailored tuxedo, joined them. "Well, you must be Mark Porringer, the bureaucrat. Don't get too many of your kind here; they mostly stay on Earth and die of boredom. My name's Leo . . . Leo Florian. I was flight engineer for a nuclear ship that set out from Okinawa spaceport in 'eighty-eight. We got caught at Beta Pic too."

Okinawa? Okinawa's a radioactive ruin. It . . . Mark looked at the man, wondering how different the Earth he came from was. "The people in this room are all from Earths similar to ours?"

Semmith nodded. "That's the idea. They've found that, at least at first, it helps to hang around with people who have more similarities than differences. Every time some new people come, we have a party like this."

"How often is that?" Mark asked, putting the tankard down on a nearby table.

"Not very," Florian said. "In fact, there are anomalously few arrivals. They've been trying to pin down the mathematics of the thing for as long as I've been here."

"Undoubtedly has something to do with the perils of the jungle," Semmith said. "Although the PacketWights try to pick suitable arrival locations for the people they capture, many newcomers die before they get to Galaxios."

Florian's eyes grew distant. "Yes, getting here can be quite a travail. But that doesn't explain why we've never gotten more than one version of a person here."

"Sure it does, Leo, if the 'Wights are—"

"You!"

Mark turned. A small, quite attractive black woman with a look of happy incredulity on her face was standing there. Strong face with prominent cheekbones and small, firm jaw. High forehead under swept-back black hair, tears spilling from bright almond eyes. "Mark Porringer," she said. "It *is* you."

For a long moment he looked at her, stunned. Mattie Wordsworth, from the long dead past. "Mattie? I thought you were—"

She threw herself against him, head against his collarbone, wiry little hands clutching at his back. "Oh, Mark." He could feel her sobbing, feel her breasts moving against his solar plexus. He squeezed back hard, remembering how he had done it in the past, adapting to her compact shape.

The last time he'd seen her, she'd been crying too, cursing him, calling him every foul name she could think of. She was a smart cookie, all right. It hadn't taken her long to figure it out. The files on the Poole incident had been easy enough to forge. For her, it only meant a demotion, a delay in her career. For him, it would have been the end, his career over, the plan destroyed.

And then she had gone on the mission to Vega and been lost.

Feeling her against him, hardly noticing anything else, except Thalia, across the room, who seemed to be watching, he pushed down the scared feeling and tried to take stock. Was it likely that this was the *same* Mattie? She may have been here for a damn long time, and any reminder of home would be emotionally charged, but . . .

He pushed her away, held her at arm's length, looked at her carefully. Semmith and Florian had melted back into the crowd. "Mattie. This is such a shock. I thought you were dead, we all did."

She wiped an eye with the back of her wrist, took a deep breath. "Yeah. The rest of the crew didn't make it. What's that they say, that the captain's supposed to go down with her ship? I ended up here instead. So did you mourn for me, Mark?"

He thought of the moment, sitting at his desk, he'd heard about it. He'd already lost her, had put her out of his thoughts completely. But still, he'd cried. "You were . . . captain of the *NR-749h*?"

She was settling down now, her eyes taking him in in the appraising way that he remembered. "Yes. Lost my first command too. But we almost made it back to Earth to warn them."

Mark nodded. "So did we."

Puzzlement on her face. "But what were *you* doing on a spaceship, Mark? I never thought you'd ever leave Earth."

"It's a long story."

"I know we had our ups and downs, but . . ." Eyes downcast now.

A surge of delicious feeling overwhelming him, he seized

her body, drew her into a bear hug. "There's no reason why we can't start up where we left off, so many years ago."

In your universe, that is.

Feeling remarkably refreshed after a good night's sleep, Wolf took a seat on a small, not particularly comfortable tan couch against one side wall of the conference room they'd been brought to, high in what Gaius referred to as Town Hall, an immense, brassy minar, far too large to be a mere minaret, spiking the better part of two kilometers into the cloudless blue sky.

Hope Ox and those damned cats are okay back in the hotel room . . . Image of the dog snuffling around the nice bamboolike catcage Gaius had found for them, scaring the little fuckheads into a helpless panic.

Looking out the broad glass window facing him, Wolf thought, Well, not cloudless, no. But those distant smudges are floating jungles, hm? I wonder where evaporated moisture goes? How far away is the end of *up*? The center of the tube?

Somewhere, dozens of parsecs away, he imagined an infinite tunnel cloud, rotating, stuck at the zero-gee axis of an infinite cylinder—how can the Topopolis be spinning around its long axis? What the fuck does long axis *mean,* in this context? *How* the fuck . . . Sharp memory of Gaius grinning at him. Why the fuck you think they *call* it a Topopolis? Just to be funny?

Well.

So here's an infinitely long cloud, bloated with water vapor, up in zero gee. When it grew big enough, the gravity gradient would pull a few condensed droplets loose, here, there, everywhere, and the rain would fall and fall, fall for millions of years, until it found a limitless ocean, down on the Topopolitan floor, where, one day, it would evaporate again and begin the long journey . . . upward.

How long did it take this ecology to form? Or did the Topopolitans build it all-up?

A snicker from Gaius. Don't be silly. The Topopolis grows from its endpoints.

Endpoints. Just two?

Snicker. Think. *Topopolis.*

He stretched, digging his boot heels into the carpet. The clothes he'd been given were comfortable, reminding him of the way he'd dressed when young, he and his father wandering the ruins of Appalachia together. Suede boots. White chinos. Canvas vest. Hand-tooled brown leather belt, done up in scenes of the desert Southwest, making him remember the rescue of Cory. Jesus! Not so long ago as all that.

Honoria looks damned sharp in her outfit too, standing over there, looking out the window, white, sleeveless tunic covering her only to mid-thigh, waist cinched in with a shiny black patent-leather belt, sandals laced up her calves. She turned away from the vista, turned and looked at him, smiled, one dimple forming briefly at the left corner of her mouth, started walking toward him, watching him watch her.

The image of grace.

Remember the look of surprise, then gratitude, in her warm brown eyes when you came to her little hotel room, unbidden. She'd been almost naked, standing at the foot of the narrow bed she expected to inhabit alone, holding up one of the dresses she'd been given, already wearing the soft white cotton underwear.

She stood still as I walked over to her, closing the door behind me.

Stood still as I undressed her, taking off what little there was to take, kneeling in front of her, pulling down those cotton panties and . . . she was standing in front of him now, looking down at his face, smiling, knowing what he was remembering.

Remember the look in her eye when I told her how sorry I was about . . . everything that'd happened.

How do you feel, Wolf? She'd asked. Do you still . . . love her?

That simple mistake that all women make.

Try to explain.

I haven't *thought* about how I feel, you see. Not in a long time. Not since . . . not since my father died. Ah. That last, however untrue it might be, maybe just barely true, seemed to make sense.

Then, the bed.

Then on to the gruesome details of a willing fuck.

Does she remember it all only as a haze of love? Or does she remember, as I do, the noisome, graphic kaleidoscope of sweating, grunting, thrusting mess and . . . She sat down beside him, snuggling close, taking his hand in her own.

Laughter from the doorway.

Ah, yes. Now here was dear old Mark, standing, chatting with Mattie, leaning in close as she grinned, putting one small hand briefly in the middle of his chest. Imagine that. What a shock to find her here, after all these years of thinking her dead. Christ, I knew her pretty well, way back when. Why didn't I know she was Mark's girlfriend, once upon a time? They were . . . apparently seeing each other, right up to the time she went away and got killed.

Mark stunned, wondering, *My* Mattie? Is she? Or from some other universe, where my Mattie came here instead of dying in a presumed starship explosion?

We never found the remains of that lost ship, did we?

In any case, this Mattie remembered *him.* Remembered him fondly indeed.

Look at the fucking twinkle in his eye. What's become of moping old Mark? Is that all it takes? Well, hell, remember what old Freud said: The only way a man can be free of neurosis is by constant, unfettered access to the pussy of his dreams.

Mark kept turning as he talked to her, turning so he could keep Thalia visible out of the corner of one eye.

Thalia standing in the corner, face expressionless, eyes dark, arms folded across her flat chest, not looking at Mark and Mattie, *certainly* not looking at Wolf and Honoria, all nice and snuggly on their couch, just maybe with a faint hint of fresh *fuck* surrounding them like an aura.

No, Thalia Jansky was watching the remaining couple in the room, Stu and Cory standing over by the window, looking out at the magic vista, whispering to each other, heads pressed together.

I've never been without. Always moved from one woman to the next and then on to the next, at will. I wonder how that other life feels?

Guess maybe Mark would have some inkling.

Gaius came through the doorway, loops of what looked like electrical cable coiled around one shoulder, followed by another man, tall, muscular, balding, with a great big nose and an undershot jaw. They walked over to the conference table and the bald guy took a good look at the silent silver keg of the TrackTrixCom, sitting where Wolf had set it down.

He said, "Mph. Looks undamaged, as you say. Let's see if we can get it running, hm?" Speaking with a slight but noticeable French accent.

Not a French-Canadian accent, Wolf thought, though, since the last war, Quebecois are about all the Frenchmen in the . . . He felt a slight pang. Well, no. If there're times without number, there could very well be Frenchmen without number, on Earths without number, and . . . hell.

While Gaius fooled with his extension cord, sorting through an octopus of alternate termini, trying to find one that fit the TrackTrixCom's power socket, the bald guy turned to face them. "Good morning," he said, "I am Dr. Pompidou, and wish to welcome you to EarthHaven."

Across the room Stu stage-whispered, "Not Munchkinland?"

Thalia said, "Shh."

Mark shouted, "*Jesus!*"

Mattie's laughter was high and delighted.

The doorway beyond them was filled with something that looked like a cross between a blond gorilla and a fairy-tale ogre. Huge hands, blue eyes, a long, skinny, naked red penis dangling between its legs as it leaned low to negotiate the entry. "Pompidou," it said, voice a low rumble, "you people really ought to be more considerate about your building codes."

It spoke English better than the Neanderthalers had, but its mouth was full of big, yellow, sound-distorting teeth.

Honoria whispered, *"Sasquatch,"* making it a three-syllable word.

The thing grimaced at her. "Yes, ma'am. Some of your folk call us that. Others say Yeti, Jotun . . . variations on a theme, we're really all the same. *We* always called our homeland Sasquatchewan, not that it really matters."

Pompidou smiled and said, "This is my colleague, Dr. Klaang. His folk evolved from Gigantopithecus."

Stu: "I thought that was a kind of extinct gorilla, not a hominid."

"Maybe on your Earth it was."

Well, Wolf thought, I don't think I can imagine this getting any stranger. Honoria, he noticed, was squeezing his hand in a deathgrip.

Stu, holding Cory's hand now, said, "Cool."

The doorway filled again, this time with . . . Pompidou said, "This is Rann, from the, ah, political . . ."

Honoria said, "*Selkie.*"

The thing in the door looked like a beautiful woman, dressed head to toe in sleek, iridescent roan fur. Slanty green eyes. Foxy face. Furry tits with bare pink nipples. Down between her legs . . . The thing that wasn't quite a woman grimaced at Wolf, then lifted her hands and wriggled them rapidly, obvious sign language. Hell, maybe even Ameslan. Deaf people in the camps were using it again, since there were no more batteries left for the cochlear implants.

Pompidou seemed to redden, not quite grinning. "Yes indeed, ah . . . Miss Rann can't form human speech sounds, though she understands well enough. She suggests the men in the room try to look at her face, if possible."

Mark smirked from his corner, making a slight sniggering sound.

Goddamn cartoon characters, every one of us.

Stu said, "Don't you have machine translators?"

Pompidou pursed his lips. "Well, the knowledge exists, but the resources . . . our machine technology is severely limited, I'm afraid."

Honoria jumped and seemed to cower against his side.

In the doorway was a small, gray-skinned biped with big, slanting, featureless black eyes, nostrils without a nose, thin gash of a mouth, terribly familiar looking. Since it too was naked, Wolf stole a glance between its legs. There was something vaguely like the shape of a vulva there, more or less like a vulval outline, seen through tight pants.

The thing said, "You may call me Witless." It had a pleasant boy-girl voice, on the boundary between baritone and tenor. "Please, my friends. It's my favorite joke."

No reaction.

Witless said, "Well, you see, I'm really not witly at all."

Silence, Pompidou smiling.

It said, "Ah, me. I guess you had to be there."

The TrackTrixCom's voice suddenly filled the room: "Oh, thank you! What a relief! I was afraid, when I suspended, I might never wake up again."

Pompidou said, "Ah! Welcome! Do you know where you are?"

The TrackTrixCom sounded cautious: "I think so. Yes."

The Saucer Man stepped forward, rubbing its hands together. "Excellent! My friend, we have several thousand questions we'd like to ask!"

Wolf grunted and said, "Hell, you think *you've* got questions."

Standing in the shade, with her back against the scaly trunk of an unknown sort of tree, breathing its faint cinnamon scent, Thalia Jansky watched the picnickers and savored a sense of her own idiocy.

There. Sitting on a floral print blanket, picking over a bowl of chips and salsa, sucking on fine glass bottles of what seemed for all the world to be bona fide Coca-Cola, Mark and Mattie sat facing each other, sitting in tailor's seat, laughing and talking as if there were no one else in the world, as if they were still *in* the world.

As if all the years and all the loss had never happened.

As if *I* never happened.

Every now and again Mattie would reach out and touch Mark's pallid forearm with her hand, dark skin etched against light, like a shadow. Each time she did, Thalia felt a sharp pang, deep inside, of futile anger. My God, I'm jealous. Wolf and Honoria were, of course, nowhere to be seen.

A lump formed under her heart.

Stu and Cory *were* down by the lakeshore, standing ankle-deep in pale blue water; water, apparently, with some actual color to it, not just a reflection of the bright sky, their shoes heaped together on a little, white sand beach.

Closer than anyone else, yet almost unnoticed, on a plain blue blanket, Gaius and Pompidou, Rann and Dr. Klaang, sat clustered around the shiny keg of the TrackTrixCom, rigged now to some sort of solar power converter, like a big clunky version of the thing you used to be able to buy for portable appliances.

From a time before the war, that's what I'm remembering. Not my memory, just . . . my grandmother's attic, finding an antique laptop computer, manufactured around 2020, sitting in a box, covered with dust, next to a thing like a windowpane that would power the computer through sunlight.

Nowadays, all it takes is a little panel of photovoltaic stamps on the rim of the fliptop monitor to . . .

Talking, talking, filling each other in.

Look at that.

Rann the Selkie-Goddess sitting with her knees drawn up, legs apart, heels braced. Gaius and Pompidou ostentatiously not looking. Gigantic Dr. Klaang . . . Oh, God, what the hell is wrong with me? I should be over there with them, *listening*!

Up in the conference room Pompidou had been blunt: "Somewhere, the Topopolitans are real. If we can get to them, plead our case . . . well, you see, the Topopolis *must* continue to form, *must* continue to engulf the universe, but with luck, *if* we can find them, talk to them somehow, let them know we're *here,* we can get them to include us in their final plan."

Then, into the silence, Stuart had whispered, "You're talking about Tipler's Omega, aren't you?"

It was the TrackTrixCom that replied, "Maybe so."

Maybe so, the Topopolitans are engaged in the process of engulfing the universe, rebuilding it into the sort of universe in which physical immortality can be real.

And it was Honoria who'd said, "I have read that book, over and over again, trying to understand. What I have understood is that if they *do* succeed, then we, along with all creation, will be reborn to eternal life. We need do nothing."

Dr. Klaang's voice had been an incongruous rumble: "If they take us with them, then we need not die."

Pompidou: "And if we never die, then we need not be reborn."

Gaius laughed bitterly: "Do *you* want to take a chance on the perfectibility of the Topopolitan emulation?"

And so, they're building a fleet, all the people of Galaxios, all the people of several other floating continents, peopled by the descendants of a whole host of intergalactic flotsam, a universe of lost souls. We can find the Topopolitans, you see. We think we know the way.

It seemed odd that Wolf had been the one to ask, "Why us? What difference can *we* make?"

Because you've been abroad in the larger universe, the wild universe, abroad in the purlieus of the Topopolis. Because your TrackTrixCom will help us where we're going.

Gaius laughed again. "Simple enough," he'd said. "Experienced starcrew are a rare and precious commodity. People in the here and now live and die, just like anywhere else."

So off we go again, off into a wild blue wonderland.

Twelve

A couple more days and Cory was glad they were on the move again. Something to do. Something more than attending meetings, listening to incomprehensible explanations about the world, the flesh, and the devil, apparently incomprehensible even to educated adults.

Maybe my mother understands all this as well as anyone.

But if they had something to do, then they'd be distracted from . . . Every time Stu touches me, I want to throw myself on him and . . . Not a pretty picture. Not pretty at all. Too many associations from the camp, ugly, ugly . . . and yet . . .

As they rode in the little cabin, car hanging under the taut bag of the little blimp, engines thrumming irregularly from somewhere behind, Galaxian topography rolling by underneath, Stu was a warm presence beside her. Every now and again he'd rub the back of his hand against her bare thigh, contriving to push the hem of her skirt up a little more each time.

Will you *stop*? Will you please stop?

Where'd you learn this trick, young Stuart? Make it up all by yourself, or are you watching Wolf interact with my mother?

Mother, who wouldn't hesitate to do what Wolf wanted, whenever he wanted it.

You know what they say about women like that.

Professor Pompidou came staggering down the little aisle, big hands on the edges of seat backs, suddenly leaning across them, pointing out the little round porthole. *"There."*

She looked.

Stu stiffened beside her.

Below them the landscape came to an abrupt end, land curving out into long arms, enclosing an embayment full of blue. Not the blue of sea, of course, not the blue of water reflecting sky, but the pale, hazy blue of empty sky itself. Well, no. Not quite empty. Far away you could see little smudges and slits, faraway things not quite hidden by the intervening density of the air itself.

And, in the bay, connected by a wickerwork of what looked like long, thin, rickety ladders, row on row of shining silver dirigibles.

"The Fleet," Pompidou said, pride in his voice.

The Fleet.

The Fleet that would take them to find the Topopolitans?

Memory of meeting after meeting, of Atlanteans and others running on and on about this and that, "bringing you up to speed," is how one of the Moderns put it. Why us? Qualified spacecrew. Rare as hell, you see. And recently abroad in the Topopolitan periphery. Contact with PacketWights. The TrackTrixCom and its net, you see . . .

The dirigible began sloping down toward some kind of landing stage.

For just as second, watching the ground rise up, Cory remembered watching an old film, watching the *Hindenburg* explode, burn, crash, while some Anglo blubbered about the

Humanity . . . remembered for a moment, then Stu touched her thigh again, making her forget.

Give me strength to resist? I feel like I've become a virgin again, just by saying no to him. Why is that?

They landed, bumping on the ground, men rushing up to seize the lanyards, and Cory thought, What're those things over there? They look like floating squids or something.

Lying between crisp, warm sheets, sleeping Mattie's arm thrown over his chest, Mark opened his eyes on the simple furnishings of the dirigible-yard hotel room, the perpetually slanting rays of light coming through the flimsy curtains on the window and leaving a swirling pattern on the walls and floor. He could smell her perfume, a delicate, flowery scent.

In the mirror on the wall opposite, she looked like a sleeping child, dark head tucked down into her pillow, one small black foot peeping out at the foot of the bed. And him, head propped up, ungainly face expressionlessly watching itself, eyes smugly meeting his.

This is more like it, he thought. I could get used to this, even with Fantasyland just outside the door. He'd fucked her just as in days of old, this other Mattie responding to him just as his own Mattie had. Better than with Thalia too. Thalia'd never really tried to figure out what made him feel good; she kept repeating over and over those things that were supposed to make a man feel good, not empathizing with him in the least. Hell, she does the same thing with the cats.

Mattie stirred slightly, pulled back her arm, turned over.

He turned onto his side, pulled himself up against her hot back, drew his legs up slightly until they were nestled against hers. The sensation of her buttocks cradling his groin made him stiffen a little. Her coarse, black hair was in his face, and the smell of it was different, more personal, slightly soapy.

He'd been able to piece together this Mattie's story, knew for certain that in her version of the world, he hadn't been forced to screw her over. In fact, it appeared that the primary difference between her world and his was that in her world, he'd been a much nicer guy, and figured out a way to preserve both their reputations. Instead of splitting up, they'd moved in together, and had been making preparations for their wedding when she'd disappeared.

And she loved her long lost Mark Porringer, the man that I could've been but wasn't.

She's determined to go on with them, deeper into the Topopolis, following these crazies on a quest for . . . what? eternal life? God? What did they call it, the all-present omniscience? Another one of these bold starship captains with a mission. Will I go? Or will I show up at the Atlantean employment commission's offices bright and early on Monday morning?

I should try harder to be the other Mark, try to see the world through his eyes. Or hers. Who knows, there might actually turn out to be a point to all this madness.

Totally unconcerned that he would be rebuffed, he cupped his hand over her breast, feeling the heft of it. She shifted, made a questioning noise. "It's morning, Mat. Or at least what passes for morning hereabouts. How about a return engagement?" Silly sounding, but he imagined that a nice version of himself would talk that way.

Mattie turned onto her back, looked up at him from delighted charcoal eyes, caressed his cheek. "Mmm-hmmm," she said. "Mark, I thought I'd never—Come here, hon."

He kissed her, feeling a pang of erotic awareness that he hadn't felt since he was a teenager. So much for old Thalia, he thought. I can be the man Mattie thinks I am, unless . . .

Unless she finds out.

Standing at the edge of the wharf, on the "waterfront," hanging ten over infinite blue space, Wolf found he could still think of it that way, despite the evidence of his eyes.

Two, three layers of suspended airships, yes, bobbing slowly up and down, wave of motion undulating sequentially through the plane, but then . . .

God almighty. Remember that first EVA? They train you in low Earth-orbit so they can judge the relationship between your imagination and your courage. Not afraid 'cause you don't see the Earth as *down,* a one-hundred-mile fall to splat-on-the-rocks, fiery wind whistling up your asshole all the way down? No-brain washout. Scared shitless because you *do*? No-balls washout.

Close by his ear, Gaius's voice whispered, "Impressive, hm?"

Wolf turned and looked at the man, saw a familiar glint in his eye, and thought, *Kindred spirit? Maybe so.* Maybe the fuck so. He said, "What happens if I fall . . . overboard?"

Gaius smiled and shrugged. "I call the coastguard, they drop a skydiver after you. He catches up in twenty minutes or so and the two of you float around on his cargo chute. In a couple of hours you're picked up by a blimp and brought back here. There's a monetary fine for that kind of fuck-up. Like a traffic ticket."

From behind them Mark said, "And what happens if no one sees you fall?"

The man looked at him, seemed disapproving.

Scary thought, hm, buddy-boy? Everything's scary to y'all, id'n it? Even with this Little Black Mattie standing by your side, holding onto your little ol' dick.

Gaius said, "I guess you'd die of thirst in a few days. 'Course, if you hit something at terminal velocity for a falling body, you'd get killed straight off. Birds and flying bugs'd take care of your carcass, bones'd turn to dust in a few centuries if they didn't land on something. Dust'd blow around on the wind for fuck-all ever."

Stu: "How far's the bottom?"

"Good way of putting it, boy. Each thread's just under a

parsec in diameter. We think we're about seventy thousand AUs above sea level here."

Seventy thousand AUs. Well, shit. Wolf said, "What the hell makes the gravity here? And what makes Galaxios float? Magic?"

Another shrug. "Actually, we think the gravity comes from the air itself. The gradient is very low—from what we've been able to figure out, which isn't a whole hell of a lot. We've calculated it runs from zero gee at the hub up to around one-point-five at the hull."

Stu said, "Wait a minute. If the air's causing the gravity, wouldn't the highest gee be at the midpoint, in a zone of high pressure air?"

Mark, sounding dubious: "No, I don't think that's right. Did you say the hull was spinning around the thread's long axis? I mean—"

Gaius burst out laughing. "Atlanteans have been publishing learned journal articles about all this shit for thousands of years. Truth is, we don't know much of anything. Our explorers have been a few AUs in every direction, everything else is rumor from people we've met along the way. Rumor, and outside observation from newcomers."

"And the continent?"

Another shrug. "Overall density of the bryophytic mass is approximately equal to that of air at local average pressure. Meaning we fucking float. Drift along in the zonal winds."

Wolf heard a strangled sound from Thalia, spun in her direction.

Gaius said, " 'Bout time you fuckin' squidlies showed up."

Squidlies? No, not like squids at all.

Floating toward them along the edge of the wharf was a vic of white creatures, around a meter long each, plump-bodied, shaped almost like blimps themselves, cluster of fat tentacles on the nose, big, wrinkled-looking eyes like old-fashioned purses with a bright liquid glint inside, giving you a sense of . . . expression. Life. Intelligence. There was a rippling wing down the horizontal centerline of each body.

"Cuttlefish," Cory whispered. "Flying cuttlefish."

You could hear the magic in her voice, the sudden joy, making Wolf want to take her and . . . Something about women's happiness, he thought. Something that draws me in.

A soft voice, speaking out of the air, said, "How do you do, ladies and gentlemen? Gaius. Rann. Professor Pompidou. Good to see you again."

Wolf looked at Gaius, who said, "Mental telepathy, I'm afraid. Scared the shit out of me at first."

"Now, now," the voice said. "We never did figure out if it was what you call telepathy." As the voice spoke, belonging, presumably, to one of the creatures, the three of them began changing colors rapidly, odd, swirling patterns, coruscations, but only on parts visible to each other. Wolf tried to figure out which cuttlefish could see which pattern on which surface.

The voice said, "Yes, it is complex. Especially since we don't actually know what's going on either. Your viewpoint is so different. Utterly alien."

"Which one of you is . . . speaking?" Thalia asked.

"We don't know," the voice said.

"Group consciousness!" Stu whispered, voice ragged with excitement.

"You're not individuals?"

"We most certainly are. And not telepathic with each other—we communicate by chromophoric articulation."

"The color patterns," Gaius said.

Wolf felt a pulse of irritation at the man having assumed his ignorance. "Then who's doing the talking?"

Silence. Then, "No one. Our scientists have theorized that cuttlefish chromophoric communication has created a sentient noosphere which is able to interact with and manipulate the nonsentient, chemically induced bioelectric and phono-mechanical noospheric components connecting individual humans."

Honoria said, "You alter our auras to make us think we hear you?"

The voice said, "Apparently. And yet we ourselves are not conscious of the speaking."

Honoria: "Then your group soul speaks to our individual souls and—" She broke off abruptly.

Wolf smiled to himself. Polite Honoria, sensitive to the feelings even of a . . . creature. And he knew enough about her theology, from his own polite listening, to know that what she'd not said was, *that makes you animals.* Like as not, they understand that anyway, given how this seems to work.

Gaius said, "The cuttlefish were here when the Atlanteans first arrived, had been here for ages, immortal and—"

The voice said, "Not immortal, my friend. We lose individuals to accident and despair. One by one by one. There are only a few thousand of us left now, where once there were hundreds of millions. One day there will be none."

Professor Pompidou said, "The cuttlefish have been building this fleet with the intention of flying to the nearest Waste Mass Dynamo and diving in. Suicide."

From the meeting, Wolf remembered discussion of this dynamo, a couple hundred thousand miles away, apparently the nearest access to the Topopolitan life support system.

"Suicide, that is," Gaius said, "until you folks showed up with a working, fully programmed TrackTrixCom."

"Yes," the voice of the cuttlefish said. "Maybe the odds have shifted slightly in our favor at last."

Gaius whispered in his ear, "Apparently they can't easily breed away from their homeworld and the total mass of the cuttlefish population."

"True," the voice said. "If we can find the Topopolitans, maybe they can help us find our way home. If we have a home, somewhere, somewhen, somehow." Mournful despair in that voice now. Hoping against hope.

The TrackTrixCom, just as disembodied as the cuttlefish group soul, said, "There could be a way."

Bachelor Officers' Quarters. An uncomfortable dinner, despite all the unique and uncomfortable company, despite all the new and fascinating things to talk about, think about, do. Uncomfortable, Wolf thought, because, despite all that, we're still us.

Stu sitting attentively beside Cory, sitting too close, looking as though he wanted to help her *eat,* for Christ's sake . . . girl half irritated, half embarrassed, half afraid, half . . . wanting. She's closed up shop on him, wondering why the hell she did what she did and . . . hell. *You* know *why,* old boy. Seen it yourself a hundred times. Back when we were out on the bare-assed branch, all the rules were in abeyance. Now?

Houses and trees and people and clothes to cover your precious little crotch. Now you have to think about what it *means,* not just how it feels. Did it feel good, little girl? Or don't you remember anymore?

Christ. I remember how she looked, back on the rubber sheet, under a skyful of magic galaxy. Maybe I shouldn't've said no. I'd've enjoyed just the one shot, one unique little snapshot out of so many hundreds, good, bad, indifferent, supreme. And not been struck mooncalf dumb if it'd been taken away for no good reason.

Honoria was looking at him, smiling. Because I'm smiling. Because she doesn't know why. Maybe she'd understand if she did know. Maybe she's the one person here who *does.*

Mark, sitting close by Mattie, as if he wanted to help *her* eat. Like father like son? Well, no. How much can you pick up from a short-duration stepfather? Just boys-will-be-boys is all. Mark sitting there with his shining face obscenely bloated. Glancing every now and again at Thalia, trying not to smirk. Got *my* pussy, you see. Better than *yours,* castrating bitch . . . Why'n hell don't you just stand on the table and pound your fucking chest, silly bastard?

And, every now and again, Thalia would look up, look at me, look at Honoria, look at her son, look back down at her plate. Never at sweet little Marky.

He'd sighed, taken a bite of a juicy, game-flavored hamburger, turned to Pompidou and wondered aloud how terrestrial animals had come to be here. Atlantean starships carry your average pet aurochs, instead of Siamese cats and a big, black Lab?

The Frenchman had laughed, not quite choking on his bouillabaisse. Earth-colonizing Saucer People brought most of our breeding stock. That's what the history books say.

Later, they went for a walk under the moons of Mars, just the two of them, Wolf and Honoria, down by the waterfront as the sky grew dim with an improbable dusk, star-beacon turning orange, streaking with vermilion, with stark, dark red, turning the windows of nearby buildings scarlet in all directions.

Like a park, like a magic park, like nothing I ever saw before, but very much like things I imagined over and over again. At some point, as they walked along, human voices fading with distance as they got deeper into the manicured nonwilderness, Honoria took him by the hand.

Why do you want to hold my hand, Honoria Suárez? Why do you want to act like you love me?

No answer given, none expected.

We don't really *know* why we do these things, now do we?

Lots of pretend answers. Storybook fables about love. Textbook fables about sociobiology, about reproductive strategies giving rise to social evolution.

In the end, she turns her face toward me, tilts her head back for a kiss, looks me in the eye and asks her silent question. *Do* I? How will I ever know, Honoria mine? How will *you* ever know.

Neither of us ever will.

So I kiss her and tell my familiar lies.

She knows they're lies, but, expecting them, accepts them nonetheless. How else will we all get along?

I put my arms around her then, feel her breasts pressing into me then, feel the tilt of her pelvis as she brings her abdomen into contact, feel the soft rub of her mons against me, under not too many layers of cloth.

I've been a bastard, cheating, mistreating, just the way they say. Am I being a bastard now? Maybe so. Why then would she pretend to love me?

I sit her down on a bench of fine, smooth pimalia wood—or is it sorapus? Certainly not skeel—kneel between her soft, smooth, eternally fit thighs, push up her skirt . . . no underpants, nothing but fine black pussyhair and sleek brown skin, nothing but the execution of her own well-laid plans, no responsibility of mine.

Isn't that the way it always goes?

I lean in, touch her gently, listen to her sigh a girlish sigh, different, unique, yet always exactly the same, from woman to woman to woman.

You are special.

You *are* special.

Honest to God you are.

That makes her hands come out and hold the back of my head. At some point we're on the ground, and I make a girlish gasp of my own, just so's she'll know how much I like it, which makes her arms hold me tight, her breath whisper in my ear.

She tilts her hips back while I thrust and grind and thrust some more, breath coming in gasps, puffing against the side of my head, blowing in my hair, and, as always, she snorts away her own orgasm, maybe thirty seconds before mine, giving me that wonderful thirty seconds of plunging away in the hot and wet of her, just me, no more responsibility, just me, then just my dick, then just my universe of sensation.

Lying on his back beside her, Wolf said, "I guess I just didn't understand what you meant to me, Honoria. I'm sorry as hell for—"

She put her hand on his thigh, gentling him, and said, "What will happen to Thalia now?"

Stark realization that it didn't fucking matter. Tomorrow, we board the dirigible fleet and go on our way to the Waste-Mass Dynamo. We've got to go, you see, because . . . because the rest of this . . .

Well. Lots of nighttime left.

Though morning will come, sure as the grave.

Thirteen

Seventh day out.

Mark carried the tray full of unknown delicacies back to the little booth by the snack bar entrance. The other tables were filled with arguing people of all sorts, half of them wildly gesticulating to drive home their points. As they approached the great mystery at the waste-mass dynamo, everyone was growing more animated, debating their particular view of what was about to happen and what it all would mean. Dr. Pompidou and Rann were questioning the Track-TrixCom at the far end of the room, and a crowd had gathered around. Mark felt some annoyance that they'd appropriated their device without so much as asking, but he supposed it wasn't important.

Mattie smiled up at him as he set the tray on the dark, inlaid table and slid into the little booth. "They're not serving dinner yet," he said, "but it's not too late for their version of afternoon tea. They have a hot table loaded with these things, blinis I'd guess you'd call them."

She took one, bit it delicately between gleaming teeth. "This reminds me a bit of a luxury cruise I went on once, graduation present to myself. I just wish we could get a little more privacy."

Mark smiled, remembering their attempted coupling the night before, the two of them crammed in the little bunk, barely able to position themselves, acutely conscious of little noises, other people's little noises, from beyond the thin partition.

Thalia was suddenly standing there, haggard-looking, wisps of hair out of place. God, she's really showing her age.

"Mark," Thalia said, face almost expressionless, "I want to talk to you. Now. Alone."

Here? He looked around at the small, crowded, noisy room. For Christ's sake. Maybe if I . . . "Anything you have to tell me, you can say in front of Mattie."

"Oh, is that so?" Little glimmer of maliciousness there, and Mark was suddenly afraid. He looked at her face, barely avoiding meeting her dead-on gaze. But the expression he had seen many times changed to one unfamiliar to him. Softly, she said, "Time is growing short. Do you mind. Please?"

Slowly he understood what was about to happen, and the burn of anger and humiliation that had been with him for weeks subsided a little. Time for the worm to turn, eh, bitch? For a long moment the idea of his having the two of them seemed awfully appealing. There was no way to tell how much Thalia remembered about the events surrounding Mattie's demotion. As much as he loved to see her squirm, he'd have to cut this scene short. Voice level, he said, "Well, yes, actually, Thalia. We do mind."

"Uh, too bad." She grabbed a stool from a nearby table and sat down, turning a hard stare on Mattie, whose smile was still in place but seemed to be wilting. "You know Mark is my husband," she said, matter-of-fact. "We're still married."

Mattie nodded. "Yes, Mark's told me everything. Considering the circumstances, I'm afraid I don't think that—"

"Thalia," Mark said, "what are you trying to do? You fucked me over with Wolf when I really needed you. You wouldn't fucking give me the time of day."

Thalia looked back and forth between the two of them. "Mark, I don't expect you to forgive me. I just want you to know I've been doing a lot of thinking lately. I've made mistakes, a lot of them, and—"

"I've heard everything now," Mattie said. "This is unbelievable. Lady, you're really something. Can it be that you're jealous someone's picked up your leavings?"

Thalia said, "I know I must seem ridiculous to the two of you. I have a feeling that we really are getting close to something . . . something important. Just listen to the conversations all around us. Mark, if we could just talk, sometime, alone, before we get to where we're going. Is that a possibility?"

Mark suddenly realized he was enjoying this immensely. The shoe was on the other foot, big-time. At one and the same moment he felt pity for his wife and was flattered by her attentions. But why was she humbling herself in front of him this way? He exchanged a look with Mattie, tried to keep the smugness out of his voice. "Thalia, I don't know why you're doing this, except maybe as some kind of penance. You know as well as I do that it's over, has been since back at the beach at Sagdeev. You made your choice then. If Wolf doesn't want you, so be it. We have to live with our choices, my dear. You have to live with yours."

"But . . ." Thalia's head sank into her hands, and she let out a little moan. "This place, these things. I can't go on without *somebody.* I really have to . . ." She suddenly looked up, eyes wet. "You knew me once upon a time, Mark. I'm not . . . responsible for the changes. I only did what seemed right. No one can blame me if it's come out so wrong."

Mattie said, "Calm down, Thalia. You look awfully tired; get some rest. Things'll seem better if you're rested."

Mark said, "Listen to her, Thal. I'm sorry things worked out the way they did between us, but it's all water under the bridge now."

Thalia looked straight into Mattie's eyes. "Mattie, one thing you should know. Mark isn't what he seems. Everything's just skin deep with him, an act. If I've learned anything, it's that everything he says is a lie. Everything. Look at him now. He's doing his best to conceal it, but you can see the little shit-eating grin under the surface."

Mattie said, "But then, why . . . ?

Thalia shook her head listlessly, muttered, "I wish I knew," under her breath, and then stood and marched out of the room, bumping between the tables as she went, gesture marred by the slow, steady back-and-forth tipping of the floor.

Mark did his best not to crow.

The travel time was measured in weeks of confinement, irritation, arguments, but at last they arrived. Five hundred miles every hour, droning on and on. Twenty days takes you as far as the moon, if there were a moon here. What's that, five years or so to Mars at its closest? If there were a Red Planet hanging somewhere in the sky.

Fortunately, the Waste Mass Dynamo was only a month out from Galaxios.

So close, if it wasn't for the 400,000 miles of pale blue air, it'd hang in the sky like a Catherine wheel. It'd been visible, like a galaxy of dark blue flame, for the past three days. Three days in which they finished off whatever'd been begun in the weeks that went before.

Wolf stood in the forward cockpit, between Pompidou and

red little Rann. Haven't given much thought to that one. Wonder what that'd be like?

Stop it.

Asshole.

Look!

For Christ's sake.

Most of the others were here. Cory and Stu. Mark and Mat. Thalia . . . Cuttlefish floating overhead, looking more or less over his shoulder, TrackTrixCom secured to the floor by his feet, trailing a power cable, hooked into the dirigible's fuel cell system.

The thing in the sky, hundreds of miles across, was visibly moving, round and round and round, fire in a thousand shades of blue, swirling in on itself, like colored water disappearing down an invisible drain, a hard violet dot right at the center.

Pompidou said, "On a clear night you can see the central light from some parts of Galaxios. Shimmers like hell."

Wolf looked back at the girl and found himself admiring the clean lines of her figure. Girl. Just a girl. Another couple of years and all that promise will have bloomed. Would I have resisted her then? *Could* I have? Isn't that the way it always goes? Me, lying on my back, looking up at—

Honoria suddenly wedged herself in at his side, taking him firmly by the hand.

The TrackTrixCom said, "Very little knowledge of the deep Topopolis has filtered out of the threads, since no one in historical memory has come back."

Gaius: "And we who've fallen in are stuck in a sea of air."

"What little we know has been handed down through galactic generations of vermin, one species giving way to another."

Stu, querulous: "So what *is* it?"

TrackTrixCom: "It appears to be in some ways similar to the objects found at the hearts of spiral galaxies, sometimes suspected to be prefatory artifacts of the Topopolis. They all may simply be entryways to a hyperspatial structure connecting and synchronizing the various parts of the Topopolis, in this instance, part of the manifold that absorbs and redistributes matter and energy throughout the complete system."

Pompidou said, "Hence the term Waste Mass Dynamo."

The TrackTrixCom said, "Yes. The galactic core entities appear to be part of an energy recovery system as well. No one has ever been sure about these smaller entities."

Long silence, then Wolf said, "So if we drive into this damned thing, how do we know we won't be turned to energy and . . . recovered?"

Glassy, gassy silence, bespeaking everyone's fears.

Gaius: "Well, we always told the cuttlefish it'd be suicide. No one *really* knows how to navigate a hyperspace manifold."

Stu said, "Isn't that what we do when we fly faster than light?"

Pompidou: "No. We only thought it was. With primitive human drives, the manifold navigates us."

Gaius laughed. "Which act may have been a form of suicide as well. Talk about your brave men dying a thousand times!"

Wolf felt a slight chill. "So we just go down the rabbit hole? What then?"

Pompidou: "If we live, if we find our way with the help of your little TrackTrixCom friend, maybe we find the Topopolitans themselves at last. Maybe we get to state our case in a court of last appeal."

"Well," the voice of the cuttlefish said, "no time like the present. You ready?"

Wolf felt the pang reform in his guts. *Ready?* For what? I'm afraid to know.

The TrackTrixCom said, "Quite. My systems seem properly connected to your navigation computer, other ships of the fleet now slaved to my command . . ."

The engines began to throb, ship accelerating, and Wolf felt Honoria's hand clutch his more tightly still. Watching the dynamo swell before them in the empty sky, he wondered about Cory's hand, about Mattie's.

Thalia, he thought, will have to tough it out alone.

As the wheel of blue fire grew to cover the sky, as the violet center grew until it looked like a world seen from space, a world or perhaps a small sun, Honoria felt the palm of Wolf's hand grow moist in hers and knew he was afraid. When she looked up at his face, there was nothing, eyes alert and bright, watching with interest as what he probably thought of as death and oblivion rushed toward them.

He looked down at her, smiled slightly, squeezed her hand and mouthed, "Sorry."

He knows that I know and doesn't mind. Most men would mind.

Wolf squeezed her hand, let it go, put his arm around her shoulder and drew her close.

The TrackTrixCom said, "All right. We'll now steer toward the core's equator, flying in the direction of rotation."

She felt the deck surge under their feet, but the symmetrical shapes in the sky gave no indication of any bank or turn.

The cuttlefish soul said, "Suddenly I feel doubt. Did we really want to die after all?"

Wolf: "Too late now, little buddy." Forced jollity in his tone, the brave man facing his fate.

Honoria looked up and saw Thalia watching them, naked, pathetic jealousy in her face. She thought, I won him back. Won him back from her, better than he was before. At least I've got that, no matter what happens next.

God won't let me down.

God's not a man.

The sky outside flashed violet.

Stark shadows of the people around her, black against impossible light.

The light inside grew hazy, becoming incandescent.

Do we die now?

Somebody screamed, a woman, high and shrill, full of utter, inconsolable fear.

Not me. I didn't scream.

I know what comes next.

I've got faith.

I . . .

Her skin seemed to grow hot, reducing the world to a tinge of pain. Pain and the tight grip of Wolf O'Malley's hand.

A pang of doubt.

Am I burning?

Burning in the Fire?

She thought she heard a voice, Wolf's voice, sincere and humble: "I love you, Honoria. I'm sorry about everything."

I believe you.

Isn't that the way it's supposed to go?

The world flashed black, then white, then the dirigible's interior returned.

She felt her feet come off the floor, felt herself and Wolf come adrift in the air.

Stu cried, "Zero *gee?!*"

Wolf's voice, hard and astonished: "*Look!*"

Honoria looked out the window, felt her heart pulse in her chest, letting her know she was still alive. Alive and seeing.

Seeing.

Crystalline spheres filling up the sky, intersecting, interlocking in impossible ways, glinting in the light of . . . of . . . The wheel of blue fire, converted somehow to ring on ring on ring of surging white wings.

Choirs of bright angels orbiting round and round and

round, spiraling inward to a center of unseeable, unknowable light.

Listen. Listen to them *sing.*

It was *true.* It was true all along.

Did you ever doubt it?

Of course you did.

No one ever truly *believes,* you see, but we're so afraid, so terribly afraid, children lost in night, night in which no mother ever comes. . . .

She looked into the Central Light and felt herself go blind.

Felt her eyes melt and trickle away down her cheeks like two huge tears.

You've seen Him.

No need to see anything else, ever again.

Listen to them sing.

Listen.

Thalia's voice, a harsh, broken whisper, said, "I don't believe it."

In her glorious blindness, Honoria felt pity at last.

Then shame.

Scream.

Scream at the light.

Not me screaming, thought Thalia Jansky. Impossible for it to be me. The brave never scream. Men never scream. Some women braver than men . . . me. But . . .

The wheel of blue fire outlined against the empty sky became a wheel of pure, radiant energy, energy that invaded her, like the fumbling fingers of an angry lover.

Flash.

Flash.

She heard a man professing his love.

Not any particular man.

Just a man.

The wheel became a fiery coal, flooding the zeppelin's

interior with stark crimson light, scarlet light, maroon light, duller and duller, hotter and hotter, covering all their faces with a patina of blood. Look around you. Stu and Cory . . . holding hands? Mark and Mattic, just the same. Wolf with his protective, oh-so-manly goddamned arm around Honoria's sleek, round shoulders, the two of them turned resolutely toward the light, faces filled with wonder.

Honoria's full of joy, no fear at all and—

The dirigible exploded like a popping balloon, reduced to pink tatters, then gone, and Thalia felt herself fall.

Scream.

That's it.

Scream.

Fay Wray in the hands of King Kong.

The audience will love it.

Falling through the brassy red sky, Thalia felt a deep calm steal over her, calm in the face of certain death. Is that what's coming? Of course it is. You knew it all along. All the others tumbling away, tumbling this way and that. All her friends and family falling away from her now, separate entities, falling alone, just like her, except . . . yes, that bastard O'Malley has kept hold of her hand.

Beyond them, Rann and Pompidou, Gaius and naked, furry Dr. Klaang, Omou, Witless the Saucer Man. And hundreds, thousands of others, the crews of all the dirigibles, which . . . makes it real.

Oh, God. This is it, isn't it?

Falling, faster and faster, toward a globe of crimson fire.

In just a minute, I'll be dead.

Which solves . . . just about everything.

She felt mirth boil up, roiling the calm, letting out the fear.

Christ, what if they're right? What if it's the Omega Point, and I live again, not *me,* the eternal me born from nothingness, but some computer simulacrum who thinks it's me and doesn't know how to tell the difference.

What's the word for *that?* Hell? At least it won't be *me* who suffers on and on. . . .

She thought about the last time she'd had sex with Wolf.

Sex?

No. Sex was what I had with Mark. With sweet little Wolfie, what I did was fuck.

Why did that make me happy?

Sharp memory of seeing Mark cry.

I made him cry more than once, didn't I?

Sharp anger.

What the fuck is *this?* Do I have to see my god damned *life* flashing before my eyes now? Is that how it ends?

Pang of unease.

Was my life so foul, I don't want to see it again?

Maybe so.

Not far away, the TrackTrixCom was tumbling end over end as it fell, a fat, featureless silver cylinder, like a pony keg at a fratboy party, empty, being used as a football. I remember. Christ, that stupid fat guy, the smelly one with all the long hair, caught it with his face, breaking his teeth, blood all the fuck over the place, him laughing, too fucking drunk to know he was hurt.

Christ.

I don't want to remember this shit!

Beyond the TrackTrixCom was a cuttlefish, falling all by itself, mantle rippling, keeping it stable, falling head down, eyes first toward the fire. Brave. Brave fucking God damn cuttlefish.

Hey, Mr. Squid! How's your fucking telepathy *now?*

The voice of the group soul said, "Not bad, Ms. Jansky."

Strange, she thought, how the flickering shadows on the cuttlefish were green, rather than red. Chromatophoric . . .

"Not so, Ms. Jansky. This individual is white with terror. The shadows are real."

Then why . . .

The voice sounded very strange when it said, "Because the Jewel of Eternity is green. Green the color of life. The color of love. The color of the Soul of All Souls."

What?

The TrackTrixCom said, "Good fire and bad. Rings of bright angels and crystalline spheres. Green jewels and eternal souls . . . *I* see the Great Counter counting me down."

What?

She looked. It was still a dull red fire, tongues of flame reaching out for her now. *Hurt.* Is it going to hurt? No answer. When she looked away from the fire, the TrackTrixCom and the cuttlefish were gone. Along with everyone else. She felt the fear pulse harder.

I didn't want to . . . face this alone.

Bitter anger.

Goddamn you, Wolf, why did you have to . . .

Mark's face, crying bitter tears as she stormed out of the house.

Stu's face, stiff with anger. We were all right alone, Mom, just you and me. Why couldn't you honor Dad's memory? She thought of him tied by the dick to Cory's bewitching little ass. Well, now you *know* why, don't you? You little shit.

Wolf's face, grinning, but with that odd look he got when filled with sexual desire, standing at the foot of some bed or another, ogling her open cunt, fixated on the space between her spread legs.

That's all I was to him? Why did it excite me so?

The fire grew close.

She screamed, I'm not ready yet!

The fire engulfed her, and that was all.

Fourteen

Wolf awoke, lying warm and snug in clean, soft sheets. There was a pillow under his head, dented in, shaped to the side of his face, warm from hours of sleep. White ceiling overhead, with some sort of textured finish, thousands of tiny little peaks, throwing tiny gray shadows, light streaming in from a set of broad glass doors, filtered by gauzy white curtains.

Outside, you can see the shadow of a balcony rail, the shadows of tall buildings beyond. I'm back in Galaxios. My God, it was all just a dream. . . .

Beside him, the covers were rumpled, where someone else, now departed, had been. When he put out his hand, the bed there was still warm. And at just about the place where you'd expect, it was damp, a spot just a little smaller than the palm of his hand. And if I bring my fingers to my nose, what will I smell. Honoria? Thalia?

How much of what I know will turn out to have been a dream? What'll I see, if I step through the curtains, step out onto the balcony? Galaxios? Or will that be Chicago out there? From another room, not far away, came the rush-hiss of a shower starting up. So. Who did I know in Chicago? And why do I think it's Chicago?

Light's not right for L.A. Perfect for Chicago. Can't be Honoria, then. Never was in Chicago with Thalia. What the hell was her name? Moira Stevenson? Something like that. And how did *she* smell? Can't remember. Too long ago, too many others in between.

I remember we had a pretty good time, though. Hell. That's what I *always* remember. He pulled the covers back and sat up, looking down at himself. Well. Don't fucking look any younger. Chicago was eight years ago. He fiddled with his dick, scratching, feeling dried bits of this and that, and thought, Well, looks like I'm having a good time now.

He put his feet over the side of the bed, stood up on a warm, carpeted floor. There was a slight sense of the air currents on his back, not too cold or anything. Just right. The sign of a damned fine air-conditioning system. Not too many of them left in postnuke America. Hell. What if *that* was a dream? Then I'm . . . somebody else.

And then? Then, buddy boy, you march right on down to the fucking nuthouse and turn your ass in.

Slightly unnerved, shower hissing and splashing in the background, he walked across the room and pulled the curtains open, listening to the very slight rumble of high-quality travois rods. Sunshine outside. A brilliant blue sky. Tall buildings surrounded by some kind of mist. No sign of landscape.

Where the hell is it misty in the morning? Chicago's mist is more like heavy ground fog. Dayton? Am I in fucking Dayton, Ohio? When he slid the door open, it was almost too smooth, making a sound that was somehow oily. He stepped outside, naked and barefoot, and it was warm, warm underfoot, warm on his back.

Perfect weather.

He looked up, looking for the sun.

There it is, a white hole into eternity.

Odd.

How come I can look right at it?

He looked away quickly, expecting to blink away the yellow phantasms of incipient retinal burn. Nothing. He went to the railing and looked over at the cityscape below. These buildings are funny-looking. Like . . . something off the cover of a cheap old book. Less angular than American architecture . . . Russian? Shit. Ain't no Russian architecture left. Blown to bits before I was born.

What the hell are those, roadways running between the buildings? Tiny dots on them, moving slowly. Not cars. Pedestrians, then. Aerial walkways. In the distance he could see a monorail moving along. Not your *real* sort of monorail, train riding on a thick beam. More the amusement park sort, hanging under a single railroad rail that was . . . What *is* supporting that goddamn thing?

Nothing I can see.

Beyond, more buildings, rising out of the lovely mist, mist stained, somehow, with pink and purple light. More walkways, trams, monorails, little things flying about, not bugs or birds. Glint of glass and metal.

Flying cars.

Soft rumble overhead. When he looked up, there was an airliner drifting along, contrail stretching out behind it.

He looked back at the cityscape again and failed to find the slightest familiar sight. Okay. If my life was a dream, and this is not, then I've got fucking amnesia. Great. He turned away from the city, intending to find out who was in the shower and . . .

Over on the next balcony, an immensely obese man sat at a picnic table. Long brown hair, tied into a thick ponytail, cascaded down his back, long beard hanging off his face, and the breastlike mounds of his chest were shiny with grease. In front of him, plates were heaped high with breakfast food. Sausage piled on eggs, French toast stacked here and there, wherever it would fit, dripping with syrup and melted butter, strips of hard-cooked bacon going over the sides of the plates like Roman warship *corvi*.

The man was eating steadily, eyes half shut, face full of orgasmic bliss. Eating and eating and eating and . . . Christ. In just a minute or so, he'll have eaten enough, if it was me, it'd make me puke.

The eating went on.

And on some more.

Wolf stepped up to the balcony rail. "Hey, buddy?"

The man paused with a fistful of scrambled eggs halfway to his mouth, turned and looked at Wolf. Nodded pleasantly, chewed slowly, swallowed hard and smiled, greasy lips parting to show eggy teeth. "Hello, neighbor!" He shook his fistful of eggs at Wolf. "Nice day!"

Wolf nodded, feeling slightly odd. "Um. Yes indeed. Uh . . ."

"What can I do for you, pal?"

"I, uh, seem to be lost." He gestured over the rail. "Could you, uh, tell me what city this is?"

The man did a classic double-take. Brayed laughter, spraying bits of egg. "*Shit!* That there's the City of God."

Wolf gaped at him.

"You're in fucking *Heaven,* pal! Don't you see the streets of gold?"

Wolf looked back at the cityscape, peering at the nearest aerial walkway. Kind of yellow-brown metallic. Maybe . . . He stepped back to the rail and leaned over, looking straight down. The sides of the buildings stretched away, fluted and straight alike, dwindling with perspective until they merged.

Now, how *high* would a building have to be before . . .

When he straightened up and looked back at the man,

he'd turned away and was eating again, shoveling food into his mouth just as fast as he could swallow it. If you listened carefully, you could hear the swift liquid sound of his chewing.

Heaven.

Wolf turned and went back into the room. The sound of the shower was going on and on, still splashing, the obvious sound of a shower with someone inside. With an empty shower, you got just a steady hiss. Okay. No time like the present. He crossed the room in a few quick strides, opened the bathroom door and went in.

Steamy. Humid. Mirror completely clouded over. Stall shower with frosted glass. Inside, a human shape. An obviously female human shape, with a lot of long dark hair on one end, another dark splotch more or less in the middle.

Wolf hesitated, feeling like a character in a movie. Should I be holding a knife? No, wait. Then we'd have to have shower curtains instead of glass.

He reached out and slid open the stall door and it was Honoria after all, slick and shining with soap, holding her breasts and smiling.

Not a *dream!* Not a dream at all . . .

She beckoned to him to climb in, and laughing, pulled him close, kissed him with a mouth that was unbelievably sweet, and whispered in his ear, "We're dead, Wolfie! Isn't it *wonderful!*"

Strange dreams. *Damn* strange . . . Mark dug himself farther into the bed and pulled the covers back over his shoulder, shifting a leg up so he was in half-fetal position. He let the warmth and comfort guide him back in the direction of sleep, trying to ignore the brightness of the room, but it was no good. His eyes opened a bit and saw Mattie's dark hair and shiny black shoulder like polished anthracite nestled amid the radiant linen. Turned away from me, but still inviting.

Big bed. Bigger than king size.

Beyond her, a sliding glass door behind a nearly transparent gold-flecked curtain, door open a crack, soft breeze stirring the curtain slightly. Outside, a spacious balcony with comfortable-looking padded chaise longues.

The furniture and decorations in the room were totally unfamiliar to him. Nothing remarkable, but . . . this isn't any room I remember. Must have been out of it last night, went to the wrong room. Jesus, this isn't just a hotel room, it's more of a suite, there's a living room out there. This isn't the EarthHaven hotel. How did I get here?

He slipped out from under the sheets and sat on the edge of the bed. Took stock. Slightly queasy feeling in his stomach, but otherwise . . . could I have drunk too much and passed out? I haven't done that since I was a kid. Little roll of fat on his belly, fat thighs pressed together, cock and balls in their nest of hair. Big arched feet sticking out, hmm, looks like those corns have finally gone away. Must be from parading around in the nude . . . Images flooding back, memories of places too bizarre to imagine. Images leading to the final descent and oblivion and . . . here.

And where the hell is this?

He stood up, took a few lumbering steps toward the living room, then changed his mind and headed for the balcony. Mattie made a little breathy moan and changed position slightly, but didn't wake up.

The glass door slid aside soundlessly, and the warm breeze swept over him, bringing in the sugar-sweet scent of Autumn Eleagnus and the sounds of a bustling city. For a moment he was surprised by the smell, carried back to the little yard of his mother's house, pictured himself there raking leaves in the cool sunshine, sniffing the air, wondering what was generating this perfumed smell when the trees were nearly bare. Not looking forward to going back in, having the defects of his performance faulted in his mother's soft, oh-so-cold way.

That was a long, long time ago.

He stepped over the door track and out onto the crinkly, indoor-outdoor carpet of the balcony. He was high up, looking out into the deep canyon of a high-rise world, sky mostly hidden by the balconies above. The buildings opposite were behemoths of dark glass and steel, like every city he had ever been in, but different, somehow streamlined and looped about with ribbons of light, shining unsupported walkways and roads piercing it everywhere. Daring the world to be offended, he went to the buffed silver railing, leaned out.

On either side of this balcony, extending into the distance, an infinite series of similar balconies. All the nearby ones were empty, but in the middle distance, far enough away to be totally anonymous, people were eating breakfast, reading old-fashioned paper newsdocs, most looking extremely content with this particular version of the world.

Not the world *I* come from, though. Mark felt a pang of disorientation, forced himself to come to grips with the situation. This is no dream; this is, for lack of a better world, reality. Bitter taste in his mouth, disappointment flooding back. Still lost.

On the balcony two apartments away there was a sudden movement and someone came out. Female, naked. Sudden rush in the pit of his stomach. Mark hunkered down behind a potted bush, watched through a chink in the leaves. She was thin, not perfect by any means, but to see any woman like this, unobserved. A delicious feeling.

Of course, it was Thalia, but somehow this realization didn't change the feeling. He watched as she tried to make sense of her surroundings, walking this way and that, white skin so pallid, making her nipples and dark pubic triangle so much more appealing. Somehow the overexposure to her naked body he'd had didn't make a bit of difference.

God. Like this, I can almost imagine that I still love her. What's the point in that?

He glanced inside, and saw that Mattie was stirring, kicking the covers off her legs, getting up. He looked back at Thalia, had a resurgence of wanting *her,* not Mattie, but forced himself to look away, go on back into the room.

Cory lay in the bed, covers pulled up to cover her breasts, watching Stu, naked, move around their hotel room, confused, wishing he was dressed, wishing she was dressed, wishing she knew what was going on, where they were, and why.

She remembered awakening, not quite darkness inside, faintly blued predawn light starting to define the world outside, outside the glass doors, beyond the curtains. She'd stretched delicately, feeling oh-so-pleasant, feeling the clean, smooth, obviously expensive sheets slide underneath her butt, feeling such decadent languor.

Maybe it was all a dream. Papa dead. Mama lost. The camps. The school. The sale. Wolf O'Malley. Starships. Mu Arae . . . *everything.*

Maybe this was her bedroom in Buenos Aires and . . .

Heart pounding softly in her chest.

I'm not alone.

There's someone in the bed beside me.

Then she'd heard that someone sigh, obviously awake, felt him, felt *him* roll over toward her, smooth hand coming under the covers, touching her belly, palpating her breasts like so much dough, felt the hand drift down across her belly while she lay paralyzed, wondering *who.*

Stu's voice sighed, "Oh, Cory . . ."

Then he'd kissed her. Kissed her like the romantic lead in a movie, while his expert fingers combed through her pubic hair, found the magic spot, called it to life, life and . . . Oh, it went on and on, not like that first time, lost in the floating forest. No more hurried, frantic boy shoving himself into her, pumping as fast and hard as he could, grunting and gasping like a man being tortured to death, spasming into her and . . . No, this went on and on, until she was so liquid inside, in her belly, in her heart, that she'd fallen back into the dream. Then he was inside her, moving just so, moving just right, that place at the bottom of his belly moving against her until her muscles clenched and she gasped, wondering how this could possibly be related to the other thing that happened.

Then it was over, and he kissed her some more, told her how sweet she was, how special and good, until she slept again in the crook of his arm.

To awaken in daylight and watch naked Stu, *boy* Stu, explore their little room. *Was* it him, or just a dream?

Every now and again, he looks at me.

Looks at me like he owns me.

Just like the fat man I imagined, as Wolf put the handcuff on my wrist and led me away. I'm afraid to get up. Afraid to get up and look outside.

Stu swung open a cabinet door and cried, "Oh, look, Cory! A 3V set! I wonder what's on now?"

Very odd inner surge indeed, and she thought, If this is Heaven, why do I feel so *bad* all of a sudden?

In the next room, there was a knock on the door.

Call it a cafeteria, though it was more like those things you saw at vacation hotels, where they stick strangers together on the theory they'll have interesting things to say to each other, breaking the bonds of humdrum familiarity. Come *on!* We're on *vacation!* Let's *talk!* Thalia remembered a day, only a couple of years gone, when she and Mark had sat side by side, silently eating, not looking at a circle of nervous, silently eating strangers, while one lone snotty young woman, no more than a girl, really, went on and on about, *So much for scintillating conversation. . . .*

Stupid.

Just like the heartworn pang she felt, walking into this huge room full of laughing, talking, *happy* goddamned *perfect* fucking strangers, only to find herself not three meters from a nice round table where with, oh, shit, how *could* it be anyone fucking else? Cory and Stu. Mattie and Mark. Honoria and Wolf.

Laughing, talking, eating, happy.

She turned to go, feeling like she was made of lead.

Stuart bounced to his feet. "Mom. *Mom!* I found the *cats!* There's a nice kennel here and they've got Merry, Neff, and Ox!"

Happy. Happy. Happy. A boy and his fucking cats.

The empty chair at the circular table was between Mark and Wolf, Mark looking up at her with a nice, arrogant smirk. Wolf at least had the decency to preserve a shadow of doubt behind his eyes. She sat down, determined to tough it out.

God damn it. I'm a grown woman. Got my*self* in this fucking mess, and now I'll just . . .

Wolf patted her on the back of one hand.

God *damn* it, you fucking, patronizing shit, I . . .

Unsaid.

Mercifully unsaid.

"Ma'am?"

Thalia jumped at the soft voice. Looked up. Jumped again. Young man. Beautiful, ascetic young man with platinum-blond hair and sky-blue eyes, shrouded in faint haze, as though in a movie scene shot through gauze, Vaseline on the camera lens, dressed all in white . . .

"Ma'am, what would you like for breakfast?"

Thalia stared, drinking him in.

"Ma'am?"

"Where are your wings?"

The waiter smiled. "In some other patchlink, I guess, though sometimes I wish . . ." The smile turned wistful. "I'm just a simulacrum, ma'am. I never really existed anywhere else."

Um. "Anywhere else? So where's here?"

Mark laughed. "Hadn't you heard? This is fucking Heaven!" Mattie nudged him in the ribs, giggling, though you couldn't tell if the downcast eyes were accompanied by a blush.

Fucking Heaven? I just bet. You look tired, Marky-poo. Surprised then at the depths of her ill will toward him. God damn it . . .

Wolf said, "Stuart thinks we're in Tipler's endpoint emulation."

Stu: "It fits, Mom. It really does. I mean, look around you."

"Emulation of what?"

"Everything!"

The whole universe. All of space and time. The universe plucked from God's imagination and thrust into the bowels of a creation-girdling machine. She looked at Wolf and said, "What do *you* think?"

He shrugged. "Doesn't really matter where we are, does it?" He grinned, somehow uneasy. "I just hope this id'n a death fantasy conjured up by a brain about to go down for the count. That'd be a pisser, huh, Thal?"

As you say, a pisser. She looked at Honoria. "You?"

The woman's face took on an obscenely serene glow as she laid one slim, tan hand on Wolf's hairy wrist. "Real."

Real. Really *Heaven,* for Christ's sake? Like in the fucking Bible? "Cory?"

A shrug.

She looked at Mattie, who smiled. "I'm with Wolf."

With *Wolf?* Not enough you stole my fucking husband, now you have to go after my first *love,* for . . . for . . . Jesus. Get hold of yourself. "Mark?"

His face got a very hard-bitten look. "Since when did you ever care what I thought? Or how I felt?"

Well. Well. Looks like I'm not the *only* one stuck in blaming mode. Somehow, that little bit of self-realization made her feel better, like a cloud lifting from the face of the sun. She looked up at the waiter. "And the truth?"

The man cocked his head to one side, cheeks dimpling as he smiled, deep amusement tainting his eyes. "Well," he said, "I recommend the scrambled eggs, Ma'am. I think you'll find them truly exceptional."

Fifteen

Breakfast done, waiting in a glass-walled antechamber for the others to do their ablutions, Stu watched Mark fidget uncomfortably, decided to step outside. The canyon between buildings here was large, and the aerial walkway that spanned the gap was a thin ribbon winding over the endless abyss.

There was a gusty breeze out here, alternating cool and warm in a pleasant way, the stronger currents causing a moment of vertigo as he imagined the unsupported span would twist in the wind and dump him off. Grabbing hold of the railing, he realized that the thing was solid enough to withstand a hurricane, if they had hurricanes in Heaven. Out of the corner of his eye he noticed Mark following him, shrugged to himself.

The sky was crowded with clouds now, rows and bunches of chunky altocumulus, the late morning sun passing behind them, backlighting them dramatically against the crystalline blue. Converging in the infinite distance, telling me how big the sky is here.

Will it ever be night here? The sun had clearly changed position since they'd awakened, but the idea of night seemed somehow incongruous. If night comes, what will we see in the sky? Will it be like the galactic core or the void? Or will there be hosts of luminous angels looking down, halos gleaming like stars?

Suddenly, Mark was beside him, hands on the railing, staring into the limitless sky. He wants to say something to me. With a start, Stu realized that the anger he'd felt at the man had shrunken away to almost nothing. Jesus, he thought, I suppose anything *is* possible.

He doesn't give a shit about Mom now that he's got this black woman. Maybe that makes the difference. Hell, miracle of miracles, we've both got women now.

Mark said, "Well, Stu, you seem to be doing pretty well for yourself. I must admit, for a while there I thought the way you were turning out, you'd never get laid."

He never talks to me like this. Stu said, "Yeah. Well, I guess things change, don't they?"

Gust of wind, carrying the smell of flowers. "You know," Mark said, "I really did have good intentions with your mother. It just . . . didn't work out."

"You should have figured that out years ago."

"Anyway, it's over now. Despite all *this,* that's one thing I'm sure of. Mattie's a . . . wonderful woman."

Is that a snigger in his voice? He's trying to tell me that the long battle between him and Mom is over, and that *he won.* Christ, why should I care?

"I know you don't like to hear advice," he said, looking down into green nothingness, "but I think I've figured out a little. If you let a woman get control of you, she'll just slip through your fingers. That was the problem I had with your mother. She knew I couldn't get by without her. Don't let that happen—"

"With Cory? Christ. What kind of advice is that?" And *who* are *you* to give *any* kind of advice, you pathetic, old—

"I'm just . . . well, if this is Heaven, and we're going to be here for a long, long time, I don't want to see you get stuck. I guess I wouldn't want to see you make the same mistakes I did. We're calling it Heaven, but it could just as easily be the other place."

"Ummm, well. What are you getting at?" Stu looked back at the cafeteria exit, felt relief that the others were gathering there.

"Just . . . be careful. That's all. Things can get out of hand before you know it."

"Mark, I'm not an idiot. I know what I'm doing. Why don't you just concentrate on getting your own life . . ." Well, maybe that's not exactly the right term. ". . . in order."

"Fuck it, Stu. You don't listen, I know that. Maybe nobody ever listens to anybody. If you won't take that advice, take this: enjoy it while you can. If this is fucking Heaven, at least enjoy it. Don't worry about it too much. Don't lose sight of the pleasure. It can happen, believe me."

What kind of game is he playing now? I'll be glad to get this kind of bullshit out of my life forever. Stu glanced up to see the others coming in a clot. He looked at them all, at the looks on their faces, and shuddered.

It was something of a relief to be back inside again, despite the glory of sun, wind, and infinite view. Not infinite. Not really infinite, Wolf thought. Too much shit in the way, just like when we were back in the Topopolis. They'd walked along, having those same old stupid arguments, over and over again. Bored, Wolf began walking along the edge, looking over the rail from time to time, feeling vertigo for the first time in his life.

Shit. I had to come to *Heaven* to get dizzy from a height?

The quality of the height was different, that's all. When

you were hanging in orbit, or even just hanging from the limb of a white oak tree, the yawning gulf under your feet had meaning. Fall off a tree and break my fucking neck or fall from orbit and burn like a meteor, it's all the same thing. This . . . Walking beside him, Honoria had smiled and said, "Don't fall off."

And what if I do? She'd shrugged. God must have something in mind, even if it's only just us.

Which had set Mark and Stu to arguing again. This is Tipler's emulation. No it isn't. We're *somewhere* in the Topopolis. Where else *could* we be?

Well . . . well . . .

Well, why are there only people like *us* here? Our kind of humans. I mean, where are the Atlanteans? Where's Rann and Professor Pompidou? Where are the cuttlefish? That's what *I'd* like to know.

Wolf himself was wondering what'd become of the TrackTrixCom. Surely, in a perfect emulation of all that'd gone before, there'd be room for a machine emulating a mind. . . . No. No, I don't fucking believe it. We're not fucking copies in some computer dream. And this ain't God's *real* fucking Heaven.

The Topopolis, then?

No. Too unlikely.

Where, then?

No point wasting time wondering. Either we'll find out or we won't.

Now they stood at the entrance to another great hall, standing at the head of a flight of broad, black marble stairs, standing at a lovely wrought-iron railing, looking down over one more vast space, an immense concourse that went on and on, until . . .

Funny. You'd think, in a room this big, the floor and ceiling would eventually merge, but it doesn't. It just goes on as far as the eye can see, broad floor covered with a pattern of red, black, and white Penrose tiles, open storefronts, a bustle of people.

Trompe l'oeil.

As far as the eye can see?

How far is that?

If there were a complete spiral galaxy at the far end of the room, would I see its dim glow from two million light-years away? Silly ass.

Cory said, "This looks just like the Alemán-García shopping mall in downtown Buenos Aires, only a whole lot bigger. You remember, Mama? The one where you and I and Daddy—" She stopped and bit her lip.

Softly, eyes far away, Honoria said, "*Lo recuerdo, Corazón.*"

Wolf caught the look in her eye, not directed at him, and felt a pang of stark realization. If she believes this is Heaven, then somewhere out there, joined to her in eternal Catholic marriage . . . He tasted the softness of the idea, and thought, For your sake, Honoria . . . Would I give her up because I loved her, or would it be easy because I don't love her at all?

Novel idea.

They started walking down the steps, together as a group, silent, and Wolf wondered if the others were just as afraid as he was.

Down on the concourse floor there were people bustling everywhere, laughing, talking, smiling, idle, walking hand in hand, arm in arm, like lovers, like friends, like family. Cory kept feeling like she'd fallen back into the past, conjuring up images of herself, walking through the mall between her mother and father, one of them holding her by each little hand, looking wide-eyed at all the stores, all the merchandise, all the people, none of it meaning much of anything, just . . . excitement. The being there. The doing.

How old was I in that memory? Five? Seven? Can't have been much more than that.

There were other, later memories, of being at the mall with her friends, girls pretending to be older than they were, whispering about boys. Older boys, of course. Boys our age weren't interested yet. She remembered how the adventure, the imagining, made her shiver so deliciously. What if they *had* been interested? What then?

She stopped in front of a storefront now, looking in. Row on row of toys, thronged by children. Children. She thought about her mother's Heaven, her conception of paradise, life after death, and thought, Is this the Heaven where dead children go? Why not simply send them to Neverland?

Behind her, Wolf, in a voice strangely soft, as unlike his own as she could possibly imagine, said, "This isn't the world I grew up in. When I was a boy, the shopping malls were gone, blown away in a war that happened before I was born. This is my daddy's Heaven. This is the world that got taken away, the one he used to . . . talk about."

And if this was really Heaven, would your daddy be here? Would mine? Stu? Is that what everyone's thinking about right now? What if this was really Heaven? She looked up and saw Thalia standing beside them, a little in the background, looking sad, not looking at the toys, not looking at the children.

Just watching all the people walk along. What would she do if her dead husband came popping out of the crowd?

She imagined the glad cries.

What if. A nice game to play, but . . . we're not in Heaven, are we? We're somewhere else.

Honoria said, "Look: Is that a hairdresser?"

Thalia looked, blinked, seemed to brighten.

Mattie said, "Hell. What're we waiting for?"

Mark said, *"Christ."*

Wolf laughed and said, "Cool it, Marky. You ain't the only one fuckin' died and went to Heaven, you know."

* * *

Inside, Wolf stood to one side, watching the women queue up for treatment, then started looking at the rest of the clientele, at what was being done to them. Not really like any of the places I ever went, the more specialized places, salons, some women go to. More like . . . like something out of ancient video history.

Row on row of people, men and women alike, not just women, sitting in metal-armed chairs, huge chrome beehives over their heads and . . . magazines. They should be reading magazines. It should be fat, middle-aged women with layer on layer of clown-lips and pancake makeup, reading magazines that told them how beautiful they were going to be.

These people all had their eyes shut, were sitting perfectly still.

As he watched, first Honoria, then Cory, finally an ever-so-slightly reluctant Thalia—why reluctant, too macho for this girly stuff?—sat down in a chair, had a beehive lowered over her head, had it switched on, sat perfectly still.

What the hell is going on here? Anything the likes of *me* can understand?

Mark, sotto voce: "And now, a word from our sponsor . . ."

Stu tittered.

One of the hairdressers walked up to them, focused on Wolf, came to stand in front of him, one hand on a slim hip, pelvis cocked, one long, bare leg extending forward toward him, smiling, looking up into his eyes.

Mark, sounding bitter: "Typical."

The woman had blue eyes, pale skin, platinum-blond hair, red lips. Her midriff was exposed by a deliberately too-short blouse, more pale skin, lying over delicately shaped muscles, her low-slung shorts exposing a perfect little whorl of navel. Above, just-right breasts, each one showing a little hump of erect nipple, below, if you looked in just the right place, you could see the outline of her vulva through a clingy weave.

Staring, Wolf tried to imagine he could tell whether or not she was shaved; decided that she was.

He felt the bottom of his belly suddenly grow heavy.

The woman smiled, with just the right touch of lewd awareness.

I know you, the look said.

She reached up and touched his cheek with slim, red-nailed fingers, making a light sandpaper sound, seemed to shiver, and said, "Come on, Mr. O'Malley. Hot towel, a nice warm shave, a trim around the edges, *then* you'll know where you are."

Mr. O'Mulley? Wolf felt a hard pang of alarm as she took him by the hand and led him to a chair.

"There there," she said, patting him gently on the shoulder. "It'll be all right. You'll see." As she let the chair back, he caught a brief glimpse of Mark and Stu watching him from the entrance, both frowning, both seeming . . . nonplussed.

The woman came and stood close by the side of his chair, blocking the view, Wolf realizing his face was now at the level of her abdomen. From this close you could see through the mesh of her shorts' weave. Skin. Bare skin. No underwear, no pubic hair. Fleshy roll on the left, fleshy roll on the right, a little bump in between.

He looked up the length of her body, seeing her face smiling down at him between the small mounds of her breasts. "So. *Is* this Heaven?"

She shrugged. "How should I know? I just work here."

Disquiet. That's the wrong answer. How could the *workers* in Heaven be unhappy? She stepped a little closer, so her body was no more than a couple of inches from his face, making him feel her warmth, radiating against his skin, making him think he could smell her, a faint, pleasantly organic tang, quickly erased, most likely just imagination.

She wrapped the warm, wet towel around his face with a

quick, practiced twirl, sudden shift of sensation itself with something akin to orgasm. A pause of heartbeats, then the towel away, practiced hands applying hot lather, then the scrape of a straight razor, pleasure with just the right tinge of pain.

When she leaned across him to work, the hard bulge of her pubic bone pressed against his shoulder.

Remember that girl? What the hell was her name? Can't remember. Thin, odd thing she was. A party. I was at a party. Sitting because I was too drunk to stand up and dance. Came and stood right next to me, stood so close I could smell her. Planted her pussy right on my shoulder cap and started rubbing, rubbing away, moving like she was dancing, skin shining, sweaty in the dim light . . .

Can't remember what happened next. Too drunk. Probably just blacked out. Woke up on the floor in the corner the next morning with a splitting headache, surrounded by snoring, stinking sleepers, dancing girl nowhere to be seen.

Went on home to tend to my sick old dad.

More hot towel.

Then she sat him upright.

"Hold still, Mr. O'Malley."

Mr. O'Malley. Not my name at all. Dad.

As she lowered a silver beehive over his head, he whispered, "This thing going to cut my hair?"

She said, *"Shhh."*

Then, *click.*

Feeling the air so still and crystalline around her, Thalia Jansky lifted the silver hood and looked around. *How odd.* Everyone motionless under their hoods, Honoria, Cory . . . prickle of surprise. Wolf? Well, one of those pretty girls could talk him into anything, sure, but Stu? *Mark,* for Christ's sake?

No sign of the pretty little attendants.

She walked slowly through the still air to the entrance of the boutique and looked back out into the mall. Bare floor. Still air. What could've happened to the people?

She stepped out onto the bare floor, which seemed cold right through the souls of her soft shoes, turned and looked nervously back into the shop. Yes, motionless people still there, sitting under their hoods.

Something's supposed to be happening to me? What? I don't know.

She caught movement out of the corner of her eye, spun, looked. Up on a distant walkway, a tiny figure was standing, leaning on the wrought-iron railing, looking toward her. A slim man with brown hair, white face, dressed in some kind of light blue uniform. Maybe the ERDA flight-crew uniform?

Seeing her look, he lifted one arm in a slow, sweeping wave.

A terribly familiar wave.

Familiar . . .

She felt a sharp scald of nausea.

No. No, this is the thing you've been trying to keep at bay all—

"God, please . . ." she whispered, then screamed, *"Winston!?"* She could hear the disbelief in her voice. The near panic.

The figure stopped waving, leaning its hands once again on the railing, as if waiting. She stood, indecisive, one hand lifted in an abortive return wave, wondering what, if anything, could be real in the here and now.

I just can't believe any of this.

When did it become impossible? At Beta Pic? No, of course not. All of that was straight out of science fiction, sure, but . . . *possible.* Eminently possible, just like rocketships, just like hyperdrive, just like . . . teleportation? Sure. So, the Pleiades, the Galactic Core, the Void, even the rubber sheet, blue galaxy hanging in the sky . . .

The Topopolis? Well, Okay. The Hanging Forest? Sure. Galaxios and Atlantis? Variations on a theme. When did it start to be fantasy? When we woke up here? *How am I supposed to know what's real, goddamn it?* She turned indecisively, hesitantly, to look back into the shop, to look at her motionless crewmates. Mark. Mark with all his doubts. Wolf, with his easy ability to make snap decisions.

When she looked back into the mall, the figure at the rail was gone.

"No . . ." Running now, decision suddenly made, sprinting across the tile floor, stumbling up the stairs . . . When she got to the top, there was no one in sight, just more empty, infinite mall.

But when she touched the black iron railing, there where two warm places, just where his hands must have been.

Whispered: "*Winston* . . ." Thought: But what do I *want* to believe?

After a while, when the warm spots cooled away and became just two more stretches of railing, she walked slowly back down the stairs, across the tile floor, back into the boutique, back to her chair, sat down and pulled the beehive down over her head.

Feeling like he was awakening from a too-long dream, Wolf opened his eyes to the darkness under the hood, but continued to sit still. Don't know what's outside. Lift the hood and . . . what? Still the mall? Or will it be Galaxios? Or will I be back on the ship, lost between the stars, back on Mu Arae, even back on Earth? Which one would I prefer?

After the dream, after the too-real dream . . .

He felt himself shiver.

Waking up with a hangover. Walking home in stark morning light, that clear, angular morning light you only see on a cloudless spring morning in North Carolina. Home to a house smelling of sickness, defeat, despair.

Finding him.

What was it he said last night?

That was all you could try to think of.

He'd said, "You go on to your party, son. Have a good time. Don't want you to think of me even *once.*"

Anguish: "Dad . . ."

A feeble grin then: "Oh, shit. Just eat some nice, hot pussy for me, hm?"

"I'll be home around midnight."

"Sure."

He shut his eyes then, seemed to go to sleep.

Now, in the impossibly sharp morning light, Wolf pried the pad of paper from the dead man's hands and tried to read the words he'd written. The pencilings were too sloppy, too smeared with sweat to be made out. All except the first line, which read, *It's 1 A.M. now, son.*

Waited as long as he could, then tried to write his last words. Then died without me.

He remembered crying for an hour, cradling the stiff, shrunken carcass in his arms, before getting up the courage to put in a call to the hospital, get someone to come and . . . take it away.

It.

My *father,* for God's sake!

Wolf grabbed the rim of the beehive and shoved it up, boutique light flooding into his eyes making him flinch. That's *not* the way it happened! When he got too sick, when the pain got to be too much, we called the medics, they put the needle in, I held him till he stopped breathing, and that was that. An honorable death, easy, so easy . . .

He died in my arms, smiling with relief.

Long silent pause, staring at the backside of one slim, pretty attendant.

Didn't he?

She turned around and looked at him, smiled, helped him

to his feet. "Well, Mr. O'Malley. Do you know where you are now?"

He pushed her away. "No. Sorry."

She shrugged, "Ah, well. It'll come to you, by and by."

He turned and walked away, out into the bustle of the mall, seething with confusion. *Why don't I understand what's going on?*

Not far away was a kiosk, one of those things you see in every mall. He remembered picking through some ruins with his father, Dad blabbing away about the good times he'd had in this very mall as a boy, way back when. They'd dug up just such a kiosk, his father reading off shop names, remembering in which one a kid would be welcome, in which one shooed away. . . .

"Barrel of Fun!" his father had said. "Christ! Wasted a lot of allowance money in *that* fucker!"

No Barrel of Fun on this kiosk, with its blinking red *You Are Here* cursor. Every time he looked away and looked back, the shape of the map changed, layer on layer, hall on hall on hall. . . .

Public library?

There's a public library here. . . .

He turned and walked quickly back to the boutique, where his friends dreamed on.

Expecting heat, Mark felt instead a cold rip of air, the cloud of tiny ice crystals stinging his wet, numbed face, ticking noise muffled by the tightly fastened hood of his anorak. Where am I? The sidewalk had been cleared, but there were still patches of ice here and there, snow piled up on the opposite side of the street like great, bleached sand dunes. At the top of the hill, a single street lamp, blazing white in a burst of mist against the dead black. Ghostly breath swirling around his face.

Is this home? Despite the fact that they'd moved when he

was four, he still thought of 1450 South Quinn Street as his home, the little twentieth century rambler among hundreds of others at the entrance to the Prep Barracks. That would explain the great dark void to his right; although even when Lake Michigan was frozen over there would be moving lights out there.

The bulk of his winter clothing felt heavy, reassuringly warm, like a little house, but his wet, cold feet were getting stiff and trickles of chill brushed on his midriff whenever he moved.

Why am I here? Don't recognize this place. He took a few, crunching steps, almost slipped.

Slowly, the idea formed. This is a dream within a dream. If I'm dreaming that I'm dreaming this, I should be able to . . . He turned around, a dance of Frankenstein monster steps, found himself looking down his long shadow into a world of dim white flecked with a spectral reflections.

The snow had drifted quite a bit in this direction, covering the concrete and crusty ice in a smoothly undulating layer. By the time he reached the tapering metal light pole, he was forcing his legs to move through snow up to his knees. He stopped, looked up; the light was a spherical bulb embedded in a heavy hood.

When he looked away, the image of the bulb was still there. He blinked, trying to make it go away, noticed a strange shape protruding from the snow, as though the drift had covered a big box of some sort. Curiosity getting the better of him, he fell to his knees, snow making a rubbing squeak. He brushed his gloved hand against the granular surface, and the snow came away without cohesion, leaving an uneven shallow gouge. Clearly, there was no box shape under the snow. He dug his hand in deep, feeling some resistance as the snow was compressed. He attacked the snow with both hands frantically, scraping, paddling snow out of the way as fast as he could.

Something. Something small . . . mobile. Through his glove he couldn't tell much about it, except that he could get his fingers around it. He clutched it gently and pulled.

Christ almighty!

He was seized by unimaginable horror. It was a female arm, slim and white, the hand perfectly manicured, a thin white-gold band on the ring finger. The hand was so delicate, so small, fingers half curled. For a long moment he just stared, then began to excavate the rest of the body.

The snow offered little resistance, but his hands passed through it without moving much. He finally got back to his feet and began sweeping with both of his hands, until the woman's face and upper torso were exposed.

Christ. It's her. This *must* be a dream.

Lying there, face perfectly composed, wearing a dress as white as the snow, was his mother. Eyes shut, bluish lips set into a smile. He pulled off a glove, touched her high, fine cheek, felt the cold biting into his fingers.

Slowly, deliberately, he took off the other glove, shrugged himself out of his coat and began to unbutton his shirt.

Wolf could see that they'd been shaken by the dreams, every one of them, good dreams, bad dreams, in-between dreams. No one had wanted to talk about their experience as they walked silently along, threading the byways of the mall.

Reduced to individuals, locked in our thoughts.

Troubled.

Heaven?

This is fucking *Heaven*?

It took a long time to get to the library, would've taken even longer if certain things hadn't . . . dawned on them. Walking along in silence, like the others helplessly wrapped in his thoughts, Wolf had been trying for the thousandth time to put that faux death scene out of his head, think about something nicer, some old fuck, the flying of some plane or glider or rocketship or another, when Cory muttered, "I've got to pee. I wish we'd see a bathroom pretty soo—"

Mark pointed. "Over there."

Men and Women.

Then, when he looked away, looked at Honoria, looked back again, the doors said, *Hombres* y *Mujeres.* Then, quickly, Men and Women again. Christ, if one of us was a relict Kraut, would I see *Damen und Herren?*

But it was, after all, a relief to stand in the urinal, peeing for a long, long time, waiting for the stream to subside. I didn't notice. Should've been in pain, with a bladder this full. Heaven? No pain till you've got the chance, then bliss to piss?

They walked on, up stairs and down, along brilliant halls thronged with anonymously well-dressed *folk,* down dark corridors, where silent dark ones skulked, consulted kiosk after kiosk . . . Then Stu: "You know, I believe I'm getting hungry."

The food court appeared not long after that, and they ate a meal at a little white table, surrounded by thousands of eaters, dishes picked from an endless variety of little windows, Chinese, Korean, Indian, Italian. . . .

Wolf ate a large pizza covered with a rubble of variety meats all by himself, washing it down with two cold, brown bottles of dark, heavy beer, and just before he finished, Mark whispered, "You know, I wish we'd get to the library soon."

Wolf paused with a mouthful of cheese, crust, and sausage, sat and looked him in the eye, holding his gaze for a long minute before starting to chew again. Think that's how it works, buddy boy? He swallowed finally, licked greasy lips, and said, "I wish you were right. I wish it'd be right around the next fucking . . ."

Honoria: "Wolf . . ."

Look. Look at how nervous they all are. Nobody wants to think that our wishes . . .

". . . right around the next fucking corner."

Thalia laughed suddenly, "And then what? Beggars will ride?"

"Only in Spain," Stu said.

They got up, walked on, and right around the next corner the mall widened out into one of its periodic enlargements, a huge, multileveled room with a big hole through the middle, going all the way up to an immense geodesic dome of frosted glass.

Wolf tipped his head back, looking up at the dome, and wondered what lay beyond, what was making all the light.

Maybe nothing?

A hollow cavity lined with big lightbulbs?

Shadows here and there, places not so bright. Maybe some of the lightbulbs have burned out. Who does the maintenance in Heaven?

In the middle of the hollow was a big stone building, looking like a cross between the famous, lion-guarded New York Public Library and some kind of Egyptian mausoleum.

"Greeks," Cory whispered. "Only Greeks had Mausoleums."

They went in. No books. No nothing particularly librarylike. Little alcoves where you could sit and read, if there'd been anything to . . . Help desks, but no attendants. Lots of very nice blue carpeting. No customers.

Mark: "Great. Fucking *great.*"

Wolf said, "You know, Mark, if you took a more positive attitude, maybe—"

Mark said, "Thank you, fucking Norman Vincent Peale."

Wolf thought, *Who?* Turned away and started trying knobs and handles on various doors. One of them proved unlocked, the door swinging open, revealing a moment of darkness inside, then a swift flood of soft blue light, and a hearty voice boomed, "Welcome! Welcome to the Great Library of Heaven! Welcome to the answers to all . . . Why, Wolf O'Malley, as I live and breathe! And Ms. Jansky too!"

Looking over his shoulder, Thalia said, "I've just got to stop having expectations. I've got to start taking things as they come."

Wolf glanced at her briefly. "Good idea." He walked across the room to the pedestal where the silver beer keg perched and said, "So. Are you *our* TrackTrixCom?"

It said, "Oh, probably not, but it's nice to think so, hm?"

Well. He hesitated, trying to frame a question, any question. . . .

The beer keg said, "I know what you want to know."

Wolf looked away, looking at the others. Expressionless. He looked back at the keg. "Then tell us."

"Sit down. Make yourselves comfortable."

Sit. Wolf looked around. They were all inside the little room now, the room seeming bigger than it had been only moments ago, and there were chairs lining the wall, enough for each of them, but no more. "Figures," he muttered, taking a seat.

Silence.

Then Honoria said, *"Well?"*

Patience, my sweet.

The TrackTrixCom said, "As you have surmised, *Señora Suárez,* this is indeed Heaven."

The look on her face was unreadable, compounded, Wolf thought, from some improbable mixture of awe and horror. What, not quite ready to meet your maker and . . . explain things away?

She stammered, "*Mi . . . mi esposo . . .*"

It was till death do us part, Honoria. He was already dead, months in his grave, when they dragged you from the alley and sold your ass to me. He'll understand. He'll understand if this is really Heaven and he was any kind of man at all. I'll shake his hand and give you back to him, honest I will.

But she was looking at him, and the look in her eyes was sorrow.

Which made him feel simultaneously uncomfortable and elated.

Mark shouted, "Wait just a goddamned minute . . ."

Thalia seemed to flinch.

Careful, Marky-boy. Think where you *might* just be.

Hmm. Makes me feel good inside to be sarcastic and full of balls, even when it's just inside my fucking head.

Mark said, "You mean *real* Heaven, like . . . like in . . ."

The TrackTrixCom said, "Well, sort of."

Honoria: "Sort of?"

Motionless, featureless, it could not squirm. Nonetheless, Wolf had a distinct feeling of . . .

It said, "What if I told you this was indeed a part of Heaven, the human part of Heaven, where all the people who ever lived, from every possible timeline, hundreds of trillions of souls, have been resurrected to eternal life?"

Silence.

It said, "What if I told you the Topopolitans succeeded?"

Stu burst out, "I *knew* it! Tipler's Paradise! We're at the Omega Point after all!"

The TrackTrixCom said, "Well, sort of."

Honoria: "Sort of." Flatter now, with just a trace of anger.

It seemed to sigh. "Heaven's such a *complex* idea, madam. Surely your own cosmology can accommodate—"

Thalia said, "So the Topopolitans managed to stabilize the oscillations of the universe and prevent the next Big Crunch from happening. Then with all eternity at their beck and call, they built a computer that encompassed—"

It said, "Sort of."

Wolf snarled, "Sort of *what,* for Christ's sake? Stop beating around the goddamn bush!"

It said, "Okay, the computer's real all right, and I suppose we're all in it. I know *I* am, at any rate. Look: there was no way the Topopolitan civilization could actually stop the

Crunch. That'd take forces larger than the universe itself, and the universe is *everything*. There are no such forces."

Wolf thought about that. Then, softly, he said, "So?"

It said, "Inside the computer, falling toward the cosmic event horizon, the value of Tau could be leveraged. Time could be made to seem as long as one wished it to be."

Honoria stood, face dark with outrage. "So," she said, "I die, die my real death, and instead of God's true eternity, thanks to these miserable *Topopolitans,* I go to the *shopping mall* for ever and ever?"

Wolf felt an urge to giggle.

"Well," it said, "just for a very long time. This universe will come to an end one day, I suppose, though, in the meantime, a transfinite number of extremely powerful coprocessors will continue to work the problem. If there's a way, there most certainly is a will."

Wolf sat back in his chair, stunned.

Very quietly, Mark said, "None of this is *real,* you know. It *can't* be. It just can't." He seemed very tired. "Somewhere, back on Earth maybe, we're all just lying in a hospital ward, unconscious, with electrodes stuck to our heads and—"

The TrackTrixCom said, "Maybe you're right, Mr. Porringer. Maybe you're right. I mean, what can *I* know? I'm just a dumb terminal, after all."

Silence.

Then Wolf said, "You mentioned a human part of Heaven. Are there others?"

"Of course there are. If you're looking for your cuttlefish friends, I can give you a very nice map. I'm sure they'll be glad to see you."

Sixteen

Looking down on the landscape passing too slowly below, Thalia said, "Why the hell are there airliners in Heaven? Why the hell couldn't we just walk through some magic door and *be* there?"

Standing next to her, Wolf put his arm around her, resting his hand lightly on her shoulder, and said, "You got to admit, it's a really *great* airliner, though. Jack Northrop's best wet dream."

She felt her stomach kink just a bit, maybe from his touch, enhanced by the sexual metaphor. Typical Wolf O'Malley. Never give a sucker an even break.

On the other hand, it *was* a great airliner, a flying wing the size of a battleship, rolling smoothly through the sky, driven by whispering jets of air, jets powered by God knows what. She smirked at that. God knows. What a laugh!

Just now they were looking down through one of the vast forward viewports, curving panels of invulnerable photo-gray glass making up most of the wing's leading edge, looking down on the landscape of Heaven. Human Heaven, she reminded herself. Cityscape, cities tens of thousands of miles across, stretches of countryside in between. Mountains. Valleys. Plains. Amber waves of grain and all that.

Even little seas that they flew over in a matter of minutes, their shadow like that of some great bird. Once, over just such a sea, Wolf had pointed down at a couple of white flecks on the water. "Look! Galleys! Is that a pentekonter?"

She squinted, wondering if he could see better than she could. Sails. Little banks of oars. "Seems like a slow way to get around."

Stu, standing next to them for a few minutes, said, "What would Odysseus be up to, once he got used to being here?"

Wolf laughed. "Anyway, what's the hurry, when you've got damn-all forever?"

Almost damn-all forever, Thalia reminded herself. Not *quite* damn-all forever. If the clock ticks at all, sooner or later we'll get where we're going.

And if it *doesn't* tick? Well.

Then they ran out of Human Heaven, landscape abruptly coming to an end at an infinite seashore, only there was no water down below, no ocean, no . . . Wolf seemed to draw away from her, drawing in on himself. "Not like looking up into an empty sky. Not like looking down past your space-suited feet at the infinite depths of the universe. No starry sky . . ."

No nothing down there. Something . . . more than infinite. Pearl-gray emptiness, sucking at us, as if . . . She said, "This is how some of those old writers imagined hyperspace would look."

He said nothing, continuing to stare, face . . . perturbed.

What, Wolf O'fucking-Malley *afraid?*

Impossible.

He said, "Courage in the face of something you don't fear is no courage at all."

She felt a little pulse of resentment. Why'd you have to say that? Why couldn't you let me look down on you for just a little while? Why the hell couldn't you *mind* being afraid?

Sometime later they passed over a little island in the sky, and a couple hundred passengers among all the thousands aboard departed, donning triangular parawings, dropping down through a hatch in the floor while the ship's engine's throttled back to a shuddering whisper, people falling in a flock of gray sails, like so many little birds, dwindling away until they were gone.

The ship flew on, hours, days, maybe even weeks, though no one aboard slept or ate, felt tired or bored or much of anything else, until another great land mass, infinite flat landscape just like the one they'd left behind, emerged from gray nothingness.

Cuttlefish Heaven. Seeing it, rolling the phrase over and over in her head, Thalia thought, Everything's so damned silly. Cuttlefish fucking Heaven, for Christ's sake.

In a little room in a tall tower in the midst of an infinite cuttlefish city, they stood in a group, indistinguishable cuttlefish floating in the air before them, waiting.

"Welcome," the familiar, friendly, sourceless voice said. "Welcome to the Great Kraaken's Waiting Room."

"Kraaken?" Stu said.

"A kind of big squid," Cory said. "Sperm whales used to eat them, before whales went extinct."

It said, "We borrowed the term from your own group soul. For the physical imagery, no more."

Mark said, "Kind of tough, picturing your God as prey. Praying to prey? I mean—"

"Not so. All things are prey, in one sense or another. Whales ate the kraaken. Humans ate the whales. Bacteria eat the humans. Viruses eat bacteria."

"Nothing eats viruses," Wolf said. "They're not alive."

The voice said, "Then maybe we should worship viruses. Certainly, there are no viruses in Heaven."

Implying, just maybe, there was a Bacteria Heaven floating somewhere far off in the hyperspace sky?

Mark: "You really think this is Heaven? You called it a waiting room."

Honoria abruptly said, "They think they're in Purgatory."

Catharsis, Thalia thought. *Purgatory.* Binge and purge. She suddenly imagined some vast cosmic bathroom, row on row of stark white toilets, toilets occupied by row on row of puking, shitting sinners. Purgation. The others looked at her as she suddenly laughed into the silence.

The voice said, "The analogy is fairly precise. In our theology, there was a vast holding tank, where components of the oversoul were somehow to ready themselves for merger with eternity."

Mark, sarcastic: "And you believe that?"

"Once upon a time, when we ourselves were a primitive folk, our group soul as yet unawakened, we believed in a heaven in which each dead soul was granted the eternal use of an entire infinite universe for itself alone; a universe full of worlds inhabited by finite-state beings whose sole purpose was the fulfillment of the dead soul."

Wolf said, "Houris."

Thalia thought, Once an asshole, always an asshole.

The voice said, "Yes. That word will do."

Stuart: "That's pretty much equivalent to Tipler's Paradise, isn't it? I mean . . ."

Thalia thought, Once he gets a stupid idea in his head, he can't get beyond it.

The voice said, "I know what you mean. In our old myth, as each dead soul, wandering the holding tank, found itself ready for true eternity, it would go to a place called the Well of the Worlds, there to pass on into its newly made universe, personally tailored for it by the Great Kraaken."

Mark said, "Well of the Worlds? I suppose it's always midnight there?"

Stu said, "Christ you're stupid, Mark! That's Well of the *Souls* you're thinking of!"

"What's the fucking difference?"

The voice said, "In any case, we have discovered that the Well of the Worlds is real. We think we know how to get there. And we have therefore built a Second Fleet."

Why am I not surprised? Thalia turned away from the cuttlefish and started looking out the window. Their city was depressingly familiar to the ones she'd seen in Human Heaven. Buildings, just maybe, with an architecture that reminded her of the little ceramic buildings you'd stick in a tankful of tropical fish.

Mark said, "Then you people are idiots too! This place isn't *real.* It *can't* be! Don't you understand? It's just some kind of very sophisticated VR! We're fucking hog-tied and living in a dream!"

Honoria, quiet: "The dream is yours, Mark. Only yours."

Mark spun about, face white with anger, eyes wide, mouth opening to go for the attack.

Wolf stepped forward quickly, putting his arm around her protectively, one hand raised toward him in a placating gesture. "Hey, people. Even if Mark *is* right, exploring this place will be a hell of a lot more interesting than just sitting around and moping, wandering the fuck around some giant shopping mall or some other useless shit, whether its forever 'til the Topopolitans' induced tau runs down, or just 'til we fucking starve to death in our VR chambers!"

Mark stood stock-still for a second, then his anger seemed to recede, bleeding away back into some pocket deep inside. He relaxed and took a step back. "Well. Well, I . . ." He looked Wolf in the eye suddenly. "Well, I guess you're right."

"Hip-hip," Thalia said, her own anger popping up from nowhere at all.

Days later, Wolf stood in twilight by the shore of an inland sea, looking across the water at the Second Fleet. Seaplanes. Why should it surprise me that the cuttlefish would build seaplanes? They were lovely things, of mirror-bright metal, each one reflecting some image of the darkling sky along the curvature of its hull, the burnished upper surface of its sharply swept shoulder wing. Big jet engines buried in the wing root, powerful, fast, turboram technology of the finest sort.

As the sky darkened, ruddy, cuttlefish-optimized light fading away, Wolf looked toward clouds of mist rising a few kilometers farther on down the shore. That was where sea met sky, where the landscape of Cuttlefish Heaven came to an end, where the waters of the sea tumbled over in a great arc of waterfall.

Flying here from the cuttlefish city, they'd passed out over this last little arm of land, swinging out over the void to approach the sea from outside, and Wolf had looked down on the waterfall, stunned, blue-gray water tumbling over the rim of the world, falling in a broad sheet into the limitless no-color depths of hyperspace, sheet breaking up into tumbling, weightless balls of water, growing smaller and smaller, breaking apart into droplets, then mist, changing to a vapor cloud that drifted inland across Cuttlefish Heaven to fall as rain.

And come here again one day.

Like the waters of a fountain.

There was another small figure standing by some trees, over on the grass, which wasn't grass at all, just as the trees weren't really trees, looking toward the mist, watching the red light boil in its depths, growing darker and bloodier as the light above faded away, red to indigo to black.

Stars? Are there stars in Cuttlefish Heaven?

Of course there are.

As he walked slowly toward her, unfamiliar constellations began to form.

No way I can tell where they lived, when they lived.

An unknown, unfamiliar galaxy, somewhere far beyond the sky.

He was almost beside her when she said, "It's beautiful."

He said, "Yes. Yes it is. I miss the stars, miss the starships, more than I want to say." When he looked away from the sky, Cory was looking up at him, and he could see the shadows under her eyes. Well, he thought, most men would show concern, would ask, *Oh, what's wrong?* He smiled and said, "You look pretty enough tonight."

Pretty girl, out crying under the alien stars.

She looked away, frowning, looking ever so serious, and Wolf thought, All they ever want is for someone to take their small-scale concerns seriously, to make them feel they're more important than all the big deeds in all the big world. She looked up at him, eyes riveted on his face, and said, "Why is everything so screwed up? Why can't we believe we're in Heaven now and let it go at that?"

He nodded, looking into her eyes, willing her to hear, Yes, I understand. Talk to me. He caught his lower lip between his teeth briefly, saw her eyes flicker briefly as she caught the movement.

She said, "Do you think I made a mistake, letting Stuart . . . I mean . . ." He thought he could see her blush, even in the near darkness. Her eyes tried to break contact with his, drifting to one side, trying for concealment, but he moved his head, keeping it in her line-of-sight.

He said, "Nothing that any of us have done is all that terrible, Cory. Life's not a puzzle we can figure out, a game we can win. Our feelings matter."

She stepped closer to his body, stepping into what was,

even in Latin culture, within his personal space, merging it with hers, getting her head more or less under his chin, where his line-of-sight couldn't go. She laid one hand on his broad chest, then laid her head beside it.

Wolf could feel her blouse brushing against his shirt, cloth on cloth.

She said, "I didn't really want to . . . you know."

He nodded, knowing she'd sense the movement and go on.

"It was just that . . . lost in that crazy sky full of endless crazy trees, alone together in the darkness, with me feeling I was without a friend. And he was, oh, close to me, my age, a boy, not a man, not so scary, not so . . ."

Innocent. Innocent and safe. But he fucked you anyway, didn't he, little girl?

Wolf nodded. Then he put his hand on her back, rubbing gently. There there, little Cory.

There was a choking sound, out in the darkness.

Wolf looked up, looking into the night.

There was a dark woman shape, running away.

Honoria.

Of course.

Cory broke away from him, crying out to her mother, running after her in the darkness.

No, wait, you don't understand . . .

Wolf stood looking out to sea, at the twinkling red-green-white running lights of the seaplanes of the Second Fleet, and thought, These things just happen. Why? Because I trained myself to make them happen.

Night fallen, Mark sat on the summit of a little hillock, looking down over the impossible sea. Now that it was dark, even he could tell that these weren't the stars of Earth, but were more uniform in brightness, tending toward orange in color. As though all but the dimmest stars had already burned themselves out. Across the darkness there were sparks of light, and each wavelet brought forth a burst of golden phosphorescence. After the events of this long day, he felt exhausted, but unable to sleep.

"Is this spot taken?"

He was surprised to see Thalia standing above him. The intermittent light glimmered on her face, erasing the signs of age and making her appear as she did when they'd first met. Her new hairdo was remarkably effective in redefining the shape of her face, making it slimmer-seeming, less blocky.

Mark had a brief image of her on the balcony back in Human Heaven, of Mattie waiting for him, expectant. He said, "Sure. What's the harm?"

As she sat, her dress fell away, exposing her legs. He remembered a time, seemingly not so long ago, when they sat together like this. On a dune at Rehoboth. When was that? Must've been after the Camp David conference in '77. Gee. Stuart hardly seemed much more than a toddler then. They'd driven down to one of the turnoffs down in the national park, gone off to watch the full moon rise, then made love at the edge of the water. After they'd screwed, Thalia on top, he just lay there, gasping, listening to the surf and watching the moonlight-washed stars. If there'd been a moment when he was completely in love with her, it was that moment.

Now look at the mess we've gotten ourselves into. And we can't go back no matter how much we want to. The fact of the matter is that I never did hate her, even at the worst of it with Wolf. I guess I even feel a little sorry for her.

"So," she said at last. "It just gets stranger and stranger."

"I guess so." Noncommittal, that. Wait her out; she wants to say something.

Thalia drew her legs up, wrapped her arms around them. "Mark, it's been a long time since we've even been friends. You're a bastard. You know it as well as I do. But there's something between us. I don't know what it is, but I can't deny it."

Husky quality to her voice, as though . . . as though she were crying. With no one to see, his desire to torment had fled. He just felt tired. Even his passion for Mattie seemed to have been swallowed up by melancholy. "Thal, I wish none of this had ever happened. That's the truth."

"Sooner or later, we're going to be devoured whole by all this," she said. "It's going to happen, it's just a question of when."

"I don't know. It's—"

Without warning, sea-shine silhouette turning into a small, dark person, Mattie, of course. Coming up the dune until her head was above theirs. Can hardly see anything but the bright eyes and teeth.

"Well well well," she said, intoning the words, "What have we here?"

Mark said, "It's nothing, Mattie."

"Oh, nothing, is it? Thalia, is it nothing?"

Thalia turned away, said, "Mattie, Mark and I were together for ten years. I think we were just saying . . . goodbye."

"Fat chance," Mattie said. "Mark. Get up and come with me right this minute or it's over between us."

Shock, moderating to dull indignation. For long seconds he hesitated, wanting both of them, really. Finally, sense came to him, and he said, "What the hell? Mattie, I never—"

"Christ," she shouted, "I *knew* it. I'm not gone ten minutes before you're back with this slut."

Mark felt a sodden fear in the pit of his belly. The emotions he'd had in Galaxios came roaring back, and he started to rise to make some motion of protest, couldn't think of one. "Mattie, no. I love *you.* This other woman means nothing to me. . . . She's been trying to get me back since Wolf dropped her, that's all. It's not my fault. Thalia, can't you understand it's over?"

"Mark, it's you who are pitiful." Which one said that? Suddenly they were both gone, disappeared into the dark night. Against the surf's loud scrape-splash he shouted, "Mattie! No. I didn't mean to . . . please . . ." Diminuendo, trailing off . . .

"Thalia?"

Shit.

He sank his butt into the sand, utterly bewildered, and rubbed a hand through his freshly trimmed hair.

Midnight or later.

Two reddish full-moon-like objects were rising simultaneously, painting a double swath of light on the water, but the fact that celestial mechanics made this impossible didn't bother him much. Back at the quay, he could see the others from a great distance, observed them moving about, changing configurations much as the cuttlefish did.

Wonder if the cuttlefish can read us the way we can them? Messages beyond our comprehension. Or too simple for us to see.

As he walked down the path into the dune hills, Cory come came up to him. Stu said, "Hi," and tried to take her arm, but she pulled away.

"Let's walk together, okay?" she said, very serious.

Stu, feeling hurt and apprehensive, said, "Sure."

"You know I like you a lot." Pause. "We've been through a lot together."

"Well, yeah," he said. "And the best is yet to come. The cuttlefish think we'll be at the Omega Point before tomorrow's out. I'm not sure I know what it'll mean, for me or for us, but—"

She stopped, turned to face him, seemed to lose courage. "It's . . . well, it's so difficult to say this. I don't want to hurt you, Stu, I really don't. But there is no 'us.' I'm not your possession."

Goddamn it. Stu felt the fear and anger gathering in him. "Jesus, Cory—" His voice broke, and he tried to calm himself down. "Jesus. I never . . . I just wanted to . . ." Words going nowhere, feeling the sting of her truth. I just wanted to take you for granted, not to have to worry. No, can't say that. "But Cory, I love you. I do." For some reason, it still didn't sound right, even though he knew it was true. "Believe me, please?"

She looked into his eyes as though searching for the lie. "It's not love. You don't even know what love is. Stu, you're still a little kid."

Wanting to bawl, No, I'm *not!* Knowing that that would confirm it. "Cory, God put us together in Heaven—" Taking a little gulp of air.

"You think that means we're married? What God joins together let no man put asunder? Jesus, it'd almost make a kind of sense. Listen to me. This has happened so fast, I haven't been thinking. That night on the branch—and afterward—was a mistake. I was lonely, I'd been—"

"Rejected," he said accusingly. "Cory, you can't seriously think—"

"I'm still confused, but I know my own heart, and it tells me I'd be a fool to let you control my future."

Stu suddenly hoped that this was some kind of test. He had a vision of Mark wilting under his mother's gaze, and let his anger grow. "You say that like you think I'll understand. There's nothing *to* understand. Wolf doesn't care about you at all." Impassive look. I've got no hold on her at all. His resolve faded: "Please, don't. Please . . ."

"Stu, you'll get over it. This may be my last chance."

"Last chance for *what?* Christ, Cory, we're going to go bodily to God's Throne tomorrow."

"Stuart, you don't know a thing."

"I thought you were different from the others," he said, "You're just another—" He choked on the inevitable last word.

Very deliberately, she turned and stalked away. When she was out of sight, he fell to his knees and started to sob.

A new day dawning, the final day, she supposed. Thalia stood in the wide entryway of the cuttlefish cafeteria, little flying squidlings drifting around her in the air, not quite bumping into her, though she was decidedly in the way. The room was . . . full of the damned things, drifting around floating balls, granular things that look a bit like huge cantaloupe . . . or, better yet, like enormous versions of those stupid port-wine cheeseball things people you barely knew were forever giving you at Christmastime. . . .

People? Gone. Gone away. Each and every one.

Forget about them. Let the living remember the dead. We dead should just forget the living and get on with the business of being . . . Christ, do I believe that?

There were people here, at tables on the floor around the edge of the room, and there, in one corner a table with all her friends, comrades, lovers, children. . . . Uh-oh. She felt herself try to control amusement, lips quirking as she tried to keep them still, saw Mark look up, face bleak, bleak face rippling quickly to anger. Oh, who cares? Who the fuck cares?

Look. Wolf sitting back from the table a bit, uncomfortable as hell, Cory sitting at the corner, eyes hollow. Honoria down by the other corner, picking at her steak and eggs. Stu, not looking at anyone, face flushed, not touching the plate in front of him.

And dear, dear, pathetic fucking Mark, not even a plate of fried whatever to keep him company, anger gone away now, eyes all hollow and sad . . . She walked over to the table, trying not to smile. Looked them over, finally let go of it and grinned. "Hey, Marky . . ." Twit the little twit by speaking in ol' Wolfie's voice. "Where's Mattie, still pissed at you?"

Wolf said, "Caught a plane back to Human Heaven, Thal. Said she was tired of our sad, sorry asses."

Thalia said, "Hmm." Not quite a laugh. "You'd think they wouldn't let prize assholes like us into Heaven in the first place."

Stu looked up from his untouched breakfast and said, "Hell, Mom. Maybe they don't."

Wolf seemed to like that. Brought a familiar glint into his eye, at least.

The seaplane had been configured for the human passengers, six big leather recliners lined up against one wall, two by two, little windows shining with ruddy cuttlefish light. Mark, first in, stepped through the foldout hatchway, took the window seat in the first row. The rest of the plane was filled with bank after bank of holsters, suspended by a kind of wire array, each cuttlefish firmly ensconced, arms outstretched, tentacles dangling. Either their chromophores were covered or they were just too excited to "talk."

Just as well. All their speculation's beginning to make my brain hurt, and doesn't accomplish a damned thing.

The rest of the human group had piled in, taken their seats, all of them studiously avoiding the one next to them. Finally, moping Stuart, last in, threw himself down beside Mark. Together again. Just like old times. Both of us missing old Thalia then. Now it's more complicated, but the same anyway.

Look at him. Going through the motions, just like me. God, I'd hoped he'd be able . . . No, stop lying to yourself. Just trying to steal a little of his hopefulness, youthful optimism, before it got smashed. You knew this'd happen. It always happens. You can't live up to people's expectations, and, somehow, he's caught it from you. I've somehow fashioned Stu in my own image. No wonder he hates me so much.

"Could I sit there?" he said in his whiny toddler voice. Always wanted the window seat, always got it.

"Nope." Turning away to look out the precious hole, he felt a surge of satisfaction. "Nothing out there to see, anyway."

A plane started up, a muted rumble, then another, then another, until the air was filled with a chorus of thunder. Finally, the engines on their own plane started, first a complaining squeal, then a chattering roar that drowned out everything. Mark felt around in the crack of his seat, wasn't surprised to find the metal buckles of the seat belt. He fastened the thing around his gut with a snap.

Remember what happened to the First Fleet? Seat belts wouldn't have helped much then. An image of plummeting, alone, frightened beyond belief, superimposed by the comforting vision of waking up next to Mattie. Mattie's gone, though. I must've screwed up, somehow, even before she found me with Thal. She could tell I wasn't the Mark she remembered. That's why she went back.

This time I wake up alone.

Still don't understand a bit of what's going on. If this is a VR simulation, I'm alone now, always have been. *Cogito ergo* . . . what? What's it mean to be, if everything is an illusion? Sudden, sheepish feeling. I remember thinking the same thing back when I first started taking philosophy. It's no more true now than then.

He could feel the plane begin to move forward, looked over at Stu, who was straining to see around him, watch the sky fill with planes. "Well, we're off," he said, not really to anyone in particular. The cuttlefish seemed to quiver with pleasure.

The plane's engine changed in pitch and the dark water dropped away.

The waterfall at the edge of the world had long ago dwindled to a line, then disappeared. Stu sat there, waiting, conscious of the hollow feeling under his sternum.

The sound of the plane's engine was a buzzing drone, resonances drifting in and out, almost making a kind of song. Out the window you could still see the tight formation of the fleet, specks lined up rank upon rank, but the featureless gray of the hyperspace sky was taking on a mottled, mother-of-pearl sheen, hints of rainbow color here and there. No way to say how high they were; he guessed that was meaningless here. The pressure in the cabin hadn't changed, though.

Mark had long ago fallen into slumber, head canted to one side, snoring softly, drool building in the corner of his mouth. Maybe I do understand him better now, at least a little. Does he feel about Mom the same way I do about Cory? Shit, that's so fucking . . . but what if it's true? Is that why he turned out the way he did, why he accepted the situation in our house?

He drew himself up, tried to stop thinking about her, just two seats back, sitting with her mother.

"Look!" His mother's voice, tense with excitement. "Something's out there."

Stu unbuckled his seat belt and knelt by the little window. From this vantage he could only see back where they'd been. Mark was wakening, blinking, wiping his mouth, making spit noises. He sat forward, blocking the way, a sudden light in his eyes, face going through surprise and delight to skepticism. "Jesus H.—" he said. Stu roughly pushed him back in his seat, stuck his eye against the surface of the window.

The opalescence of the sky gathered from all directions to coalesce into an enormous deck of clouds, like the top of a world-girdling cumulonimbus, very dense and solid-seeming, edges trailing into long streamers of feathery cirrus. All of it lit in awesome red-gold radiance, fresh blood mixed in equal parts with molten gold, sky fading to purplish in the distances. Colors more intense than any sunset, cloud details sharper and finer. Stu gasped, pushed Mark farther out of the way, craned his neck painfully. At the center of it all was a hazy white globe, haze encompassing a hundred iridescent halos of light. The globe nestled among the cloud tops like a caught moon.

"It's the Omega Point," he whispered. "It must be."

"What the hell do you think, Stu, that it's an actual *point?* That's ridic—"

Wolf said, "Jesus, did I ever imagine a Heaven like this?"

Through the narrow opening between the seat and window, Stu could see all of them, faces pressed up against their windows, staring wide-eyed, slack-mouthed. Stu said, "You see someone?"

Cory said, "Don't you? In front of the gate, that's San Pedro, with his book."

Honoria said, "Daughter, you must be imagining. It's not a man. Not a man at all."

Thalia: "I don't see anything but a palace, marble, I suppose. It looks like it was designed by M. C. Escher."

"Looks like a golf course to me," Mark said. "Or maybe a cemetery. It's pretty clear we're each getting a different view. VR'd work that way, wouldn't it?"

A cuttlefish nearby squirted from its holster, then another, then another. Soon the cabin was filled with them, jetting about, bodies dark with communication. The air was saturated with their joyful thoughts about the nearness of the Great Kraaken and the culmination of their lives. "He's here. Look at the mighty clusters on his olfactory crest, the brightness of his eye. This is truly the moment we have been waiting for."

"Well," Wolf said, "I wonder what happens next. If we

go to our own various versions of Heaven, I doubt we'll be together anymore."

Thalia said, "Does that mean . . . it's goodbye? Forever?"

Stu said, "Maybe not. The Omega Point Theory seems to say—"

"Your theory only applies to you, son," Wolf said. "Honey, if this is the End, I guess I want to tell you that—"

Eyes pinned to the great milky globe growing as they approached, Stu thought he heard a string quartet playing somewhere. Haydn? In the bright white center of the thing, a translucent shape, coming into focus. A man's face, a bland, bald, shit-eating grin plastered across it.

Squid voice-not-voice: "Here he comes, to devour us along with our vessels. Goodbye, humans, it's been nice knowing you."

The engine stopped, the plane began to tip violently, and things went dark. Stu fell hard against a bulkhead, and, amidst golden sparks and flashes, lost consciousness.

Wolf O'Malley floated serenely in the empty hyperspace sky, waiting patiently for the end to come. All around him, stretching out to the ends of the universe, floated . . . others. Honoria, with her hands over her face, weeping. *Dios. Dios mio,* forgive me . . . Stu, staring intently at *something,* whispering to himself. Listen . . .

". . . of *course* an image of God created for *me* by the Omega Point entity would have a human face. Of *course* it would. All those fairy tales they tell little kids . . . What *else* would I see? Fucking *Santa?* Eight tiny reindeer?"

Keep talking boy. Soon you'll convince yourself.

He smiled.

So how come *I'm* not afraid? Big hairy coconuts, a-swingin' between my manly thighs? Heh. Nope. Just don't believe any of this shit. Guess that puts me in the same category as brave Mr. Porringer, hm?

Mark was hanging motionless, staring, face empty of emotion. Jeez. Almost looks like he's . . . nailed up to an invisible cross. Beyond him, Cory? Cory, why are you looking at me? Soft, silent voice: *She's just a child, Wolf. That's why you didn't fuck her, remember?*

Christ. *Is* it? Is *that* the reason? I've fucked plenty of fifteen-year-old girls in my time.

Yes, but some of them were women. Cory's just a child, despite . . . everything that's happened to her.

Wolf tried to remember the girls he'd fucked, some when young himself, when it was a . . . *legitimate* sort of thing. Others when he was older, eventually much older. Can't remember them. All gone, like trying to remember the shape and feel of your fist, from, oh, how about your thousandth masturbation? Which one was that, old boy?

Is that all I am? An old boy?

The voice seemed to snicker.

Well, lookee there. Good old Thalia staring at me too, with something of that same yearning in *her* eyes. So *are* they all stupid, dear voice of infinity?

Silence.

What, cat gotcher tongue?

The voice said, *They've come and sucked your dick for you, Mr. O'Malley. What more did you want?*

Don't know. Do you?

Sure, but I'm not telling.

Are you really God? The real honest-to-God God? Or just Stuie's pathetic Omega Point?

Silence.

Beyond the people, familiar people and strangers alike, there was a sea of cuttlefish, stretching on and on, dwindling away to tiny dots, like black stars in a gray sky. There was a bigger black dot nearby, hanging, looking at him with a double red glint from liquid glowing eyes.

I'll be damned. Ox. Good old Ox. Man's best friend.

The voice said, *Why, Wolfie, I'm surprised at you. I thought pussy was a man's best friend.*

Tell me, God: Dogs got souls?

Think you've *got a soul, Mr. O'Mulley?*

No.

Guess that makes you a soulless monster, now doesn't it?

Guess so. Looking at the dog, Wolf remembered waking up from a sound sleep, finding the dog's heavy, hot body pressed against his back, breathing slowly, softly, also asleep.

Why did that make me feel so damned good?

The voice said, *Better than waking up with your leg over a sleeping woman, woman breathing in your face, nice, wet, freshly fucked pussy under your hand?*

Yeah.

The voice said, *Probably because you think the dog loves you, and the women do not.*

So that's what I think, is it?

What do you think? (Suspicious echoes: *do* you think, do *you* think, do you *think?*)

I don't know.

Me neither.

What happens next?

Silence.

How come you don't answer my questions?

The voice said, *So far, they don't have answers. Next question.*

Wolf thought, None of them? Damn. He said, How about that last bit? Dog really love me? How about the women?

Silence.

Damn. Not even *one* of the—

The voice said, *Ox really loves you.*

Great. Just great.

The voice said, *I thought of an answer to what comes next.*

From not far away, Honoria screamed.

Hyperspace exploded to black.

Seventeen

Fiat lux . . .

They fell in darkness, one by one.

Honoria calling out in a babble of Spanish. God. Corazón. Her husband. In that order. Then her voice faded, as though she were falling away, the others remaining.

Stu's voice, cracking with excitement and fear: "Mom! Mom, can you hear me? Where are you?"

Male voice: "Stuart!"

Uncertain: "Wolf?"

"No. Mark."

The wind was starting to roar now, a sure sign they were falling faster and faster.

"Stu?"

Silence.

"Stu? Thalia?"

Her voice said, "I don't want this. Oh, God, I don't want this. . . ."

What did you want, then? Do you know?"

"Thalia! This isn't *real!* Just hang on! It's all a *dream!* We're going to wake up soon!"

Silence.

"Thal?"

Silence.

Distant barking.

Good old Ox. Always faithful.

Cats. Would the cats yowl as they fell? No. Watched a cat thrown from an eighty-foot cliff once. Went to its death watching with interest, paws outstretched, perfectly stable, as the ground came up from below.

Mark yelled, "Oh, God. *Anybody?*"

Afraid to be alone, Marky? Me too. Wolf called out, "Just us chickens." Listen to that. Accent as thick as can be: *Jes us chickens.*

Mark seemed to whimper: "Oh, God . . ."

Wolf said, "Okay. I'm ready to wake up. Any time now, Marky-boy."

"Fuck you."

Still falling, all alone now, utterly calm, Wolf started to sing, wind whistling along in his hair: "Nobody loves me, everybody hates me, I'm gonna eat some . . ." Well. Shit fire. Why'd it have to come to this, anyway?

Silence.

No answer.

. . . *et seq. noctem.*

After dinner, Honoria went to her room, the room she'd been sharing with Wolf for so long now, and stood looking out the window at that Sagdeevan landscape, as unthinking as it was possible to be. The meal, spiced red rice and chick peas, mixed with sauteed sweet onion, overloaded with the bits of almost-raw garlic Wolf loved, was like acid lead in her stomach, a burning weight just under her breastbone. A bitter taste on the back of her tongue.

So this is it? My salvation and Corazón's; the rest of our lives?

Outside, the sunset landscape was beautiful, in a barren yet peaceful fashion. Bare hills, with just that fuzz of algal green, as though the world were like moldy bread too long on the shelf. Dots of green, fuzzed with white, here and there. Empty, off-color sky.

I'd like to go home again. As if my home wasn't . . . here. She could see the wind was blowing outside, rippling the walls of the plastic greenhouse tent in which her garden grew. If I were out there, I could feel the wind in my hair, feel it blowing fresh and cool on my cheeks.

No. The winds of Sagdeev are warm like sweat. And you'd be wearing an oxygen mask.

She heard the damned dog padding by in the hallway. God. A monster. Already, it'd laid one great, steaming pile of turds on the kitchen floor for her to find in the morning. Wolf had laughed, praising Ox for having the good sense to do it on the kitchen tile instead of the living room carpet.

Too much trouble, you see, to put on his own mask, the dog's, and take him out for a midnight stroll.

She could hear voices in the background. Wolf's, a low rumble. Corazón's lighter, finer. Laughing. Then silence. Then Wolf again.

There was a pain under her breastbone, and momentarily she hoped it was a fatal heart attack. No such luck. Only dyspepsia.

Outside, Mu Arae, looking not at all like the sun, was a vast red ball hanging just above the western horizon, sinking into the sullen green-brown mist that hid the end of the sky. The mist, edgeless, not at all like clouds, was cutting the star to pieces and shapes, blocking out its light.

There was a dark fleck on its surface, which she imagined might be a sunspot. It moved away, dissipating. A bird? No. No birds here. Airplane. Helicopter . . .

She turned away and looked at the bed. *Bed.* Why doesn't it turn my stomach, just the way this awful supper has? But she remembered how happy she'd been to see Wolf again, once she'd gotten over the joy of Cory's return. *Cory.* Gringo nickname she's taken to heart.

Not quite the same little girl anymore.

She remembered Wolf coming to bed with her, that first night home, oncc they'd gotten those awful Porringer people settled. Pathetic Mark. Disgusting Stuart. This bitch Thalia Jansky, too proud to take her husband's name . . .

I got undressed for him, throwing my clothes carelessly aside, just the way he likes. Got undressed in the order he prefers, like a dancing whore, smiling as his eyes grew greedy. Kicking off my shoes. Slipping out of my skirt, letting it ease down over my hips, letting him see the curve of my hip, keeping the tail of my blouse oh-so-carefully over the only thing he really wants to see.

I can tell.

Turned my back. Stretched, so the blouse rode up and showed my ass. Heard him sigh. Unbuttoned it, facing away. Played with my breasts, even though all he would see was the suggestive movements of my elbows. Let the blouse fall down my back to the floor. Walked to the bed. Turned around.

Wolf still standing by the door, ridiculous hump in the front of his pants.

Lay myself down on the bed, legs half spread, watching him look, seeing the hunger in his eyes. You know what to do, the eyes seemed to say. Do it now.

Lay back. Spread my legs. Pulled them up. Put my hands under my knees so I'd be all the way open, first for his eyes, then for the rest of him. The world came back and she was looking at herself in the mirror. Face a blank. I was expecting to see tears. No tears.

There was a scuffling noise from somewhcre else in the

house. Then Cory's voice, raised, high-pitched. Alarmed? Something. Then Wolf laughed—I know that laugh—and the scuffling noise was repeated.

Honoria turned away from the mirror, opened the bedroom door and went out into the hallway. Rustling and scuffling. Living room. Wolf chuckling in a workmanlike way. Cory . . . inarticulate words. She walked down the hall, stopped in the nice archway Wolf had built his last time home, just to please her.

Wolf was standing in the middle of the room, back toward her, elbows out, unbuttoning his shirt. Beyond him, Cory was sprawled on the floor, wearing her white blouse, white tennis shoes, white socks, white shorts a scrap of cloth beyond her, up on the couch. She was sitting up on her elbows, feet braced on the carpet about a half meter apart, lips of her vulva popped open so you could see her opening.

Looking up at Wolf, she seemed . . . hypnotized.

Field mouse. Black snake. Moment of truth.

Honoria turned away, feeling as though the whole world had receded to an infinite distance. Turned and walked into the kitchen, stood by the sink, looking out the little window, little window there only so she'd have something to look at while she did her mindless woman's work. It was almost night now, sky deep indigo, shading to black, freckled with a few bright stars, occluded by ragged black clouds. Some of the highest clouds were still tinted orange by the setting sun. Mu Arae. Not the Sun . . .

From the living room, obviously frightened, Cory said one strangled word, something halfway between *oh* and *no.* Wolf's voice muttered, reassuring words no doubt. There. There now. This feels so good. So good.

She remembered the first time he'd spoken them to her, the first night after he'd bought her. Nothing special, she thought then. Just one more dick; after so many you stopped counting them. But he was . . . gentle enough. Pleasant enough. Kind enough. Generous enough. After a while the words came true.

From the living room she could hear Wolf starting to pant.

There were lighter sounds as well. The sounds of Cory, breathing aloud.

She took the kettle. Filled it with bottled water. Put it on the stove. Turned the burner on. Watched it begin to glow bright orange. I always hated electric stoves. Gas is so much nicer.

From the living room, Wolf said, "Oh, Cory . . ."

Oh, Cory.

Cory, panting with . . . No. It's just the weight of him bouncing on her belly that makes her breathe like that.

Took out her cup. Dropped in a tea bag. Opened the silverware drawer to get one of the nice silver spoons Wolf had brought from Earth one day. Family heirloom, he'd said. The monogram was R. My mother's family . . . She took out the long, slim, serrated bread knife, slid the drawer silently shut, turned and walked back into the living room.

Wolf's buttocks, fuzzed with short black hair, were pouched with muscular effort as he curled his hips under so he could thrust himself all the way in, then pull out again, not quite far enough to slip free. All she could see of Cory was two long, slim white legs wrapped around the outside of Wolf's thighs, white tennis shoes resting on the back of his knees.

That and the top half of her head. Black hair. White forehead shining with sweat. Wide, staring eyes.

Staring right at me.

She stepped close, Cory's eyes following her movement, put the knife in position above Wolf's heaving back, holding the hilt in her left hand, putting the heel of her right over the pommel. Shoved as hard as she could, pushing it in as far as it would go.

Wolf jerked and grunted, tried to get up, pushing off with his arms. Fell back. Cory grunted as his weight fell on her.

When Honoria tried to pull Wolf away, he was too heavy, Cory dragging along under him, eyes blazing. She stopped, panting heavily, then reached down and tried again. Cory squawked, a horrible croaking sound, and Honoria realized that the knife had gone right through Wolf and thrust several centimeters into her daughter's chest as well.

As she watched, Cory's lips worked, trying to form a word, a sentence. Then the eyes went empty and there was nothing more.

From the kitchen, the teakettle began to whistle.

The ship lurched horribly, upended, and there was a noise like tearing paper. Stu clung to the straps that held him in the bunk, fingers straining, and watched in horror as the other stack of bunks began to distort, pulling from the wall. Mark and Honoria had identical fearful, staring expressions. Shit. Corazón, beneath him, let out a pathetic little bleat.

Again the ship changed course, and his stomach somersaulted. Mom and Mattie must be fighting to avoid the debris. When it happened, they were ascending at maximum power on a course that would take them behind the moon in a few hours. From 200,000 kilometers out, the Earth's bright ball had passed through the circular maw of the world-destroyer like a butterfly being snagged by a net. And what came out the other side . . . he still couldn't believe it. There wasn't even an explosion, just an expanding red-pink sphere, glowing brightly, smooth at first, then coalescing into moon-size droplets as the light faded. What's the opposite of accretion? Deaccretion? Earth had been reduced to planetesimals in less time than it takes to pop a balloon.

They were still accelerating, but the stuff was moving outward at tremendous speed, and had caught up with them in a matter of minutes. The last thing Stu'd seen was a metal blob of unknown size, surface cooling, crinkled but shiny like the crust forming on a bead of solder, shooting right at them. Now the screen showed nothing.

Mattie's voice over the intercom: "Brace yourselves. We're going in."

Mom said, "Stuart, I love you."

"Mom—" he said.

There was a loud crash and the straps bit deep into him. His head snapped forward, then back, and a thousand pounds of his own weight crushed him against the barely padded mattress. He could hear the blood rushing through his ears, bloodred pulsing in his visual field, darkening, fading to black.

Then, after what seemed a second, helical spirochetes of golden light filled his eyes, forcing him back to consciousness. Throbbing silence, made palpable by the absence of the roar of the nuclear engines. Tiny gravity here, probably not acceleration, just enough to keep things from floating away.

Where the other set of bunks had been there were only a few strands of twisted, broken metal. Various modules had broken off from the kitchenette and workstation, and a small leak from the sink was pumping a slow-motion arc of water globules into the air. He shouted, "Mom?" then, "Mattie, anybody?" No response.

With a deeply uncomfortable sensation in his stomach, he looked past his feet at the "down" end of the cabin. What a mess. It looked like the in-basket of a metal recycler, tangled wires threading a heap of cans, food trays, and miscellaneous instruments, bent, sharp-ended poles sticking out at odd angles. The bunks had been smashed against the wall, and all he could see was their spring-lined bottoms.

Stu carefully undid the straps holding him in, noticing for the first time that his fingernails were bleeding, starting to ache. When he had the last one unfastened, he levered himself around, grabbed hold of the retractable ladder, swung himself over to it. Corazón was still strapped in her bunk, eyes closed, dribble of blood in one nostril. "Cory?" he said, and she opened her eyes slowly and looked at him. Blank look in those dark, beautiful eyes.

"We crashed. I'm afraid Mark and your mother . . ." Stu motioned at the jumble at the other end of the cabin. "They must have been . . . I'm going up to see what happened there." He pulled himself hand over hand to the control room hatch, saw with horror that the mechanical indicator showed total decompression on the other side.

Jesus. It's getting . . . hot.

Cory had undone herself and was clambering toward the down end. "Are you sure you want to do that?"

She pulled the bunk down, and there was Mark, looking like a smashed bug in a puddle of his own blood. Silently, she pried the corner of the other bunk loose, looked into the crevice, and started to retch. Stu got himself upright, feeling the heat coming through the bulkhead on his feet, went to her, pulled her away, not knowing what to say. She clutched at him, began to cry without noise, chest heaving against him.

This is it. This the end. Stu imagined that the air was already less satisfying. He wondered what his life would have been like if they'd been able to get to Sagdeev, as they'd planned. If he could have gotten to know Cory better. An image of her smiling, red-gold Australian sunset glinting in her dark hair, laughing at a little joke he'd managed to make up.

He hugged himself against her cool body, feeling the cloth bunch up, and the soft resilience underneath. Squeezed her as hard as he could, the area behind his eyes clotting with pain. Wanting to throw himself desperately against the walls, claw his way through the indestructible metal, he clung to her instead, and began to cry.

Under control now, she stroked his head.

* * *

Easter Sunday.

Corazón Suárez O'Malley watched the bright landscape, silver and gold trees, amber grasses of Alii Nui VI pass on by, watching out the armored glass rear window of the limousine as it rolled down the empty concrete highway. Overhead, Alii Nui, Great Mother, was a brilliant green disk in the sky, pale yellow-green sky, ten times the size of the Sun, but shedding no more light.

In the distance you could see the white skyscrapers of downtown Redburgh, just peeking over the hills. By the side of the road, a gang of Sixian laborers, like pulpy softshell crabs the size of big dogs, armed with picks and shovels, hammers and wheelbarrows, labored. The gangly young man guarding them held a double-barrel, ten-gauge shotgun under one arm.

The dumptruck driver, also human, portly and rather older, had a pistol holstered at his hip, but his arms were folded across his chest as he half leaned, half sat on the truck's front bumper, hat tipped low over his eyes, as if asleep.

From the front seat, Jorge the driver said, "Senator be coming home from Earth tomorrow, ma'am?"

Ma'am. Always the polite fiction. Always. She could see his black eyes looking at her in the rearview mirror, smoldering with . . . something. Beyond him, on the horizon, were a range of silver-gray mountains almost vanished in the haze, above which she could see a brilliant speck rising into the sky, the noonday shuttle from O'Malley Cosmodrome.

She said, "Yes, Jorge."

Eyes burning on her, he said, "And so, of course . . ."

She looked back at him, frowning. Getting to be a little possessive are we, Jorge? Have to think about that. She said, "Of course. I'll have to be clean as a whistle for him by tomorrow night. You know that." *Clean as a whistle.* Funny

Anglo turn of phrase. Whistles are always full of spit. Like me.

They pulled off the highway and through the gates of the cemetery, pulled into a parking space, and Jorge got out to open the door for her. His eyes were still angry. She put one hand on his arm and said, "I'll be back in a few minutes. And the senator will have to go back to Earth next week. The Porringer confirmation hearings . . ."

She walked away without another look, making a mental note to talk to Luisa about finding another driver, about finding a suitable posting for Jorge . . . elsewhere. Candlehaven. That's the one. They say it's such a *nice* frontier world. Give him some land. A little seed money. Find some nice girl who'll volunteer to be his wife, someone who can be trusted to be subtle, not tip him off that it was a put-up job.

The grave was freshly mowed, fresh flowers at the base of the stone.

She made a mental note to have the groundskeeper tipped. What's his name? Grenzman? And he has two nice little girls. See that they each get a jumbo Easter basket delivered this afternoon.

"Hello, Mama. Nice to see you again."

The gravestone was silent, and there was a cool breeze blowing, stirring her dress, playing in her hair.

Hard to imagine her under the ground like that, all these years, in her box. Stone cold . . . and nice of Wolf to bring her along, without my even asking, when we moved here from Sagdeev. Of course, he moved Ox's grave too, but . . . nice. He can be nice when he needs to be.

Politicians need niceness on tap.

Doesn't have to be sincere.

Just nice.

She had a momentary memory of Wolf the Starship Pilot, as he had been, twenty years ago. Handsome. Oh, so handsome. Movie star handsome, making Miz Jolsen sweat when she saw him. God. I haven't thought about that in a long, long time.

Wasn't hard for him to get me down on the living room floor. I had an orgasm before he was done. Surprised me. Surprised both of us.

Then, over his shoulder, while I waited, dazed, for him to finish, my mother, the knife, my scream . . . Wolf pulling out, springing to his feet, erect penis sticking out, oh-so-stiff.

Got the knife away from her.

Got her calmed down.

Both of us blubbering, saying how sorry we were, how it just *happened.*

Came to me in the night, came to me in my bed, oh-so-nice and . . . Twice. I remember we did it twice, fell asleep in each other's arms. And in the morning, of course, Mama was dead, lying naked in a tub full of cold, bloody water.

Buried her out back, not far from where we buried Ox about five years later. By then, you couldn't really tell where she was anymore. Wolf said he had to dig up the whole damned yard to find them both, get them out of their body bags and into decent coffins.

Inspector general.

Mark, Thalia, Stu . . . Beta Pictoris . . . The BeauHun ship . . . the Federation of All Worlds. Welcome. Welcome star-farers . . . Remember the hero's welcome we got? Remember the parades? The medals? Dinner with the President and her husband?

It was at that dinner I told Wolf I was pregnant, probably from that first night we spent together. Angel O'Malley conceived just about the time Mama climbed into the tub and started screwing up her courage while Wolfie screwed me, putting the razorblade to her wrist.

Mental note to make *sure* Angel was home tomorrow.

I think I remember the water running as she filled the tub. I didn't care. Wolf had his mouth on me.

Funny, Wolf looks a little bit like the President's husband now, sixty-seven years old, hair silver and black, still handsome, even if he is forty pounds heavier. . . .

Election next year.

How would it feel to be First Lady of the Human Race?

She put her own little bouquet down beside the larger, nicer one the graveyard had provided, turned and walked away, down to where Jorge was waiting by the car.

The wind from the Pacific was cool and, as always, moist. Mark could feel the wet cedar planks of the deck giving slightly under his weight as he crossed to the stairs, looked back to where it was pulling off from the cabin wall. Got to get someone in to fix it soon, or the whole damn thing'll come loose. The buzz of the generator was harsher than usual, cutting through the sound of wind and waves. That too. Through the bedroom window he could see that Corazón had turned on her lamp, was reading in bed. Damn woman never wants to get out of bed these days.

For that matter, neither do I. But it's the first of June, time to collect my paycheck.

He stepped off into the unruly green-brown mass of unmown lawn, crossed the twenty yards or so to the beach.

It was less than half a mile to the post office, but he was feeling pretty stiff, so when he came to the barrier of broken, piled-up driftwood, he found a big, bleached bole and took a seat, facing out to sea. It was nearly noon, and the morning fog was burning off now. Low clouds, wispy and darker, twisted below the steely gray overcast, coming ashore.

Still, the overcast was bright, so it would be classified as a fine day hereabouts. Slice-of-Cake sea stack loomed clear and dark, wedge shape topped with a ragged copse of windblown evergreens, and the lesser rocks were just visible as a variety of unlikely shapes beckoning out beyond the booming surf.

Of all the places in the world to come, this is the one I picked. Olympic Peninsula. La Pull. Thought it was the most beautiful beach in the world when I first saw it. Still do, for that matter. And the Northwest continues to escape the worst of it. It was the right choice. I made *all* the right decisions, dammit. I've *got* mine. Then why does it still seem so . . . hopeless?

Shit. Pull yourself together, boy. You've got it made. O'Leary would be proud of you. You've escaped through a hole in the electrons, just like him. You've gone to Goldbrick heaven. Even Dad—image of his father goggling into viddies after the snafu that abolished his job—no, can't picture him smiling down on me. Mama, of course, would have me turn myself in, go to jail for what I'm doing. If there are any federal prisons anymore, which I doubt.

He got up, laboriously crawled over the larger branches in his way, imagining as he did his first day here, that the driftwood was some kind of dinosaur graveyard, and the wood enormous bones. The beach was smooth, almost neutral gray, penetrated here and there by dark humpback rocks. He looked back at the cabin, lonely little shack, really, small and forlorn-looking beneath the gigantic rain-forest cedars. This is what I wanted.

Fuck you, Mama. The world has gone to hell. You want me to try and hold it together?

In the distance, reflected in the wetness left by the incoming waves, more sea stacks, Moptop, Butte, and little Seal's Tail. Well, gotta get a move on. The post office closes at one.

Really, it couldn't have worked out better. Who would've guessed that printing checks and sending them out would be the last things the U.S. government could do with any reliability? All the electronic systems just broke down, but the good old USPS keeps on.

Don't want to think about Cory, do you? Christ, you bought her, own her by any reasonable definition. Why can't you control her? Oh, she's so sweet, says the things she knows I want to hear, then just gives them that little twist at the end that says *I'm* the schmuck, not her. She won't make dinner anymore, the kitchen's a disaster area. And how long has it been since she sucked me off? Weeks, maybe a month. She'd be gone in a second if I didn't give her her allowance. I doubt that the Company would even go after her anymore.

I'm gonna have to deal with that girl. Jesus. Maybe I should just kick her out.

The first signs of the village were appearing now, dirt tracks, old, abandoned houses. Mark jumped a little freshwater stream that crossed the beach, getting some water in one of his shoes, then climbed across some broken rocks, careful not to step on the anemones crowding the little pools in the crevices. In a moment he was on the main road, paved with gravel and broken oyster shells. He looked out to sea one more time, as if searching for something, then headed inland.

The Post Office and General Store was a neat, dark green building standing under a stand of enormous old redwoods. Inside, set away from the shelves of canned and dry goods, there was a small room behind a little, wooden partition, with an old, gray-haired lady of obvious Native American descent sorting a few letters into a wall of pigeonholes, singing a little chant as she worked. As he came up to the counter, she turned, said, "Well, Mr. Porringer, I was wondering if you were going to make it today. Here's your mail." He took a handful of thin plastic envelopes, left without saying a word.

The check looked like it always did, and he ripped open the envelope, double-checked the amount, a big number which was indexed to inflation and approximately trebled every month. All right. Now what's this?

It was a letter from his mother. Unusual, nowadays. He ran a finger down the seam and it folded open.

A cold grue formed in his stomach. Christ almighty. She *can't* do that! I don't have any room. I—

His mother, fleeing from Chicago, was on her way.

The laundry had just started filling, a cold wash of her best clothes, what few were left, when the power failed for the third time that morning. Feeling exhausted, Thalia opened the washer's lid and looked in. It was half full of soapy red water, water with a slight reddish tinge. Oh, great. That mean's the filter's failed again and I'll have to wash them all over.

And my bath. Christ I was looking forward to . . .

Well. No electricity, no continuous coil. Which, without the filter, would be red with rust anyway. There'd be some warm, clean water in the reserve tank, but not enough for a bath.

As she bent down to check the clothes in the dryer, Wolf's ratty old blue jeans, still wet from the previous load, she caught a whiff of herself. Armpits and hours-old come.

Her eyes felt grainy, sensation compounded by tired anger. I can never get back to sleep when he wakes me up like that. Wish the hell I could just sleep right through it the way Lisa says she can when Donny gets after her. Not that Wolf wouldn't like that.

This morning, he hadn't shaken her or anything. She'd just woken up as he pushed her onto her back, pushing her thighs apart, sticking his fingers in so he could check the lay of the land. Sometimes I wish I was dry, the way some women . . . Hell, he'd probably just hurt me if I wasn't wet enough for him.

Shove it in and not care.

Once upon a time, she'd complained about the quickies. What happened to the old times, Wolf, when you used to excite me until I could hardly stand anymore? Old memories now, of young people in Youth Service, charged up with what was happening to them, all around them.

She went in the bathroom anyway, stood in front of the clouded, black-flecked mirror and started to get undressed. Saggy tits and fat belly. Is that what happened? Can't I excite him anymore? Then why . . . Oh, hell. Maybe he just shuts his eyes and imagines, just like he's jerking off with a magazine in one hand and his dick in the other.

Is that all I am to him?

Tired. Tired of asking that question. What difference does it make?

She turned on the water and watched the tub fill. When the stream coming out of the tap started to turn pink, she turned it off and got in. Three inches deep. Warm as spit, at best. She put her finger up her vagina and agitated, trying to get his residue gone.

Not that it'll matter. He'll come home, eat supper, then want my ass in the bed so he can forget his day, so he can get to sleep, rest up for the dawn fuck and then off to the salt mines.

Wolf, at least, had become tanned, fit and muscular from years working on a roadgang. Tanned. Hell, his tan's so heavy it makes him look black, when the light's just right. She felt a stir down below and sullenly pulled her finger out, swishing it clean in the water.

Who cares? Who the fuck cares?

Another stirring, something in her heart. I wish . . . long, shallow memory of those old days, Youth Service, flying, loving each other, following the news of the space program, ERDA probing the asteroids. We got married, applied to ERDA, even got accepted for astronaut training, but . . .

I thought I'd kill myself when the program was canceled, six weeks before we were scheduled for our first flight. Goddamned politicians.

And now, twenty years later . . .

There was the sound of their old pickup truck in the driveway, engine shuddering to a stop. Thunk of truck door. Bang of the house's screen door. Now what? She heard Wolf walk across the living room, stepping, as always, on the one board that creaked.

Just to remind himself it's still there, though he'll never bother to fix it.

She heard the refrigerator door open and close. Heard the whispery pop of a beer opening. Oh, God. Two, three beers, and he'll be after my cunt.

The bathroom door opened silently and Wolf was standing there looking at her, naked in three inches of water, legs spread, crotch nicely soaped up. He stood holding the doorframe with one hand, beer in the other, face flat and expressionless.

She looked back at him, waiting for it to start.

Hell, maybe it'll be fun for once, doing it in the tub with soap to play with.

He said, "I just got fired."

She felt a pang grip her heart. *Fired?* Then how will be pay the mortgage? How . . . She had a brief vision of them living in public housing. "How . . . uh . . ."

"Congress held a secret vote last night and canceled funding for Public Works. They sent us all home. Not even going to get the pay they owe us for the fourteen days we worked this month."

His face crumpled suddenly and he started to cry.

Reeling from a thousand lives lived all at once, Wolf floated alone in gray hyperspace. All those lives really mine? All the way from Wolf the hero-savior of humanity to Wolf the homeless bum living under a bridge? That'd been a good one, Wolf almost happy living outdoors, smoking cheap cigars and drinking sour wine.

And far from the worst. In some of those lives, he was a corpse under the ground, while other people, people important to him, had lived on and on.

Is this life that I remember living really the best of all possible lives? In the universe of Many Histories, I seem to have slipped from track to track, avoiding most pitfalls.

In some lives, he'd apparently lost the knack of getting into women's pants. One particular nightmare . . .

Image of an obese Wolf, standing alone in his dirty kitchen, carefully carving into the soft, sweet-smelling flesh of a ripe Santa Claus melon, cutting an almond-shaped opening that, through long practice, was just the right size, angling in just so, using a long-handled spoon to scoop out a narrow tunnel that went just above the pocket of seed.

Then he'd carried the thing to his bed, laying a plastic garbage bag over the sheets, centering the melon on it, then arranging his five pillows into the rough shape of a woman's torso, no need for arms, legs, head. Standing there at the foot of the bed, looking at his creation while he played with himself. Getting harder and harder to get it up these days.

When he was ready, he climbed aboard, thrusting into the melon, thrusting and thrusting, panting, sensation almost as good as he remembered women being, especially if you warmed it in the microwave for a few seconds.

Hanging in nothingness, Wolf shook his head, grinning. Imagine. Imagine being that man.

He shouted, "*Heellllooooooo* . . ."

Not even an echo.

What did I see? Was I supposed to learn something from visiting that . . . that . . . ocean of despair? What could it have been I was supposed to learn? Why don't I know?

And, finally, that other question. Are the others hanging alone too, each one in his or her own empty universe? Are *they* wondering what the hell it's all for?

Funny. I can *see* what the others should have learned. Thalia. Mark. Stu. Honoria. Even Cory. But me?

No.

He pictured Thalia floating alone and imagined her grim satisfaction as she contemplated the cruel lessons Wolf O'Malley should have learned. *That'll teach you . . . bastard.*

He smirked.

Will she realize I learned nothing, just like her?

Slow, reluctantly dawning light.

Well. Not so.

I learned the other people's lessons, now *didn't* I?

Jesus.

Goddamned *sneaky* son of a bitch.

You got to admire a God like that.

Eighteen

Suddenly, Wolf was sitting in an old plastic chair, legs crossed, magazine in his lap. It was a little stuffy in the room, no windows, fluorescent light overhead making him squint. Maybe the air-conditioning was on the fritz, air blowing, but not much cool. There were other people in the room, but Wolf felt curiously uncomfortable about looking at them. Keep your head down, that's the ticket, pretend you're invisible, that you're all alone here.

The thick magazine sprawled in his lap was open roughly to the middle, to somewhere around . . . he squinted. Page 21,468? Um. Not enough paper here for there to be . . . He closed it, staring dully at the cover. It was a deep hologram, full of misty light and half-resolvable images.

The title seemed to be something like *Times Without Number,* but when he looked again, it was something else. He opened to the first page, and was gratified when it said page 1. Well. Flipped to the middle. Page 4,274,556 . . .

Flipped to the last page.

There was a lazy-8 down in the corner. And the last words on the page? "The keys to. Given! A way a lone a last a loved a long the" . . . Wolf felt a dull blast of rage that faded as quickly as it came.

He shut the magazine and looked up, shoving shyness aside as pointless. Mark was there, sitting in a plastic chair, thick magazine open in his lap, listlessly turning pages. Thalia, sitting with her own magazine shut, slouched in the chair, head tipped back, eyes open to the ceiling. Honoria had her magazine open to somewhere near the beginning, wide eyes scanning right, left, right again.

Wonder if hers is in Spanish.

Cory was looking down at her open magazine, eyes far away, not reading. Apparently feeling his gaze, she looked up and met it. Smiled slightly. Hi, Wolf. Stuart was reading his magazine with evident interest, but every now and again he'd glance up, always at Cory.

Wolf took a quick look around the room. No cat cage. No big dog. Felt a pang of sorrow. They were the best part, after all.

A wingless woman in a white robe, pretty young thing with pale skin, pale eyes, platinum-blond hair, slim hips, pert little tits, opened the door and looked in on them. "Mr. Porringer?" she said in a marvelous contralto. "God will see you now."

Mark, bless his heart, looked scared as hell as he followed her into the impenetrable light behind the door. Wolf thought, What will I feel when my turn comes? How much courage is required?

Mark slowed, felt the angel's hand more firmly on his arm. The bright white light was pouring out from every direction, sourceless, casting no shadows.

No. The sound of the word hung there in space and time, echoed in his mind like a solid, iron bell. It had been his motto, his watchword, and now, on the threshold of God's examination room, it seemed to become his entire self.

"Come on, Mr. Porringer, there's nothing to be afraid of." Tugging a little.

Mark made an insincere little chuckle. "It's not *nothing* I'm afraid of. I'm a nihilist, after all. The only thing that I've ever really believed in is myself."

"Not true, Mr. Porringer. You've always believed in the disapproval of others."

Surprised, hurt, he looked into her little upturned angel face. "It's not my fault if—"

"Please come along. Just another few steps."

Imagining Wolf snickering, or God Himself looking askance, he reluctantly started to walk.

Bubbles of light seemed to engulf him, cleansing him. Hazily at first, green light, then foliage. He came out in a little sun-dappled ravine, breezes ruffling the leaves one against another, causing the dapples to open and close, light and dark intermingling. Pine trees, skinny branchless boles covered with the big curling scales, here and there caked with yellow resin. He raised his head and took a deep breath through his nose, enjoying the smell of turpentine and dust on this hot summer noontime. On either side, higher up, were the rows of blocky tract houses that marked the edges of civilization.

You could hear the sound of children beyond the impenetrable thicket of greenbrier and blackberry bushes, but he knew the path and automatically searched it out. Dark, footpacked dirt led the way.

One path led to another, and he could see the bright clothing of other kids through the trees. They were playing at the edge of the creek, yelling encouragement to the two who had climbed halfway up the eroded red cliff face on the far side of the water. One of the kids slipped, fell backward, rolled down the slope, finally came to rest butt first in the rocky shallows of the creek.

Everyone was laughing, including the wet, rust-covered boy.

Why am I here? I never liked those kids much, just barely got along with them.

He hung back, suddenly realized that, although the geography of the creek was exactly as he remembered it, these were *different* children. Not Kenny Quiroz or Walter Barr or David McClanahan, whose faces were still etched into his soul.

Maybe . . . with these kids, he could . . . what? Make friends better? Not end up being tormented, continually having to defend himself from the little devils? He vividly recalled a time, when he was maybe twelve, and Kenny and David had stolen his baseball cap, tossing it back and forth, keeping it away from him until he collapsed into tears. He never *had* gotten that cap back.

Maybe this time it'll be different.

Slowly, he came out from behind the fallen tree and said, "Hi."

God will see you now?

Thalia sat dully, watching Mark rise and go through the door. God? No God here. No God anywhere. Not if I had to live any of the lives I saw, every life I saw. Even my real one. Chicago childhood secure from all evil. Youth Service. The lost promise of Wolf. *Wolf.* Christ, I thought it was a nickname, stupid nickname for a man who . . .

She had a sharp memory of young Wolf standing in the shadows before her, the two of them surrounded by the loud Brazilian night. Grinned. Unzipped his fly. Didn't expose himself, just . . .

I remember that remarkably pleasant clench in my crotch, realizing I was going to . . . go right along with the gag.

No gag at all.

Wolf. Then home again, service all done. Case Western, where I stayed and studied till I was thirty-one years old. B.S. in aerospace engineering. M.S., Ph.D. in metataxial physics. Met Winston there. Love. Whatever the hell I know of love, that's where the memory lies.

Stuart born when I was a freshly minted postdoc.

All those lovely years, blurred with activity.

Winston.

God, has he been gone five years already?

She remembered how she'd cried, hiding up in the avionics space of her latest ship after the message came. Just a piece of paper. There's been an accident. Your husband of twelve years is dead.

Not just dead, but utterly gone.

Not even remains left behind.

"Mrs. McCray?"

Thalia looked up. The angel girl was standing in the open doorway, eyes infinitely wise and sad. "God will see you now."

As she stood up, putting her magazine aside, Thalia Jansky thought, Mrs. McCray. She called me Mrs. McCray. . . .

Mrs. Winston McCray.

Stranger who never existed.

Stuart, voice frightened, said, "Mom?"

Thalia followed the angel girl through the door and disappeared into the white light.

Found herself walking along wet brown sand by a flat gray sea. The sea, covered with irregular runnels of white foam, stretched away from her, not to a distant horizon, just disappearing into mist. The sky overhead was hazy blue-gray, featureless, sunless. The land . . . Wet sand. Wet beach sand. Line of dunes making an irregular edge against the sky, hard to make out . . . What would I see if I climbed up there?

There was no wind, the air cool, a little too damp for comfort.

So what's this, another dose of humility. Another dose of misery?

Another . . . lesson?

Why does it always have to be lessons? Always punishment. Always . . . in the distance, outlined against sea, mist, sky, was the tiny black shadow of a man, walking toward her?

God will see me now?

Is that what this is?

I don't believe it. I don't believe any of it.

Mark was right all along.

Just a dream.

Her heart beat fast nonetheless.

She squinted toward the shadow, felt a surge of breathless . . . *Winston?* Started walking toward the shape, wishing it would resolve, that she'd be able to see . . . it's like I'm walking into the setting sun, glare hiding . . . no sun here. No sun at all.

Something wrong with the shape. Winston McCray was a tall, spare man, balding even when young, with a long, narrow, jut-jawed, *Grapes of Wrath* sort of face. The shadow was of a shorter, blockier, better proportioned man. A man with broad shoulders, muscular arms, narrow hips, long, thick legs . . .

Oh, God.

Wolf?

Is *Wolf* the one?

A sudden realization: the possibility that she'd loved him all along, that even Winston McCray had been . . . a poor substitute.

God, I do not want that to be the truth.

At least let me have truly loved Stuart's father.

She stopped, staring at the man, who was now only two meters away, also motionless, no longer a shadow. Tall, dark, craggy face just beginning to need a shave. Dark brown, curly hair, flecked with bits of gray, mostly around the temples.

She said, "You're not Wolf O'Malley either."

He smiled. Said nothing.

Some bitter sarcastic voice, a part of her, snarled, *Oh, great. The strong, silent type.* "So who are you supposed to be? God, for Christ's sake?"

The man laughed, slightly irregular teeth white in the gray light, skin crinkling nicely around his light brown eyes. "Thalia, you're a card, you know that?"

A . . . *card?* "Well who the hell *are* you, then?"

He said, "I'm your missed connection, Thal. That's all."

She felt an odd hollow form, like a lump in her throat.

He said, "Aw, don't look so sad."

Sad?

Then he said, "Come on, Thalia Jansky. That life's still waiting for you to live it."

When he held out his hand, she stepped forward and took it in her own.

And he said, "Let's go home now. They're all waiting for you."

No need to ask who.

Honoria knew her turn would come next. She shut the magazine and put it aside, reached out and patted Corazón's hand, smiled at all the others. Well, at the few others, now that Mark and Thalia were gone. Pathetic Stuart, looking all forlorn. Cory. Wolf . . . Only four of us?

It seemed like so many more.

The door opened and the angel appeared, bearing with her the usual cascade of white light. "Ms. Suárez?"

Honoria bounced lightly to her feet, smiling, ready to go, turned, surprised, to see Corazón standing right beside her, confused. *Ms.* . . . Worthless *inglés* word. She turned to the angel, and said, "*¿Señora o Señorita Suárez, por favor?*"

The angel laughed, pleasant, human, not like a bell at all. "*Tanto mejor.*"

Honoria took her daughter's small, cool hand and they stepped forward together, not hearing Wolf's whispered farewell, walked through the door and up the long grassy slope of a tree-capped hill under a deep, burnished, utterly empty blue sky.

When they got to the crest, stopping in the shade of broad, dark green olive trees, Honoria put down her picnic hamper, took the soft old blanket from Corazón's arms and spread it on the grass. Down the long hill there were other blankets and other parties of picnickers; beyond them, a broad, silver-blue stream; beyond that, beyond the red tile bridge they'd crossed, a parking lot full of shiny, colorful new cars. Beyond the road, the forest. Beyond the forest, the towers of the city.

I know that city, she thought. It's not Buenos Aires.

For some reason, she couldn't remember its name.

Corazón, who'd asked for this picnic to celebrate her eleventh birthday, was unpacking the hamper, pausing to uncap a bottle of orange-cream soda and take a long swig.

"Ahhh . . . It's *delicious,* Mama. Can we . . ." She gestured at the tinfoil-wrapped chicken, the insulated pot of *paella.*

Honoria stroked her soft brown hair, smiling. "Don't be so impatient! It won't be much longer. . . ." She looked back at the parking lot, then scanned the roadway anxiously.

Down on the hill, a tall man and his little boy were flying a kite. You couldn't see the string from this far away, but the red and yellow kite was sailing nicely, hanging almost a hundred meters up, dangling a long white tail, the traditional tail of rags.

When she looked back toward the road, the familiar green car was just pulling into the parking lot. Honoria stood and waved, and the man, getting out of the car, spotted her right away, waving back, waving vigorously, loping across the bridge.

Corazón screamed, *"Daddy!"* and started running down the hill to meet him. When they met, the girl climbed him like a tree, hugging him with her arms and legs. Sitting on the blanket, Honoria was glad her belief had never wavered.

Stu was flipping through the magazine, not looking at it, strong feeling of realization washing over him. He'd never see his mother again, never argue with Mark again, never . . . well, in a sense, Cory was gone anyway, but . . . he felt as though he'd had his whole life snatched away from him before it had really had a chance to start. He glanced at Wolf, saw the expression of impatience, looked away.

"Mr. McCray?" He looked up to see the pretty angel standing there, arm out, delicate white hand ready to take his. Any last words? He said, " 'Bye, Wolf." Stood, walked.

Through the door the world was almost as white as the light dwindling behind him. He was walking up the middle of an asphalt road streaked with ice and dark rivulets of meltwater. Although the air was cold, it was very still, and the hot sun hanging in the dark blue sky seemed to be magnified. He took a big deep breath, and the air burned his nostrils and lungs on the way down.

All around, deep snow, the deepest in years, a meter of it or more, speckled with glitter. The ground was thick with ice cream frosting, and where objects had been before there were just empty contours. Parked in their driveways, most cars looked like they had swollen to twice their size.

Stu recognized the neighborhood despite the shroud. This was just down the street from the house he'd grown up in. Over the years, his mother had brought him back here again and again.

Around the corner he heard the hollow scraping sound of shoveling snow, and watched a big lump of snow sail up to fall into an accumulating pile. The shoveler was hidden behind the big green arborvitae.

That's my driveway. A strange anticipation seized him, and he began to run, first a step or two, then full speed.

In the driveway, chopping some ice out of the crack at the edge of the sidewalk, was a man, thin-looking despite the heavy blue coat, little navy knit cap pulled onto his head. He looked up, gave him that characteristic little smirk, and said "Stuart. Your turn."

Scared to believe it, Stu looked down at himself, certain that he'd find himself a little boy, and that this was the winter before his father had died.

No. I'm still fifteen. I feel fifteen. He looked at the house and saw his mother in the big picture window, smiling, waving. Everything right with the world, he took the shovel and dug in.

All alone, as expected.

When his turn came, Wolf followed the angel girl through the door and into the light, looking not toward the supposed infinite, but down, toward her slim hips, which moved just the way he liked women's hips to move.

Grin. Grin, you bastard. This is all your life's been about. No sense trying to change now.

Men of evil will everywhere, not so much bewitched into behaving by the promise of some postmortem reward as terrorized by the possibility of punishment. Who the hell was it said every man commits adultery in his heart? Can't remember. Doesn't matter.

He remembered that most pathetic iteration of himself he'd been shown, the lonely old melon-fucker. Looked down at the angel girl's rear end and imagined her delicately, deliciously naked.

So. Am I supposed to think that's more pathetic than carving a cunt from a melon?

Typically, instead of turning naked on command, the girl was displaced by a narrow track of dried mud, tall green grass on either side, giving way to dense piny woods on the left, sun-drenched fields on the right.

There were clumps of trees here and there, casting pools of dark shade, a tall, irregular hill beyond, concealing the horizon, and the sky was clear, blue, slightly tawny with faraway haze.

I know this place.

Of course you do.

In the distance, beyond the edge of the hill, were distant mountains.

Well. If I keep walking, I can be there in no time flat.

There. That's the way. One foot after the other, putting the landscape behind you. After a while he started to sweat, to breathe deeply, to feel wonderful.

Alive.

That's what this is.

I'm alive.

Alive the way a dog is alive, running free, emptied of all thought. Just . . . being. He began to run.

It'd been a wonderful night. The beer. The music. Dancing. Cutting a girl from the herd, taking her out in the moonlight. Then away, to her trailer park home, to her bed. Undressing her in the almost-darkness, just enough light to see what was what. Then holding her close and . . . finally just doing it.

Being alive, like an animal. Just like now.

What difference can the rest of it, all that petty human bullshit, make?

He stumbled to a stop at the top of a hill, bending over, holding his side, gasping for breath, dripping sweat, slowly calming down. All right. All right. Go on down. It'll be all right. You'll see.

He walked slowly down the path toward the half-collapsed

old house. Some said it'd been a nice place, before the war, but there'd been a heavy shockwave come through here when Asheville got it, freakishly focused by the shape of the hills, knocking it askew on its foundation. Weather'd done the rest.

There was a old car in the driveway, up on cinder blocks, undergoing its fifth or sixth renovation, a car that would run again when the work was done, run for another few years, then need another iteration of this same task.

Someday, he thought, there'll be no more parts. Then it won't run anymore.

Image of that time: house overgrown and empty, car a rusted-out shell, this whole place gradually disappearing under kudzu, weeds, sapling trees.

Not now, though.

The old man was sitting in his chair up in the shade of the porch, hair scruffy and gray, whiskers at least three days beyond the need of a shave, smoking his pipe, reading a newspaper. Ox was at his feet, sound asleep, looking more like hassock than dog.

When Wolf sat down beside him, the old man passed him a part of the paper he was finished with and, as he opened it to read, he thought, All the things we've lost, they're all out here, somewhere.

Happily ever afterward, then?

Wolf laughed.

What other meaning does *forever* need to have?

And so . . .

And so the soap opera theme music swelled from the scenery, covering everything, and . . .

Bang.

Wolf awoke to an empty space, soft gray-silver mist in all directions, lit through and through with pearly light, like the inside of a dense, dense cloud, lit by the light of a noonday sun. I remember this, he thought. Remember it from one of those lives. More than one of them. Thousands, millions . . .

Flying my ship through the opaque upper atmosphere of some impossible gas-giant, shadows in the mist like living things, like . . . I remember bursting free of the clouds, bursting free into the clear upper air, hurtling above towering cumulonimbus, only to find it wasn't the sun at all, but a thousand silvery moons, silvery moons hanging in a midnight sky packed with layer on layer of stars.

I was alone in that life, and didn't mind.

That felt good, didn't it?

They all did. All those lives.

Even the bad ones, the pathetic melon-lovers, the bad men who cheated and stole, the killers with blood on their hands, looking grimly down on dying men with slashed-open throats . . . we all loved our lives, even when we hated them.

Even when they hated us.

Lives without number.

No way to count them all.

Layer on layer of lives receding, receding until . . .

Hello, Wolf.

That you, God?

Of course. Who else would meet you here?

Did I learn my lesson?

Did you?

You could run through every one of an infinite number of lives, lives of an infinite number of people, looking for lessons learned, lessons to be learned, nitpicking, nitpicking, losing your way in the details.

Every forest has its trees.

Every lesson learned is no more than an arrow, pointing the way to . . .

All my life, in all of my lives, I was helpless, saw myself

as helpless, before the forces that shaped me. What I lacked was the power to change, rather than to *be* changed.

Simple enough, God said.

And the others? What were their lessons?

No different from yours. When people make bad choices, they tell themselves it was the choice they *had* to make. I had to steal that candy bar. The store's economic policies forced it on me. I had to kill that man. It was his life or mine.

Excuses are always lies.

Until we learn that, we remain helpless victims.

And you? Does God transcend change?

Nothing transcends change. Nothing but the scale of our victimhood.

Is that a disappointment? Wolf thought, Why don't I know yet? Surely . . . He said, Tell me how there could be a God. Help me to believe.

The essence in the featureless clouds seemed to smile. Belief is the one thing that remains unnecessary. Ask yourself rather, How do the starships fly?

Wolf thought, How? Mechanistically? Stochastically? Philosophically?

Yes.

Wolf said, Length, breadth, height, duration. All the attractoral dimensions of phase space interact and . . . the starships evade the restrictions of conformal time by moving through probabilistic time.

You can only travel faster than light, then, by traveling through time. Since conformal time enforces its limits through paradox, you can only evade paradoxical time travel by ejecting yourself from the one universe and inserting yourself into some other, infinitely similar universe at some earlier time.

A universe that is, for its own internally consistent reasons, ready to receive you.

God said, The possibility of probabilistic time travel, as a means of evading conformal paradoxes, requires the existence of a discontinuity space. You leave one universe, phase space shifts around you chaotically, until the appropriate destination space comes into being.

Wolf said, Good enough for magic starships, but . . .

Probabilistic time contains all the conformal times that can exist.

So if God *can* exist, God *will* exist?

The essence in the clouds seemed to titter. That doesn't account for anything at all, now does it?

No.

Do you exist, Wolf?

I thought so at one time. Now . . .

Now you're afraid you are just the figment of some greater being's imagination. No more than an ephemeral mote in the eye of an incomprehensible, probabilistic God. Is that it?

In a nutshell.

And yet . . . How could there be such a thing as a mind?

Lots of theories, Wolf thought. No shortage of ideas. I always liked Memetics best. The quantum mechanical structures of the brain spontaneously bring forth chaotic memes, nothing more than quantum states at first, most lethal, most instantly erased, all the rest fit into the existing ecology of the mind by the universal laws of Mendel-Darwin evolution.

And in due course, once communication systems, however primitive, have evolved, memes escape from the minds they made, escape as free-range memes into the evolving noösphere? God asked.

Yeah. That's the theory.

If the quantum-mechanical ecology of the brain mandates a mind, then the quantum-mechanical ecology of the universe, in the presence of all potential probabilistic states, mandates a God.

Wolf laughed. If the starships fly, then QED.

- Returns must be accompanied by receipt
- Returns must be completed within 30 days
- Merchandise must be in salable condition
- Opened videos, discs, and cassettes may be exchanged for replacement copies of the original item only
- Periodicals and newspapers may not be returned
- Items purchased by check may be returned for cash after 10 business days.
- All returned checks will incur a $15 service charge

BORDERS®

- Returns must be accompanied by receipt
- Returns must be completed within 30 days
- Merchandise must be in salable condition
- Opened videos, discs, and cassettes may be exchanged for replacement copies of the original item only
- Periodicals and newspapers may not be returned
- Items purchased by check may be returned for cash after 10 business days.
- All returned checks will incur a $15 service charge

BORDERS®

- Returns must be accompanied by receipt
- Returns must be completed within 30 days
- Merchandise must be in salable condition
- Opened videos, discs, and cassettes may be exchanged for replacement copies of the original item only
- Periodicals and newspapers may not be returned
- Items purchased by check may be returned

BORDERS
BOOKS AND MUSIC
270 DAIRY ROAD
KAHULUI MAUI HI 96732
(808) 877-6160

STORE: 0153 REG: 02/73 TRAN#: 7504
SALE 01/15/2001 EMP: 00050

TOP TEN
6271980 MM T 6.99
BLUE RAIN
6267574 MM T 6.99

5910691 MM T 6.99

Subtotal 20.97
HAWAII 4.166% .87
3 Items Total 21.84
CASH 22.00
CASH .16-

01/15/2001 06:08PM

Mahalo for visiting Borders Maui

Visit our website at www.borders.com

Online access available in store!

God said, *Quod erat demonstrandum.* In a nutshell, of course.

So the Topopolitans didn't need to make an Omega Point God, because the universe, on its own, had already made one for them?

Quite right.

And what about me?

What about all of you?

Do we matter?

God said, Everything matters, Mr. O'Malley. That's why excuses always fail.

For Wolf, as for all men, time began again with a rush of white light.